THE VAN

RODDY DOYLE

ISIS
LARGE PRINT
Oxford

Copyright © Roddy Doyle, 1991

First published in Great Britain 1991
by
Martin Secker & Warburg Ltd.

Published in Large Print 2014 by ISIS Publishing Ltd.,
7 Centremead, Osney Mead, Oxford OX2 0ES
by arrangement with
Vintage
one of the publishers in The Random House Group Limited

CIP data is available for this title from the British Library

ISBN 978–0–7531–9262–7 (hb)
ISBN 978–0–7531–9263–4 (pb)

Printed and bound in Great Britain by
T. J. International Ltd., Padstow, Cornwall

This book is dedicated to
John Sutton

Thanks to
Brian McGinn and Will Moore
for their help, advice and recipe for batter

Let's Twist Again (Mann/Appell) used by permission of Carlin Music Corporation, Iron Bridge House, 3 Bridge Approach, London NW1 8BD. *Barbara Ann* (Fassert) © Warner Chappell Music Ltd. Reproduced by permisssion. *Hippy Hippy Shake* (Chan Romero) © 1959, Jonware Music Corp, USA. Reproduced by permission of Ardmore and Beechwood Ltd, London WC2H OEA. *California Girls* (Brian Wilson) © Irving Music Inc. Used by permission of Rondor Music (London) Ltd. *Give It a Lash, Jack* used by permission of GOAL.

Jimmy Rabbitte Sr had the kitchen to himself. He felt a draught and looked up and Darren, one of his sons, was at the door, looking for somewhere to do his homework.

— Oh —, said Darren, and he turned to go back into the hall.

— D'yeh need the table, Darren? said Jimmy Sr.

— Eh —

— No, come on. Fire away.

Jimmy Sr stood up. His arse had gone numb on him.

— Jesus —!

He straightened up and grinned at Darren.

— I'll go somewhere else, he said.

— Thanks, said Darren.

— Not at all, said Jimmy Sr.

Jimmy Sr left Darren in the kitchen and went out to the front step and sat on it. Christ, the step was cold; he'd end up with piles or the flu or something. But there was nowhere else to go until after the dinner. All the rooms in the house were occupied. He rubbed his hands; it wasn't too bad. He tried to finish the article in the Press he'd been reading, about how people suffered after they got out of jail, with photographs of the Guildford Four.

A car went by. Jimmy Sr didn't know the driver. The sun was down the road now, going behind the school gym. He put the paper down beside him on the step and then he put his hands in under the sleeves of his jumper.

He was tempted to have a bash at the garden but the grass was nearly all gone, he'd been cutting it so often. He'd have looked like a right gobshite bringing the lawn-mower for a walk around a baldy garden, in the middle of November. There were weeds in under the hedge, but they could stay there. Anyway, he liked them; they made the garden look more natural. He'd painted the gate and the railings a few months back; red, and a bit of white, the Liverpool colours, but Darren didn't seem to care about that sort of thing any more.

— Look, Darren. Your colours.

— Oh yeah.

Jimmy Sr'd noticed small patches where some dust and bits of stuff had got stuck to the wet paint. He'd go over it again, but not today. It was a bit late.

The car went by again, the other way this time. He got a better look at the driver but he still didn't know him. He looked as if he was searching for a house he didn't know. He was only looking at the even numbers across the way. He might have been the police. That would've been good, watching the guards going in and arresting Frano Traynor again. It had been great gas the last time they'd done it, especially when Chrissie,

Frano's mot, started flinging toys down at them from the bedroom window and she hit Frano with Barbie's Ferrari.

— Jesus; sorry, love!

— You're alrigh', said Frano back, searching his hair for blood.

That would have killed the time till the dinner.

But the car was gone.

There was nothing else happening, no kids on the street even. He could hear some though, around the corner, and a Mr Whippy van, but it sounded a good bit away, maybe not even in Barrytown. He took his change out of his pocket and counted it: a pound and sevenpence. He looked at his watch; the dinner'd be ready soon.

Darren read the question he'd just written at the top of his page.

— Complexity of thought and novelty in the use of language sometimes create an apparent obscurity in the poetry of Gerard Manley Hopkins. Discuss this view, supporting the points you make by quotations from or references to the poems by Hopkins on your course.

Then he tore out the page and wrote the question out again, in red. He read it again.

Starting was the hard bit. He brought the poetry book in closer to him. He wrote Complexity, Language and Obscurity in the margin.

He could never start questions, even in tests; he'd sit there till the teacher said Ten minutes left and then he'd fly. And he always did alright. It was still a bit of a fuckin' drag though, starting.

He read the question again.

His ma would come in to make the dinner in a minute and then he'd have to find somewhere else.

He read one of the poems, That Nature is a Heraclitean Fire.

Darren didn't know when Tippex had been invented but Gerrah Manley Hopkins had definitely been sniffing something. He couldn't write that in his answer though.

Down to business.

— Right, he whispered. — Come on. Complexity.

He started.

— In my opinion the work of the poet and priest —

He crossed out And Priest.

— Gerard Manley Hopkins is —

Then he stopped.

— Fuck it.

He'd just remembered; he shouldn't have written In My Opinion. It was banned. Crosbie, their English teacher, wouldn't let them use it.

He tore out the page.

Upstairs in her bedroom Veronica, Darren's mother, was doing her homework as well.

The door was locked.

—You're not even inhalin' properly, said Linda.

— I am so, Linda; fuck off.

4

Tracy took another drag, held the smoke in her mouth for a bit, then blew it out, in behind the couch. She couldn't blow it out the window cos her daddy was out there sitting on the step. Linda grabbed the Major from her and took a drag, a real one, and held it much longer than Tracy had — and got rid of it when they heard the stairs creaking. She threw the fag into her Zubes tin and shut it and nearly took the skin off her fingers. They beat the air with their copy books.

They waited. They looked at the door.

But it didn't open.

— Get it before it goes ou', Tracy whispered.

Linda giggled, and so did Tracy. They shushed each other. Linda opened the tin.

— Jesus, she said. — I've crushed it.

— Let's see.

It was their last one.

— Ah Jesus, said Linda. — I'm gaspin'!

— So am I, said Tracy.

— Yeh can't be. You don't even inhale.

— I do, Linda.

— Yeh don't. Your smoke comes ou' too puffy.

— That's just the way I do it. It is, Linda. —God, I'm gaspin'.

— Yeah, said Linda. — Does tha' look like Mammy's writin'?

Tracy looked at the writing on the inside cover of one of Linda's copies.

— Yeah, she said. — Sort of —

— Look it, said Linda.

She took the copy from Tracy and showed her the other inside cover.

— That's wha' it was like when I started, she told Tracy.

She turned back to the first cover.

— This's much better, isn't it?

— Yeah, said Tracy, and she meant it.

She read it; Please Excuse, about ten times down the page, getting smaller and closer near the bottom, not like her mammy's yet but not like Linda's usual writing either, much smaller, hardly any holes in the letters.

— She'll kill yeh, Tracy told Linda.

— Why will she? said Linda. — I haven't done annythin'. I'm only experimentin'.

She wrote Please.

— Is tha' like it?

— Yeah, said Tracy.

They'd forgotten that they were gasping. Tracy crossed out History in her homework journal. She'd just finished it, five questions about the pyramids.

— Jesus, she said, reading what was next on the list.

— Wha' Irish story are yeh doin', Linda?

— I'm not doin' anny, said Linda

She showed Tracy another Please and a new Excuse.

— Is tha' like it?

— No.

— Ah but, Mammy —

— No, I said.

— Daddy —?

— Yeh heard your mammy, said Jimmy Sr.

— But —

— No buts.

The twins, Linda doing all of the talking, had just asked if they could get a new video for Christmas. They'd had none in the house since Jimmy Jr, the eldest, had taken his with him when he'd moved out a few months ago.

— No buts, said Jimmy Sr. — We can't afford it, an' that's that. And, we've no place to put it —

— With the telly —

— Don't interrupt me, righ'!

He was really angry, before he knew it; nearly out of his seat. It was happening a lot these days. He'd have to be careful. He stopped pointing at Linda.

—We're not gettin' one; end o' story. Now I want to enjoy me dinner. For a change.

Linda raised her eyes to heaven and shifted a bit in her chair, and thought about walking out of the kitchen in protest, but she stayed. She was hungry.

So was Gina, Sharon's little young one.

— Shut up, Sharon told her. — Wait.

She put the chips in front of Gina, then lifted them away.

— Now, if yeh throw them around, Sharon warned her, — I'll take them back off yeh, d'yeh hear me?

Gina screamed.

— An' Grandad'll eat them on yeh. Isn't tha' righ', Grandad?

— Wha'? said Jimmy Sr. — Chips, is it? Come here, I'll eat them now.

He leaned over to Gina's chair.

— Give us them here. Lovely.

Gina screamed, and grabbed the plate. Sharon managed to keep the chips on the plate but got ketchup on her hand.

— Ah, bloody —

— Buddy! said Gina.

Sharon wiped her hand on Gina's bib.

The Rabbittes got dug into their dinners.

— Lovely, said Jimmy Sr.

Tracy had an announcement.

— There's a piece o' paper hangin' up in the toilet an' yis are all to put a tick on it every time yis flush the toilet.

— Wha'? said Jimmy Sr.

Darren came in.

— Good man, Darren, said Jimmy Sr. — Were yeh watchin' abou' the Berlin Wall there?

— Yeah, said Darren as he sat down.

— Terrific, isn't it? said Jimmy Sr.

— Yeah, said Darren.

Jimmy Sr wondered, again, why Darren wouldn't talk to him properly any more.

— Darren, said Tracy. — Every time yeh flush the toilet you're to put a tick on the paper hangin' up on the wall.

— What's this abou'? Jimmy Sr still wanted to know.

— There's a biro for yeh to do it in the glass with the toothbrushes, Tracy told them.

— Okay, said Darren.

— Hang on, said Jimmy Sr. — What are we to do? Exactly. Tracy raised her eyes.

8

— Jesus, she said to Linda.

— Don't Jesus me, you, said Jimmy Sr. — An' anyway, that's a curse. Swearbox.

— It's not a curse, said Tracy. — It's a name.

— Not the way you said it, said Jimmy Sr.

He picked up the marmalade jar with the slit in its lid and rattled it in front of her. The swearbox had been his idea, to force him to clean up his act in front of the baby.

— Come on, he said.

— I haven't anny money, said Tracy.

— Yeh have so, said Linda

— Fuck —

— Ah ah! said Jimmy Sr. — Double.

Veronica took over.

— That's the last time you'll use language like that in this house, she told Tracy. — D'you hear me? And you as well, she told Linda.

— I didn't say ann'thin'! said Linda.

— You know what I mean, said Veronica. — It's disgraceful; I'm not having it. In front of Gina.

Gina was busy with her chips.

— That's righ', said Jimmy Sr. — Yis know how quickly she's pickin' up things.

— I on'y said Jesus, said Tracy very quietly, standing up for her rights.

— I didn't say ann'thin', said Linda.

— You're becoming a right pair of —

Veronica didn't finish. She stared at them, then looked away.

— Bitches, said Sharon. — If Gina starts usin' dirty language I'll kill yis.

— I didn't say ann'thin', Linda told her plate.

Jimmy Sr studied the piece of burger on his fork.

— Eh, he said. — Should it be this colour?

— Yes! said Veronica.

— Fair enough, said Jimmy Sr. — Just askin'.

He chewed and swallowed.

— Second time we've had these yokes this week, he said, sort of to himself.

Veronica let her knife and fork rattle off her plate. Jimmy Sr didn't look at her.

— Anyway, he asked Tracy, — why am I to put a tick on this piece o' paper when I go to the jacks?

— It's for school, said Tracy, as if he was some sort of a thick. — Geog'aphy.

— Wha' has goin' to the jacks got to do with geography?

— I don't know, said Tracy. — Somethin' to do with water. Miss Eliot says we're to do it.

— Why does Miss Eliot want to know how often I have a —

— Swearbox! said Linda.

— Starebock! said Gina.

— I didn't say it, said Jimmy Sr.

He turned back to Tracy.

— Why does she want to know how often I use the toilet facilities?

— Not just you, said Tracy. — All of us have to.

— Why?

— Geog'aphy.

10

— It's to see how much water all the class uses, Linda told him.

— Why? Darren asked.

— I don't know! said Linda. — It's thick. She's useless. Tracy's to do the toilet an' I'm to do the sink an' the washin' machine but I'm not goin' to. It's thick.

— Is that your homework? said Veronica.

— Yeah, said Linda.

— Then you're to do it.

Linda said nothing.

— I'd still like to know wha' Miss Eliot wants with all this information, said Jimmy Sr. — She might blackmail us; wha', Darren?

— Yeah. —Yeah.

— The Rabbittes go to the jacks twice as much as everyone else, wha'. She'll want to know how often we change our underwear next; wait an' see.

— Stop that, said Veronica. — It's their homework.

Darren was beginning to grin, so Jimmy Sr continued.

— An' after tha' we'll find bits o' paper stuck up beside the beds, wha'.

— Stop!

Darren laughed. And so did Jimmy Sr. He spoke to Gina.

— We'd run ou' of paper if we had to tick off every time you go to the jacks, wouldn't we, Honey?

Gina threw a chip at him, and hit. He pretended he was dying. Sharon picked up the chip before the dog, Larrygogan, got to it and she made Gina eat it.

— There, she said.

But Gina didn't mind.

— Do you not do maps and stuff like that? Veronica asked Linda and Tracy.

— No, said Linda. — Sometimes only.

— Nearly never, said Tracy.

Veronica shrugged.

Jimmy Sr belched.

— Lovely dinner, Veronica, he said.

— You liked those yokes, did you? said Veronica.

— They were grand, said Jimmy Sr. — Much nicer than the ones yeh get in the chipper or the shops.

— Yeah, well, said Veronica. — When I start getting some proper money again you won't see them so often.

— No no, said Jimmy Sr. — They're grand.

They looked at each other.

Then Gina dropped her plate on Larrygogan.

— Ah Jesus, said Sharon.

— Starebock! said Gina.

Jimmy Sr stood on some chips when he was trying to wipe the ketchup off Larrygogan.

— Ah Jaysis —

— Starebock!

And Sharon slapped her.

— Ah leave her, leave her, said Jimmy Sr. — It's only chips.

— She does it on purpose.

Gina started some serious screaming. Sharon wanted to kill her, but only for a second. She lifted her out of her chair and rocked her. But Gina wasn't impressed.

— Jive Bunny, Gina, said Jimmy Sr. — Look it.

— OH —

He started twisting.

— Look at Grandad, Gina, said Sharon.

— LET'S TWIST AGAIN —

LIKE WE DID LAST Jaysis!

He slid on a chip and nearly went on his arse, saved by the table. Gina stopped screaming, to watch. Jimmy Sr, steadying himself and taking off his shoe, looked at Gina and sniffed victory. But Gina was getting ready to start again; he could tell by the way her cheeks were twitching.

— Righ', he said to the rest. — Hawaii 5–10.

He made a trumpet out of his fists and started.

— DEH DEH DEH DEH —

DEHHH DEH —

Linda, Tracy, Darren, even Veronica made trumpets and joined in. Gina danced in Sharon's arms and forgot about screaming. Larrygogan cleaned the chips off the floor and he cleaned the plate as well.

Jimmy Sr sat watching the television. There was no sound on. The three other lads watching it all had earphones but Jimmy Sr couldn't see another pair anywhere. He could've asked the young one behind the desk over there what he'd to do to get a pair of earphones for himself but he didn't want to. She looked busy. Anyway, they mightn't have been free. And anyway as well, what was on didn't look that good; just fellas in togas talking; a play or something.

Jimmy Sr was in the ILAC library, in town.

It was terrific here, very nice.

He'd never been in here before. It was great. There was a lot more to it than just the books. You could get tapes or records out or even those compact discs, or just listen to them in here. He'd go over there, to the music part, after this. There was a language resource centre, a room where you could learn more than sixty languages in one of those booth things. Or you could use the computer — he looked at the brochure again — to enhance your computer literacy skills. There was even a reading machine for if you had sight problems. Having one of them beside the bed would have been very handy for when you came home scuttered at night.

He didn't drink much any more; just the few pints twice a week.

He'd go over and have a look at the machine in a minute.

He was definitely joining. He had his application cards here. It was lovely here. You could stay here for ages and never get bored. You could even borrow pictures and bring them home.

That was a bit fuckin' stupid when you thought about it; sticking a picture up on your wall for a fortnight and then having to bring it back again; on a bus or on the DART, sitting there like a gobshite with a big picture on your lap, of a woman in her nip or something.

Still though.

It was gas watching your men here watching the telly, and not being able to hear. One of them had laughed a minute ago, like he was trying not to, but the chaps on the telly had looked deadly serious. She'd asked him —

your woman at the desk — if he was a householder when he'd asked her how you joined.

He didn't know.

He told her it wasn't for himself he was asking, and she gave him the cards and told him that he'd have to get a householder to sign the back of them.

He sort of knew. But the problem was, he didn't know — not exactly — if you actually had to own your house or if renting was enough. And he rented his, so if he'd said Yeah, I am a householder and he'd found out that he wasn't one when he was filling in the card at the desk he'd've felt like a right fuckin' eejit. In front of the young one there. She looked younger than Sharon.

Bimbo, one of his mates, owned his house. Jimmy Sr'd get him to sign it, to be on the safe side.

There was a thing he'd seen downstairs in the shopping part of the ILAC on his way up here; a studio, a small one you went into and sang a song — for six quid. The twins would've loved that.

Maybe they wouldn't have, but; not any more. They'd have been too embarrassed. There was a list of the songs you could sing along to. New York New York was one of them. That was his song; he always sang it at weddings and on bank holiday Mondays in the Hikers.

Six quid. Veronica would fuck him from a height if he came home with a tape of himself singing and she found out how much it'd cost.

He got up. He was going to have a look at the books. When he joined up he could take out three at a time and keep them for three weeks, but he'd only take out one or maybe two. He wasn't that quick of a reader.

15

And anyway, he'd want to come here more than just once every three weeks so if he took out one book at a time he could come back more often than that.

There was a sign — a handmade one — on the desk that said that you could get an Action Pack for the Unemployed but there weren't any on the desk. You had to ask for one.

He wondered what was in them. Action Pack. Probably just leaflets.

And a compass and a fuckin' hand grenade and one of them cyanide tablets for if you were caught behind enemy lines.

He'd ask for one the next time. The young one was dealing with some people at the desk and one of them looked like he was going to start getting snotty with her.

She was a nice-looking young one, lovely; not what you'd have expected. With a few buttons open at the front, fair play to her.

He went over to the books. He wanted to find the Sports shelf. He was thinking of getting a couple of greyhounds.

Veronica and Jimmy Sr were alone, sitting on their bed. Jimmy Sr watched Veronica putting on socks and then her boots.

— We could always get a few bob from a lender, I suppose, said Jimmy Sr.

— No, said Veronica.

— A few bob only —

— No, said Veronica.

—You're righ'; you're right, o' course, Veronica, said Jimmy Sr. — We'd only be gettin' ourselves into —

— I'd die before I'd go looking for help from one of those crooks, said Veronica.

— You're dead right, yeah. I just thought —Will Leslie come home, d'yeh think?

Veronica didn't want to answer this. But she did.

— I doubt it, she said.

—Yeah, said Jimmy Sr.

Les was in England, somewhere. They thought.

— What abou' Jimmy? said Jimmy Sr.

— Ah yeah, said Veronica.

She studied the soles of the boots.

— Where else would he go? said Veronica. — If I pushed a bit harder my fingers would come through, look it.

Well, don't push then, Jimmy Sr nearly said, but he stopped himself.

— Would he not go to — em — Aoife's parents' place? he said.

Aoife and Jimmy Jr were living in a bedsit in Clontarf.

— He'd better not, said Veronica. — If he does he needn't come home for his Sunday dinner again.

She stood up.

— With his washing.

— Yeah, said Jimmy Sr. — At least we won't have to buy anythin' for him.

— Something small, said Veronica.

— Very small, said Jimmy Sr. — So that's the twins an' Gina is all we have to get presents for really. An'

Darren. An' somethin' small for Sharon as well. That's not too bad.

Veronica wasn't convinced.

— Well —, she said.

She was at the dressing-table mirror now.

— What about all the food and the drink? There's a lot more than just the presents. And there's other presents as well, you know. Gerry's kids and —

— I'll tell Gerry and Thelma and Pat they're not to send ours any presents an' we won't send theirs any.

— God, said Veronica. —I never —

— Sure, they can't afford it either, said Jimmy Sr.

He didn't want Veronica to finish. There was no point. He'd heard it before. It only made him angry now and he'd end up shouting. It wasn't fair.

— No one can, said Jimmy Sr.

Veronica said nothing.

— We were always broke at Christmas.

— After it though, said Veronica.

— Ah — ! said Jimmy Sr.

It wasn't fuckin' fair.

— Ah sorry, said Veronica.

She turned to look at him properly.

— I didn't mean anything.

— Ah, I know. — I don't blame yeh. It's just —

He looked at her looking at him.

— We'll manage, he said.

— Yes, said Veronica.

— I'll win the turkey in the pitch 'n' putt annyway, he said.

— You always do, said Veronica.

— An' maybe a hamper as well, wha'.

— That'd be great.

Neither of them wanted to talk any more about Christmas. It was still months away anyway; weeks. And Veronica had to go. She checked her folder.

— Eh —how're the oul' classes goin', Veronica? said Jimmy Sr.

— Grand, said Veronica.

Veronica was doing night classes, two Leaving Cert subjects.

— Are yeh the oldest? said Jimmy Sr.

— No!

— I'd say the maths is hard, is it?

— It's not too bad, said Veronica.

That was a lie, only a small one though because it was getting easier. She was getting used to it, being in the classroom and having the teacher, a young lad Jimmy Jr's age, looking over her shoulder all the time. And Darren was going to give her a hand.

— I was thinkin' I might do a few classes meself, Jimmy Sr told her.

— You're too late, Veronica told him. — You'll have to wait till next year.

She wasn't sure if that was true — she thought it was: really — but she wanted to do it on her own, even going up to the school on her own and walking home; everything.

She had to go.

— Bye bye so, she said. — Are yeh stayin' up here?

— I am, yeah, said Jimmy Sr. — I'm goin' to read one o' me bukes.

The twins were in the front room — he could hear them — and Darren would be in the kitchen but he didn't mind staying up here. He'd lie back — it wasn't that cold; just nice — and read.

— I got three bukes ou', he told Veronica. — Look it.

But she was gone.

— See you later, she said from the hall.

— Okay, love, said Jimmy Sr. — Good luck. D'yeh have all your eccer done now?

But she didn't answer. She was gone. He heard the door.

Fair play to her.

He picked up one of his books. The Man in the Iron Mask. By Alexandre Dumas. Lousy cover. He could have drawn better himself.

He remembered something. He got his thumb-nail and dragged it across the plastic covering. It worked, left a line of little grooves across the plastic. He did it again. The sound was the same as well, as when he was a kid.

That was gas —

He got up.

He'd make himself a cup of tea — it was just a bit chilly up here — and then he'd get going. Fifty pages before Veronica got home.

— Mind your house!

That wanker over there had been roaring that since the start of the match. He probably didn't even know what it meant, the stupid oul' bollix. The ball was down at the Barrytown goal, about the first time it had gone in that direction in the second half.

It was Saturday afternoon. Jimmy Sr was in St Anne's Park, watching the Barrytown Utd Under 18s; watching Darren.

Five-nil for Barrytown was the score. The opposition were useless. Jimmy Sr couldn't even remember what they were called. Darren didn't bother dashing back to help defend, and he was dead right. The last time this shower had seen the net shake was when their keeper farted.

The ball was coming back up. Darren went to meet it. No one came with him.

— Good man, Darren! Away yeh go!

Darren stopped the ball. Normally he'd have had two or three men up his arse by now or, with the ground this soggy, someone sliding towards his ankle. Now though, two of their defence ran around him on their way back as if they didn't want to get in his way because it was rude, so Darren held onto the ball for a while, turned and crossed where the centre line should have been.

— Give us a display of your silky skills, Darren!

That was the Barrytown keeper, Nappies Harrison.

The sweeper was waiting for Darren. That was what he'd called himself; the sweeper. — We're playin' three central defenders, he'd told Darren in the first half. — Like Arsenal. He was waiting for Darren on the other side of a puddle, hunched as if he was going to dive into it. Kenny Smith was to Darren's left, shouting for the ball. Darren lobbed the ball over the sweeper, ran around him (—Yeow, Darren!) and dug the ball out of the muck with his toe and sent it over to Kenny, hard so it wouldn't get stuck again.

— Good play, said their sweeper; Jimmy Sr heard him.

Darren knew he'd be praised after the match for his unselfish play (— That's the Liverpool way, lads) but he'd given the ball to Kenny because he couldn't be bothered bringing it any further himself. He heard the ironic cheer. They'd scored again; an Anto Brennan diving header that he hadn't really needed to dive for.

Darren strolled back across the line. He hated these sort of games, when they won without sweating. They'd be beaten next week; it always happened.

— Come on now, lads, the oul' guy at the side shouted.

— Make the score respectable, come on.

—Will yeh listen to him, said Kenny.

—Yeah, said Darren. — Fuckin' pitiful.

Most of them wouldn't turn up for training on Tuesday night because of this win; their emphatic victory.

The ball was in the centre circle. The ref picked it up and blew his whistle; game over, ten minutes early.

— Thank fuck, said Pat Conlon. — It's fuckin' freezin'.

— I was goin' for me hat-trick, Kenny complained.

— Ah, fuck off complainin', said Pat. — Anyway, yeh'd never have got another two.

— No problem to me against these cunts.

The sweeper was waiting for Darren at the sideline, with his hand out.

22

— Good game, he said.

— Yeah, said Darren. — Thanks.

— Best team won.

— The pitch wasn't fit for playin' on, said Darren.

His da was waiting for him as well.

— Well done, Darren.

— Thanks, Da.

He ran along the edge of the gravel path to the gates of the park.

— Bring your ma with yis the next time, he heard Kenny telling the sweeper, and he heard his da laughing.

Darren got into the back of one of the three Barrytown cars.

— Push over, there, he said.

— Ahh! Hang on; me leg!

— Good man, Darren, said Mr Reeves, his da's friend; Bimbo. — Is that everyone now?

— No; Kenny.

— Kenny! Darren roared. — Come on.

— They were useless, weren't they? said Mr Reeves.

— Pitiful, said Darren.

Hurry up, he wanted to say. Hurry up!

Kenny climbed in the back on top of the three lads already in there. There were two more in the front, and Bimbo.

Darren got the door shut.

— Jaysis, said Bimbo. — We're nearly scrapin' the ground. Did yis have your dinners at half-time or somethin'?

They laughed. The car moved. They cheered.

But Bimbo braked.

Darren's da was at the front passenger window.

— Will youse go with Billy, lads? he asked Muggah McCarthy and Pat Conlon.

— Okay, said Muggah, and Darren's da got in when the two of them got out.

— Off yeh go, he said to Bimbo.

Kenny leaned over (— Ah, Kenny! Watch it!) and rolled down Darren's window. He roared at the other team as they climbed into their mini-bus.

—Yis dozy cunts, yis!

— Here; none o' tha'! said Bimbo.

He braked again.

—Yeh can get ou' here if you're goin' to start tha'.

— Disgraceful behaviour, said Darren's da, and he winked back at them.

— Sorry, said Kenny.

They nudged each other. Bimbo got the car going again.

— Did yeh get this yoke off the Vincent de Paul, Mr Reeves? said Nappies.

They laughed.

—Yeah, said Kenny. — It's pitiful, isn't it, Darrah?

— Fuck off, said Darren.

His da laughed.

— Gettin' locked tonigh', men? said Anto.

— Fuckin' sure, said Kenny.

He started singing.

— HERE WE GO
HERE WE —

— Shut up in the back, said Bimbo.

24

The windows were steaming up. Darren rubbed his and watched the people walking along the sea front, looking out for young ones.

— D'yeh see her? said Kenny. — Jaysis.

He turned to look out the back window and kicked Anto in the mouth.

— You're dead, said Anto.

He checked for blood. There wasn't any.

— That's pitiful behaviour, said Nappies. — Isn't it, Darren?

Darren gave Nappies the finger.

— Swivel, he said.

Nappies was sitting on Anto's lap. His right ear was nearly pressed to the roof.

— Hurry up, Mr Reeves, will yeh. Me neck's nearly broke.

— Well, men, said Anto. — Where're we goin' tonigh'?

— The Nep, said Nappies.

— No way. Yeh fuckin' hippy.

— There's nothin' wrong with the Nep, said Anto. — It's better than the field youse drink in.

— Yeah, man.

— Right on, Anto.

— Will yeh be wearin' your flares, Nappies?

— He's pitiful.

— Yis haven't a clue, Nappies told them.

— Where's the Nep? said Bimbo.

— Town, said Nappies.

— My God, said Bimbo. — Would yis go tha' far for a drink?

— Fuckin' eejits, said Jimmy Sr.

— It's cos they're afraid their oul' ones'll catch them if they drink in the Hikers, Anto told Bimbo and Jimmy Sr.

— Don't start, you, said Nappies. — My ma knows I drink.

— Yeah; milk.

— Fuck off.

— Does she know yeh smoke hash as well, Nappies? Kenny got a couple of digs from Darren, to shut him up.

— Where do the rest of yis go? Bimbo asked them. He wasn't being nosy.

— The Beachcomber, said Anto.

— Yeh do not, said Nappies. — Don't start. They wouldn't let yeh in.

— Would they not now? said Anto. — D'yis hear him?

— What's it like inside then? said Nappies, — if yeh've been in there. Tell us; go on.

— Better than the fuckin' Nep anyway.

— You were never in there; I knew it.

— Fuck off, you.

— Fuck off, yourself. The state o' yeh. You'd get drunk on a barman's fart.

— Fuck off.

— Language, lads. — Do none of yis go up to the Hikers at all?

— I do, said Kenny.

— Yeh do in your brown, said Anto. — He asked yeh do yeh drink in the Hikers, not do yeh sit on the wall outside.

26

— Don't start, said Kenny. — I do drink there.

— When?

— Yeah; go on.

— With me da.

— Yeah; the day yeh made your Confirmation.

— Fuck off.

— Yeah, Kenny; your oul' lad drank your money on yeh.

Darren enjoyed this, even with his da there; the lads slagging each other. He rubbed the window. He couldn't open it because Kenny's feet were in the way. They were turning off the sea front. It was a bit fuckin' childish though; not the slagging, the subject matter. The theme.

— Anyway, said Kenny, — knacker drinkin's better than drinkin' in a pub. Specially if you've a free house.

— That's not knacker drinkin'! said Anto.

They didn't even shave, most of them in the car. Darren did, and he was younger than some of them. And he'd been in the Beachcomber. And the Hikers. It was no big deal. He was working tonight in the Hikers — but he'd drunk in there as well when he wasn't working — and then he was going on to the Grove. The Grove was a dump. It usen't to be that bad but there were just kids there now and the music was pitiful; it used to be great. But he was meeting Miranda there after work, so it was okay.

— Hey, Darren. Where're you goin' tonigh'?

— Workin', said Darren.

She was fifteen but she looked much older; she wasn't skinny at all. She'd done her Inter; six honours;

27

two less than Darren. She'd great hair, black that went up and out and down, and huge eyes and no spots, not in the light in the Grove anyway. He'd only seen her in the Grove so far. He wasn't really going with her.

— Here we are, lads.

They were outside the community centre.

— Thanks, Mr Reeves. You're a poxy driver.

Darren opened the door and Kenny fell out onto the road, on purpose; he always did it. Darren climbed out.

— Jesus; me legs.

— Yeah. We should have a bus.

— Will you get us one for Christmas? said Bimbo.

— Here, Mr Reeves, said Pat. — We'll rob the 17A for yeh.

The two other carloads had arrived. Their manager, Billy O'Leary, got out of his car.

— Righ', he said. — Yis listenin'?

He zipped up his bomber jacket and rubbed his hands. Bimbo and Jimmy Sr went over and stood beside him.

— Yis listenin'? —Righ'; good win there but, let's face it, lads. They were spas.

He let them laugh, then frowned.

— Next week'll be a different kettle o' fish. Cromcastle are always a useful side so we can't afford to be complacent.

— Wha'? said Kenny.

— We're not to act the prick, Muggah told him.

Miranda was a bit of a Curehead —

— Darren, said Billy. — Terrific game, son.

— I thought he was pitiful, Pat whispered.

28

They sniggered.

— Fuck off, you, said Darren.

— Listen now, lads, said Bimbo.

— Terrific, said Billy. — One-touch stuff, he told the team. — Get the ball and give it to someone who can do more with it.

— That's the Liverpool way, Muggah whispered.

— I heard tha', said Billy. — And you're righ'; it is.

— wha' abou' me, Billy? said Nappies. — Didn't I have a terrific game as well.

— Yeah, said Kenny. — Pullin' your wire.

— Yis listenin'!? said Billy. — Now listen, I want yis all at trainin' on Tuesday, righ'. No excuses. Annyone not goin' to be there?

No one's hand went up.

— Good, said Billy. — On time as well, righ'. I want to work on some set pieces for Saturday.

— Yeow, Billy!

— Fuck up a minute. Even if it's rainin' there's still trainin', righ'.

— Fair enough.

— Okay.

— Okay, boss.

— Righ'; off yis go home, an' fair play; yis were very good there today. I was proud o' yis.

— We're proud o' you as well, Billy, said Pat.

— Come here you, Bollockchops, said Billy.

They roared.

— What's happened your long throw, pal? Billy wanted to know. — My mother's cat could throw the fuckin' ball further than you did today.

They roared.

— Too much wankin', son, said Billy. — That's your problem.

He ran at Pat.

— Show us your palms there. Come on; hands ou'.

Darren watched Pat jumping over the low wall into the shopping centre carpark. Billy couldn't follow him over.

— See yis, said Darren, quietly.

He headed for home, still wearing his boots and gear. He hoped there'd be hot water. There often wasn't these days.

She was a bit of a Curehead but not that bad: she had a mind of her own. It was just the look, the image she followed, the hair and the Docs. She was into the Cure as well but not only the Cure.

He was walking on the Green, to keep his boots off the concrete.

She was into —

— There's Darren Rabbitte an' his legs.

It was Anita Healy from Darren's class, and her friend, Mandy Lawless.

— Howyis, said Darren.

He grinned and pretended to pull his jersey down over his legs.

— They're nicer than yours, Mandy, said Anita.

— That's true, said Darren. — Yours are hairier though, Mandy.

Anita screamed.

— Fuck off, you, Rabbitte, said Mandy.

She pretended to kick him and Darren grabbed her. She screamed Let go as if she didn't really mean it, and he did. They stood there for a bit.

He saw his da coming.

— Seeyis, he said.

— See yeh, Darren.

Anita shouted after him.

— Mandy said you're a ride, Darren!

— I did not, Anita. Fuck off.

Darren kept going.

Jesus. Mandy wasn't a bad-looking bird — woman. She was a bit Kylie-esque but she'd great legs, real woman's legs. And tits too. She often took her jumper off in school and wrapped it round her waist, even when it wasn't all that hot. Darren liked that, and it annoyed him as well sometimes.

He started to run.

It was Monday. Jimmy Sr was reading to Gina. He had her for the afternoon because Sharon had wanted to go into town. He had been going to play a round of pitch 'n' putt.

— Can yeh not bring her around with yeh in the buggy? Sharon had said. — From hole to hole.

— Are yeh jokin' me, Sharon? he'd said. — They wouldn't let me in. Ah, she'd be too much of a distraction. She'd be hit by a ball. Some o' the wankers tha' go down there are cross-eyed.

— Can yeh not play tomorrow instead? she'd said.

— I am playin' tomorrow, Sharon, he'd told her. — I have to. I'll have to win a turkey between now an'

Christmas an' there's not tha' many weekends left when yeh add them up. I need all the practice I can get. —Okay, okay. Give her to me here.

Veronica wouldn't take her. She had to read six chapters of Lord of the Flies and summarise them; that was her excuse.

— She won't stop yeh from readin', Veronica, for Jaysis sake.

— Take her with you or stay at home, she'd said. — I've other things to do.

So he was stuck with Gina. He didn't mind, not too much. The afternoon off would be good for Sharon. She wasn't looking the best these days, kind of pale and hassled looking. Give her a few hours in the shops and she'd be grand.

Gina was on his lap, trying to grab the book.

— The king is a beau, my good friend, he read. — An' so are you, too, wha'ever — Ah ah; just listen — wha'ever you may say abou' it. Porthos smiled triumphantly. Let's go to the king's tailor, he said — I'll smack yeh if yeh do that again, Gina.

— Smack!

—Yeah. —Now. —An' since he measures the king, I think, by my faith! I may allow him to measure me.

He closed the book.

— I think, by my faith, it's a load o' bollix. — Here.

He put Gina down and got up — Jaysis! — and picked her up.

— Up we get. You're a righ' little buster, aren't yeh?

— G'anda.

32

— That's me. We'll go for a walk, will we? an' find someone to annoy.

He picked up the book. Only thirty-nine pages gone and over four hundred to go still and it was shite. He was sure it was good, brilliant — a classic — but he fuckin' hated it. It wasn't hard; that wasn't it. It was just shite; boring, he supposed, but Shite was definitely the word he was looking for. And he'd have to finish it because he'd told Veronica he was reading it, told her all about it, shown it to her; the fuckin' eejit.

— Better get your anorak, he told Gina.

She pushed his chest and he put her down. She ran to the door — they were in the front room — reached up and got the door open.

Jimmy Sr noticed her pile of video tapes on the shelf; Postman Pat, The Magic Roundabout — that was a great one — five of them, presents from people. And no video to play them in. God love her.

He walloped his leg with the book.

— The Man in the Iron fuckin' Mask.

Maybe he'd tell Veronica he'd finished it (— He escaped, Veronica) and start one of the other ones he'd got out of the library. He was useless; couldn't even read a book properly.

He went down to the kitchen, and the bell rang.

— wha' now?

He went back up the hall. Veronica had no problem reading and finishing her books. He made out Jimmy Jr's shape through the glass.

— What's he doin' here?

He only came on Sundays, since he'd left and shacked up with that Aoife young one; a good-looking young one: too good for that waster.

He opened the front door.

— Howyeh, said Jimmy Jr.

He got past Jimmy Sr.

— Forgot me washin' yesterday, he said. — No kaks or nothin'.

Jimmy Sr followed him down the hall into the kitchen. It was empty; Veronica was swotting up in Sharon's room and the rest were still at school. Jimmy Jr held up the bag with his washing in it. It had Ibiza printed on the side of it, and a little map.

— Here, he said.

— Would Aoife not do your washin' for yeh? said Jimmy Sr.

— No way, said Jimmy Jr.

— Yis divide the work between yis?

— No, said Jimmy Jr. — She told me to fuck off an' do me own washin'.

They laughed a bit.

— She's dead righ', said Jimmy Sr.

— When was the last time you washed annythin'? Jimmy Jr asked him.

— Don't start. I do me fair share.

— Yeah, yeah, yeah. Course yeh do. — I'd better go. I've to make the fuckin' dinner.

— My Jaysis, tha' young one has you by the bollix alrigh', said Jimmy Sr.

He followed Jimmy Jr to the door.

— Come here, said Jimmy Jr. — Could yeh use tha'?

It was a fiver.

— Eh —

— Go on, said Jimmy Jr.

He put it into his da's cardigan pocket.

— A few pints, he said.

— Thanks.

— No problem. See yeh.

— Thanks.

— Shut up, will yeh. See yeh.

— Okay. — Good luck, son.

Sharon found him.

— Did yeh not hear me? she said.

Jimmy Sr was standing facing the door when she walked into the bedroom. He'd been in there since Jimmy Jr'd left.

— Wha'? said Jimmy Sr. — Were yeh lookin' for me, love?

— I was screamin' up at yeh nearly, Sharon told him. — From downstairs. Did yeh not hear me? she asked him again.

— I must have fallen asleep. Dozed off. I was just —

— Are yeh alrigh'?

He looked miserable, and small and kind of beaten looking.

— I'm grand, he said.

He looked around him, as if for a reason for being there.

— The tea's ready, Sharon told him.

— Oh, lovely.

— What's wrong?

— Nothin', Sharon. Nothin'. — Nothin'.

He smiled, but Sharon kept gawking at him.

— There is somethin', isn't there? she said.

— Ah, look —

— I can tell from your —

— Get off me fuckin' back, will yeh!

— Sorry I spoke.

She grabbed the door on her way out.

— I'll be down in a minute.

— Please yourself, she said, and she slammed the door.

She heard wood splitting in the middle of the slam but she didn't stop. She went back downstairs.

In the bedroom Jimmy Sr opened his mouth as wide as he could and massaged his jaws. He was alright now. He'd thought his teeth were going to crack and break; he couldn't get his mouth to open, as if it had been locked and getting tighter. And he'd had to snap his eyes shut, waiting for the crunch and the pain. But then it had stopped, and he'd started breathing again. He felt weak now, a bit weak. He was alright though. He'd be grand in a minute.

He closed his mouth. It was grand now. He'd say sorry to Sharon for shouting at her. He stood up straight. He'd go down now. He took the fiver off the bed and put it in his pocket.

He had young Jimmy's fiver and two more quid Veronica'd given him so he could buy a round. If only Bimbo and Bertie were there the fiver would be enough and he'd be able to give Veronica her money back but if

Paddy was there he'd need it. It was a quarter past ten, early enough to get three or four pints inside him and late enough to make sure that his turn to put his hand in his pocket didn't come round again before closing time.

He came off the Green, crossed the road. The street light here was broken again. The glass was on the path. It was always this one they smashed, only this one.

It was funny; he'd been really grateful when young Jimmy had given him the fiver, delighted, and at the same time, or just after, he'd wanted to go after him and thump the living shite out of him and throw the poxy fiver back in his face, the nerve of him; who did he think he was, dishing out fivers like Bob fuckin' Geldof.

He was grand now though. He had the fiver and he was out on a Monday night.

— There's Jimmy, said Malcolm, one of the Hikers' bouncers.

— Howyeh, Malcolm, said Jimmy Sr.

— Chilly enough.

— Who're yeh tellin'.

He pushed the bar door, and was in.

— The man himself, said Bimbo.

He was pleased to see him; Jimmy Sr could tell. He had a grin on him that you could hang your washing on. There was just himself and Bertie up at the bar, new pints in front of them. Bertie turned and saw Jimmy Sr.

— Ah, he said. — Buenas noches, Jimmy.

— Howyis, said Jimmy Sr.

There was nothing like it, the few scoops with your mates.

— A pint there, Leo, Bimbo shouted down the bar, — like a good man.

Leo already had the glass under the tap. Jimmy Sr rubbed his hands. He wanted to whoop, but he put his hands in his pockets and looked around.

He nodded to a corner.

— Who're they? he said.

— Don't know, compadre, said Bertie. — Gringos.

They were looking over at three couples, all young and satisfied looking.

— They look like a righ' shower o' cunts, said Jimmy Sr.

— You don't even know them, sure, said Bimbo.

Bimbo fell for it every time.

— I wouldn't want to fuckin' know them, Jimmy Sr told Bimbo. — Look at them. They should be upstairs.

The Lounge was upstairs.

— I speet on them, said Bertie.

— Yeh can't stop people from comin' in if they want, said Bimbo. — It's a pub.

— 'Course yeh can, said Jimmy Sr.

— He's righ', compadre, Bertie told Bimbo.

— How is he? said Bimbo. — A pub is a pub; a public house.

Leo arrived with Jimmy Sr's pint.

— Now, said Leo.

— Good man, Leo, said Jimmy Sr. — Fuck me, it looks lovely.

They agreed; it did.

The head of the pint stood higher than the glass, curving up and then flat and solid looking. The outside of the glass was clean; the whole thing looking like an ad. Jimmy Sr tilted the glass a little bit but the head stayed the way it was. They admired it.

— My Jaysis, said Jimmy Sr. — wha'.

They got down off their stools and headed for an empty table.

— Anyway, said Bimbo. — Anyone should be able to come into a pub if they want.

— No way, said Jimmy Sr.

They sat down at their table and settled themselves in; sank into the seats, hooshed up their trousers, threw the dried-up, twisted beermats onto the table beside them — they were dangerous.

There wasn't much of a crowd in.

— Come here, Bimbo, said Jimmy Sr. — Do yeh think annyone should be allowed in here? Annyone now?

— Eh — , said Bimbo.

He didn't want to answer, but he had to.

— Yeah.

— Then what's Malcolm doin' outside then?

He had him.

— In the fuckin' cold, said Jimmy Sr.

— Si, said Bertie. — Poor Malcolm.

— He's gettin' well paid for it, Bimbo told Bertie.

Then he got back to Jimmy Sr.

— That's different, he said. — He's only there to stop messers from comin' in. He's not goin' to stop them just cos he doesn't like them.

— Me bollix, said Jimmy Sr. — How does he tell tha' they're messers?

He had him again.

— He can tell.

— How?

— Si.

— Ah look it, lads, said Bimbo. — Anyone — not messers now, or drug pushers or annyone like tha' — annyone tha' behaves themselves an' likes their pint should be allowed in.

They could tell by the way he spoke and looked at them that he wanted them to agree with him; he was nearly begging them.

— No way, said Jimmy Sr. — No fuckin' way.

Bertie agreed.

— Si, he said.

— Ah; why not?

— Look it, Jimmy Sr started, although he hadn't a breeze what he was going to say.

— Compadre, Bertie took over.

He sat up straight.

— Say we go into town, righ'; we go into town an' we try an' get into one o' those disco bars, righ'?

— Yeah, said Jimmy Sr.

— Would we be let in, would yeh say? Bertie asked Bimbo.

— I wouldn't want to go into one o' them, said Bimbo.

— Answer me question, said Bertie.

Bimbo thought about it.

It wasn't the pints Jimmy Sr loved; that wasn't it. He liked his pint — he fuckin' loved his pint — but that wasn't why he was here. He could do without it. He

WAS doing without it. He only came up about two times a week these days, since he'd been laid off, and he never missed the drink, not really. Every night at about nine o'clock — when he heard the News music — he started getting itchy and he had to concentrate on staying sitting there and watching the News and being interested in it, but it wasn't the gargle he was dying for: it was this (he sat back and smiled at Bimbo); the lads here, the crack, the laughing. This was what he loved.

— Well? Bertie said to Bimbo.

Being on the labour wouldn't have been that bad if you could've come up here every night, or even every second night, and have got your batteries charged. But there you were; he'd a family to feed and that. He was only here now because one of his young fellas had given him a fiver.

— I wouldn't say we'd get in, said Bimbo.

— I agree with yeh, said Bertie. — The hombres at the door would tell us to vamoose an' fuck off. And —

He picked up his new pint.

— they'd be right.

He disappeared behind his pint. Jimmy Sr and Bimbo waited for him.

— Now, said Bertie, and he was looking at Bimbo, — why would they be righ'?

Jimmy Sr loved this.

Bimbo took up his pint, and put it down on the mat again.

— I give up, he said. — I don't know.

— Yeh do know, said Bertie. — It's because we've no righ' to be there. Amn't I righ'?

— Yeah, said Jimmy Sr.

— Disco bars aren't there for the likes of us, Bertie told Bimbo. — They're for young fellas an' signoritas. To go for a drink an' a dance an' wha'ever happens after, if yeh get me drift.

They laughed.

— It's not our scene, said Bertie.

He swept his open hand up and across from left to right, and showed them the room.

— This is our scene, compadre, he said.

— Fuckin' sure, said Jimmy Sr.

Bertie was really enjoying himself. He pointed the things out to them.

— Our pints. Our table here with the beermat under it stoppin' it from wobblin'. Our dart board an' our hoops, over there, look it.

He stamped his foot.

— Our floor with no carpet on it. Our chairs here with the springs all stickin' up into our holes. We fit here, Bimbo, said Bertie. — An' those fuckers over there should go upstairs to the Lounge where they fuckin' belong.

— Ah well, said Bimbo after he'd stopped laughing. — I suppose you're righ'.

— Oh, I am, said Bertie. — I am.

— Yeh are, o' course, said Jimmy Sr. — Come here but, Bertie. You were in one o' them before, weren't yeh? In a disco bar.

— I was indeed, compadre, said Bertie.

— Were yeh? said Bimbo. — wha' were yeh doin' in one them places?

— Watchin' the greyhound racin', said Jimmy Sr.

— Yeh know wha' I mean, said Bimbo. — Don't start now.

— wha' d'yeh think he was doin' there, for fuck sake? Bimbo ignored him.

— Excuse me, Bertie, he said. — Why were yeh in the disco bar?

— There was nowhere else, Bertie told him.

He waited.

— wha' d'yeh mean?

— There was nowhere else to go cos all the other canteenas were shut; comprende?

— No. Not really.

— I got into Limerick after —

— Limerick!?

— Si.

— wha' were yeh doin' there?

— Ah now, said Bertie. — It's a long story, an' it doesn't matter cos it's got nothin' to do with the disco bar.

— Yeah, but why were yeh in Limerick? Jimmy Sr asked him.

— You're beginnin' to annoy me, compadre, said Bertie.

— I was only askin', said Jimmy Sr. — My round, lads.

— No, hang on, Jim, said Bimbo. — I'll get this one.

— It's my round but.

— You're alrigh', said Bimbo. — Don't worry 'bout it. Bimbo stood up so that Leo could see him.

— No, hang on, said Jimmy Sr. — Sit down.

— Not at all, said Bimbo. — You're alrigh'.

— Sit down!

Bimbo didn't know what to do.

— I'll buy me own round, said Jimmy Sr. — Righ'?

People were looking over at them, and wanting something to happen. Leo was at the end of the bar, ready to jump in and save the glass.

Bimbo sat down.

— o' course, Jim, he said. — No problem. I just — Sorry.

— You're alrigh', said Jimmy Sr.

He patted Bimbo's leg.

— Sorry for shoutin' at yeh, he said. — But I'll pay me own way, alrigh'.

— Yeh'd better, said Bertie.

Jimmy Sr smiled.

— Sorry, Jimmy, said Bimbo. — I didn't mean —

— No, Jimmy Sr stopped him.

He stood up.

— Three nice pints here, Leo!

He had a look at his watch on his way back down: he was safe; there wouldn't be time for another full round.

— wha' were yeh doin' in a shaggin' disco bar? Bimbo asked Bertie. — Of all places.

— He told yeh, said Jimmy Sr.

— No, said Bimbo. — He didn't; not really. He only said he was in Limerick.

— Correction, said Bertie. — I told yeh, there was nowhere else to go to.

— Why was tha'?

— Jesus, he's thick, Jimmy Sr told Bertie.

— Everywhere else was shut, Bertie told Bimbo. — By the time I got my burro corralled an' I'd thrown a bit of water on me face an' dusted me poncho it was past closin' time; comprende?

— Yeah, said Bimbo.

— So, said Bertie. — There was this disco bar in the hotel —

— Did yeh stay in a hotel? Jimmy Sr asked him.

— Si.

— Jaysis, wha'.

— Nothin' but the best, said Bertie.

— Was it dear?

— Twenty-six quid.

— Are yeh serious? said Bimbo. — For the one night only?

— Oh, si.

— My God, said Bimbo. — Breakfast?

— Ah, yeah, said Bertie. — 'Course.

— Was it one o' them continental ones, Bertie? Jimmy Sr asked him.

— Fuck, no, said Bertie. — I speet on your continental breakfast. A fry.

— Lovely, said Bimbo. — Was it nice?

— Alrigh', said Bertie.

— That's gas, said Bimbo. — Isn't it?

— Wha'? said Jimmy Sr.

— Bertie bein' in a hotel.

— I still want to know wha' he was doin' in fuckin'
Limerick, said Jimmy Sr.

— Now, Leo shouted from the bar.

— That's me, said Jimmy Sr.

He was up and over to the bar in a second.

— wha' was it like, an'annyway? Bimbo asked Bertie.

— What's tha'?

— The disco bar.

— Oh, tha'. Grand. It wasn't too bad at all.

Jimmy Sr was back.

— Get rid o' some o' them glasses there, Bimbo, will
yeh. Good man.

He lowered the pints onto the table.

— Look at them now, wha'.

— tha' man's a genius, said Bimbo.

— Si, said Bertie.

— How come they let yeh in? Bimbo asked Bertie.

—What's this? said Jimmy Sr.

— The disco bar.

— Oh, yeah.

— I was a guest, compadre, Bertie told Bimbo. — I
was entitled to get in.

— Is tha' righ'?

— Si. I made a bit of an effort.

He held the collar of his shirt for a second.

— Know wha' I mean?

—Yeh brasser, yeh, said Jimmy Sr.

— Fuck off, you, said Bertie. — I'll tell yeh one
thing. It works.

—Wha'?

— Makin' the effort. Dressin' up.

46

Jimmy Sr made his face go sceptical.

— I'd say it does alrigh', he said.

— I'm tellin' yeh, said Bertie.

— Maybe, said Jimmy Sr.

Bimbo was a bit lost.

— He's tryin' to tell us he got off with somethin', Jimmy Sr told him.

— Ah no, said Bimbo. — You're jokin'.

— He is, o' course, said Jimmy Sr.

— I'm sayin' nothin', said Bertie.

Bimbo was looking carefully at Bertie, making sure that he was only messing. Bimbo didn't like that sort of thing; Bertie was married. But he thought he was having them on; he could tell from Bertie's face, looking around him like he'd said nothing. He was definitely codding them.

Bertie caught Bimbo looking at him.

— A big girl, she was, he told him.

— Ah, get ou' of it, said Bimbo.

Jimmy Sr was looking at Bertie as well. He was the same age as Bertie, a few years older only. Bertie hadn't got off with any young one in Limerick; he could tell. But he kept looking.

Jimmy Sr was having problems with one of his laces. The knot was tiny and his fingernails weren't long enough to get at it properly. He'd have to turn the light on; he could hardly feel the knot now it was so small. He'd no nails left either, all bitten to fuck.

— Christ!

He didn't roar it or anything, but it exploded out. And he threw his head up because his neck felt like it was going to burst. He was sitting on the bed, bent over.

His nails usen't to be like this.

He tried to pull the fuckin' shoe off. His neck was getting sorer. He shut his eyes.

— Is that you?

Now he'd woken Veronica.

— Can't get me fuckin' poxy shoe off.

But it was good that she'd woken up. He slumped, then stretched and rubbed his neck.

— Sorry, he said.

— How was it?

— Grand.

— How are all the lads?

She always said Lads like they were kids, like he went out to play with them.

— Grand, he said. — Bimbo was askin' for yeh.

— And what did you tell him?

— Eh —

That was a hard one.

— I said yeh were fine, said Jimmy Sr.

— Did you cross your fingers when you said it?

— Ah, Veronica.

— Ah, Jimmy.

It was alright; she wasn't getting at him.

— I'll have to get into bed with the fuckin' shoe on; look. Veronica sat up and turned on the lamp beside her.

— What's wrong? she said.

— Me shoe; look it.

She looked.

— Can you not tie your laces properly yet?

And she put his foot in her lap and got going on the knot. He nearly fell off the bed turning for her.

— You're useless, she said. — You really are.

For a split second he was going to straighten his leg quick and put his foot in her stomach, the way she spoke to him like that; for a split second only. Not really.

— There.

She had it done already.

It was nice as well sometimes, being mothered by Veronica.

— Thanks very much, he said.

He got up with the rest of them in the mornings, even though he didn't have to; got dressed and all. Only Darren and the twins had to get out of the house early these days, and not that early because the school was only up the road, but it was still mad in the kitchen. He liked it though. He knew chaps that wouldn't bother their arses getting up, and wives as well who stayed in bed and let their kids get themselves off to school. He wasn't like that.

First thing, after he had a piss, he sneaked into Sharon's room and took Gina out of her cot. She'd be waiting for him. It was thick, but he held his breath when he was opening the door until he saw that she was still alive. Every morning; he couldn't help it. She grabbed his neck and the two of them sneaked back out

49

of the room because they knew that they weren't to wake Sharon.

Then they'd hit the twins' room. Veronica stuck her head in and roared at them on her way down to the kitchen and his and Gina's job was to follow Veronica and make sure that they were getting up.

— Yis up, girls?

It was a stupid question because they never were. He'd put Gina down on the bed and she jumped on them and that made them stop pretending that they were still asleep. It was like having a bag of spuds hopping on you. Once, Gina's nappy had burst, and that had got them up quick. When he heard Linda or Tracy telling Gina to stop he got out of the room because they didn't like him to be there when they got out from under the blankets.

He went downstairs by himself. He looked into the front room to see that Darren was up. He didn't look in really; he just knocked. Darren had been sleeping in the front room since they'd decided that Sharon needed a room of her own, for Gina. It was terrible; there were two less in the house — Jimmy Jr and Leslie — and still poor Darren had to sleep on the couch. They'd been going to build an extension in the back; he kept meaning to find out if the Corporation would do it.

This morning Darren was coming out when Jimmy Sr got to the door.

— Howyeh, Darren.

— Howyeh.

— Y'alrigh'?

— Yeah.

— Good. Did yeh tidy up the blankets an' stuff yet?

— Yeah.

— Good man.

He got out of Darren's way and let him go into the kitchen first. Next he unlocked the back door and let Larrygogan in. The fuckin' hound had a hole bored through the door nearly, from scraping at it every morning to get in, and whining. But Veronica never let him in; she didn't seem to hear him. Jimmy Sr had watched her sometimes when the dog was crying and whining outside — it was fuckin' terrible, like a baby being tortured or something — but Veronica didn't notice it; he'd watched her.

When he opened the door the dog was all over him, hopping around him; thanking him, Jimmy Sr sometimes thought. The dog was no thick. He could nearly talk, the noises he made sometimes when he wanted a biscuit or a chip. He didn't just growl; he had different growls that he used, depending on how badly he wanted something, and whimpers and other stuff as well. And sometimes he just looked at you — just looked — and you couldn't help thinking of one of those starving kids in Africa. He was a great oul' dog, Larrygogan was.

— Ah Christ!

His fuckin' paws were wet, and dirty. He jumped at Jimmy Sr again. Jimmy Sr grabbed the dog's legs just before they landed on his trousers.

— Get his towel, Darren, will yeh.

— Okay, said Darren.

Jimmy Sr looked out the open door while Darren was getting him the dog's towel from under the sink. It was pissing out there, and cold. Not real wintery cold, but the stuff that got inside you and made every room in the house seem miserable, except the kitchen when it was full. The poor dog was wringing, like a drowned rat; half his normal size because his hair was all stuck to him. He barked. Then he shook himself. His back paws started slipping on the lino, so Jimmy Sr let go of his legs.

— Here.

Darren threw the towel to Jimmy Sr.

— Good man, said Jimmy Sr.

He opened the towel — it was manky but dry — and got ready to dry the dog's back, and this was the bit the dog loved. Jimmy Sr dropped the towel and missed Larrygogan by a mile because Larry was in under the kitchen table, sliding and barking.

— Come ou' till I dry yeh.

Larrygogan put his chin on the floor and barked at Jimmy Sr.

Jimmy Sr always thought that that bark, the real cheeky one, sounded like Get fucked. And the way his ears jumped up when he said it — not said it, not really; just barked — but he looked like he was saying it, giving cheek to Jimmy Sr, his master. It was gas.

— Come on ou' here, yeh renegade, yeh.

The dog barked again.

— Here, Darren; go round there an' shove him ou' to me.

Jimmy Sr stared at Larrygogan.

— You're fucked now, he said.

— Stop that, said Veronica.

— Sorry, Veronica, he said.

He loved this.

Darren was at the other side of the table. He got down on his knees and stretched in under the table and pushed Larrygogan — Larrygogan was chin down, arse up — but Larrygogan pushed back against Darren's open hands. The dog's paws slid a bit but he stayed put, and Darren had to climb in under the table. He was bursting his shite laughing now, and so was Jimmy Sr.

— Mind he doesn't fart on yeh, he told Darren.

— Oh Jaysis, said Darren, and he couldn't push properly any more because he was laughing so much.

Larrygogan was winning.

— Ah, leave him, said Jimmy Sr.

He stood up.

— Let him catch his death. He deserves to die, the fuckin' eejit of a dog.

Darren got out and up from under the table. They grinned at each other but then Darren sat down and started reading his book. Jimmy Sr shut the door. Larrygogan charged out to the hall.

He still had a good breakfast these days, the fry and loads of toast and a bowl of Cornflakes as well sometimes if he still felt a bit empty. They used to have Sugar Puffs and the rest of them; every time there was a new ad on the telly the twins had to have a box of the new things. But they only had the Cornflakes now. They were the best. Tea as well, loads of it. He only had coffee later on in the day, and sometimes he didn't bother. He didn't need it. Tea though, he loved his cup of tea; twenty bleedin' cups.

He had a mug for work that he'd had for years; he still had it. It was a big plain white one, no cracks, no stupid slogans. He put two teabags into it; used to. My God, he'd never forget the taste of the first cup of tea in the morning, usually in a bare room in a new house with muck and dirt everywhere, freezing; fuck me, it was great; it scalded him on the way down; he could feel it all the way. And the taste it left; brilliant; brilliant. He always used two bags, squeezed the bejesus out of them. The mug was so big it warmed more than just his hands. It was like sitting in front of a fire. After a few gulps he'd sip at it and turn around and look at his work. He always got a few walls done before he stopped for the tea. Even if the other lads were stopping he kept going, till he felt he needed it; deserved it. He'd look around him at the plastering. It was perfect; not a bump or a sag, so smooth you'd never know where he'd started. Then he'd gulp down the rest of the tea and get back to it. The mug was outside in the shed, in a bag with his other work stuff. He'd wrapped toilet paper around it.

— You'll get drenched goin' to school, Darren, he said.

— Yeah, said Darren.

— Still, said Jimmy Sr. — It'll save yeh the bother o' washin' yourself, wha'.

— Yeah, said Darren.

Darren looked at the rain hitting the window.

— Jesus, he said.

54

— Stop that, said Veronica.

— That's the real wet stuff alrigh', Jimmy Sr told Darren.

— I've P.E. today, Darren told him.

— Is tha' righ'? said Jimmy Sr. — Ah, they'll never send yeh ou' in tha'; they couldn't.

— They did the last time.

— Did they, the cunts?

Veronica put his plate in front of him and then walloped him across the head.

— Sorry, he said.

He took out tenpence and dropped it in the swearbox.

— D'yeh want a note for the teacher? he asked Darren.

— He does not, said Veronica.

— No, said Darren. — I don't mind. It might stop.

— That's very true.

Darren got back to his book and his breakfast. Jimmy Sr picked up his knife and fork.

— wha' have we here? he said.

Darren kept reading. Veronica was busy. So he just chopped a bit of sausage off, put it on a piece of toast, closed the toast over on it and bit into it. The marge was lovely and warm.

The twins came in.

— You're to sign this, Linda told Jimmy Sr.

— Get back upstairs and get that stuff off, said Veronica.

— Ah, Mammy —

— Go on! — You too, she told Tracy.

Tracy followed Linda out into the hall.

— It's not fair! they heard Linda.

— wha' was tha' abou'? Jimmy Sr wanted to know.

— They were wearing eye-shadow, said Veronica.

— Oh.

— They were sent home last week for having it on, said Veronica.

— It's crazy, said Darren. — It's pitiful.

Jimmy Sr wasn't sure.

— They're a bit young, he said.

— Sixth years aren't allowed to have it on either, Darren told Jimmy Sr.

— Ah then, said Jimmy Sr. — Then you're righ', Darren. That's just stupid.

— It's a school rule, said Veronica.

— That's right as well, o' course, said Jimmy Sr.

Darren was standing up, putting his book marker carefully into place so it wouldn't fall out.

— If everybody had that attitude, he said, — nothing would ever change.

Jimmy Sr didn't know what to do. He liked hearing Darren talk like that, but he was being cheeky as well; to his mother. There was something about the way Darren spoke since his voice broke that left Jimmy Sr confused. He admired him, more and more; he was a great young fella; he was really proud of him, but he thought he felt a bit jealous of him as well sometimes; he didn't know. Anyway, he wasn't going to be let talk like that to his mother. That was out.

But the twins were back.

— You're to sign this.

Linda had spoken to him.

— Wha'?

— Here.

— Yeah, said Jimmy Sr. — Why but?

He took Linda's homework journal from her.

— Don't know, said Linda. — You're to just sign it.

Jimmy Sr looked at the cover; Big Fun, Wet Wet Wet, Brother Beyond, Tracy loves Keith. He looked at the back; Linda loves Keith.

— Lucky Keith, he said. — Where am I to sign?

Linda took the journal and found the right page.

— Here, she said.

There was a page for each week, divided into sections for subject, homework and teachers' comments.

— You don't have to read them, said Linda.

— Homework not done, Jimmy Sr read. — Persisted in talking. — Homework not done. Cheeky. Stabbed student with compass. — Homework should be done at home.

He looked up.

— Fuckin' hell, he said. — An' that's only Monday.

— Let me see, said Veronica. — My God.

Linda pointed at one of the comments.

— I wasn't cheeky. She just said I was but I wasn't. An' he — tha' one there — he hit me with his ruler so I had to get him back but she didn't see him hittin' me, she on'y seen —

— Saw, said Veronica.

— She only saw me gettin' him with the compass. An' I did not stab him. I on'y —

57

— Shut up! said Jimmy Sr.

He looked at Veronica.

— Give us a pen, he said to Linda. — Where's your journal till I see it, he said to Tracy.

— It's in school, said Tracy.

— Why's tha'?

— A teacher kept it.

— Why?

— He just did.

Jimmy Sr looked at Veronica again.

— You're grounded, he told the twins. — The two o' yis.

He saw Parent's Signature, and signed the dotted line.

— Till when? said Tracy.

— Till I say so, said Jimmy Sr. — Who told yeh to get me to sign this?

— Miss McCluskey.

— Elephant Woman, said Darren, on his way out.

— Don't start now, said Jimmy Sr.

He stared the twins out of it.

— I'm warnin' yis, he said. — If one o' yis laughs I'll tan your arses for yis.

Tracy started; she couldn't keep it in. And that got Linda going.

— Here, said Jimmy Sr.

He walloped her with the journal, but not too hard.

— I'm checkin' your homework every nigh', d'yeh hear me. An' —

He shouted after them.

— if I see anny more bad comments I'll —

The front door slammed.

— crucify yis! — The pair o' them'll be pushin' buggies before they're fifteen.

— Oh God, said Veronica. — Don't.

He looked at Veronica, carefully.

— I'll check their eccers every nigh', don't worry. An' we won't let them out at all after their tea, an' that'll sort them ou', wait an' see, Veronica. Fair enough?

— Okay.

— I'll do everythin'. I'll even sleep in the same bed as them.

— Jesus, said Veronica. — We've enough trouble in the house without that as well.

Jimmy Sr laughed.

— Good girl, he said. — An' you can sleep with Darren. How's tha'?

He loved the breakfasts. Pity they went so quick.

He got up.

Where was Gina?

— No rest for the wicked, he said.

— They're not real computers annyway, sure they're not.

— Not at all, said Veronica. — They're only toys.

Jimmy Sr and Veronica were doing a bit of Christmas shopping. It was Thursday morning and more than three weeks to go, so Donaghmede Shopping Centre — where they were — wasn't too bad, not too crowded. They hadn't really said it, but they were looking for things that looked good and cost nothing. It reminded Jimmy Sr of when he was a kid and he used to walk along with his head down and pray, really pray, that he'd find money on the path, and he'd close his eyes turning a corner and then open them and there'd be nothing on the ground in front of him.

— And they're very bad for your eyes, said Veronica.

— Is tha' righ'? said Jimmy Sr. — Oh yeah; I read somethin' abou' tha' somewhere, I think. — Ah well, then. We'd be mad to get one for them.

They'd just been looking at the computers in a window. They were for nothing, dirt cheap; great value they looked. You linked them into the telly and then you could play all kinds of games on them. Jimmy Sr had played Space Invaders once, years ago; only the once, so he hadn't really got the hang of it, but he'd enjoyed himself. These things looked better; more colours and varieties. It would have been good to have one at home, a bit of gas. And, as well as that, it was a computer, after all; there were probably other things you could do with them, not just play games. Only they couldn't afford one of the fuckin' things. Last year now, last year they'd have bought —

— Sure, who'd we give it to? said Veronica.

— The twins. I suppose.

— They wouldn't be interested, said Veronica. — They'd hate you if you gave them one of them.

She laughed.

— I'd love to see the look on their faces if they thought they were getting a computer game for Christmas.

Jimmy Sr laughed as well now.

60

— Yeah, he said. — I just thought they looked the business, yeh know. Darren?

— He'd be insulted.

She was right.

— You'd be the only one who'd use it, said Veronica.

He made himself smile.

— True, he said.

— We'll get you an Airfix instead, said Veronica.

It was crying alright; she was crying.

Jimmy Sr was outside Sharon's room. He'd come up for his book.

Sharon snuffled.

Jimmy Sr held the door handle. He was going to go in.

But he couldn't.

He wanted to, but he couldn't. He wouldn't have known what to do any more.

He went back down to the kitchen very carefully, and stepped down over the stair with the creak in it.

Veronica had been in already to have a look at her. It was his turn now. One, two —

He grabbed the handle and went straight into the front room.

— Sorry, Darren; for bargin' in on yeh — Oh, hello.

— Hi.

She smiled. God, she was lovely.

He held his hand out to her.

— Darren's da, he said. — Howyeh.

She blushed a bit; lovely.

— This is Miranda, Darren told Jimmy Sr.

— Sorry, said Jimmy Sr. — I didn't catch —

— Miranda, said Darren.

— Miranda, said Jimmy Sr. — Howyeh, Miranda.

— Fine, thank you, said Miranda.

— 'Course yeh are, said Jimmy Sr.

— Were yeh lookin' for somethin' in particular? Darren asked him.

He had one of his smirks on him, one of his they-treat-me-like-a-kid ones. But he was chuffed as well, you could tell.

Jimmy Sr patted him on the head.

— I am indeed, Darren, son, he said. — I'm lookin' for Gina.

— She's not here.

— No, that's true, Jimmy Sr agreed. — But Miranda is, wha'. Bye bye, Miranda.

He shut the door after him. She was a cracker alright. Veronica'd said she was lovely but women always said that other women were lovely and they weren't; they hadn't a clue. Miranda though, she was a —

A ride; she was. It was weird thinking it; his son was going out with a ride; but it was true. He could've given himself a bugle now, out here in the hall, just remembering what she was like and her smile; no problem.

He'd never gone out with a young one like that.

He went back into the kitchen to tell Veronica he liked her.

There were days when there was this feeling in his guts all the time, like a fart building up only it wasn't that at

62

all. It was as if his trousers were too tight for him, but he'd check and they weren't, they were grand; but there was a little ball of hard air inside in him, getting bigger. It was bad, a bad sort of excitement, and he couldn't get rid of it. It was like when he was a kid and he'd done something bad and he was waiting for his da to come home from work to kill him. He used to use his belt, the bollix. He didn't wear a belt; he only kept it for strapping Jimmy Sr and his brothers; under the sink he kept it, a big leather thing; he'd take ages bending over, looking for it and then testing it on the side of the sink and saying Ah yes as if he was pleased with it; and he'd stare at Jimmy Sr and make him stare back and then Jimmy Sr'd feel the pain on the side of his leg and again and again and it was fuckin' terrible and it was worse if he took his eyes off his da's eyes, the fuckin' sadistic cunt, so he had to keep staring back at him; it was agony, but not as bad as the waiting. Waiting for it was the worst part. If he did something early in the day and his mother said she was going to tell his da, that was it; she never changed her mind. He'd go through the whole day scared shitless, waiting for his da to come home, praying that he'd go for a pint first or get knocked down by a car or fall into a machine at work or get a heart attack, any fuckin' thing.

And that was how he sometimes — often — felt now, scared shitless. And he didn't know why.

— Did yeh ever read David Copperfield, Veronica? said Jimmy Sr.

— No, said Veronica.

63

She was reading Lord of the Flies at the kitchen table.

— Did yeh not? said Jimmy Sr. — Ah, it's very good.

The best thing he'd ever done was give up on that Man in the Iron Mask fuckology.

— Look at the size of it but, he said. — Eight hundred pages. More. Still though, it's the business. There's this cunt in it called Mr Micawber an', I'm not jokin' yeh — D'yeh want to read it after me, Veronica?

Veronica finished the note she was taking, about Piggy getting his head smashed. She knew what he wanted her to say.

— Okay, she said.

— Do yeh? said Jimmy Sr. — Fair enough. I'd better finish it quick so. I've to bring it back to the library on the twenty-first of December.

He checked the date.

— Yeah, he said.

— We've loads of time, said Veronica.

— 'Course we have, said Jimmy Sr.

He was delighted. He didn't know why, exactly.

— Do you want this one when I'm finished with it? Veronica asked him.

— Okay, said Jimmy Sr. — That's a good idea. A swap, wha'.

— Yes, said Veronica.

He looked at her reading and stopping and taking her notes. He wondered if maybe he should take notes as well. He sometimes forgot what —

No; that would just have been thick; stupid.

— I'll go up an' get a few more chapters read before the tea, he told Veronica.

— Grand, said Veronica.

— They're stupid fuckin' things annyway, said Jimmy Sr.

— Ah — I know, but —

Veronica wasn't convinced.

Jimmy Sr picked up one of the cards.

— For instance, he said, — look at this one, look it. Dessie an' Frieda; they only live around the fuckin' corner, we see them every fuckin' day!

Veronica's face was the same.

— Annyway, said Jimmy Sr. — It's you says tha' we can't send any, not me.

Veronica's face hardened. Jimmy Sr got in before she could.

— You said we can't afford them, he said. — I don't mind.

— We can't afford them, said Veronica.

— There, said Jimmy Sr. — Yeh said it again. We can't afford them. So we won't send any. — So wha' are yeh whingin' abou'? It's your idea.

Veronica sighed. She just looked sad again.

— That's not fair, she said.

— How is it not fair? Jimmy Sr wanted to know. — How is it not fair!?

Veronica sighed again.

— How!?

— You're blaming me, said Veronica.

— Yeah, said Jimmy Sr. — An' you're blamin' me.

—What d'you mean? said Veronica.

—Yeh are, said Jimmy Sr. —You've decided tha' we haven't the money to buy Christmas cards an' you're probably righ'. But then you put this puss on yeh — It's not my fault we've no fuckin' money for your fuckin' Christmas cards!

— I never said it was.

— No, but yeh looked it; I have eyes, yeh know.

He stood up.

— Ah, Jimmy —

— Ah, nothin'; I'm sick of it; just — fuck off!

Jimmy Sr was holding a bottle of Guinness. He had a can of Tennents in his other hand and an empty glass between his knees, so he was having problems. That was the worst thing about not being at home; just that; you weren't at home, so you couldn't do what you wanted. You had to watch yourself.

He was in Bimbo's house.

If he'd been in his own gaff he wouldn't have been sitting like this, like a gobshite, too far back in the armchair — he couldn't get out of the fuckin' thing because his hands were full. He didn't want to put the can or the bottle on one of the arms of the chair because the wood was at an angle like a ski jump and very shiny; he could smell the polish. And Bimbo's kids were flying around the place, in and out, like fuckin' — kids. And this fuckin' tie he had on him, it was killing him; it was sawing the fuckin' neck off him. It was the shirt, a new one Veronica'd given him; she said he'd put on weight. It wasn't fuckin' fair: he was drinking far less but he was getting fuckin' fatter. She said he was anyway. She'd probably said it because it was either that or admit that she'd bought him the wrong size of a shirt. Anyway, he was fuckin' choking and he couldn't loosen the poxy tie because his fuckin' hands were full —

Jesus tonight!

It was Christmas morning. They did this every Christmas, went to one of their houses and had a few scoops before the dinner. It was good; usually. He wasn't sure, but he had a good idea that it was really his and Veronica's turn to have the rest of them in their house; he wasn't sure. Bimbo had just said, Will yis all be comin' to our place for your Christmas drinks? a few days ago and Jimmy Sr hadn't bothered saying anything because there was no point; they hadn't the money to buy the drink for them all.

They'd only a few cans for themselves at home, and Jimmy Jr was bringing some more. He was supposed to be anyway.

He leaned forward as far as he could go and put the Tennents on the floor; he could just reach it. That was better. Now he could organise himself a bit better. He rescued the glass from between his knees and held it for the Guinness.

Bimbo's mother-in-law was still looking over at him.

Let her, the bitch.

He wished Bertie would hurry up. He was good with oul' ones like that. He told them they were looking great and he wished he was a few years older and that kind of shite. Jimmy Sr was no good at that sort of thing, not this morning anyway.

She was still looking at him.

He smiled over at her.

— Cheers, he said.

She just looked at him.

Jesus, he didn't know how Bimbo could stick it. Where the fuck was Bimbo anyway? He was by himself in here, except for Freddy Kruger's fuckin' granny over there. He said he'd be back in a minute. And that was hours ago. He was playing with one of the kids' computers, that was what the cunt was doing; leaving Jimmy Sr here stranded.

Veronica was inside in the kitchen with Maggie, Bimbo's one.

— That's a great smell comin' from the kitchen, wha', said Jimmy Sr.

Her mouth moved.

—What's tha'? he said, and he leaned out.

Maybe she hadn't said anything. Maybe she couldn't help it; she couldn't control her muscles, the ones that held her mouth up. Ah Jaysis, this was fuckin' terrible; fuck Bimbo anyway.

He heard feet on the path.

— Thank fuck.

It was out before he knew it. And she nodded; she did; she'd heard him; oh Christ!

She couldn't have; no. No, she'd just nodded at the same time, that was all. Because, probably, her neck wasn't the best any more, that was all. He hoped.

The bell rang; the first bit of Strangers in the Night.

She definitely hadn't heard him.

Stupid fuckin' thing for a bell to do, play a song. Anyway, they didn't even need a bell. This house was the exact same as Jimmy Sr's; you could hear a knock on the door anywhere in the house.

Bertie came in.

— Compadre!

Jimmy Sr got up out of the chair.

— Happy Christmas, Bertie.

They shook hands. Bertie's hand was huge, and dry.

Vera, the wife, was with him; a fine thing, Jimmy Sr'd always thought; still in great nick.

— Howyeh, Jimmy love, she said, and she stuck her cheek out, sort of, for him to kiss.

He kissed it. It wasn't caked in that powdery stuff that a lot of women wore when they were out. Mind you, Veronica didn't wear that stuff either.

The room was fuller now; Jimmy Sr, Vera, Bertie, Bimbo and two of his kids, and the mother-in-law over there in her corner. Jimmy Sr felt happier now.

— What'll yeh have, Vera? said Bimbo.

— D'yeh want a Tennents? Jimmy Sr asked Bertie.

— Oh si, said Bertie.

— Bimbo gave me one, Jimmy Sr explained, — an' then he asked me if I'd prefer a bottle o' stout an' I said Fair enough, so —

He picked the can up off the floor.

— I didn't open it or annythin'.

— Good man, said Bertie. — Gracias.

— Will yis have a small one with them? Bimbo asked Jimmy Sr and Bertie.

Jimmy Sr looked at Bertie and Bertie shrugged.

— Fair enough, yeah, said Jimmy Sr. — Good man.

This was the business now alright. He grinned at Vera, and lifted his glass.

— Cheers, wha'.

— What did Santy bring yeh, Jimmy? Vera asked him.

— This, said Jimmy Sr.

He showed her his new shirt.

— Very nice.

— It's a bit small.

— Ah no; it's nice.

Bertie had found Maggie's mother.

— Isn't she lookin' even better than last year? he said to them.

— Def'ny, said Jimmy Sr, but he couldn't look at her.

— They're in the kitchen, Jimmy Sr told Vera.

— Good for them, said Vera.

Bimbo came back with the small ones and Vera's drink, a gin or a vodka.

— The cavalry, said Bertie. — Muchos gracias, my friend.

— The girls are in the kitchen, Bimbo told Vera.

— Good, said Vera.

Jimmy Sr reckoned she'd had a few already. Maybe not though: she wasn't really like the other women, always making fuckin' sandwiches and tea and talking about the Royal Family and Coronation Street and that kind of shite. She kept their house grand though; any time Jimmy Sr had been in it anyway.

Bertie leaned in nearer to Bimbo.

— There's a funny whiff off your mammy-in-law, he told him.

Bimbo looked shocked.

— She might be dead, said Bertie.

Jimmy Sr burst his shite laughing. Poor Bimbo's face made it worse. Vera laughed as well. She just laughed straight out; she didn't cluck cluck like a lot of women would've, like Veronica would've.

— Go over, Bertie told Bimbo. — I'm tellin' yeh, compadre, the hum is fuckin' atrocious.

— My God, said Bimbo, dead quiet. — Is she after doin' somethin' to herself?

— Go over an' check, said Bertie. — It might have been just a fart, but —

Bimbo looked around, to make sure that none of the kids was around to witness this.

— Hang on, said Jimmy Sr. — I can smell somethin' meself now alrigh'.

— Isn't it fuckin' woeful? said Bertie.

— Oh God, said Bimbo.

— This could ruin your Christmas dinner, compadre, Bertie told Bimbo.

Bottled Guinness got up into Jimmy Sr's nose.

He went out into the hall to sort himself out and to laugh properly. This was great; this was the kind of thing you remembered for the rest of your life.

— You'll never get it out o' the upholstery, said Bertie.

Jimmy Sr wanted to go out into the garden and roar, really fuckin' howl.

One of Bimbo's kids — Wayne he thought it was — ran into the room to tell his da something —

— Get ou'! said Bimbo.

And then.

— Sorry, son; go in an' tell your mammy I need her.

— Tell her to bring a few J-cloths, said Bertie.

— No! don't, Wayne, said Bimbo. — Off yeh go.

Wayne came out, looking like he'd just changed his mind about crying, and galloped down to the kitchen walloping the side of his arse like he was on a horse.

When Jimmy Sr went back into the room Bimbo was over at his mother-in-law, pretending he was looking for something on the shelf behind her. Vera pointed at Bertie and whispered to Jimmy Sr.

— He did this to his brother last night, she said. — The exact same thing.

Bimbo came back. They got in together, to consult.

— I can't smell annythin', said Bimbo.

— Can yeh not? said Bertie.

— D'yeh have a cold? Jimmy Sr asked Bimbo. — It's gettin' worse.

— It's not, is it? said Bimbo. — God, this is desperate.

Maggie and Veronica arrived, and most of Bimbo's kids.

— What's up? said Maggie. — Ah howyeh, Vera.

— Howyeh, Maggie. Happy Christmas. Happy Christmas, Veronica.

— And yourself, Vera; happy Christmas.

— Never mind Christmas, said Bimbo.

He nodded his head back; he didn't want to look. He whispered.

— We've an emergency on our hands.

— How come? said Maggie.

Jimmy Sr was having real problems keeping his face straight. So was Vera. Bertie though, he looked like a doctor telling you that you had cancer.

— Your mother — , said Bimbo.

— She has a name, you know, said Maggie.

— That's not all she has, signora, said Bertie.

That was it; Guinness, snot, probably some of his breakfast burst up into Jimmy Sr's mouth and nose; it didn't get past his teeth — he was lucky there — but something landed on his shirt; he didn't care, not yet; his eyes watered —

— Fuck; sorry.

And he laughed.

Veronica had her handkerchief out and was trying to get the snot off his shirt.

He laughed like he was dying of it; it was hurting him but it was fuckin' great. Veronica was tickling him as well and that made it worse.

Veronica started laughing at him laughing.

They were all laughing now, even Bimbo. He knew he'd been had but he didn't mind; he never did; only sometimes.

Jimmy Sr felt a fart coming on, and he didn't trust himself with it; he couldn't, not the way he was, helpless from the laughing and sweating and that; he'd have ended up being the one who'd ruined Bimbo's Christmas — by shiteing all over his new carpet.

— Eh, the jacks, he said.

— Off yeh go, said Bertie.

It took him ages to get up the stairs; he had to haul himself up them.

He had a piss while he was up there, and gave his hands a wash; he always did when he was in someone's house.

He was some tulip, Bertie; he was fuckin' gas.

Jesus, the water was scalding.

He dried his hands, and looked at his watch: half-twelve. That was good; they'd stay another hour and a half or so. The crack would be good.

Vera; she was a fine-looking bird. She looked after herself — whatever that meant. She looked healthy, that was it. She looked healthier than Veronica. She was a good bit younger than Veronica, maybe ten years. But she looked like she'd been a young one not so long ago and poor Veronica looked like she'd never been a young one. It wasn't just age though.

Bimbo had an electric razor.

He had two of them, two razors, the jammy bastard; an ordinary-looking one and a thin yellow one that didn't look like it could've been much good. Jimmy Sr picked up the yellow one: Girl Care. What the fuck —

She was a bit of a brasser, Vera, but Jimmy Sr liked that.

It was Maggie's, that was it; for her legs or — only her legs probably. He pressed a small rubber button, and it came on but there was hardly any noise out of it. He put his foot up on the bath and lifted his trouser leg and pulled down his sock a bit; new socks, from the twins.

— One from each o' yis, wha', he'd said when he'd unwrapped them, earlier at home.

He looked at the door; it was alright, it was locked.

He slowly put the Girl yoke down on top of a couple of long hairs, there on his shin: nothing. He massaged another bit of his leg with it, and then felt it. It was smooth alright but — it was smooth there anyway. There was a clump of about ten hairs growing out of a sort of a mole yoke he'd had since he was a kid.

They were real wiry, these hairs, and blacker than the other ones. He wouldn't put the head of the razor straight down on top of them; he'd just run the thing over the mole quickly and see what it did.

He looked at the door again. Vera probably used one of these, when she was shaving her legs —

— Ah fuck this!

He threw the Girl Care back onto the shelf over the sink.

God, he was a right fuckin' eejit. Shaving his legs; for fuck sake!

He was sweating.

He'd better get back down to the others.

Shaving his fuckin' legs.

He felt weak, hopeless, like he'd been caught. Was something happening him?

He turned on the cold tap.

No, fuck it; he'd only been curious, that was all; he'd only wanted to see if the fuckin' thing worked, that was all.

The cold water was lovely on his face. Nice towel as well; lovely and soft. Maggie had probably put it into the bathroom just before they'd arrived, just for them. It wasn't damp and smelly, the way it would've been if the whole family had been through it that morning.

Fair play to Bimbo; and Maggie. They had the house lovely.

He felt better now. That hot wetness was gone. He was grand now.

He unlocked the door and went downstairs.

It was nice. The window was open and it wasn't cold at all. There was no one out on the road; no voices or cars. No one would've been out on Christmas Day night; there was nowhere to go, unless they'd been out visiting the mother or something and they were on their way home.

Veronica was asleep.

That was the first time they'd done the business in a good while; two months nearly. Made love. He'd never called it that; it sounded thick. Riding your wife was more than just riding, especially when yis hadn't done it in months, but — he could never have said Let's make love to Veronica; she'd have burst out laughing at him.

He wasn't tired. He hadn't drunk much. There hadn't been that much to drink, but that didn't matter; he wouldn't have wanted it anyway. Anyway as well, he'd had a snooze after they got back from Bimbo's while Veronica and Sharon were getting the dinner ready.

Veronica had caught him feeling her legs to see if they were smooth, to see if she shaved them.

— What're you doing?

— Nothin'.

She hadn't really caught him; he'd have been doing it anyway. But he'd had to keep feeling them up and down from her knees up to her gee after she'd said that, so she wouldn't think he'd stopped just cos she'd said it.

They were smooth, except on her shins. They were a bit prickly there.

Young Jimmy'd come for the dinner. In a taxi, no less. Fair play to him. And five cigars for Jimmy Sr from Aoife, his mot. That was very nice of her; he'd only met her the once. She was a nice young one, too nice for that —

That wasn't fair. He was alright, young Jimmy. He was staying the night, downstairs with Darren. And Darren was well set up as well, with a lovely-looking young one.

Aoife and Miranda.

Two lovely names. There was something about them; just thinking of the names, not even the girls themselves, got him going. They were models' names.

Veronica wasn't what you'd have called a sexy name. Or Vera.

Vera wasn't too bad though. There was no saint called Vera as far as he knew.

Veronica shifted and moved in closer to him. That was nice. He felt guilty now; not really though. He put his hand on her back.

That fucker Leslie hadn't got in touch; not even a card. Even just to tell them where he was; and that he was alive. He'd been caught robbing a Lifeboat collection box out in Howth. He hadn't even been caught, just seen by an off-duty cop who knew him. And that was why he'd left, for robbing a couple of quids' worth of fivepences and twopences. Last August that was. He'd spent two nights in Veronica's sister's in Wolverhampton, and that was it; they hadn't heard from him since. On the run. He was only nineteen. He'd have gone eventually anyway; he was always in trouble and never at home, and you couldn't be held responsible for a nineteen-year-old. They were better off without him. Jimmy Sr had taken the day off work to go with Leslie to court the first time, about five years ago now, for trespassing on the tracks.

Poor Veronica had bought a present for him, just in case; a jumper. But she hadn't put it under the tree. It was up in the wardrobe over there, all wrapped up. She hadn't said anything when he didn't turn up yesterday or even today. She'd been in good form all day. You never knew with Veronica.

Jimmy Sr would throw the little shitehawk out on his ear if he turned up now. No, though; he wouldn't.

Trespassing on the tracks. Then he'd gone on to the big time, robbing fuckin' poor boxes. He was probably sleeping in a cardboard box —

It hadn't been a bad day; not too bad at all. Fair enough, probably nobody got the present they'd really wanted — the faces on the poor twins when they'd seen their presents, clothes. They used to get new clothes

78

anyway, their Christmas clothes; their presents had always been separate. Still, they were happy enough with the clothes. They'd been changing in and out of them all day. They were getting very big, real young ones. Gina was the only real child left in the house.

Jimmy Sr had got David Copperfield for Darren, and he'd liked it; you could tell. To Darren From His Father; that was what he'd written inside it. He saw Darren reading it after the tea.

They'd had their turkey as well, same as always; a grand big fucker. They'd be eating turkey sandwiches for weeks. He'd won it with two Saturdays to spare, and a bottle of Jameson. His game had definitely improved since he'd gone on the labour.

He got a tea-towel for Veronica, with Italia 90 on it. She liked it as well. She showed it to Sharon and the two of them laughed. He gave out to her later when he caught her using it to dry the dishes and she'd laughed again, and then he had as well. That was what it was for, he supposed. But she could have kept it for — he didn't know — a special occasion or something.

— Jimmy, love, she'd said. — Christmas is a special occasion.

Then she'd shown him how to use it; for a laugh. It had been a good oul' day.

You got used to it. In fact, it wasn't too bad. You just had to fill your day, and that wasn't all that hard really. And now that the days were getting a bit longer — it was January — the good weather would be starting soon and he'd be able to do things to the garden. He had plans.

The worst part was the money, not having any of it; having to be mean. For instance, Darren had gone to Scotland with the school when he was in second year, but the twins wouldn't be going anywhere. They'd come home soon and ask and he'd have to say No, or Veronica would; she was better at it.

Unless, of course, he got work between now and then.

Only, it was easier to cope if you didn't think things like that, getting work. You just continued on, like this was normal; you filled your day. The good thing about winter was that the day was actually short. It was only in the daylight that you felt bad, restless, sometimes even guilty. Mind you, the time went slower, probably because of the cold.

It hadn't been cold at all yet this winter, not the cold that made your nose numb. Inside in the house during the day, when they didn't have a fire going — when the kids were at school — and they didn't have any heaters on, except in Sharon's room for Gina, it was never really cold, just sort of cool, damp without being damp. It wasn't bad once you were dressed properly.

He'd had to take his jacket off a good few times when he was out walking with Gina it was so warm. He did that a lot, went out with Gina. He even took her to the pitch 'n' putt once, and some fuckin' clown had sent a ball bouncing off the bar of her buggy when Jimmy Sr was teeing up at the seventh, the tricky seventh. God, if he'd hit her he'd have killed her, and

80

he'd only said Sorry and then asked Jimmy Sr did he see where his fuckin' ball had gone. Jimmy Sr told him where the fuckin' ball would go if he ever did it again. But it had scared him.

Mind you, at least he'd had something to tell Veronica when he got home, something genuine. Sometimes he made up things to tell her, little adventures; some oul' one dropping her shopping or some kid nearly getting run over. He felt like a right prick when he was telling her but he kind of had to, he didn't know why; to let her know that he was getting on fine.

He went into town and wandered around. He hadn't done that in years. It had changed a lot; pubs he'd known and even streets were gone. It looked good though, he thought. He could tell you one thing: there was money in this town.

— Si.

Bertie agreed with him, and so did Bimbo.

Young ones must have been earning real money these days as well; you could tell by the way they dressed. He'd sat on that stone bench with the two bronze oul' ones chin-wagging on it, beside the Halfpenny Bridge; he'd sat on the side of that one day and and he'd counted fifty-four great-looking young ones going by in only a quarter of an hour; brilliant-looking women now, and all of them dressed beautifully, the height of style; they must have paid fortunes for the stuff they had on them; you could tell.

He'd read three of your man, Charles Dickens' books now; they were brilliant; just brilliant. He was going to do some Leaving Cert subjects next year, next September; at night, like Veronica. He read the papers from cover to cover these days. He read them in Raheny Library, or Donaghmede if he felt like a change. He preferred Raheny. And he watched Sky News in the day. He couldn't keep up with what was happening these days, especially in the Warsaw Pact places. They were talking about it one day, him and Darren and Sharon and Veronica, and even the twins, at their dinner; they were talking about it and he'd noticed one thing: the twins called Thatcher Thatcher and Bush Bush but they called Gorbachev Mr Gorbachev: that said something. Because they could be cheeky little bitches when they wanted to be.

Sky News was good, better than their other poxy channel, Sky One. But he wouldn't pay for it when they had to start paying for it later in the year sometime. It wasn't worth it, although he didn't know how much they were going to charge. And that reminded him: there'd been a bill from Cablelink stuck up on the fridge door for weeks now. It could stay there for another few; fuck it.

He'd made a list of things to do in the house and he was doing one a week. He'd fixed the jacks yesterday, for example; tightened the handle. It was working grand again now. That sort of thing. But nothing mad. He wasn't going to become one of those do-it-yourself gobshites, fixing things that didn't need fixing, and then invading the neighbours and fixing their stuff as well, and probably making a bollix of it. Once the weather got better and the days got a bit longer, he'd be out there in the garden, ah yes; he wouldn't notice the days flying past him then. He had plans.

He had loads of things to keep him going. The money was the only thing. He'd be going past a pub in town and he'd have the gum for a pint — he always did when he heard the voices and the telly on — just one pint, but he couldn't go in; he couldn't afford it. Or he couldn't buy an ice-cream for Gina when they were out, not that he'd let her have an ice-cream in this weather, but that kind of thing; it was irritating. It was humiliating.

Still though, money wasn't everything. He was happy enough.

Bimbo was crying.

Jaysis.

Bimbo; of all —

— What's up? said Jimmy Sr.

But that sounded bad, like nothing big was happening. The man was crying, for fuck sake.

— What's wrong with yeh?

That was worse.

— Are yeh alrigh'?

Better.

He sat down, in front of Bimbo, at the other side of the table. He blocked Bimbo from the rest of the bar so no one could see him, unless they were looking.

— Ah, I'm —

Bimbo tried to smile. He wiped his cheeks with the outside of his hand.

— I'm grand.

It was like Bimbo remembered where he was. He sat up and lifted up his pint. Jimmy tasted his; it was fine, the first in five days.

— I got a bit o' bad news earlier, said Bimbo. — It knocked me a bit.

He shrugged.

Bimbo's parents were already dead. Jimmy Sr knew that because he remembered that they'd died very close to each other, a couple of weeks between them only. Maybe Maggie's mother had snuffed it but — Bimbo was a bit of a softy but he wouldn't break out crying in his local for Maggie's mother; she'd been as good as dead for fuckin' years. One of the kids —

Oh fuck. He wished Bertie was here.

Bimbo spoke.

— I was let go this mornin'.

— Wha'?

— Let go. — I'm like you now, Jimmy, wha'. A man o' leisure.

— You were —?

— Yeah; gas, isn't it?

He could see Bimbo's eyes getting watery again. Poor Bimbo.

— How come? said Jimmy Sr, hoping that it might get Bimbo talking instead of crying.

— Oh. Ten of us got letters. The oldest, yeh know. In the canteen, on our way ou'.

Bimbo was a baker.

— The chap from the office said tha' they had to compete with the big boys. That's wha' he called them, the big boys.

84

— The fuckin' eejit.

Bimbo hardly ever said Fuck.

— They need our wages to compete with the big boys — wha'.

— That's shockin', said Jimmy Sr.

Bimbo was twirling the stout in his glass; he didn't know what he was doing.

— Any chance they'll take yeh back when they've — yeh know?

— He said Yeah, the young fella from Personnel tha' gave us the letters. I didn't believe him though. I wouldn't believe him if he — tha' sort o' fella, yeh know.

Bimbo sat up straight again.

— Ah sure —

He grinned.

— We'll keep each other company anyway, wha'.

— Ah yeah, said Jimmy Sr. — Fuckin' sure.

There was that about it. He stopped himself from thinking that this was good news, but he nearly couldn't help it.

It was shocking though. Bimbo was younger than him and he was being fucked out on his ear because he was too old.

— My father, God rest him, got me in there, said Bimbo.

— That's righ'.

— His brother, me Uncle Paddy, he worked there.

— Yeah.

— I'll never forget comin' home the first week with me first wage packet. I ran all the way, nonstop all the way with me hand in me pocket to stop me money from fallin' ou'. An' a bag o' cakes tha' had been sent back. Fruit slices. Fly cemeteries. I was more excited abou' the cakes than I was abou' the money, that's how young I was. I knew I'd be king o' the castle when me sisters saw the fruit slices. Marie's little one has epilepsy, did I tell yeh?

Marie was one of Bimbo's sisters, the one Jimmy Sr liked.

— No; is tha' righ'?

— Yeah; Catherine. She's only six. Sad, isn't it?

— Jesus, yeah. — Six?

Bimbo started crying again. His face collapsed. He rubbed his nose. He searched for a hankie he didn't have. He gulped. He smiled through it.

— What am I goin' to do, Jimmy?

They got locked, of course. Bertie was great when he arrived.

— That's great news, compadre, he told Bimbo. — You were always a poxy baker anyway, wha'.

And Bimbo burst his shite laughing; he was delighted. And Bimbo's laugh; when Bimbo laughed everyone laughed. Veronica always said that Bimbo's laugh lassoed you.

— Three nice pints, por favor, Bertie roared across to Leo, the barman. — An' John Wayners, lads?

— Jaysis, said Jimmy Sr.

He hadn't much money on him. Still though —

— Fair enough, he said.

— Okay, said Bimbo. — Me too.

— Good man, said Bertie. — An' Leo? he roared. — Three Jamesons as well.

And then Paddy turned up.

— How much of a lump sum will yeh be gettin'? Paddy asked Bimbo when he came in.

— Jesus Christ, said Jimmy Sr. — He isn't even sittin' down yet an' he wants to know how much money you're gettin'.

Bimbo laughed.

— I couldn't give a shite how much he's gettin', said Paddy.

— Then wha' did yeh ask him for then?

— I only asked him, said Paddy. — Fuck off.

— A couple o' thousand, said Bimbo.

— Don't tell him, said Jimmy Sr.

— Around three, said Bimbo. — I don't know. They're tellin' us on Monday.

— We'll meet up here at teatime on Monday so, said Bertie.

— Ah yeah, Bimbo assured them. — We'll have to have a few pints out of it alrigh'.

— You'll go to pieces without somethin' to do, Paddy told Bimbo.

— Shut up the fuck! said Jimmy Sr.

He gave Bimbo a quick look, but Bimbo didn't mind.

— You'd make a great doctor, Bertie told Paddy, — d'yeh know tha'. I can just see yeh. You have cancer, missis, your tit'll have to come off.

— Oh Jesus, said Bimbo.

—Yeah, said Jimmy Sr, when he'd stopped laughing.
—Will he be alrigh', Doctor? No, missis, he's fucked.

They laughed again.

— wha' will yeh do but? Paddy asked Bimbo.

—There's loads o' things he can do, said Jimmy Sr.

— Like?

— Doin' up his house, eh —

— His house is already done up, said Bertie. — It's
already like Elvis's gaff; what's it — Graceland.

Bimbo laughed at that, but he was pleased.

— His garden, said Jimmy Sr.

— His garden's like —

— It's not like a human garden at all, said Bertie.

— There's loads o' things he can do, Jimmy Sr
insisted.

— Yeah, said Paddy. — I'm sure there is. Wha'
though?

— He can clean the church on Monday mornin's,
said Bertie.

They roared.

— Some oul' one tried to get Vera to start doin' tha',
said Bertie. — Help cleanin' the fuckin' church on
Monday mornin's.

— I wouldn't say that'd be Vera's scene exactly, said
Jimmy Sr.

— Not at all, said Bertie. — She doesn't even help to
dirty the fuckin' place on Sunday mornin's.

Bertie knocked back half of his pint.

— Ahh, he said.

— My turn, said Bimbo.

— The first of many, said Bertie.

— Leo, Bimbo shouted. — When you're ready. Three —

— Four, said Paddy.

— Four pints an' four small ones like a good man, please!

They said nothing for a bit.

— Ah yes, said Bertie.

He was getting them ready.

— I know wha' I'd do if I got a lumpo sum like Bimbo's gettin', he said.

One of them had to say it. So —

— Wha'? said Jimmy Sr.

— I'd bring it into the Gem, righ'.

— Eh — , righ'.

— An' I'd wave it under Mandy's nose an' let her sniff it a bit.

Jimmy and Paddy started laughing.

— Then I'd bring her round the back, behind the fridge, righ'.

— Oh God.

Bimbo started laughing now.

— An' I'd — die happy.

They laughed on top of what they were laughing already; Bertie sounded so sincere.

— My Jaysis, compadres, said Bertie when he'd recovered a bit, — I'm not jokin' yis.

Paddy nodded. He liked Mandy from the Gem as well.

They all liked Mandy.

— You're a dirty fucker, Jimmy Sr told Bertie.

— I said nothin' tha' yis don't all think when yis go into tha' shop. Tha' signorita. My fuckin' Jaysis.

— She's only sixteen, abou', said Bimbo.

— So?

Bimbo shrugged. It didn't matter; they were only messing.

— I was in there this mornin', said Bertie. — She is unfuckinbelievable; isn't she? I was gettin' me Sun. She's as good lookin' as anny of them Page Three brassers.

— She's better lookin', said Jimmy Sr.

— Si, said Bertie, — She fuckin' is. I said it as well; I told her.

— Yeh didn't, said Paddy.

Bertie stared Paddy out of it for a second. Then he got back to Mandy.

— I opened it up at page three, righ', an' I showed it to her. Tha' should be you, I told her.

— Did she say ann'thin' back to yeh?

— Si. She told me to fuck off. But she was delighted, yeh could see.

— She's a lovely-lookin' girl alrigh', said Bimbo.

— I made her get a packet o' crisps for me as well, said Bertie. — I hate the fuckin' things.

They laughed. They knew what was coming next.

— Just to get her to bend over, yeh know. Caramba, lads, I nearly broke the counter with the bugle I had on me. When she gave them to me I said Salt an' vinegar so she had to do it again.

— She'll be fat by the time she's eighteen, said Paddy.

90

— No, said Jimmy Sr. — No, she won't.

— Why not?

— She's not like tha', said Jimmy Sr. — She's not like those young ones tha' look like women when they're fourteen an' then they're like their mothers before they're twenty. She's not like tha'.

He wondered if he should have been talking like this, if he was maybe giving something away. But Bertie agreed with him.

— Si, he said.

— My twist, said Jimmy Sr.

He wanted to get up. Halfway through talking there he'd felt dirty; kind of. And then stupid. Talking about young ones like that, very young ones. But when Bertie joined in it was safe. Darren was doing lounge boy tonight though. If he heard —

He stood up.

— Same again over here, Darren, please!

— Wha'?

— Leo knows. Just tell him the same again.

It was getting crowded. Leo was skidding up and down behind the bar.

— So annyway, Bimbo, said Bertie when Jimmy Sr was sitting back down. — Compadre mio, that's wha' I'd do if I was you.

— How though? said Paddy.

— Wha'?

— How would yeh do it?

— The same way I've always done it.

— No, I don't mean the ridin', Paddy explained. — I mean gettin' her to do it. How would yeh manage tha'?

91

— No great problem there, compadre, said Bertie. — I'd show her the money an' tell her I'll give her some of it if she'll say hello to the baldy fella; there'd be nothin' to it.

— Ah fuck off, said Jimmy Sr.

— Wha'? said Bertie.

— Yeh can't just do tha'.

— Why not?

— Cos the girl's not a fuckin' prostitute, that's why not.

— No, Bimbo agreed.

— Listen, compadre, said Bertie. — All women are prostitutes.

— Ah now — , said Bimbo.

— Will yeh listen to him, said Jimmy Sr.

— He's righ', said Paddy. — I had to buy my one a Crunchie before she'd let me ou' tonigh'.

Bertie addressed Bimbo.

— Don't misunderstand me, compadre, he said. — Not just women. All men are brassers as well.

— I'm no brasser, chum, said Jimmy Sr.

— Fuck up a minute, said Bertie. — wha' I'm sayin' is, is tha' everyone has his price.

— Ah, is that all? said Bimbo.

— If you think — , said Jimmy Sr.

He was talking to Bertie.

— If you think tha' you can just walk into the shop an' put the money on the counter there an' Mandy will drop her —

— Watch it, Jimmy, here's Darren.

— Here's the cavalry, lads, said Bertie.

— Make room there, will yis, said Darren.

— Certainly, certainly.

They got all the dead glasses and put them on the table behind them, so Darren could put the tray on their table.

— D'yeh know Mandy from the Gem, Darren? said Bertie.

Jimmy Sr tried to kick him but he got Bimbo instead, but not hard.

— Yeh, said Darren. — Mandy Lawless.

— Nice, isn't she?

— She's alrigh', yeah.

— Keep the change, Darren, said Jimmy Sr. — Good man.

Darren took the money and counted it.

— You're a pound short, he told Jimmy Sr.

— Is tha' right'? said Jimmy Sr.

He'd never get rid of him before Bertie opened his mouth again. He gave Darren a fiver.

— Yeh can pay me back later, he told him.

— No, said Darren. — I have it here.

Ah sufferin' Jesus!

But Bertie said nothing, and Paddy didn't either. He was looking around him, looking for something to moan about.

— There y'are, said Darren.

Jimmy Sr took the notes and left the silver and copper in Darren's hand.

— Good man.

— Thanks very much, Da.

— No problem.

— I'll tell yis though, said Jimmy Sr when Darren
was gone. — Yis should see his mot. Darren's mot.

— Is she nice? said Bimbo.

— Lovely, said Jimmy Sr. — Fuckin' lovely.

— Go 'way. That's great.

— Miranda, her name is.

— Oh I like tha', said Bertie. — Mirr-andaah. Si;
very nice. Is she a big girl, Jimmy?

— She's a daisy, said Jimmy Sr.

— An' you're a tulip, said Paddy.

— Fuck off, you, said Jimmy Sr.

— Lads, lads, now, said Bertie, and he leaned
forward to get between Jimmy Sr and Paddy as if to
break up a fight, even though there wasn't one. — Birds
in their little nest, said Bertie.

— wha' abou' them? said Paddy.

— They agree, said Bertie. — Righ'?

Paddy didn't argue with him.

— Now, said Bertie. — If yeh had, say, a thousand
quid, righ' —

They sat up. They loved these ones.

— An', Bertie continued, — yeh knew for a fact tha'
the most gorgeousest woman — now, the best fuckin'
thing yeh'd ever seen in your life, righ'. An' yeh knew
for a fact —

Bimbo started laughing.

— Shut up, you. — Yeh knew for a fact tha' she'd let
yeh get up on her if yeh gave her it, the money. Would
yis give her it?

— All of it? said Jimmy Sr.

— Si, said Bertie.

He looked around at them. They were thinking about it, even Bimbo.

— wha' would she give me for half of it? Paddy asked him.

They roared.

—Where is it? said Jimmy Sr.

They were outside in the carpark, watching poor Bimbo getting sick. He was finished now, for the time being anyway. But he still looked very pale around the gills.

They'd been the last to leave; out of their trees, especially poor Bimbo. He could hardly talk. Darren had been giving the air a few squirts of Pledge, to let the manager think he'd done the cleaning.

— Tan ver muh, Darr-n, Bimbo'd said, and that was as much as he could manage.

They were outside now.

— Oh God, said Bimbo again, for about the thousandth time.

— You're alrigh', said Bertie.

— Terrible waste o' fuckin' money tha', said Paddy.

He was looking down at what had come out of poor Bimbo.

Jimmy Sr had to agree with Paddy.

— Still though, he said. — He got the good ou' of it.

— True, said Paddy.

Jimmy Sr didn't feel too bad at all, considering he was out of practice. He was swimming a bit. He'd had to hold on to the wall there when he thought he was going to fall. He was pleased with himself though.

Bimbo straightened up.

— Are yeh alrigh' now, son? Bertie asked him.

— He is, o' course, said Jimmy Sr. — Aren't yeh?

Bimbo didn't say anything for a bit. Then he spoke.

— Yeah. — Yeah —

— Are we goin' or wha'? said Paddy.

The plan was, they were all going down to the seafront with a couple of sixpacks. They'd decided this after Paddy had been complaining about all the kids that were down there every night.

— All ages, he'd told them. — Polluted out of their heads.

— That's shockin', Bimbo'd said.

And then Bertie'd said that they should go down there themselves after they were flung out of the boozer, and that was where they were going now. So —

— Are we goin' or are we? said Paddy.

— Lead the way, compadre, said Bertie.

— Ah, I don't — , said Bimbo. — I don't know if —

— Come on for fuck sake, said Jimmy Sr. — The fresh air will fix yeh.

— There — , said Bimbo. — There's nothin' wrong with me.

— Come on then, said Jimmy Sr.

— Are — Hey, lads, said Bimbo. — Are — are we goin' on a boat?

— Will yeh listen to him, said Paddy.

Bimbo started singing.

— Ah shite! said Paddy.

— WE COME ON THE SLOOP JOHN B —

— Ah si, said Bertie.

He liked this one, so he joined in with Bimbo.

— ME GRAN'FATHER An' ME —

— Where's it gone? Jimmy Sr asked Paddy.

— Wha'?

— The chipper van, said Jimmy Sr.

— wha' about it?

— Where is it?

— I don't know!

— LET ME GO HOME —

— LEHHHHH' ME GO HOME —

— I want some fuckin' grub, said Jimmy Sr. — Shut up, will yis.

And then he joined in.

— I FEEL SO BROKE UP —

I WANNA GO HOME —

They were finished. Bimbo looked much better. He started again.

— BA BA BAH —

— Hang on a minute, Bimbo, said Jimmy Sr.

— BA BARBER ANN —

— Shut up!

Jimmy Sr nearly fell over, the shout had taken so much out of him.

— We've no fuckin' chipper, he told them.

— That's righ', said Bertie. — I thought there was somethin' missin' alrigh'.

There was always a van outside the Hikers, not just at the weekends either; always.

It wasn't there tonight though. Bimbo looked up and down the road for it, and behind him.

— He must be sick, said Bimbo.

— He must've eaten one of his own burgers, said Bertie.

— What'll we do? said Jimmy Sr.

— No problem, amigo. We'll go to the chipper.

He meant the real chipper, the one not on wheels; the one over the Green between the Gem and the place where the Bank of Ireland used to be.

— No, way, said Jimmy Sr.

He shook his head and nearly went on his ear again.

— What's wrong with yeh? said Bertie.

— WEEHHL —

THE WEST COAST FARMERS' DAUGHTERS —

— Shut up, Bimbo.

— The chipper's down there, said Jimmy Sr. — Righ'?

— Eh — si.

— An' the fuckin' seafront's up there, said Jimmy Sr.

— Si.

— So there's no way I'm goin' all the way down there, then all the way back up here again.

— Paddy'll go for us an' we'll wait for him.

— I will in me brown, said Paddy.

They sat on the carpark wall.

— May as well liberate these an' annyway, said Bertie, — wha'.

He got his sixpack out of its paper bag.

— While we're makin' up our minds. Alrigh', Bimbo?

— Yes, thank you.

— Annyone got an opener?

— I fuckin' told yeh we should've got cans, said Paddy.

— I told yeh.

— Fuck off.

— The cans don' taste as nice, said Jimmy Sr.

— Si, said Bertie. — Correct.

He stood up and put the neck of the bottle to the edge of the wall.

— Let's see now, he said.

He tried to knock the cap off the bottle.

— You're goin' to break it, said Paddy.

— Am I? said Bertie.

He lifted the bottle and held it out so the froth ran over his hand but not onto his clothes.

— Well done, Bertie, said Jimmy Sr.

— There y'are, Bimbo, said Bertie, handing him the opened bottle.

— My turn next, said Jimmy Sr.

— Do your own, said Bertie.

He put the top of the bottle to the edge of the wall, then pulled it down but he missed the wall and scraped his knuckles and dropped the bottle.

— Shite!

— Watch it.

A Garda car was crossing the road towards them.

The guards didn't get out but the passenger opened his window.

— What's goin' on here?

Bertie took his knuckles out of his mouth.

— We're waitin' on your wife, he said.

Paddy started whistling the Laurel and Hardy music. Jimmy Sr nudged him but Paddy didn't stop.

— None of your lip, said the garda to Bertie.

Jimmy Sr didn't like this sort of thing.

Bertie went closer to the car and leaned down. He held his top lip.

— This one? he said.

Then his bottom lip.

— Or this one.

Paddy stood up now as well.

Bimbo whispered to Jimmy Sr.

— Do we know — know his wife?

Jimmy Sr didn't know what he'd do if the cops got out of the car. He'd never been in trouble with the guards, even when he was a kid; only through Leslie.

The driver spoke.

— Mister Gillespie.

Bertie bent down further and looked past the passenger.

— Buenas noches, Sergeant Connolly, he said.

Bimbo got down off the wall and started picking up the broken glass.

— You're looking grand and flushed, said Sergeant Connolly.

— That's cos we've been ridin' policemen's daughters all nigh', Sergeant, said Bertie.

Jimmy Sr wanted to get down and run.

Paddy leaned down beside Bertie to see the faces on the gardaí. He hacked, like he was getting ready to spit, but the passenger didn't budge. He wouldn't even look at him.

Sergeant Connolly spoke.

— You wouldn't know anything at all about a small bit of robbery of Supervalu in Baldoyle this afternoon, Mister Gillespie? he asked Bertie. — Would you, at all?

—Yeah, said Bertie. — I would.

—What?

—They got away, said Bertie.

The sergeant laughed. Jimmy Sr didn't like it.

—You can come over to me house now an' search it if yeh like, Bertie told the sergeant.

—We already did that, said the sergeant.

The passenger grinned.

— wha' are you fuckin' grinnin' at? said Paddy.

Bertie moved forward a bit and crowded Paddy out of the way.

— Did yeh find annythin'? he asked Sergeant Connolly.

— Not really, said the sergeant. — But — tell your lovely wife Thank you, will you, like a good man. — I forgot to thank her myself. Good night now. Safe home.

The car moved away from the kerb and back across the road, and around onto Chestnut Avenue.

— The cunts, said Paddy.

—Where's there a bin? said Bimbo.

— Over here, Bimbo, said Jimmy Sr. — Look it.

He took Bimbo's arm and made him come with him. He wanted to get home — and get Bimbo home — before the cops came back.

— See yis, he told Bertie and Paddy.

—Where're you goin'? said Paddy.

— Home, said Jimmy Sr. — I'm knackered.

— Good nigh', compadre, said Bertie. — Here; bring one o' the sixpacks here, look it.

— No, said Jimmy Sr. — No, thanks, you're alrigh'. See yis.

He wanted to get the fuck home. He couldn't handle that sort of thing at all. He didn't want the guards thinking anything about him. And Bimbo; the two of them not working and that. Your man, Connolly, would start thinking that they were working for Bertie. And they'd raid the fuckin' house or something. Veronica —

— Are we goin' home, Jimmy? said Bimbo.

— Yeah.

— Good.

The next couple of weeks were great. He had to admit that. If he'd been looking for someone to be made redundant it would have been Bimbo. That didn't mean that he'd wanted Bimbo to get the sack; not at all. What he meant was this: he couldn't think of better company than Bimbo, and now that Bimbo wasn't working he could hang around with Bimbo all day. It was fuckin' marvellous.

He didn't think he was being selfish. At first — during the first week or so — he'd felt a bit guilty, a bit of a bollix, because Bimbo was so miserable and he was the opposite. He couldn't wait to get up and out in the mornings, like a fuckin' kid on his summer holliers. But he didn't think that way any more. Because he was helping Bimbo really. He wasn't denying that he was delighted that Bimbo wasn't working — not that he'd told anyone — but he didn't have to feel bad about it because, after all, he hadn't given poor Bimbo the sack and he'd never even wished it. And if Bimbo ever got his job back or got a new one he'd be the first one to slap him on the back and say Sound man. And he'd mean it as well.

But Bimbo was sacked; it was a fact. He was hanging around doing nothing. And Jimmy Sr was hanging around doing nothing, so the two of them might as well hang around and do fuckin' nothing together. Only, with the two of them, they could do plenty of things. Playing pitch and putt by yourself on a cold March morning could be very depressing but with someone else to go around with you it could be a great bit of gas. And it was the same with just walking along the seafront; and anything really.

Jimmy Sr hadn't felt bad, really bad, in a while; not since before Christmas. He hadn't felt good either, mind you; just — settled. Now though, he felt good; he felt happy. Bimbo was helping him and he was helping Bimbo. The day after the night they'd got locked — the day after Bimbo'd been sent home — Jimmy Sr called for him and took him out for a walk. Maggie patted Jimmy Sr's arm when he was going out the front door. It was a Saturday, a day when Bimbo would have been at home anyway, but he could tell that Bimbo didn't think it was an ordinary Saturday. He had a terrible hangover as well. But the walk had cheered him up and Jimmy Sr took him into Raheny library and got him to fill in a card and he showed him what books were where.

On Monday, the first real day, Jimmy Sr called for Bimbo at nine o'clock and made him come out for a game of pitch and putt. He had to threaten to hit him over the head with his putter if he didn't get up off his hole but he got him out eventually. He even zipped up his anorak for him. And Maggie filled a flask for them, which went down very well cos it was fuckin' freezing. They gave up after six holes; they couldn't hold the clubs properly any more because they'd no gloves, but they enjoyed themselves. And Jimmy Sr showed Bimbo what was wrong with his swing. He was lifting his head too early. They watched a bit of snooker in the afternoon, and played Scrabble with Sharon until Gina upended the board, the bitch, when they were looking at something in the snooker.

On Wednesday — it was pissing all day Tuesday — Jimmy Sr brought Bimbo into town. Bimbo had only been on the DART a couple of times before, so he enjoyed that. And some little cunt flung a stone at their carriage when they were going past the hospital in Edenmore, and that gave them something to talk about the rest of the way; that and the big new houses off the Howth Road in Clontarf that were so close to the tracks the train nearly went through them.

— Imagine payin' a fortune to live tha' close to the tracks, said Jimmy Sr.

— Thick, said Bimbo.

Jimmy Sr pointed out the houses he'd plastered.

He brought Bimbo up to the ILAC Centre and he got a young one behind the counter to put a programme about volcanoes on the telly and they watched a bit of that. They went for a cup of coffee, after Jimmy Sr had taken out a couple of books and he'd explained to Bimbo about the computer strip yokes inside the books and on Jimmy Sr's card and how the young lad at the check-out only had to rub a plastic stick across them to put the names of the books beside Jimmy Sr's name inside in the computer. They still stamped the date you had to bring them back by the old way.

They went for a coffee downstairs. The coffee was lovely there but Bimbo had insisted on having tea. He could be a cranky enough little fucker at times. Jimmy Sr was going to make him have coffee — because it WAS lovely — but then he didn't. They looked out at what was going on on Moore Street. They enjoyed that, watching the oul' ones selling their fruit and veg and the young ones going by. They saw a kid — a horrible-looking young lad — getting a purse out of a woman's bag. He'd done it before they knew what they were seeing, so there was nothing they could do. The woman didn't know yet either. She just walked on along, down to Parnell Square, the poor woman. The kid had probably done it to get drugs or something. They didn't say anything to each other about it. It made Jimmy Sr think of Leslie.

— Taste tha' now, Bimbo, said Jimmy Sr.

He held his mug out for Bimbo to take. Bimbo took it, and sipped.

— There. Isn't it lovely?

— Oh, it is, said Bimbo. — It is, alrigh'.

— Bet yeh regret you didn't get a mug of it for yourself now, wha', said Jimmy Sr.

They went home after that.

They did something every day nearly. The weather was weird. It was lovely one minute; they'd have to take their jackets off, and even their jumpers. And then it would start snowing — it would! — or hailstoning.

— Snow in April, said Bimbo, looking up at it.

He liked it, only he was cold. They were in under the shelter at the pond in St Anne's Park. Bimbo didn't want to lean against the wall because he could smell the piss; it was terrible. They had Gina with them, in her buggy.

— It's mad alrigh', said Jimmy Sr.

— It was lovely earlier, said Bimbo.

— That's righ', said Jimmy Sr. — It's the fuckin' ozone layer; that's wha' I think's doin' it.

— Is April not always a bit like this? said Bimbo.

— Not this bad, said Jimmy Sr. — No.

He made sure that Gina's head was well inside her hood.

— The greenhouse effect, he said.

— I thought tha' was supposed to make the world get warmer, said Bimbo.

— It does that alrigh', Jimmy Sr agreed with him.

— Yeah; but it makes it go colder as well. It makes the weather go all over the shop.

— Yeh wouldn't know wha' to wear, said Bimbo. — Sure yeh wouldn't.

He put his hands up into his sleeves.

— Yeh'd be better off goin' around in your nip, said Jimmy Sr.

They laughed at that.

— At least yeh'd know where yeh stood then, wha', said Jimmy Sr.

— I'd need shoes though, said Bimbo.

106

— An' somewhere to put your cigarettes, wha'.

They laughed again.

— I'm never happy unless I have me shoes on me, said Bimbo. — Even on a beach.

— Is tha' righ'?

— Or slippers.

Then it stopped. And the sun came out nearly immediately and it was like it had never been snowing, except for the snow on the ground. But that was disappearing quick; they could see it melting and evaporating.

— I love lookin' at tha' sort o' thing, said Bimbo.

—Yeah, said Jimmy Sr.

He checked on Gina. She was still asleep.

— Just as well, wha', he said. — She makes enough noise, doesn't she, Bimbo?

— Ah sure, said Bimbo. — That's wha' they're supposed to do at her age. She's lovely.

— Isn't she but, said Jimmy Sr. — If the rest of her is as good as her lungs she'll be a fine thing when she grows up.

They got going. They had a read of the newspapers in the library, to get in out of the cold, on their way home. But they had to leave because Gina started acting up.

They didn't meet much at night; once or twice a week only.

— Look, said Bimbo one morning.

He took something out of a brown envelope with a window in it.

Jimmy went over and turned so he could see it. Bimbo didn't really hold it up to him; he just held it.

It was his redundancy cheque.

— Very nice, said Jimmy Sr.

Bimbo put it back in the envelope and went into the kitchen and gave it to Maggie. Then they went out.

Bimbo put a lot of the lump sum into the house. He got aluminium windows for the back; they already had them in the front. And he put his name down for the gas conversion, the Fifty-Fifty Cash Back. Jimmy Sr helped Bimbo put new paper up in his kitchen and Veronica went through him for a short cut when she saw the paste in his hair and he told her how it had got there. He had to promise to do their own kitchen before she'd get off his back, but they didn't have the money to buy any paper or anything so it had been an easy enough promise to make.

They went out to Howth as well sometimes, and had a walk down the pier and along the front. They were going to get fishing rods.

Then a great thing happened. Bimbo helped out a bit with Barrytown United. He just went to the Under 13 matches cos Wayne, one of his young lads, was playing for them now; he was usually the sub, and Bimbo minded their gear and their money for them. And he sometimes drove some of the Under 18s to their matches, and home again. Anyway, he got a chance of two tickets to one of the World Cup warm-up matches, against Wales, in Lansdowne.

— Not two tickets exactly, he explained to Jimmy Sr.

— wha' does tha' fuckin' mean? said Paddy.

108

— Was I talkin' to you? said Bimbo. — We get into the game for nothin', he told Jimmy Sr, — but we have to do a bit o' stewardin'. Nothin' much though.

— Wha'?

— I don't know, said Bimbo. — Exactly. Are yeh on?

— Okay, said Jimmy Sr.

— Ah good, said Bimbo.

— They'll fuckin' lose, Paddy told them. — Wait an' see.

— Fuck off you, said Jimmy Sr.

Jimmy Sr loved soccer but he hadn't been to a game in years, and now he could go to an international for nothing.

— The tickets are like gold dust, he told Veronica.

They got the DART straight across to Lansdowne. Jimmy Sr had Darren's Ireland scarf on him. Darren still went to all the matches but he didn't bother with the scarf any more. So Jimmy Sr had it.

— How many stops after Amiens Street is Lansdowne? Jimmy Sr asked Bimbo.

Bimbo looked up at the yoke with the stations on it over the window.

— Eh — three — , said Bimbo. — Yeah; three.

— Good, said Jimmy Sr. — I could do with a slash.

They'd had a pint in the Hikers; just the two.

— We'll have one when we get there, said Bimbo.

— Grand, said Jimmy Sr. — No hurry.

— There's a big jacks under the stand.

— Grand, said Jimmy Sr.

When they got to Lansdowne they had to put on these white jackets with Opel on them and they followed this fat fella, and he brought them up into the East Stand and what they had to do was show people where their seats were. It was easy. You'd want to have been a fuckin' eejit not to have been able to find your own seat. He slagged Bimbo; said he'd buy him a torch and a skirt so he could get him a job in a cinema. — Can I help you, sir, he'd heard him saying to one fuckin' eejit who couldn't find his seat.

Then they went down to the side of the pitch just after the game started, inside the barriers — it was great — and they watched the game. It was a shite match, woeful; but he enjoyed it and the weather stayed good. He took off his Opel jacket and the fat fella told him to put it back on, but he said it nicely, so Jimmy Sr did put it back on. Coming up to full time the fat fella told them to turn around and face the crowd and stop any young fellas from climbing over the barriers when the whistle went. Then Ireland got a penno, and they had to watch that; and that gobshite, Sheedy, missed it — Southall saved it — and he turned back, and the crowd went fuckin' mad, and he turned back around and the new fella, Bernie Slaven, had scored a goal and Jimmy Sr'd fuckin' missed it. He had to watch it on the telly later on that night. He didn't know why he'd faced the crowd anyway; there was no way he was going to try and stop anyone from climbing over the barriers. They could chew their way through the barriers for all Jimmy Sr cared; it was none of his business. He enjoyed the whole day though. Mick McCarthy came over near to where himself and Bimbo were just before the end to take one of his famous long throws and Jimmy Sr

110

nodded at him and said Howyeh, Mick, and McCarthy winked at him. He was a good player, McCarthy, a hard man.

They were going to get into the Russia game as well for nothing at the end of the month. That was definitely something to look forward to; it would be a much better match.

— Definitely, said Bimbo.

They were on the DART home.

— I don't know, said Jimmy Sr. — I'd say tha' glasnost shite has made them soft, d'yeh know tha'. They don't have to worry abou' bein' sent to the salt mines if they lose any more.

—We'll see, said Bimbo.

So they filled their time no problem. Sometimes that was all they did; fill it — they just fucked around doing nothing till they could go home for their dinner or their tea. That wasn't so good. And sometimes Jimmy Sr could tell that Bimbo had the blues. And sometimes as well he had the blues himself. But they were good for each other, him and Bimbo.

And now — today — all Bimbo's practice had paid off; he'd won the pitch and putt. And instead of winning a poxy voucher for the butchers or something he'd won a trophy, a huge one with a golfer on top of it; not cheap looking either, like a lot of them were. No, it was very nice, and Bimbo was fuckin' delighted; he was fuckin' glowing.

They'd had a few pints to celebrate and now they were going out to the van to get a few chips and a bit of cod, because they were too late for their tea and too hungry to wait for Maggie and Veronica to rustle up something for them.

— Are yeh righ'? said Jimmy Sr.

Bimbo was collecting his clubs and his trophy, trying to work out the handiest way to carry them all.

— Here, said Jimmy Sr. — Give us them.

He took the clubs from Bimbo. He was fuckin' starving.

— Seeyis now, said Bimbo.

He was saying goodbye to everyone.

— Will yeh come on! said Jimmy Sr. — For Jaysis sake.

They went out into the carpark. It was still bright; it was only eight o'clock. The sky was red over where the sun was.

— Isn't tha' lovely? said Bimbo.

— I'm havin' a burger as well, Jimmy Sr told him.

But the van wasn't there.

— Ah fuck it!

And then they remembered that the van hadn't been there in a long time; months in fact. They only missed it now when they wanted it.

They headed over the Green to the real chipper.

— Prob'ly just as well really, said Bimbo. — You never know wha' you were gettin', out o' tha' van. — It's funny though —

He was having problems keeping up with Jimmy Sr.

— tha' van was a little gold mine, he said.

Jimmy Sr agreed with him.

—Yeah, he said.

— Maybe he's sick, said Bimbo.

112

He nearly went through a puddle.

— Or maybe he's dead.

— Good, said Jimmy Sr.

— A little gold mine that place was, Bimbo said again.

— It can't have been tha' much of a gold mine if it's not there annymore, said Jimmy Sr.

— Maybe, yeah, said Bimbo. — I'd say he's just sick or dead.

— I'll be dead in a minute meself if I don't get a bit o' grub into me, said Jimmy Sr. — Come here, Bimbo, he said. — You'll have to be careful yeh don't get complacent just cos you've won once. I'm not bein' snotty now —

— I know tha'.

— It happens a lot o' fellas. They stop workin' at their game, just cos they've won one poxy trophy; no offence.

— Don't worry, Bimbo assured him. — It's not goin' to happen to me.

— Good man. — We wouldn't want a job now, wha'. We're too busy.

Bimbo smiled back at him.

There were bad times as well, of course. Of course there were. Poor oul' Bimbo got the blues a bit, the way he used to himself before he got the hang of it, being a man of leisure. He — Bimbo — got the Independent every morning. It was supposed to be the best paper for jobs, and he went straight to the back pages. He hadn't a hope in shite of getting a job out of it, he knew it himself; they knew nobody who'd ever got a job out of a paper. But he still got it and went down the columns with his finger and got ink on it and then on his face, and then got depressed when there was nothing for him. God love him, Jimmy Sr had to stop him from writing away for a job in McDonalds; there was a huge ad for them in Saturday's paper.

Jimmy Sr called for him. They were playing against each other in this week's pitch and putt. And he was at the kitchen table starting to write the letter.

Jimmy Sr read the ad.

— You're not serious, he said when he was finished.

Bimbo finished writing his address.

— You're not fuckin' serious, said Jimmy Sr.

— I knew yeh'd say tha', said Bimbo.

He kept his eyes on the paper but he wasn't writing anything. His address was the only thing on the paper so far.

— wha' d'yeh think you're at? Jimmy Sr asked him.
— Well?

He took care to make sure that what he said sounded just right, not too hard and not too sarcastic.

— I'm just writin', said Bimbo. — To see wha' they say, like.

— They won't want you, said Jimmy Sr. — They're lookin' for young ones an' young fellas tha' they can treat like shite an' exploit. Not grown up men like you, like us.

— I know, said Bimbo. — I know tha' —

— They wouldn't have a uniform to fit yeh.

Bimbo had something he wanted to finish saying.

114

— I want to see wha' they say, yeh know. Wha' they write back.

— They won't bother writin' back, said Jimmy Sr.

— They might, said Bimbo.

— Jaysis, Bimbo; for fuck sake. You're a fuckin' baker.

— There now, said Bimbo.

He pointed his biro at the paper.

— If I put tha' in the letter, that I'm a baker, they might be impressed — I don't know — not impressed; they might just think that I've experience an' — you'd never know.

— Ah Bimbo.

— I'm only writin' to them.

He stood up.

— I'm only writin' to them. — I'll do it later.

Bimbo won; he won the pitch and putt.

—Yeh cunt yeh, said Jimmy Sr.

They didn't have a pint after; it was a bit early. They just went home.

Jimmy Sr knew Bimbo; if he was offered one of those jobs he'd take it. — It's a start, he'd say; and he wouldn't give a shite who saw him in his polyester uniform. He'd even wear the fuckin' thing to work and home, not a bother on him. And Veronica would ask him why he couldn't get a job like Bimbo — but that wasn't the reason he wanted Bimbo to cop on to himself. Veronica knew that if Jimmy Sr ever got offered proper work he'd jump at it, even if it was less than the dole. He couldn't let a friend of his — his best friend — allow himself to sink that low. A man like Bimbo would never recover from having to stand at a counter, wearing a uniform that didn't fit him and serving drunk cunts and snot-nosed kids burgers and chips. They weren't even proper chips.

They were at Bimbo's gate.

—You're not goin' to write tha' letter to McDonalds, said Jimmy Sr. — Are yeh?

— Ah —

— You'd just be wastin' the fuckin' stamp, for fuck sake.

— No, said Bimbo. — I don't think I'll bother.

— Good man, said Jimmy Sr. — See yeh later.

— See yeh, said Bimbo.

Jimmy Sr went on, to his own house. He wondered would the front room be free this afternoon. Darren was doing a lot of studying for the Leaving, and Jimmy Sr wasn't going to get in his way. Liverpool were playing Chelsea on RTE. Maybe Darren would be going out, meeting his mot.

He'd forgotten his key. He knocked on the glass. Bimbo probably would write off to McDonalds even though he'd said he wouldn't. He knocked again. He wouldn't rest until he got himself one of those fuckin' uniforms. He hid his eyes from the sun with his hand and looked in the window of the front room. There was no one in there. He knocked again. He should have got a knocker, one of those brass ones on the door. Bertie had one on his, and one of those spy-hole things. There was no one in.

— Fuck it annyway.

116

He'd go down to Bimbo's for a bit, and watch the —
Hang on though, no; there was someone coming down
the stairs. He could hear it, and now he could make out
the shape. It was Veronica. She must have been asleep,
or studying. She was doing the Leaving as well in a
couple of weeks, God love her. Fair play to her though.
He was going to do the same himself next year.

Veronica opened the door.

—Wha' kept yeh? said Jimmy Sr.

Jimmy Jr came around with four cans of Carlsberg, still
lovely and cold from the off-licence fridge. Jimmy Sr
put his nose to the hole in his can.

— I always think it smells like piss when yeh open it
first, he said. — Not bad piss now, he explained.

—Yeah, Jimmy Jr agreed.

He got his jacket from behind the couch and took
out two packets of Planter's Nuts and threw one of
them to Jimmy Sr.

— Open them an' smell them, he said.

Jimmy Sr did.

—Well? said Jimmy Jr.

— They smell like shite, said Jimmy Sr.

— Yeah, said Jimmy Jr. — Fuckin' gas, isn't it? An'
they still taste lovely.

Jimmy Sr took a swig and trapped the beer in his
mouth and only let it down slowly. That way he didn't
belch. The remote control needed a battery so Jimmy
Sr couldn't turn up the sound without getting up, and
he couldn't be bothered. He'd turned it down when
young Jimmy had come, to ask how he was and that,

and how Aoife was. There'd been one more goal since
then; Ian Rush had scored it. He didn't need George
Hamilton or Johnny Giles to tell him who'd scored it
cos he'd seen it himself. He was sick of those two. Giles
was always fuckin' whinging.

—They're a machine, said Jimmy Sr. — Aren't they?

—What's that'?

— Liverpool, said Jimmy Sr. — They're like a
machine. Brilliant.

—Yeah, said Jimmy Jr.

He didn't follow football much.

— A well-oiled machine, said Jimmy Sr. — There's
nothin' like them.

—Yeah, said Jimmy Jr. — I'm gettin' married.

— They always do the simple thing, said Jimmy Sr.
— It's obvious but no one else fuckin' does it.

— I'm gettin' married, said Jimmy Jr.

— I heard yeh, said Jimmy Sr.

— And?

— And is she pregnant?

— No, she fuckin' isn't!

— That's grand so, said Jimmy Sr.

He held out his hand to Jimmy Jr.

— Put it there.

He'd have killed him if he'd put her up the pole; she
was too nice a young one to have that sort of thing
happen to her, far too nice.

They shook hands.

— Did you tell your mother yet?

— No. No, I wanted to tell you first. There's another
goal, look it.

— Barnes, said Jimmy Sr. — Brilliant. Pity he hasn't an Irish granny. — Why?

— Why, wha'?

— Don't start, said Jimmy Sr. — Why did yeh want to tell me first?

Jimmy Jr was concentrating on the telly.

— I just did, he said. — Eh, I'll go in an' tell Ma.

— She'll be delighted.

— Yeah, said Jimmy Jr.

He got up and went out.

Liverpool had scored again but Jimmy Sr only noticed it when the replay came on and even then he didn't really pay attention to it. He didn't know who'd scored it.

— What're her parents like? Sharon asked Jimmy Jr.

— Good question, said Jimmy Sr. — Look carefully at her mother cos that's wha' she'll end up lookin' like.

— Will you listen to him, said Veronica.

They were all having the dinner, Darren and the twins as well. It was very nice. Not the food — it was nice as well, mind you; lovely — the atmosphere.

Young Jimmy had brought a bottle of wine. He poured a glass for the twins as well, just a small one, and Veronica didn't kick up at all. Jimmy Sr looked at her. She couldn't keep her eyes off young Jimmy.

— They're alrigh', said Jimmy Jr.

He put down his knife and fork, making noise on purpose.

— No, they're not, now that I think of it, he said.

They cheered.

— He's a bollix — , said Jimmy Jr.

119

— Stop that, said Veronica.

— Sorry, ma, said Jimmy Jr. — He is though.

They laughed, Veronica as well.

— An' she's — , said Jimmy Jr. — I think she's ou' of her tree half the time.

— Go 'way, said Jimmy Sr. — Is tha' righ'? Drink?

— No, said Jimmy Jr. — I don't think so.

— Tippex, said Darren.

— Stop that, said Veronica.

— She looks doped, said Jimmy Jr. — When yeh go into the house she smiles at you abou' ten seconds after she's been lookin' at you, yeh know. It'd freak you ou'.

— Maybe she's just thick, said Jimmy Sr.

—You'll be meetin' her soon annyway, said Jimmy Jr. — so you'll be able to judge for yourself.

— That's righ', said Jimmy Sr. — Is she good lookin'?

—Who? Her ma?

— o' course! said Jimmy Sr. — Who d'yeh think I meant? Her da?

They laughed.

— I couldn't give a shite wha' her da looks like, said Jimmy Sr.

— Excuse me, said Veronica. —You'd better not give a shite what her ma looks like either.

—Yeow, Ma!

They roared. Veronica was pleased.

Jimmy Sr really did want to know what Aoife's ma looked like. He didn't know why; he just did — badly.

— Well? he said.

He put some more salt on his spuds. They were good spuds, balls of flour.

— Is she?

— Yeah, said Jimmy Jr. — I s'pose she — No, not really —

— Ah Jaysis —

— It's hard to say. She an oul' one. She was probably nice lookin' once alrigh'. Years ago but.

— Can she not be good looking if she isn't young? Veronica asked Jimmy Jr.

— Eh —

— 'Course she can, said Jimmy Sr.

— Yeah, Jimmy Jr agreed. — But she —

— Be careful wha' yeh say, son, Jimmy Sr warned him.

— Some old women are lovely lookin', said Sharon.

— That's true, said Jimmy Sr. — A few o' them.

He glanced over at Veronica.

— What abou' you? said Darren to his da. — Look at the state o' you.

Jimmy Sr looked at Darren. Darren was looking back at him, waiting for a reaction. Jimmy Sr wasn't going to take that from him, not for another couple of years.

He pointed his fork at Darren.

— Don't you forget who paid for tha' dinner in front of you, son, righ'.

— I know who paid for it, said Darren. — The state.

Jimmy Sr looked like he'd been told that someone had died.

— Yeh prick, Jimmy Jr said to Darren.

But no one said anything else. Linda and Tracy didn't look at each other.

Jimmy Sr took a sip from his wine.

— Very nice, he said.

Then he got up.

— Em — the jacks, he said.

He had to sit down again and shift his chair back to get up properly.

— Back in a minute, he said.

— Yeh fuckin' big-headed little prick, yeh, Jimmy Jr called Darren when they heard Jimmy Sr on the stairs, going up.

— Stop that! said Veronica.

— Wha' did yeh go an' say tha' for? Sharon asked Darren, and wanting to slap the face off him.

— Stop, said Veronica.

— I was only jokin', said Darren.

It was true; mostly.

Jimmy Jr grabbed Darren's sleeve.

— Stop!!

Veronica looked around at them all.

— Stop that, she said. — Now, eat your dinners.

They did. Sharon kicked Darren under the table but didn't really get him.

Then Linda spoke.

— Are they rich, Jimmy?

— Who?

— Her ma an' da, said Linda.

— Yeah, said Jimmy Jr. — They are, kind of. — Yeah. — I suppose they are.

They were all listening for noise from upstairs.

— What did you do in school yesterday? Veronica asked Tracy.

Tracy was stunned.

— Eh —

— Nothin', said Linda.

— The usual.

— Tell us about it, said Veronica.

— Ah, get lost —

— Go on.

— Yeah, said Sharon. — Tell us.

— Well — , said Linda.

She knew what was going on, sort of. They weren't to be waiting for her daddy to come down.

— Well, she said. — We had Mr Enright first class.

— Lipstick Enright, said Darren.

— Shut up, you, said Jimmy Jr.

— Linda fancies him, Tracy told them.

— I do not you, righ'!

Veronica started laughing.

— I used to — , said Linda. — I'm goin' to kill you, Tracy, righ'.

Jimmy Sr was coming down; they heard the stairs.

— Why did yeh stop? Sharon asked Linda. — Fancyin' him.

Linda teased them.

— I just did, she said.

— She — , Tracy started.

— Shut up, Tracy, said Linda, — righ'. I'm tellin' it.

— Tellin' wha'? said Jimmy Sr.

He'd combed his hair.

— Why she doesn't fancy Mr Enright annymore, Sharon told him.

— Oh good Jaysis, he said.

They all laughed, hard.

He washed his face, put his hands under the cold tap and rubbed water all over his face and put them under again and held them over his eyes. God, he felt much better now. He was looking forward to going home. He had to wipe his face in his jumper because there was no towel. It was like when you ate ice-cream too fast and you had a terrible fuckin' headache, a real splitter, and it got worse and worse and you had to close your eyes to beat it — and then it was gone and you were grand, not a bother on you. For a while after the dinner, he'd had to really stretch his face to stop himself from crying. And that passed and he'd thought he was going to faint — not faint exactly — He kept having to lift himself up, and sit up straight and open his eyes full; he couldn't help it. He didn't blame Darren; it was a phase young fellas went through, hating their fathers. He wouldn't have minded smacking him across the head though.

He was grand now, wide awake. The pint had helped, nice and cold, and the taste had given him something to think about. He was grand.

— Come here, you, he said to Bimbo when he got back from the jacks. — The only reason you beat me today was because I let yeh take your first shot again at the seventh.

— Oh, said Bertie. — The tricky seventh; si.

124

— I beat yeh by two shots, said Bimbo.

— So?

— So I'd still've beaten yeh.

— Not at all, said Jimmy Sr. — Yeh went one up at the seventh. D'yeh admit tha'?

— Say nothin', compadre, said Bertie.

— Yeah, Bimbo said to Jimmy Sr.

He was dying to know what Jimmy Sr was going to say next.

— Yeh went up after I let yeh take your shot again. Yeah?

— Yeah.

— Well, that had a bad psychological effect on me. I shouldn't've let yeh. I'd've hockied yeh if I'd won tha' hole like I should've. — Like I really did when yeh think about it.

— Nick fuckin' Faldo, said Paddy.

— That's not fair now, said Bimbo.

He sat up straight.

— That's not fair, Jim, he said. — I beat yeh fair an' square.

— No, Bimbo, sorry; not really.

Bimbo was annoyed.

— Righ', he said. — Fair enough. — I wasn't goin' to mention it but —

— Wha'?

Jimmy Sr was worried now, but he didn't show it.

— Wha'? he said again. — Go on.

— I seen yeh kickin' the ball ou' o' the long grass on the ninth.

— Yeh cunt!

125

— I seen yeh, Bimbo insisted.

— Yeh poxbottle fuck yeh; yeh did not!

— I did, said Bimbo.

— Serious allegations, said Bertie after he'd stopped laughing.

— He's makin' it up, said Jimmy Sr. — Don't listen to him.

Bimbo tapped his face with a finger, just under his left eye.

— He's makin' it up, said Jimmy Sr. — It's pat'etic really. He's just a bad loser.

— I won, sure! said Bimbo.

— Not really, yeh didn't, said Jimmy Sr.

— You're the loser, excuse me, said Bimbo. — And a cheater.

— Yeh'd want to be careful abou' wha' you're sayin', Jimmy Sr told him.

He knew well they all believed Bimbo; he didn't give a fuck. He was enjoying himself.

— I'm only sayin' what I saw, said Bimbo. — Yeh looked around yeh an' yeh gave the ball a kick, then yeh shouted Found it! And then yeh said, I was lucky, it's landed nicely for me.

Bertie and Paddy were roaring.

— Fuck yeh, said Jimmy Sr. — Wha' were yeh lookin' at me for annyway?

— You'll have to buy a round because o' tha', compadre, Bertie said to Jimmy Sr.

— Fair enough, said Jimmy Sr.

He had a tenner that Jimmy Jr'd given him.

— Four pints over here, he roared at the young fella who was going past them with a trayload of empty glasses. — I'd still have beaten yeh, he told Bimbo.

— But I won, said Bimbo.

— It's tha' baldy bollix, Gorbachev's fault. The grass should've been cut there; he's useless. There's always dog-shite in the bunkers as well.

— Annyone want a kettle jug? said Bertie.

— Free?

— No, said Bertie. — No, I'm afraid not. I can give it to yeh at a keen price though.

— How much? said Paddy.

— Fifteen quid, said Bertie. — Thirty-five in the shops. — Two for twenty-five.

— How many have yeh? Jimmy Sr asked him.

— Ask no questions, compadre, said Bertie. — Not tha' many. A small herd. Well?

— No, said Jimmy Sr.

He looked around to see if there was anyone listening or watching.

— No, Paddy said. — We don't need one.

— No, Bimbo agreed.

— Fair enough, said Bertie. — No problem.

—Yeh wouldn't have a chipper van to sell, I suppose, said Bimbo, — would yeh, Bertie?

— No, said Bertie, like Bimbo'd just asked him if he'd any bananas.

Jimmy Sr and Paddy stared at Bimbo.

— Just a thought, said Bimbo.

And he left it at that.

Bertie loved a challenge.

—Wha' abou' a Mister Whippy one? Bertie asked Bimbo.

— I think I could get me hands on one o' them.

— No, said Bimbo.

—You've your heart set on a chipper one?

—Yeah. — Not really; just if yeh see one.

— Si, said Bertie. — I'll see what I can do.

Jimmy Sr looked at Bimbo. But Bimbo was just looking the way he always did, friendly and stupid looking, no glint in his eye or nothing.

— Bimbo's talkin' abou' gettin' himself a chipper van, he told Veronica.

— I knew he liked his food, said Veronica. — But I didn't know he was that bad.

Jimmy Sr didn't get it at first.

— Ah yeah; very good.

Jimmy Sr had no luck trying to get anything out of Bimbo.

— It was just an idea, that's all.

That was about as much as he'd tell him.

They were in Jimmy Sr's front room watching Blockbusters.

— If Bertie finds one will yeh buy it? Jimmy Sr asked him.

— B M — , said Bimbo.

The girls' team on the telly got to the answer before Bimbo.

— Are yeh listenin' to me? said Jimmy Sr.

— M T, said Bimbo.

— Mother Teresa, said Jimmy Sr.

— Let's see; — you're righ'.

— 'Course I'm righ'.

— They've won, look it. You'd've won if you'd o' been on it, Jimmy.

— What's the prize?

— A trip to somewhere.

— Would yeh take the van if Bertie found one for yeh? Jimmy Sr asked him again.

— Edinburgh; that's where it's to. That's not all tha' good, is it?

— Better than nowhere, said Jimmy Sr, defending the prize he could've won.

— That's right, o' course. They look happy enough with it annyway, don't they?

Jimmy Sr looked at the two girls on the telly.

— Wouldn't mind goin' with them, he said.

The weather was glorious. All week the sun had been blazing away, none of the chill that you often got when it was sunny in May.

They were sitting on Jimmy Sr's front step, Jimmy Sr and Bimbo, lapping up the sun. Bimbo had his eyes closed and his face shoved up to catch the sun, daring it to burn him.

— Lovely, he said.

— Fuckin' sure, said Jimmy Sr. — You can really feel it, can't yeh?

— God, yeah.

— Great drinkin' weather, said Jimmy Sr.

Bimbo didn't answer. He agreed with Jimmy Sr but he'd been talking with Maggie about them dipping into his redundancy money; they'd both been doing it, for clothes — Wayne had made his Confirmation two weeks ago — and Easter eggs and things that they'd always had. They'd taken all the kids to the pictures on Wayne's Confirmation day and that had set them back nearly forty quid after popcorn and ice-creams, forty quid that they didn't have, so it had come out of the lump sum. Maggie'd take a tenner out so they could have nice steak on a Sunday. And Bimbo'd been helping himself to the odd tenner so he could go up to the Hikers now and again. And the aluminium windows and the other bits and pieces. But it was stopping. This morning they'd had a meeting and they'd agreed that it had to stop or there'd be nothing left for when they really needed it. So the last treat they were giving themselves was three tickets for Cats, for himself and Maggie and her mother; they had them bought since last week, before the decision, so they were going to go ahead and go.

— Oh, here we go, said Jimmy Sr. — Look it.

Bimbo opened his eyes and looked at the ground till he got used to the light.

— Ah yes, said Jimmy Sr, nearly whispering.

There were three girls passing; girls about sixteen or seventeen. You could tell that they knew that Jimmy Sr and Bimbo were there. One of them looked in at them and away quickly. Bimbo felt sweaty suddenly and that annoyed him because it was Jimmy Sr that was really looking at them, not him.

— They're only young ones, he said.

— There's no harm, said Jimmy Sr.

130

He felt like a bollix now; he'd have to control himself — especially when the Child of fuckin' Prague was sitting beside him.

— They're goin' home for their tea, said Bimbo.

Jimmy Sr saw him shiver when he said it.

— An' to do their homework, said Bimbo.

— Those young ones aren't in school annymore. They left —

— I know, said Bimbo. — Those particular girls aren't goin' to school annymore but —

— They work in tha' sewin' factory in Baldoyle, said Jimmy Sr.

— They're still only young girls, said Bimbo. — Kids.

— Ah, rev up, said Jimmy Sr.

The sewing factory girls got a half day on Fridays. The first time Jimmy Sr'd looked at them on a Friday, from his bedroom window, he'd felt the blood rushing through his head, walloping off the sides, like he was watching a blue video and he was afraid that Veronica would come in and catch him. There was a gang of them — all of them seemed to be in denim mini-skirts — outside Sullivans. Derek and Ann Sullivan's daughter, Zena, worked in the sewing factory. There was about six of them laughing and hugging themselves to keep out the cold; it was months ago and young ones like that never dressed properly for the weather. All of them had haircuts like your woman, Kylie Minogue. Jimmy Sr liked that. He thought curly hair was much better than straight. He'd looked at them for ages. He even dived back onto the bed when one of them was looking his way. He'd been afraid to go back and look

131

out the window. But he did, and then they went, their heels making a great sound; he'd always loved that sound — he always woke up when he heard it. He'd felt like a right cunt then, gawking out the window; like a fuckin' pervert.

But he was only looking, day dreaming maybe. There was no harm in it, none at all. He wasn't going to start chasing after them or following them or — he just liked looking at them, that was all.

They were coming back up the road. He could hear them, their heels. Bimbo'd been wrong; they weren't going home to their mammies for their tea. He'd tell him that when they went by, the fuckin' little altar boy.

They were two gates away now. He'd see them in a minute. He'd look the other way so Bimbo wouldn't think anything. Not that he cared what Bimbo thought.

He'd see them now if he looked.

He'd say something to Bimbo, just to be talking to him when they went by.

— Will Palace beat United tomorrow, d'yeh —

— Compadres!

It was Bertie. He stayed at the gates and looked at the young ones' arses when they'd gone by, not a bother on him; he didn't give a shite who saw him.

— How's Bertie? said Bimbo.

He wouldn't give out to Bertie for looking at the young ones, of course; no way.

Bertie stayed at the gate. He was wearing an Italia 90 T-shirt. He held the collar and shook it to put some air between him and the cloth.

— Are yis busy, compadres?

— What's it look like? said Jimmy Sr.

Bertie opened the gate and nodded at them to get up.

— Come on till I show yis somethin'.

It was filthy. He'd never seen anything like it. They walked around it. It was horrible to think that people had once eaten chips and stuff out of this thing; it was a fuckin' scandal. There was no way he was going to look inside it.

He looked at Bimbo but he couldn't see his face. Bimbo was looking under the van now. For what, Jimmy Sr didn't know; acting the expert. The last place Jimmy Sr would have wanted to stick his face was under that fuckin' van; it would probably shite on top of you. It was like something out of a zoo gone stiff, the same colour and all.

It didn't even have wheels. It was up on bricks.

Bimbo stood up straight.

Bertie came out from behind the van, rolling a wheel in front of him.

— The wheels are new, compadres, he told them. — There's three more behind there, he said. — In perfect nick.

He let the tyre fall over onto the grass.

— wha' d'yeh think? he asked Bimbo.

— Which end does it shite out of? said Jimmy Sr.

Bertie got in between Bimbo and Jimmy Sr. Bimbo was still looking at the van, moving a bit to the left and to the right like he was studying a painting or something. Jimmy Sr went over so he could get a good look at Bimbo.

Bimbo looked excited and disappointed, like a light going on and off. Jimmy Sr looked at the van again.

Ah Jesus, the thing was in fuckin' tatters. The man was fuckin' mad to be even looking at it. He couldn't let him do this.

— Maggie'll have to see it, Bimbo said to Bertie.

Thank God for that, thought Jimmy Sr. It saved him the hassle of trying to stop Bimbo from making a fuckin' eejit out of himself. Maggie'd box his ears for him when she saw what he was dragging her away from her work to see.

Bimbo's face was still skipping up and down.

— I'll get her, he said. — Hang on.

Jimmy Sr and Bertie waited in the garden while Bimbo went and got Maggie. The garden was in rag order, as bad as the van. You could never really tell what state a house was in from the front. Jimmy Sr had walked past this house dozens of times — it was only a couple of corners away from his own — and he'd never noticed anything about it. He'd never noticed it at all really; it was just a house at the end of a terrace. It was only when you came round the back that you realised that there was a gang of savages living a couple of hundred yards away from you. It wasn't just poverty.

— I don't know how annyone can live like this, he said.

Bertie looked around.

— It's not tha' bad, he said. — A bit wild maybe.

— Wild! said Jimmy Sr.

He pointed at a used nappy on the path near the back door.

— Is tha' wild, is it? That's just fuckin' disgustin'.

He looked around nearer to him — he was sitting on one of the wheels — as if he was searching for more nappies.

— They should be ashamed of themselves, he said.

— It's not They, compadre, Bertie corrected him.

— wha' d'yeh mean?

— It used to be They but now it's just He. — She fucked off an' left him. An' the kids.

— Jaysis, said Jimmy Sr. — That's rough. Why?

— Why wha'?

— Why'd she leave him?

— I don't know, compadre, said Bertie after a bit. — He's an ugly cunt but.

— Did you ever see her? Jimmy Sr asked him.

— No, said Bertie. — But the kids are all ugly as well.

— Ah well then, said Jimmy Sr.

He had his back to the van, on purpose, kind of a protest. He looked over his shoulder at it.

— You've some fuckin' neck though, he told Bertie.

— Wha'? said Bertie.

— Tryin' to get poor Bimbo to throw his money away on tha' yoke, Jimmy Sr explained.

— I'm not trying to get Bimbo to throw his money away on annythin', said Bertie. — He asked me to look ou' for a van for him an' that's what I did.

Jimmy Sr took his time answering Bertie. He had to be careful.

— How did yeh find it? he asked Bertie.

— I followed me nose, said Bertie.

They laughed.

Jimmy Sr knew now that Bertie wouldn't push Bimbo into buying it. Anyway, Maggie would never let Bimbo buy it.

— It hasn't been used in years, he said.

— No, Bertie corrected him. — No, it's not tha' long off the road. A year about only.

He looked at the van from end to end.

— She's a good little buy, he said. — Solid, yeh know. Tha' dirt'll wash off no problem.

Jimmy Sr changed his mind; the cunt was going to make Bimbo buy it.

— There's more than dirt wrong with tha' fuckin' thing, he told Bertie.

— Not at all, compadre, said Bertie, — I assure you.

— Assure me bollix, said Jimmy Sr.

— Hey! said Bertie.

He was pointing at Jimmy Sr. Jimmy Sr'd been afraid that this was going to happen. But sometimes you had to stand up and be counted.

— Hey, said Bertie again, not as loud now that he had Jimmy Sr looking at him. — Listen you, righ'. You ask annybody — annybody — that's ever dealt with me if they've anny complaints to make abou' their purchases an' what'll they tell yeh?

Jimmy Sr didn't know if he was supposed to answer.

136

— No signor, they'll say, said Bertie. — Quality, they'll say, is Bertie Gillespie's middle name. My friend Bimbo, he asks me to find him a chipper van an' I find him a fuckin' chipper van. It needs a wash an' its armpits shaved, but so wha'? Don't we all?

Jimmy Sr shrugged.

— I was only givin' me opinion, he said.

— Jimmy, said Bertie. — You've bought things from me, righ'? Many products.

— That's righ', said Jimmy Sr.

— Did annythin' I ever gave yeh stop workin' on yeh?

— Never, Bertie, Jimmy Sr assured him. — Linda's Walkman broke on her but tha' was her own fault. She got into the bath with it.

— Well then, said Bertie. — If I say it's a good van then it's a good fuckin' van. It's the Rolls-Royce o' fuckin' chipper vans; si?

— Okay, said Jimmy Sr. — Sorry.

— No problem, said Bertie. —What's keepin' Bimbo annyway?

He stood up and hitched his trousers back up over his arse. Jimmy Sr stood up and did the same thing with his trousers, although he didn't need to; he just did it — cos Bertie'd done it. He put his hands in his pockets and shoved the trousers back down a bit.

They looked at the van.

—Where's the window? said Jimmy Sr.

— You're beginnin' to annoy me, said Bertie, — d'yeh know tha'?

— No, I didn't mean it like —

137

— Who wants the van annyway? You or Bimbo? It's nothin' got to do with you, chum.

— I only fuckin' asked! said Jimmy Sr. — For fuck sake.

— Maybe, said Bertie.

— I only asked, said Jimmy Sr. — I did. I was only fuckin' curious. Where's the fuckin' window, that's all. It has to have one.

Bertie thought about this.

He went over to the van. He tapped it, at about chin level.

— No, he said.

He moved down a bit and tapped again.

— No, he said again.

He moved further down.

— It must be here somewhere, he said.

He tapped again.

— No.

He looked at his knuckles.

— Jesus, it's fuckin' dirty alrigh', he said.

He stepped back and looked carefully at the side of the van from left to right.

— It must be round the other side, he told Jimmy Sr. — Does it have to have a window?

— 'Course it does, said Jimmy Sr.

This was great; no fuckin' window.

— Why? said Bertie.

— How else can yeh serve the fuckin' customers? said Jimmy Sr. — Get up on the fuckin' roof?

— Oh, said Bertie. — You mean the hatch, compadre. It's round the back. A fine big hatch. Yeh could serve a small elephant through it.

138

— Ventilation, said Jimmy Sr.

— Que?

— Yeh'd want a window for ventilation, said Jimmy Sr.

— Me bollix yeh would, said Bertie. — Why would yeh? You've the hatch, for fuck sake. It's as big as a garage door.

— Doesn't matter a shite wha' size it is if there isn't a through draught.

— There's the door for gettin' in an' ou' as well, said Bertie. — That'll give yeh your through draught.

Jimmy Sr studied the van.

— I don't know, he said.

— Look it, said Bertie. — Let me at this point remind you of one small thing; uno small thing, righ'. It's a van for selling chips out of, not a caravan for goin' on your holidays in; comprende? It doesn't matter a wank if there's a window or not. Unless you're plannin' on —

— Oh God.

It was Maggie.

— Ah, said Bertie. — There yis are. Use your imagination, signora, he told Maggie as he stepped aside to let her have a good look at the van.

Maggie stayed where she was, as if she was afraid to go closer to it. She brought her cardigan in closer around her shoulders. Bimbo was beside her, looking at her carefully, hoping, hoping.

Like a kid, the fuckin' eejit; buy me tha', Mammy, he'd say in a minute, the fuckin' head on him. If she did let him buy it Jimmy Sr'd — he didn't know what he'd do. Fuck them, it was their money.

Bertie's outstretched hand showed Maggie the van from top to bottom and back up again.

— A few minutes with a hose an' maybe, just maybe, a few hours with a paint scraper an' it'll be perfect. The Rolls-Royce o' chipper vans.

Jimmy Sr didn't know why he didn't want Bimbo to buy it. It just sort of messed things up, that was it. It was a shocking waste of money as well though.

— Have yeh looked inside it? Maggie asked Bimbo.

— Oh I have, yeah, said Bimbo. — No, it's grand. It's all there, all the equipment. It's a bit, eh —

— What abou' the engine? said Maggie.

Bertie got there before Bimbo.

— wha' engine would tha' be, signora?

There was a window. They found it when they got it back to Bimbo's. Two days after he bought it.

It was like a procession, pushing and dragging the van through Barrytown, Bimbo and Jimmy Sr and some of their kids although the twins were no help at all, just worried about getting their clothes dirty. Mind you, you didn't even have to touch the van to get dirty from it, you only had to stand near it. It took them ages to get the wheels on it and then getting it around to the front without knocking a lump off the house took ages as well and it was nearly dark by the time they were on the road to Bimbo's. The weather was great, of course, and everyone on the left side of the street was out on their front steps getting the last of the sun and by the

140

time they'd got to the corner of Barrytown Road there was a huge fuckin' crowd out watching them. Jimmy Sr kept his head down all the way, except when they were going down the hill just at the turn into Chestnut Avenue and he had to run up to the front to help Bimbo stop the van from taking off on its own, past the corner. They'd had to dig their heels in or else it would've gone over Bimbo and his young one, Jessica. He should have let it; that would have taught Bimbo a lesson about how to spend his money. Anyway, they got the useless piece of rusty shite to stop just after the corner and there was a really huge crowd by now and they cheered when they missed the corner, the cunts. They backed it back and Wayne, one of Bimbo's young fellas, got the steering wheel around; the sweat was running off the poor little fucker, and they got it onto Chestnut Avenue and the cunts at the corner cheered again. No fear of the lazy shites giving them a hand, of course.

There really was a huge crowd out. It was a bit like Gandhi's funeral in the film, except noisier. It was more like the Tour de France, the neighbours at the side of the road clapping and whooping, the cynical bastards.

— Hey Jimmy, are yeh pushin' it or ridin' it!?
And they all laughed, the eejits, like sheep.
— Yeow, Jimmy!
— Hey, look it! Mister Rabbitte's wearin' stripy kaks!
God, he wanted to kill someone when he heard that. Veronica was right; he should never have tucked his shirt inside his underpants; she'd been saying it for years. He tried to stand up straighter when he was

pushing to make the underpants go back down in behind his trousers but he was probably too late, and he couldn't put a hand behind and shove them back down; that would only have been giving in to them.

— Here, lads, look at the skidmarks!

Some people would laugh at anything. A kid had his ghetto blaster on full blast; it was like a jaysis circus. Only a couple of gates left and they'd be at Bimbo's gate and it would be over. The worst part but, was earlier, going past the Hikers, not only because he'd have loved a pint but because loads of the lads came out with their pints and sat on the wall laughing and slagging them. Larry O'Rourke was offering 3/1 that Jimmy Sr would die before they got to Bimbo's. Ha fuckin' ha. By Jaysis, the next bank holiday that fucker got up with the band and started doing his Elvis impressions Jimmy Sr would let him know who he really sounded like; Christy fuckin' Brown.

— Come on, three to one Jimmy snuffs it. Anny takers?

— That's a fuckin' big pram he's pushin', isn't it?

Jimmy Sr looked up to see who'd said that and it was Bertie.

He couldn't believe it. He'd only enough breath in him to say one thing back at them.

— Fuck yis.

He got a bit more air in.

— Yis cunts.

They were there. Just one last big push up onto the path and into Bimbo's drive and it was over.

142

Jimmy Sr couldn't stand up straight for a while, his back was killing him. The sweat was worse though. He was wringing. His shoes squelched, his shirt was stuck to him, his arse was wet. He sat down on the grass. The twins wanted money for helping.

— Get lost, he managed to say.

— Ah, that's not fair —

— Fuck off!

Jimmy Sr got the sweat out of his eyes and looked at Bimbo and Maggie looking at the van. Not a bother on Bimbo, of course; he didn't even look dirty. He had his arm around Maggie's shoulders and the two of them were gawking at the van like it was their first fuckin' grandchild. Bimbo was anyway; Maggie didn't look as delighted. You couldn't blame her. If her first grandchild was in the same state as the van she'd want to smother it, and nobody would object. Then they looked at each other and started laughing and then they looked at the van and stopped laughing, and then they started again. It was nice really, seeing them like that.

Then Bimbo noticed Jimmy Sr on the grass.

About fuckin' time.

— tha' was great gas, wasn't it? he said.

— Eh — yeah. Yeah.

— D'yeh know wha' I think? said Bimbo then.

And he waited for Jimmy Sr to give him the green light.

— Wha'? said Jimmy Sr.

— It doesn't look nearly as bad here, away from that other place.

He was talking through his arse, of course, but Jimmy Sr gave him the answer he was dying for.

— You're righ', yeh know, he said.

— The more I look at it, said Bimbo, — the more I think we're after gettin' a bargain; d'yeh know tha'.

Ah, thought Jimmy Sr, God love him.

— Yeh might be righ' there, he said.

— This sounds stupid now, said Bimbo.

Maggie had come over now as well.

— But I think that it's a godsend tha' there's no engine in it. We got it for nothin'.

— Umm, said Maggie.

They'd got it for eight hundred quid. Maggie'd put her foot down at seven hundred and fifty until Bertie'd introduced her to the owner with one of his motherless children, the youngest, in his arms.

— Poor Jimmy looks like he could do with a drink, Maggie told Bimbo.

— He's not the only one, said Bimbo. — Wait now till I do somethin' first.

He went through to the back of the house and came back with two bricks and put them behind the back wheels.

— There now, he said. — She's rightly anchored.

He tapped one of the bricks with his foot and it didn't budge.

— tha' should hold it annyway, he said.

He was pleased with his work.

— I'll put a chain on the gate later, he told Maggie. — To make sure tha' no young fellas decide to rob it durin' the nigh'.

144

— Good thinkin' tha', said Jimmy Sr.

There actually were a few young fellas in Barrytown that nearly would have robbed even as worthless a pile of shite as poor Bimbo's van, just for the crack. They'd've robbed themselves if there was no one else, some of the little bastards around here.

Jimmy Sr was feeling normal again.

— Could yeh manage a pint, Jim? Bimbo asked him.

— It's abou' the only thing I could manage, said Jimmy Sr.

— Come on so, said Bimbo. — Wha' abou' yourself, Maggie?

— No, said Maggie. — Thirtysomething's on in a minute.

— She never misses it, Bimbo told Jimmy Sr when they were going to the gate. — She won't video it either. She has to watch it live.

That was when they found the window. Bimbo's kids were inside in the van exploring and Wayne put his foot through it. Bimbo got them all out and checked Wayne's foot. It was grand, no cuts or anything. Then he told the kids to stay out of the van cos it was dangerous until they got all the grease off the floor and, to the two youngest, that it was full of spiders that bit you and then he pretended to lock the door with one of his house keys.

He was good with the kids; they'd all listened to him.

— Now, he said when he'd done it.

He patted the door and wiped his hand on his trousers and they went up to the Hikers.

Jimmy Sr needed bubbles. Darren was working in the bar, collecting the glasses and that, and he recommended Budweiser. Jimmy Sr was looking suspiciously at the glass. He lifted it and took a sip, then a bigger one and then a much bigger one.

— It's not tha' bad, he said.

The seat was nice and cold against his back.

Bimbo was very giddy, looking around him all the time, shifting, waving at every wanker that walked in.

— Settle down, will yeh, said Jimmy Sr.

— Wha'?

— You're like a performin' flea there, Jimmy Sr told him. — You're makin' me fuckin' nervous.

— Sorry, said Bimbo. — It's just — . Ah, yeh know. He lifted his pint.

— Well, Jim, cheers, he said for the third time.

— Yeah, said Jimmy Sr.

— Will yeh have another one? Bimbo asked him.

— There's no —

— Go on.

— Fair enough, said Jimmy Sr. — Thanks very much; there's no need. — Make it Guinness but, will yeh.

— Good man, said Bimbo. — Darren! Two pints o' Guinness, like a good man, please.

— Poor Darren'll be doin' his Leavin' durin' the World Cup, Jimmy Sr told Bimbo. — Isn't tha' shockin'?

— Ah that's shockin', said Bimbo.

— Fuckin' terrible, said Jimmy Sr.

146

And Darren arrived with the pints and Jimmy Sr let him take the rest of the Budweiser.

— It's like drinkin' fuckin' Andrews, he sort of apologised to Bimbo.

— Not to worry, said Bimbo.

He gave Darren a big tip when he was going.

— I was thinkin', said Bimbo. — We'll have to have the van ready in time for the World Cup.

Jimmy Sr didn't like the sound of that. We'll.

He said nothing.

— The pubs'll be jammered, said Bimbo.

He still said nothing.

— An' there'll be no cookin' done, said Bimbo. — 'Specially if Ireland do well.

— They will, said Jimmy Sr. — Don't worry.

— It's a great opportunity, said Bimbo. — Everyone'll be watchin' the telly for the whole month.

— So will I, said Jimmy Sr.

— Yeah, said Bimbo. — It should be smashin'.

They drank. It was good to be back on the Guinness. They'd have a chat now about the World Cup. Jimmy Sr felt good now. He sang softly.

— OLÉ — OLÉ OLÉ OLÉ — Did yeh hear tha' song yet, Bimbo?

— Which; the Ireland one?

— The official one, yeah.

— Ah, I did, yeah, said Bimbo.

— Isn't it brilliant? said Jimmy Sr.

— Terrific.

Jimmy Sr tried to do Jack Charlton.

— Put them uunder presheh.

— D'yeh want to be me partner, Jim? said Bimbo.

— Wha's tha'?

He'd heard Bimbo alright but he was confused.

— Would yeh think abou' becomin' me partner? said Bimbo.

He looked serious in a way that only Bimbo could look; deadly serious.

— We'd make a great team, said Bimbo. — I was talkin' to Maggie about it.

— Jaysis — , said Jimmy Sr. — Eh, thanks very much, Bimbo. I don't know —

— Will yeh think about it annyway? said Bimbo.

— I will, Jimmy Sr assured him. — I will. — Thanks.

— No, said Bimbo. — You'd be doin' me a favour.

— Oh, I know tha', said Jimmy Sr.

They laughed, and that gave Jimmy Sr a chance to wipe his eyes. He said it again.

— Thanks very much.

He took a big breath.

— Fuckin' hell, he said then. — What a day.

Wait till Veronica heard.

— McDonalds can go an' fuck themselves, he said to Bimbo. — Isn't tha' righ'?

Bimbo laughed, delighted.

— That's righ'.

They laughed again.

— Bimbo's Burgers, said Jimmy Sr. — How does tha' sound?

Bimbo clapped his hands.

— I knew it! he said.

148

He held his hand out, and Jimmy Sr took it and didn't let go of it for ages.

Then he dropped Bimbo's hand.

— Hang on though, he said.

He looked very worried.

— Do I have to help you clean it?

He watched Bimbo deciding if he was joking or not and then the two of them roared and shook hands again.

Veronica was lying beside him, nearly asleep, God love her; she'd been studying all night for her exams. She'd told him how to make chips and it seemed easy enough.

These were good chips, the ones he was eating now. They always were in the summer. There'd be a terrible smell of vinegar in the bedroom in the morning though.

He'd brought a sausage-in-batter tonight as well. He held it up to the light coming in where the curtain stopped short of the wall, to get a decent look at it. He looked down at Veronica.

— Veronica? he whispered.

He didn't want to talk to her unless she was awake anyway.

— Mmmm? said Veronica.

— Are yeh awake?

— What?

— Only if you're awake.

— Go on, said Veronica.

— How do they make these? said Jimmy Sr.

He brought the sausage down to the pillow so she could see it properly.

Veronica snorted, kind of.

— I don't know, she said. — I don't think they make them. I think they just find them.

She found his knee and gave it a squeeze.

There was only a month to go to the start of the World Cup so, as Bimbo said, they had it all to do. It wasn't even a full month, a bit less than four weeks.

They walked around the van again.

— Righ', said Bimbo. — We'll never get it cleaned up by just lookin' at it.

So he went through the house to the back and got his hose and rigged it up to the tap in the kitchen and brought the hose out to the front through the hall.

— Wha' colour is it annyway? Jimmy Sr asked.

— White! said Bimbo.

— How d'yeh know?

— All chipper vans are whi'e, said Bimbo. — Stand back there, Jimmy.

He roared into the hall.

— Righ'! Turn her on.

Someone inside turned on the cold tap and Bimbo pointed the hose at the side of the van. The water came out in two gushes and then in a steady stream and Bimbo went up close so the water would drum against the wall of the van. It made an impressive sound, and brought some of the neighbours out to watch. Bimbo sprayed right across; he put his thumb to the nozzle and aimed at one spot and held the jet of water at it for ages — but he might as well have been pissing at it for all the good it did.

— Okay! Turn her off! — Turn her off!!

He sounded annoyed.

The water slowed down and stopped altogether.

—Will yeh switch it on to the hot tap!? Bimbo yelled.

Maggie answered.

— I used up all the hot doin' the clothes.

— Ah, God almighty, Bimbo said quietly.

He let the hose drop. They studied the side of the van.

The dirt was still there, solid as ever, only shinier now because of the water. It looked even worse that way, almost healthy and alive.

— How did it get greasy on the fuckin' outside? Jimmy Sr asked.

— God knows, said Bimbo.

—Yeh could understand the inside, said Jimmy Sr.

— Yeah, said Bimbo. — Yeah.

—What'll we do now? Jimmy Sr wanted to know.

Bimbo scraped a clot of grease off with his fingernail.

— It does come off, he said.

Jimmy Sr did the same.

—Yeah, he said. — Fuckin' hell though, Bimbo. It's goin' to take fuckin' years.

— Not at all, said Bimbo.

They got paint scrapers, five of them, from Barney's Hardware and attacked the van with them, and then they started getting somewhere. Once you got the blade in under the grease and the dirt it came away easily enough. It was a little bit disgusting alright but at least they could see that it was working, the grease was coming off, and that made up for it. But the feel of it was horrible, and the smell; it was hard to describe, fuckin' terrible though. Jimmy Sr could smell it on his hands even after putting some of Veronica's Oil of Ulay all over them. And his clothes; he'd have roasted himself if he'd sat too close to the fire after a day's work. Veronica said she'd never seen dirt like it; she said it the first four days he came home, but she didn't say it like she was annoyed, more like she was fascinated.

They concentrated on the outside. They were both too scared to look carefully inside, but they didn't say anything. They just did their work. They scraped all day and when they started sliding because of the grease on the ground they stopped and hosed the path and went at it with the yard brush. Bimbo got sawdust from the butchers and sprinkled it on top of the grease and that way they didn't have to interrupt the work too often. It was manky work though, messy and slow. But Maggie said it wouldn't go on for ever and she was right; it just felt that way. He'd get up at eight and go down to Bimbo's and look at the bit he'd done the day before and it was like he'd never touched it; it was still filthy and shiny. But, then again, he'd be scraping away, breathing through his mouth, listening to the radio or chatting with Bimbo, and he'd see that there was no more grease to scrape off in this part; he'd reached the end, there was just white paint, a small island of it.

He felt brilliant the first time that happened and he didn't stop working till eight o'clock.

They were getting there.

There was more than just the cleaning of the van, of course. They had to become chefs before the end of the month, which was no fuckin' joke. The first time he made chips, at home, he put far too much oil into the pan and nearly set fire to the fuckin' kitchen when he lowered the chips into it. It frightened the shite out of him. But Veronica was a good teacher, very patient; she even let him make the dinner one night, which was very decent of her. He made a bit of a bollix of it — burnt fuck out of the burgers; it was like eating little hubcaps — but no one complained. She showed him how to peel spuds without peeling the skin off your hands as well, how to always peel out, away from your body, so you didn't stab yourself.

He cut his wrist the first time he did it; not cut it exactly, more scraped, but it was very fuckin' sore all the same. He nearly went out the window when Veronica put Dettol on it but they laughed later in bed, imagining trying to kill yourself with a potato peeler scraping away till you hit an artery, and then start on the other wrist, quick before you fainted. They hadn't laughed together like that in ages.

She'd a good sense of humour, Veronica had. The only time she got annoyed was when he peeled all the potatoes in the house, practising. He didn't blame her but, like he told her, they were running out of time. Another thing she showed him that he'd never known before; you put the chips you didn't want to use immediately in water to keep them fresh and the right colour.

— God, he said. — The simple things are the most ingenious, aren't they?

He caught Sharon grinning at him when he was practising his peeling.

— Fuck off, you, he said.

And he brought the bucket and the spuds up to the bedroom so he could do his practice in peace. Later on, Sharon asked him if she could work in the van some nights, when it was on the road. And he said Yeah.

It would do her good.

— She'd be a good worker, said Jimmy Sr.

He wanted to clout Bimbo, the way he was looking at him, like he'd farted at mass during the Offertory; that sort of look.

— I know tha', said Bimbo. — I never said different, Jimmy, now.

— Well then —?

— Staff appointments should be a joint decision, Jimmy. Between the two of us.

— It's only Sharon, for fuck sake.

— Still, though —

He was right really. But —

— D'yeh want me to sack her, is tha' it? Before she's even started.

— Ah, Jimmy —

— Ah, me arse.

But Bimbo was right, Jimmy Sr could see that. He just hated losing.

— I'll tell her we don't want her, Jimmy Sr told Bimbo, like he was giving in to him.

— Not at all, said Bimbo. — No way.

— Wha' then? said Jimmy Sr. — I'm fuckin' lost.

— Just, in future we'll make these decisions together, said Bimbo. — Is tha' alrigh'?

—Yeah, said Jimmy Sr. — No problem. Sorry abou' —

— Ah no, said Bimbo. — No. No.

They got back to work and didn't say anything to each other for a good while.

The roof wasn't as bad as the sides but it was very tricky. There was no grease up there but that didn't mean that you couldn't fall off. Bimbo did fall off but he landed on the grass, so it wasn't too bad; there was no real damage done. Still, the noise he made when he hit the ground was terrifying, like a huge thump. Jimmy Sr was on his hands and knees up there, afraid to budge. Maggie felt Bimbo hitting the ground from where she was in the house and she came out and got him up on his feet and gave out shite to him once she knew that he wasn't dying on her. Poor oul' Bimbo was a bit shook after it, so they called it a day. The only problem was getting down off the fuckin' roof. Jimmy Sr's leg couldn't find the ladder and he was shaking like fuck, but he got down eventually and he took Bimbo off for a pint. They took a look back at the van when they got out to the path, just to see what it looked like from a distance, and it didn't look too bad at all; it wasn't as white as it could've been, like new teeth, but it was definitely white.

They went on a reconnaissance mission. That was what Bimbo called it, but he was only messing. They went to a chipper; not the one they normally used cos the crowd in there were a snotty bunch of fuckers and

155

Jimmy Sr hadn't got on well with them since Leslie threw a dead cat over the counter into the deep fat fryer. That was years ago, long before Leslie went to England, and they still held it against him. Actually, it was gas when it happened. Jimmy Sr and the lads had gone in after closing time and the old fella, the one the kids called the Fat Leper, told Jimmy Sr what Les had done with the cat and Bertie changed his order from a batter burger to a smoked cod. — Just to be on the safe side, compadres, he said. Jaysis, they howled. And the Fat Leper barred the lot of them. And Bertie offered to buy the cat if that would make him feel any better, as long as he didn't expect him to eat it as well. Anyway, the barring order only lasted one night — they were cute fuckers, the Italians; you don't make your fortune by barring your best customers — but they still glared at Jimmy Sr. The Fat Leper didn't; he'd died last year, but the rest of them did. Even the ones that had been in Italy when it had happened.

So they went to a different chipper, one in Coolock. It was kind of exciting going in; stupid really, but Jimmy Sr couldn't help thinking that he was a bit of a thrill seeker. Bimbo went ahead of him. It was empty except for them.

— So far so good, said Bimbo.

There were two young fellas behind the counter, one of them opening the bags they put the chips into, putting a line of them on top of the counter, at the ready. Good thinking, thought Jimmy Sr, and he made a mental note of it. The other one was leaning against the back wall, scratching his hole. There were more of them inside, behind the yellow and red and blue plastic strips they always put over doorways in chippers but there was only the two lads on duty.

— Howyeh, lads, said Bimbo.

— Yeah? said the hole scratcher.

— Two singles, said Bimbo. — Like a good man, please.

— Large or small?

Bimbo looked at Jimmy Sr.

— A large'll do me, Jimmy Sr told him.

— Two large, said Bimbo.

They stood there at the low part of the counter, where they put the vinegar on the chips and took the money. They leaned over and tried to see the lads in action, but the chips were already done so all they did was bag them.

— That all? said the other one.

— Yeah, said Bimbo, — thanks. We're just after the dinner.

Jimmy Sr nudged him.

— Wha'?

— Go on, said Jimmy Sr. — Ask him.

It would be too late in a minute.

— Eh, lads — ? said Bimbo.

They looked at him.

Jimmy Sr had to nudge Bimbo again; he was fuckin' useless.

— Where d'yis get your chips? Bimbo asked them. — Eh, if yeh don't mind me askin' now.

— In the ground, said the hole scratcher, the smartarsed little prick, and the two of them laughed.

Jimmy Sr had to drag Bimbo away from the counter.

— Come on.

— Wha' abou' the chips? said Bimbo.

— Fuck them, said Jimmy Sr.

He pushed Bimbo out the door. The two behind the counter were annoyed now because they'd two singles wrapped and ready and no home for them. Jimmy Sr gave them the fingers.

— Go back to your own country, he said. — Fuck the EEC.

He felt a lot better after that. He went back to give them more.

— An' bring Tony Cascarino with yis, he said. — He's fuckin' useless annyway.

And he left the door open, so one of them would have to come around and close it cos it was quite chilly out.

Bimbo told Maggie what had happened and she kind of took over that department.

— Joint decisions, me bollix said Jimmy Sr, but he didn't mind; he just said it to make Bimbo feel guilty, because he deserved it.

Maggie was brilliant. She got them a cash-and-carry card, no problem to her. Fellas Jimmy Sr knew would have killed their mothers for one of those cards, to get at the cheap drink, but Maggie went off one afternoon and came back with one. She'd a great business head on her.

— A revelation, said Bertie.

— Ah yeah, said Jimmy Sr. — Hats off to her.

Bimbo was chuffed.

She found out about permits and licences and that, stuff that Jimmy Sr couldn't've been bothered looking

158

into, and Bimbo wouldn't've been able to. She said she'd organise the stock, and all they'd have to worry about was getting the van in order, and then manning it. She said she'd look after the whole legal side of the operation. It was a load off their minds, both Jimmy Sr and Bimbo agreed on that.

— I didn't even know yeh needed a fuckin' licence, Jimmy Sr admitted.

— Oh God, yeah, said Bimbo. — Yeh need a licence for nearly everythin', so yeh do.

Jimmy Sr supposed that it was only right; if you needed a licence for a dog or a telly it was only proper that you had to have one for a chipper van as well.

— It's not so much the van, said Bimbo. — It's more what yeh do in it, if yeh get me.

The outside of the van was looking well now. Bimbo's brother, Victor, was a panel beater and he was going to do a job on the dints, the worst ones anyway. There were a few bald patches but a lick of paint would make them hard to find. The neighbours still stopped and looked at them working, but they'd stopped slagging them.

— We've got it looking smashin', said Bimbo.

Jimmy Sr rubbed his fingers down the side, and there was no track left after it. He wouldn't have been able to do that last week; his finger would've got stuck.

— Now for the inside, said Bimbo.

— Oh fuck, said Jimmy Sr.

They all got together in Bimbo and Maggie's kitchen. Veronica came with Jimmy Sr so there was the four of them, and Maggie's mother. It was nice.

— Now, said Maggie. — What I thought we'd do tonight was finalise the menu.

—Wha' menu? said Bimbo.

—Yeah, said Jimmy Sr.

He was worried; he didn't want to be a fuckin' waiter.

Bimbo nearly whispered over the table to Maggie.

— It's only a van.

Veronica started laughing, and Maggie did as well.

Jimmy Sr wasn't sure what was happening, but he couldn't help thinking that he was being hijacked, himself and Bimbo.

—The menu, lads, said Maggie — a bit sarcastically, Jimmy Sr thought — is the list of things that the customer chooses from.

— Like on the wall behind the counter? said Jimmy Sr.

— Exactly, said Maggie.

Jimmy Sr nodded, like he'd known that all along; he was just checking.

They got down to business. Maggie had stuff already done in under the grill, like on a cookery programme on the telly. She divided a burger in five and they each had a little bit. Jimmy Sr thought that this was a bit mean, until he tasted it.

— Jesus!

Enough said; they all agreed with him. Maggie had a list; she even had one of those clipboard things. She put a line through the first name.

—Wha' are they called an' annyway? Jimmy Sr asked Maggie.

— Splendid Burgers, said Maggie.

— My God, said Veronica.

They tasted five more. Maggie's mother was still only on the second one when the rest of them had finished.

— Would annyone like a glass o' water? said Bimbo.

— Please, said Veronica.

— Yeah, me too, said Jimmy Sr. — I thought the third one was the nicest.

— I don't know if nicest is the word, said Veronica, — but —

— What abou' you, Bimbo? Jimmy Sr asked.

— Yeah. I think so, he said. — Not the last one annyway; the fifth one.

— Fuck, no.

Maggie's mother caught up with them.

— What do you think, Mammy? Maggie asked her.

— Very nice, she said.

— Which but? said Jimmy Sr.

— Oh, she said. — Is it a quiz?

And Veronica kicked Jimmy Sr's leg before he could say anything back.

— Will we go for the Champion Burger so? said Maggie.

— Is tha' the third one? said Jimmy Sr.

— Yeah.

— Def'ny then, said Jimmy Sr. — They were bigger as well.

— That's only because o' the way I cut it, said Maggie. — I gave you the biggest bit.

— Still though, said Jimmy Sr. — I thought it was head an' shoulders above the others.

— Champion? said Maggie. — Goin' once — twice — Champion, it is.

Jimmy Sr was delighted; he'd won. He knocked back his water and got up to get more.

— What's next? said Bimbo.

— Spice-burgers, said Maggie.

Herself and Veronica started laughing again.

They were all feeling a bit queasy by the time they'd finished — very fuckin' queasy actually — but it was great crack all the same. Fresh cod-in-batter, small bricks of the stuff, was next, followed closely by smoked cod-in-batter.

— It's not really smoked cod at all, yeh know, Maggie told them. — It's black mullet.

Veronica took her bit out of her mouth when she heard that but Jimmy Sr thought it was grand. His philosophy was that he didn't give a shite what it was so long as it tasted alright, and he made that point to the rest of them. Bimbo didn't agree with him.

— I don't think yeh should sell somethin' if it's really somethin' else, he said.

— Fair enough, said Jimmy Sr. — Put Black mullet-in-batter up on the, eh, menu an' see how many yeh sell.

— Maybe if we can't get real smoked cod we shouldn't sell it at all.

— Yes, said Veronica.

— People like smoked cod! said Jimmy Sr. — I love a bit o' smoked cod.

— But it isn't really smoked cod.

— So wha'?

Veronica wanted to say something.

— Does it have to be all these processed things? she asked. — Could you not get your fish in Howth and prepare it yourselves.

— Too dear, I'm afraid, said Maggie.

She consulted her clipboard.

— An' anyway, said Jimmy Sr. — As well as tha', how would we smoke the cod an' tha'? We don't know how. We're not — fuckin' Amazon tribesmen or somethin'.

He took another hunk of the mullet and chewed fuck out of it.

— Well, I think it's fuckin' lovely, he said.

And bloody Veronica started laughing again.

Maggie was gas once she had a few scoops inside in her. She made her mother try out two different types of ketchup.

They watched her putting a little fingerload of the second ketchup onto her tongue.

— Now, Mammy, said Maggie. — Was tha' one any less disgustin' than the last one?

— Oh yes, she said. — Definitely.

They'd polished off the few cans that Bimbo had hidden under the stairs (— I'd've sworn tha' there was more in there), so they went for a few pints before closing time, to get rid of the taste of all the gunge and shite they'd been experimenting with all night.

Maggie's mother stayed at home.

— I think the last spice-burger must've floored her a bit, said Bimbo.

— Ah yeah; God love her, said Jimmy Sr.

Veronica burst her hole laughing when he said that. She was really enjoying herself. Jimmy Sr held her hand for a bit when they were going up the road.

They were both nervous going in. The World Cup was only two and a bit weeks away now. They climbed in and stood there, sweating already before they'd done anything. They breathed through their mouths, air that hadn't been used in months; it smelt a bit like old runners, but far worse than that.

— No rust, said Bimbo, after a fair while.

— Everythin' else though, said Jimmy Sr.

— How'll we manage it? said Bimbo.

Jimmy Sr had an idea; he'd had it since he'd started sweating.

— A couple o' kids would be better in here than us, he said. — Much more effective.

Bimbo didn't look too keen.

— We'd just get them to take off the first layer, Jimmy Sr explained. — An' then we can do the rest ourselves easily. We won't be gettin' in each other's way.

It was Saturday; no school.

— I'll get Wayne up, said Bimbo.

— Good man, said Jimmy Sr. — Bribe him.

— I'll have to, said Bimbo. — Wayne loves his bed.

Wayne grew up that day; he earned his first day's wages. God, he was great. Early on, only a little while after he'd started, he got out of the van and got sick, and climbed back in again, not a bother on him. He didn't even want a glass of water when Bimbo said he'd get one for him. Bimbo got another of his young fellas,

Glenn, when he came home from his football and that made two of them inside and Bimbo and Jimmy Sr outside handing buckets of hot water into them. It was a lovely day, the sun was powerful and a nice breeze as well. Wayne was small and Glenn was tiny.

— Made for this kind o' work, said Jimmy Sr.

Bimbo agreed with him.

— They're good in school as well though, Jimmy, he said. — Glenn is tops in his class.

— Yeh can see that alrigh', said Jimmy Sr. — He's a man's head on him.

He looked in at them again.

— D'yeh know wha'? he said. — If they'd been around a hundred years ago they'd've spent all their time up fuckin' chimneys.

Bimbo looked in as well; he couldn't help laughing, but he was beaming, delighted with himself.

— Now now, lads, he said.

They were throwing water at each other.

— D'yeh know what I was thinkin'? said Jimmy Sr.

They were sitting on the grass, keeping an eye on the lads.

— Wha'?

— We should have a big paintin' there beside the hatch, said Jimmy Sr. — An' another one to match it on the other side.

— What sort of a paintin'? said Bimbo.

— I don't know, said Jimmy Sr. — A burger or somethin', an' a few chips beside. Like an ad. Not a painting paintin' like the Mona Lisa or annythin'. A sign.

165

Glenn slid out of the van headfirst but he was going fast enough to miss the path and land on the grass. He laughed and got up to do it again. Bimbo grabbed him by the kaks; he was only wearing his runners and his underpants.

— No messin' now, Glenn.

But they were sliding around like Torvill and Dean in there, not on purpose; they couldn't help it. Then Bimbo had a brainwave. He got sheets of sandpaper — he had loads of them, of course — and tied them to the soles of their runners, and it worked.

He kept looking in at them and their feet.

— Take it easy, Bimbo, will yeh, said Jimmy Sr. — You're not after inventin' fuckin' electricity.

— You're only jealous, Bimbo told him.

— Fuck off, will yeh.

By the end of the day the two lads were shagged but they'd done a great job. Maggie gave out shite; she said she'd never be able to get the rings off the bath. She'd soaked the two of them till their skin was wrinkly and they still looked grey.

— Take a look at wha' they did though, said Bimbo.

Maggie looked into the van. And she had to admit it; they'd done a great job.

They climbed into the van.

— They did a smashin' job, didn't they? said Bimbo.

It was Monday morning, bright and early.

It was still manky, there was still a very funny smell — it was worse now that the van was much cleaner;

166

more out of place — but it looked a hell of a lot better than it had two days ago.

The door was at the back of the van. The driver and passenger seats were separate; you had to get out and walk round to the back to get into the van bit. There was a step up to the door. When you came in the hatch was on your right. It was wide enough for two using their arms and elbows, with a good wide counter, although you'd have to lean out a bit to get the money. The door of the hatch was like the emergency exit at the back of a double-decker bus, but without the glass. You pushed it out and up. The hotplate and the deep fat fryer were behind the hatch, on the other side of the van. There was a small window above them, without the glass since Wayne had put his foot through it. There was a sink at the back and not a lot else; a few shelves and ledges. The sink was behind where the passenger seat was.

— What's the sink for? Jimmy Sr wanted to know.

— For washin' stuff, o' course, said Bimbo.

— But there's no fuckin' water, said Jimmy Sr.

— Yeh'd have to have a sink, said Bimbo.

— But there's no fuckin' water, Jimmy Sr said again.

— Well, it's there for somethin', said Bimbo. — We'll figure it ou'. — We'll go at it from the top down.

— Righto, said Jimmy Sr.

Bimbo was on the left wall and Jimmy Sr on the right, the one with the hatch in it. He'd skip over the hatch and finish before Bimbo and give out shite to him for being a slowcoach, for the laugh.

— Just a squirt gets the dirt, said Bimbo when they were starting.

It was a doddle compared to what they'd had to do outside.

— How much did yeh give the lads? Jimmy Sr asked Bimbo.

— Nothin' yet, said Bimbo. — Sure, they asked me could they do it again there yesterday. They had a great time, so they did.

They laughed.

— They'll learn, said Jimmy Sr. — Let's get a bit o' light in here, wha'.

He figured out how to open the hatch.

— Now.

He pushed it out, and it fell off and Jimmy Sr nearly fell out after it. It made an almighty clatter when it hit the ground. Bimbo nearly fell off his perch. He dropped his Jif into the deep fat fryer.

— God, me heart, he said.

Jimmy Sr was swinging off the counter. His legs found the floor and he felt safer.

— Fuck your heart, said Jimmy Sr. — I nearly had a shite in me fuckin' trousers. Come here, swap sides.

— No way!

They weren't happy with the look of the deep fat fryer. But they'd done their best with it.

— Still though, said Bimbo. — It might be dangerous.

— Not at all, said Jimmy Sr. — It's just wear an' tear, that's all.

They were in Bimbo's kitchen having their elevenses.

— The hotplate looks very well now, said Bimbo.

— It does alrigh', Jimmy Sr agreed. — Yeh'd ride your missis on it it's so clean.

— Shhh! said Bimbo.

Glenn was coming through with tins of pineapple rings.

— It's the man from Delmonte, said Jimmy Sr. — Good man, Glenn.

— These're the heaviest, Glenn told him.

— No problem to yeh, said Jimmy Sr.

Glenn ran out into the garden so he could get to the shed before he had to drop the tray of pineapple rings. They heard the clatter of tins hitting the path.

— He didn't make it, said Jimmy Sr.

Bimbo lifted himself up to look out the window.

— No, he said. — He did.

They'd two freezers out in Bimbo's shed — Bertie'd got them for them; grand big freezers, nearly new — and all the stuff went into them; the blocks of cod, the blocks of lard, the burgers, anything that would go bad.

The kids were bringing cartons of Twixes and Mars Bars out to Maggie now.

— I have them counted, she warned them.

Jessica went to the kitchen door and yelled out.

— There's nothin' left!

— Come here, said Maggie.

In a few seconds the kids came charging through with two Twixes and two Mars Bars apiece.

Bimbo made a grab at Glenn.

— Give us a Twix.

Glenn got away from him and into the hall, bursting his little shite laughing. Maggie shut the kitchen door.

She threw a burger onto the table. It bounced; it was rock solid.

— What d'you think of tha'? she said.

— It's a bit hard, said Bimbo.

Jimmy Sr picked it up. It was the whole thing, the bun and all.

— What's the idea? he said.

— There's onion an' sauce an' a slice o' gherkin already in there, she said. — And you can get them with cheese as well.

She sat down.

— All yeh have to do is throw it in the microwave, she said.

— That's very good, said Bimbo.

— We don't have a microwave, said Jimmy Sr.

— Can't yis get — ? said Maggie.

— We've no electricity, said Bimbo.

They looked at one another.

— Oh Christ — , said Jimmy Sr.

— Now, said Jimmy Sr. — Look at this now; there's nothin' to it. Anny fuckin' eejit could do it.

They were in the Rabbitte kitchen.

He had the mixing bowl on the table in front of him. He poured water from a milk bottle into the bowl.

— Water, he said.

He sprinkled some flour from a packet in on top of the water, then got a bit braver and poured half the packet in.

— An' flour, he said. — Yeh with me so far?

— Water an' flour, said Bimbo.

170

— Good man.

He picked up the whisk.

— This is the hard part, he said. — The hard work. I'm doin' it by hand, he explained, — cos that's the way we'll have to do in the van.

He attacked the mixture with the whisk, holding the bowl to him the way Veronica'd shown him.

— I'm tellin' yeh, he said. — It gets yeh sweatin'.

He stopped and looked.

— It's blendin' well there, d'yeh see? he said. — We need a bit more water though, to get rid o' the lumps.

Bimbo went to the sink and filled the milk bottle.

— Nearly there, said Jimmy Sr.

He poured in some more water, and prodded the lumps with the whisk and then his fingers.

— There's somethin' else supposed to go into it but I can't remember what it is.

He started whisking again.

— Doesn't matter though, he said. — This'll be grand.

He stopped and showed Bimbo the result.

— There, he said. — Batter. Not bad, wha'.

It looked right.

— Is tha' all there is to it? said Bimbo.

— That's it, said Jimmy Sr. — Except for the thing I'm after forgettin'. Let's see if it works now.

He'd already put an open can of pineapple rings on the table.

— Remind me to replace this one, will yeh, he said. — Veronica'll go spare if she goes to get it on Sunday and it's not there. — Let's see now —

He took a ring out and let it down onto a sheet of kitchen roll.

— Yeh dry it first; that's important.

He dabbed the top of the ring with the edge of the roll.

— Tha' should do it.

He held up the ring and picked the bits of fluff off it.

— It's only the paper, he said. — Harmless.

— Yeah.

— Righ'; fingers crossed.

He lowered the pineapple ring into the batter, and let it sink in completely. He got a fork and searched for the ring, and found it.

— Our father who art in heaven — Fuckin' brilliant! Look it; completely covered.

— That's great, said Bimbo.

— An' all yeh do then is drop it into the fryer. — That's great now; the batter's just righ'. If it was too watery it wouldn't've stuck an' if it was too thick the hole in the ring would've disappeared. But that's just righ' now. Perfect.

— We'll cut them up into different sizes, said Jimmy Sr.
— People prefer tha'.

That was what they were doing now, peeling the spuds and cutting them up and throwing them all into a big plastic bin full of water; out in the shed.

— When we've the money, said Jimmy Sr, — maybe we should get a chip machine like Maggie was talkin' abou' and just cut up a few o' the spuds by hand an' mix them in so people'll think they're all done tha' way.

172

— Yeah, said Bimbo.

Jimmy Sr looked into the bucket and gave it a kick to flatten out the chips.

— There's enough in there now, I'd say, he said.

— Good.

They took a handle each and carried the bin through the house out to the van. They'd a job getting it up the step, and in; the water made it very heavy and it was slopping over the sides. They were all set; tonight was the night. Everything in the van was gleaming; nearly everything. They'd had to buy some new equipment, some of the trays and the basket for the deep fat fryer. Bimbo bought it; Jimmy Sr hadn't a bean to his name. They put the bin under the sink. That was the best place for it, because it got in the way anywhere else and the sink was fuck all use to them.

— We should just pull it ou' altogether, said Jimmy Sr.

— Ah no, said Bimbo. — Not now annyway.

The thing got on Jimmy Sr's wick, a sink with no water; it was about as useful as an arse with no hole. He let it go though. They'd other things to do today.

— Will we put the rest of the stuff in? said Bimbo.

— We might as well, said Jimmy Sr.

They didn't want to leave anything in the van for too long. Some of the stuff from the freezers would go soft or even bad if they took it out too early. The timing was vital.

— The difference between a satisfied customer and a corpse, Jimmy Sr'd said.

They'd laughed, but it wasn't funny.

173

They got out, and stopped to look at the burger on the side of the van again. It was a huge big burger, a bunburger with BIMBO'S BURGERS above it and TODAY'S CHIPS TODAY under it.

The bottom bit was Maggie's idea.

— I still don't like tha' ketchup, said Jimmy Sr. — It's too like fuckin' blood. It'll put people off.

— Ah no, said Bimbo. — It's nice an' bright.

Maggie's brother's kid, Sandra, had done it; she went to some painting college or something.

— The bit o' meat stickin' ou' as well, said Jimmy Sr. He pointed to it.

— It's like a fuckin' tongue hangin' ou'.

— Well, to be honest with yeh, Jimmy, said Bimbo.

— I've never seen a tongue made o' mince.

— It's the same colour as —

— Look it, said Bimbo. — She put all those little black speckles on it to make it look like mince.

He went over and touched them, showing them to Jimmy Sr.

— They just make it look like it's gone off, said Jimmy Sr.

— It was your bloody idea in the first place, said Bimbo.

— D'yeh want to know why I don't like it? said Jimmy Sr. — An' annyway, I do like it. It's just the colours I don't like. D'yeh want to know why?

— Why then?

— Cos the young one tha' done it is a vegetarian, that's why.

174

He had him now. Sandra'd told him that, when he was talking to her while she was painting; a lovely-looking girl, she was, but a bit snotty; a good laugh though.

Bimbo looked lost.

— Sabotage, yeh dope, said Jimmy Sr.

— Wha'?

— Sabotage, said Jimmy Sr. — Animal rights.

— Wha' d'yeh mean?

— Is it not fuckin' obvious?

— Eh — no.

— A vegetarian, righ', paints a picture of a burger an' wha' does she do? — She paints it horrible colours to put people off buyin' anny.

— Sandra?

— They're all the same, said Jimmy Sr. — Fanatics, for fuck sake. Sure, they're puttin' bombs under people's cars over in England, just cos they experiment with animals.

— Hang on now, said Bimbo. — We're not experimentin' with animals.

— No, said Jimmy Sr. — But we're slappin' them up on the hot plate an' fryin' fuck ou' o' them. An' then gettin' people to eat them.

Bimbo gave this some thought. He looked at the burger.

— Ah, I don't think so, he said.

— Please yourself, said Jimmy Sr. — It's your fuckin' money. Come on or we'll be late.

They put the cartons of Twixes and Mars Bars in under the hot plate, and the cans of Coke and 7-Up.

175

They put piles of spice-burgers on the shelf over the fryer. They had the flour and a line of milk bottles full of water for the batter, at the ready on the shelf beside the sink; they'd had to go scouting for real glass bottles. They'd a box for the money. Bimbo put the big red Kandee sauce bottle and the salt and vinegar on the counter. They had ten packs of Bundies. Maggie'd got them in Crazy Prices. Jimmy Sr opened a pack and took one out.

— These are the nicest part o' the burger, he said. — Aren't they?

— They're lovely alrigh', said Bimbo, and he took one as well. — We'd better not eat all of the supplies though.

— An army marches on its stomach, Jimmy Sr told him.

There was a ream of small bags on a piece of string, for the chips, and Jimmy Sr hung that on a hook beside the fryer, and put a pile of big brown bags on the counter. Bimbo folded up their aprons nice and squarely and put them on the counter beside the brown bags.

— It's not a fuckin' pinnie, Jimmy Sr'd said when Veronica caught him trying his one on up in the bedroom. — It's an apron, righ'.

Maggie'd got the aprons, World Cup ones. It was good thinking, and a lot better than those ones with recipes printed on them or something. These just had Italia 90 on them, and the cup.

— It's not a cup but, said Bimbo. — It's a statue. I never noticed that before.

— Look it, said Jimmy Sr. — Which sounds better; World Cup or World Statue?

— I get yeh, said Bimbo.

They kept the fish in the freezer till the last minute. If you didn't dip the cod in the batter when it was still like a piece of chipboard you ended up with a fuckin' awful mush that floated on the top of the cooking oil. They piled the rectangles of cod and black mullet onto the aluminium trays.

— Yeh'd nearly need gloves for this, said Jimmy Sr. — These things are fuckin' freezin'.

He walloped a piece of cod against the side of the freezer and examined it: there wasn't a mark on it.

— That's a good piece o' fish, tha', he said. — It won't let yeh down.

The trays were cold, but not that heavy. Still, they rushed through the house so they could put them down in the van and blow on their hands.

— Beep beep, said Bimbo, to get Maggie's mother out of his way as he barrelled through the kitchen, trying to carry his tray without having to use too firm a grip. He rested it against his chest and his shirt was getting wet.

Maggie followed them out.

— Good luck now, she said.

Jimmy Sr climbed up into the driver's seat. The van was hitched up to the back of Bimbo's jalopy with a bit of rope, in the driveway and halfway out onto the path. Bimbo had wrapped an old cardigan around his bumper, for a buffer. He'd wanted to use Wayne, with one foot on each bumper, but Maggie wouldn't let him.

Bimbo got in and started the car. Maggie put her head down to him, he rolled down the window and she gave him a kiss.

— Jaysis, said Jimmy Sr, softly. — Come on, come on.

They were off.

Bimbo'd only gone a couple of feet and he had to stop cos there were two cars passing. The van rolled into the back of him, but only gently. Then they were out on the road, heading up to the Hikers. A couple of kids ran beside him, and one of them kicked the van. They disappeared; Jimmy Sr knew they were scutting on the back, the fuckers.

There was an awkward bit coming up, a bit of a dip just before they got onto the main road, Barrytown Road. If there was traffic coming Bimbo would have to stop for it and Jimmy Sr would go into him; it couldn't be helped. That was what happened, except it was worse. There was nothing coming so Bimbo kept going out across the main road turning to the right but this fuckin' eejit on a motor bike came out of nowhere from behind a parked van and Bimbo had to brake and Jimmy Sr couldn't brake, of course, so he went into Bimbo, and he heard stuff falling off the shelves behind him.

— Fuck it!

He listened.

Nothing else fell. Maybe it wouldn't be too bad.

Bimbo got going again and they made it to the Hikers without anything else happening. He started stopping about fifty yards before the Hikers, so that when he stopped he'd nearly stopped already anyway, going so slow that the van didn't bump into him at all this time.

Jimmy Sr listened to hear if there was anything rolling around inside in the back. He couldn't hear anything.

Bimbo got the bricks out from the back seat of the car and put them behind the wheels of the van. Jimmy Sr opened the door at the back.

— Ah, Christ.

Water fell onto his shoes, not much of it; most of it was at the back, on the floor, along with some of the spice-burgers and the fish. The bin hadn't turned over but there was an awful lot of water there, too much to call a puddle. The spice-burgers were the worst; the water had made them soggy and they were falling apart; they'd have to throw them out. The fish, though, weren't too bad.

They got the cartons up off the floor before the water could get at them. There was no other damage.

Still though, it was depressing.

Jimmy Sr leaned over and poked one of the fish with a finger. It was still good and hard.

— We need a mop, said Bimbo.

— We need a fuckin' engine, said Jimmy Sr. — Come on. We'll clean it up an' go in an' watch the match.

They cleaned up the mess, shoved all the bits of spice-burger and the water and the rest out onto the road with a bit of cardboard, and dried the floor with a tea-towel. Jimmy Sr gave the fish a good wash with some of the water from the milk bottles. He threw out the really dirty ones; where the dirt had got into the fish.

—There now, said Bimbo when they'd finished. — It wasn't as bad as it looked.

— Come on, said Jimmy Sr. — Or all the good places'll be taken.

— Sheedy gets it back — and Sheedy shoOTS!

The place went fuckin' mad!

Ireland had got the equaliser. Jimmy Sr grabbed Bimbo and nearly broke him in half with the hug he gave him. Bertie was up on one of the tables thumping his chest. Even Paddy, the crankiest fucker ever invented, was jumping up and down and shaking his arse like a Brazilian. All sorts of glasses toppled off the tables but no one gave a fuck. Ireland had scored against England and there was nothing more important than that, not even your pint.

—Who scored it!? Who scored it?

— Don't know. It doesn't fuckin' matter!

They all settled down to see the action replay but they still couldn't make out who'd scored it, because they all went wild again when the ball hit the back of the net from one, two, three different angles, and looking at poor oul' Shilton trying to get at it, it was a fuckin' panic.

Word came through from the front.

— Sheedy.

— Sheedy got it.

— Kevin Sheedy.

— WHO PUT THE BALL IN THE ENGLISH NET —

180

SHEEDY —
SHEEDY —

God, it was great; fuckin' brilliant. And the rest of the match was agony. Every time an Irishman got the ball they all cheered and they groaned and laughed whenever one of the English got it; not that they got it that often; Ireland were all over them.

— Your man, Waddle's a righ' stick, isn't he?

— Ah, he's like a headless fuckin' chicken.

A throw-in for Ireland.

— MICK — MICK — MICK — MICK — MICK —

They all cheered when they saw Mick McCarthy coming up to take it. And there was Paddy Mick-Mick-Micking out of him and only an hour ago he'd been calling Mick McCarthy a fuckin' liability.

— OLÉ — OLÉ OLÉ OLÉ —

— OLÉ

— OLÉ —

There was ten minutes left.

— Ah Jaysis, me heart!

— No problem, compadre.

Jimmy Sr was about ten yards away from where he'd started when Sheedy'd scored. He didn't know how that had happened. He tried to get back to his pint.

— 'Xcuse me. — Sorry there; — thanks. — 'Xcuse me. — Get ou' o' me way, yeh fat cunt.

His pint was gone, on the floor, or maybe some bollix had robbed it. He looked over at the bar. He'd never get near it; it was jammered. Anyway, Leo the barman was ignoring all orders; he was looking at the big screen and praying; he was, praying.

— Look it, Jimmy Sr pointed him out to Bimbo.

He had his hands joined the way kids did, palm against palm, like on the cover of a prayer book, and his lips were moving. When everyone else cheered Leo just kept on praying.

— How much is there left?

— Five, I think.

— Fuck.

He looked around him. There were a lot of young ones in the pub. They hadn't been paying much attention to the match earlier but they were now. There was one of them, over near the bar; she was in a white T-shirt that you could see her bra through it and —

There was a big groan. Jimmy Sr got back to the match.

—What's happenin'?

— They have it.

Gascoigne got past two of the Irish lads and gave it to someone at the edge of the box and he fired — Jimmy Sr grabbed Bimbo's arm — but it went miles over the bar.

They cheered.

— Useless.

— How much left now?

— Two.

—Take your time, Packie!

— ONE PACKIE BONNER

THERE'S ONLY ONE PACKIE BONNER —

— Up them steps, Packie!

— Ah, he's a great fuckin' goalkeeper.

— ONE PACKIE BOHHHH-NER —

182

— He's very religious, yeh know. He always has rosary beads in his kit bag.

— He should strangle fuckin' Lineker with them, said Jimmy Sr, and he got a good laugh. — How much now, Bimbo?

Before Bimbo answered the Olivetti yoke came up on the screen and answered his question; they were into time added on.

They cheered.

— Come on, lads; go for another one!

— Ah, Morris; you're fuckin' useless.

— Fuck up, you. He's brilliant.

— ONE GISTY MORRIS

THERE'S ONLY ONE GISTY MORRIS —

— Blow the fuckin' whistle, yeh cunt yeh!

They laughed.

Jesus, the heat. You had to gasp to get a lungful; that and the excitement. He couldn't watch; it was killing him.

— OLÉ — OLÉ OLÉ OLÉ —

Jimmy Sr was looking over at the young one again when he got smothered by the lads. They went up — the ref had blown the whistle — and he stayed down. But he grabbed a hold of Bimbo and hung on. Everyone was jumping up and down, even Leo blessing himself. The tricolours were up in the air. He wished he had one. He'd get one for the rest of the matches.

Bertie was back up on the table doing his Norwegian commentator bit.

— Maggie Thatcher! — Winston Churchill! —

— WHO PUT THE BALL IN THE ENGLISH NET —

SHEEDY — SHEEDY —

— Queen Elizabeth! — Lawrence of Arabia! — Elton John! Yis can all go an' fuck yourselves!

They cheered.

Jimmy Sr was bursting; not for a piss, with love. He hugged Bimbo. He hugged Bertie. He hugged Paddy. He even hugged Larry O'Rourke. He loved everyone. There was Sharon. He got over to her and hugged her, and then all her friends.

— Isn't it brilliant, Daddy?

— Ah, it's fuckin' brilliant; brilliant.

— I love your aftershave, Mister Rabbitte.

— OLÉ — OLÉ OLÉ OLÉ —

— Jaysis, said Jimmy Sr when he got back to Bimbo. — An' we only fuckin' drew. Wha' would happen if we'd won?

Bimbo laughed.

Everyone in the place sang. Jimmy Sr hated the song but it didn't matter.

— GIVE IT A LASH JACK
GIVE IT A LASH JACK
NEVER NEVER NEVER SAY NO
IRELIN' — IRELIN' — REPUB-ILIC OF IRELIN'
REV IT UP An' HERE WE GO —

— It's a great song, isn't it? said Bimbo.

— Ah, yeah, said Jimmy Sr.

It was that sort of day.

— We'd better get goin', I suppose, said Bimbo.

— Fair enough, said Jimmy Sr.

He was raring to go.

— Red alert, he shouted. — Red alert.

184

They came charging out of the pub, the two of them. Jimmy Sr let go of a roar.

— Yeow!!

His T-shirt was wringing. Fuck it though, he was floating.

Bimbo got the back door open and hopped in; really hopped now; it was fuckin' gas.

Jimmy Sr stopped.

— Listen, he said.

They could hear loads of cars honking. And there were people out on the streets, they could hear them as well.

He climbed into the van. Bimbo was fighting his apron.

It was getting dark. They had two big torch lights, the ones well-prepared drivers always had in case they had to change a tyre at night. Jimmy Sr turned them on.

— OLÉ — OLÉ OLÉ OLÉ. They're grand now, aren't they?

— Terrific, said Bimbo.

Bimbo had already rigged up the Kozengas canisters to the fryer and the hotplate. The canisters were outside, at the back beside the steps, cos there was no room for them inside. That made Jimmy Sr a bit nervous; he didn't like it. Kids were bound to start messing with them, disconnect them, or worse, start cutting the tubes and before you knew it Jimmy Sr, the van and half of Barrytown would be blown to shite. Still, there was no room for them in here. He had a quick look outside; there was no one at them.

— OLÉ — OLÉ OLÉ OLÉ —

185

Jimmy Sr got the box of matches and took one out. He didn't like this either. He stuck the match into the hollow tube of a biro. He got down on his hunkers in front of the hotplate. He lit the match, turned on the gas, pressed in the knob and held the biro to the jet in under the hotplate. He heard the gas go whoosh and he got his hand to fuck out from under there. He'd never get used to doing that. The smell; fuck it, he'd singed his hair again.

— I fuckin' hate tha', he said.

He got the deep fat fryer going as well, but he didn't need the biro this time. He threw a slab of lard onto the hotplate and topped up the cooking oil in the fryer; everything under control.

— WE ARE GREEN — WE ARE WHI'E

WE ARE FUCKIn' DYNAMI'E

LA LA LA LA — LA LA LA — LA — May as well open the hatch, wha', he said.

— Righto, said Bimbo.

It was the moment they'd been waiting for but they pretended it wasn't. Bimbo was dipping the bits of fish into the deep fat for a few seconds to make the batter stay on them, a trick they'd picked up the last time they'd gone to a chipper; it made a lot of sense. You could pile them up and it didn't get messy and you could have the fish ready to fling back into the fryer whenever anyone ordered one. That was what Bimbo was doing when Jimmy Sr unfastened the hatch and pushed it back and got the steel poles in under it to hold it up and made sure that they were secure. Jimmy Sr concentrated on what he was doing. He didn't want

186

to look too soon, to see how many were outside waiting.

There was no one.

They said nothing; they just kept doing their work. Jimmy Sr didn't have much to do. He spread the melted lard all over the hotplate. He was using one of the wallpaper scrapers they'd left over after cleaning the van. There was a hole in the corner of the plate where the fat dripped down through, onto the cans of drinks and the Mars Bars and Twixes.

— Oh shite, said Jimmy Sr when he saw what was happening.

He looked around for something, and took the cup off the top of Bimbo's flask and put it under the hole, balanced on top of the cans. It worked. Jimmy Sr scraped some of the lard over to the hole and got down to check that it all dripped into the cup. It did. That was good.

He stood up; still no one outside. He couldn't hear honking horns any more. It was like a fuckin' ghost-town out there.

Still though, it was early days yet.

— Go easy on the fish there, Bimbo, he said. — We don't want to be stuck with a load of it at the end of the nigh'.

It was beginning to look like they'd be stuck with a lot more than just a couple of dozen cod. Still though —

— OLÉ — OLÉ OLÉ OLÉ —

Getting the fish to stay inside the batter was easier said than done. Bimbo'd just scooped out a smashing

187

piece of batter, lovely and crispy; but it was empty. He was rooting around in the oil for the fish.

A couple of people, kids mostly, walked by and gawked in, and kept walking, the fuckin' eejits.

Jimmy Sr checked the fryer. It was ready and waiting. The chips were in the basket. He picked it up and shook it; just right. He got a burger and threw it on the hotplate, just to be doing something. The noise it made at the beginning was a bit like something screaming. He pressed it down hard with the fish slice, and it screamed again; it wasn't a scream really, more a watery crackle.

He turned to keep an eye on the hatch and caught Bimbo helping himself to a Mars Bar.

— Jesus Christ, Bimbo; could yeh not wait till we've sold somethin'!

The head on Bimbo, snared rapid.

— I was a bit hungry —

— Haven't yeh half Ireland's fuckin' fish quota over there with yeh?

He was joking but suddenly he was annoyed.

— I didn't want to touch them, said Bimbo. — In case —

— No one else fuckin' wants them, said Jimmy Sr.

He was thinking of something good, something nice to say when — Jaysis! — there was a young fella at the hatch. He could see the top of his head.

He jumped over to him.

— Yes, son?

— A choc-ice, said the young fella.

Sharon climbed into the van in time to hear her da.

— Wha'? — Fuck off ou' o' tha' or I'll —

Sharon started laughing.

— Do yeh not sell choc-ices? said the young fella.

Bimbo looked out at him. The poor little lad was only about ten.

Jimmy Sr leaned out and pointed.

— What's tha'? he asked the young fella.

He was pointing at the sign.

— A big burger, said the young fella.

— That's righ', said Jimmy Sr. — Wha' does it tell yeh?

— Bimbo's Burgers, the young fella read. — Today's chips today.

— That's righ', said Jimmy Sr. — It doesn't say annythin' abou' choc-ices, does it?

— No.

— No, it doesn't, sure it doesn't. So, fuck off.

Jimmy Sr went back to his burger. It was stuck to the hotplate.

— Shite on it!

Bimbo took over at the hatch.

— We've no fridge, he explained to the little young fella.

— Yeh can get choc-ices an' stuff in other chippers, Mister, the young fella told him.

— Yeah, said Bimbo; he was whispering — but we've no fridge, yeh see. We've no electricity.

He looked around at Jimmy Sr. He was trying to get some lard in under the burger so it would slide off the plate.

— Here, he said to the young fella.

189

He handed him down the rest of his Mars Bar, then shooed him off.

— Thanks very much, Mister.

— Shhhh!

Jimmy Sr's neck was going to snap; that was how it felt. There were still little bits of the burger soldered to the hotplate; the scraper kept sliding over them, the useless fuckin' thing! He'd get them off if it fuckin' killed him!

— Yeaahh!

Sharon and Bimbo kept well away from him. That wasn't easy in a space as big as two wardrobes. You couldn't go anywhere without someone getting out of your way first. Bimbo handed two milk bottles over Jimmy Sr's head to Sharon.

— We need more water, love, he told her.

Sharon was lost.

— Pop over the road an' she'll fill them for yeh, Bimbo told her. — Rita Fleming; Missis Fleming. D'yeh know which house she's in?

— Yeah.

She didn't do anything yet though. She thought she'd been told to go over to the Flemings with two milk bottles and ask Missis Fleming to fill them for her, but she wasn't sure.

— I asked her earlier, said Bimbo. — There's no problem. So long as it's not too late.

— Can I not just run home —

— Do wha' you're told, said Jimmy Sr.

— Who rattled your cage? said Sharon.

— Customers! said Bimbo. — Quick, love; off yeh go.

He said it just when Jimmy Sr got the last lump of burger off the hotplate; his timing couldn't have been better.

— Great stuff, said Jimmy Sr.

Sharon looked out the back door, and there was a gang of women coming towards the van, getting their money out of their handbags.

— There's loads of them, she said, and she ran across the road to Flemings.

Jimmy Sr got the basket of chips — he'd been waiting all night to do this — and dropped it into the oil, and nearly fuckin' blinded himself.

— Ahhh!!! — Jaysis!! — Me fuckin' —

He thought he was blinded. Little spits of fat stung all his face; he kept his eyes clamped shut.

— Are yeh alrigh'?

Bimbo didn't sound all that worried.

— Me eyes, said Jimmy Sr.

— Oh, that's shockin', said Bimbo. — Here, he said. —Wash them.

He handed Jimmy Sr one of the milk bottles.

— Jesus, said Jimmy Sr.

He poured a small amount of the water into his palm and gave his face a wipe. That was better. The stinging was gone. It was no joke though; he'd have to be careful. He didn't want to end up like the Phantom of the fuckin' Opera.

He was ready. He lifted the basket and shook it, and carefully dropped it back in; he wasn't sure why but

191

he'd seen it being done all his life; to check if the chips were done, he supposed.

— Nearly ready over here, he told Bimbo. — Action stations, wha'.

Sharon was back with the milk bottles, full.

— Good girl, said Jimmy Sr. — Yeh missed me accident.

— They're takin' their time, said Sharon.

She was talking about the women outside, who were still approaching the van very slowly.

— Oul' ones are always like tha', said Jimmy Sr. — Yeh'd swear it was fur coats they were buyin'.

— What'll I do now? Sharon asked.

— Help Bimbo with the orders, said Jimmy Sr. — I'd say. We'll have to play it by ear.

She nearly pushed him up onto the hotplate getting her apron on, but he said nothing.

— How're yis all? Bimbo said out the hatch, and Jimmy Sr went over to have a look at the oul' ones himself.

There was a big crowd of them alright, a good few quid's worth, if they ever made their fuckin' minds up. He could tell; they were coming home from bingo. They were real diehards. Imagine: going to bingo on the night Ireland were playing their first ever World Cup match, and against England as well.

— wha' are yis havin', girls? said Jimmy Sr.

No joy; they were still making their minds up. Jimmy Sr got back to his post. The chips were done. He gave the basket a good fuckin' shake, and another one for good measure, and emptied the chips into the tray.

He'd another basket ready with more chips and he lowered that into the fryer, but he stood well back this time. The going was getting very hot though.

The women were up at the counter now.

— A fresh cod, Sharon called back to him.

— Yahoo! said Jimmy Sr, and he slipped the cod into the fryer. Jesus, the noise; like having your ear up to a jet engine.

— Another one.

— A smoked, said Bimbo.

They were in business now alright.

Another five cods, three smoked ones, a spice-burger and an ordinary burger; now they were working.

— Chips just, said Sharon.

— Comin' up.

He got the scoop in under the chips and got a grand big load into the bag, filled it right up. Good, big chips they were, and a lovely colour, most of them; one or two of them were a bit white and shiny looking.

— There yeh go.

He held them out for Sharon, and she dropped them.

— Not to worry, he said.

He filled another bag.

Bimbo was still taking orders.

— Three spice-burgers, two smoked cod —

Jimmy Sr sang.

— An' A PAR-TRIDGE IN A PEAR TREE.

The fryer was getting very full now. Some of the yokes at the top were hardly in the cooking oil at all. He skidded on the chips Sharon had dropped and nearly went on his arse. He kicked them out the back door but some of them were stuck to the floor. The fuckin' heat, the sweat was running off him. There was too much for one man here.

— Gis a hand here, Sharon.

Sharon left Bimbo at the counter.

— Righ', Bimbo, shout ou' those orders again till we get them sorted ou'.

He heard Bimbo.

— Wha' was it you ordered, love?

— I told yeh, said some oul' wagon. — A cod an' a small chips.

— Got yeh, Jimmy Sr called back. — Hope she fuckin' chokes on them, he said to Sharon.

Sharon was managing the chips and Jimmy was taking the other stuff out of the fryer. He had one of those tongs yokes but you had to be careful with it cos if you held the fish too tight it fell apart on you and if you didn't it dived back into the fryer and you had to jump back quick or suffer the fuckin' consequences. But he thought he had the knack of it. He dropped the cod into a small greaseproof bag and Sharon took it and put it into the big brown bag, along with the chips. They worked well together, Sharon and Jimmy Sr. They didn't bump into each other. It was like they were two parts of the same machine.

The only problem now was Bimbo. He was good with the oul' ones and he handled the salt and vinegar like a professional, but he couldn't count for fuck.

— A cod an' a small — . Eh, — that's, eh —

— One sixty-five, Sharon called back to him.

— Good girl, said Jimmy Sr.

They were nearly through with the oul' ones; there were no more orders coming in. It was coming up to closing time though and then there'd be murder, with a bit of luck.

— One eighty, Sharon called.

She was sharp, that girl. She didn't even have to think first.

He couldn't make up his mind if the last spice-burger was done yet. He blew on it and poked it with a finger; it left a mark.

— Grand.

He dropped it into its bag and gave it to Sharon.

— I'll give poor Bimbo a hand, he said.

Most of the women were still out there but away from the counter, up against the carpark wall eating their stuff. There were only a few left at the counter.

— Wha' was yours? he asked one of them.

— A chips an' a spicey burger.

She was tiny. He nearly had to climb out over the counter to see her.

— Large or small? said Jimmy Sr.

— Large, she said.

— An' why not, said Jimmy Sr.

This was good crack. Sharon handed him the bag.

— The works?

— Oh yes.

He did the salt first, shook the bag to make sure it went well in. He looked at the women. They were real bingo heads alright; all the same, like a gang of twenty sisters.

— That's enough, said the little woman.

He showed her the vinegar bottle.

— Say when, he said.

She had a nice enough face, he could see now.

— There y'are now, he said, and he held the bag for her to collect.

— Thanks v' much. How much is tha'?

— Eh —

— One twenty-five, said Sharon.

— One twenty-five, said Jimmy Sr.

He waited while she put tenpences and twentypences up on the counter.

— Sorry —

— No no, said Jimmy Sr. — Take your time.

— I want to get rid of my change.

— Well, yeh came to the righ' place, love.

There was a nice breeze coming in. Jimmy Sr held his arms out a bit, but nothing too obvious.

Bimbo was nearly having a row with the last of the women.

— D'you take butter vouchers? she asked him.

— No, he said. — God, no.

— They take them in the newsagents, she told him.

You couldn't help feeling sorry for her. She'd probably held back till the end so the other women wouldn't hear her. Still though, they weren't running a charity.

— Only money, Bimbo told her.

— Or American Express, said Jimmy Sr, and he gave Bimbo a nudge. — We'll give yeh a shout when we start sellin' butter, he told the woman, for a joke. She didn't

196

laugh though, and he felt like a prick. His face was hot and getting hotter. Still, if she could afford to go to bingo then she could afford to pay for her supper.

That was it. They'd all been served, and they were all stuffing their faces, beginning to move away. Jimmy Sr, Bimbo and Sharon watched them.

— Tha' was grand, said Bimbo. — Wasn't it?

— Money for jam, said Jimmy Sr.

They looked around. The place was in bits already.

— I'll do more batter, said Bimbo.

— Good man, said Jimmy Sr. — But make it a bit stronger, will yeh. It keeps comin' off the fish.

Sharon got down and started wiping the mushed-up chips off the floor. One of the bingo women came back.

— Yes, Missis? said Jimmy Sr.

— D'yeh sell sweets? she asked him.

She was one of those culchie-looking women, roundy and red.

— Mars or Twix just, Jimmy Sr told her.

— A Twix.

— Comin' up, said Jimmy Sr.

He got the Twix out from under the hotplate and wiped the grease off it with his apron.

— There y'are, he said. — Best before April '92. You've loads o' time, wha'.

She laughed, and then Jimmy Sr saw it.

— Oh good shite.

It was a stampede, that was what it was, coming out of the Hikers.

— Yeh'd better be quick with tha' batter, he said to Bimbo.

197

— Why's tha'? said Bimbo, and he looked out.
— Oh, mother o' God.
Sharon looked.
— Jesus, she said. — I'm scarleh.
Jimmy Sr gave the woman her threepence change.
—Yeh'd want to get out o' the way there, he told her.
— You'll be fuckin' trampled on.
The woman did a legger.
There was an almighty crowd coming out, pouring out of the place, still going Olé olé olé olé. It was mostly the younger ones. There was suddenly a couple of hundred people in the carpark, and then one of them saw the van.
— Yeow!!
They stopped Oléing and looked at the van.
— Charge!
— Oh my fuck — , said Jimmy Sr. — Red alert; red alert.
It was like Pearl fuckin' Harbor. Jimmy Sr had half said — Form a queue there, when they hit the van.
— Oh, mother o' shite!
It hopped; they lifted it up off the road. One of the bars holding up the hatch skipped and Jimmy Sr just caught it before it fell and skulled someone outside.
— A cod an' a large!
— Curry chips, Mister.
— Howyeh, Sharon!
— OLÉ — OLÉ OLÉ OLÉ
— I was first!
— Are yis Irish or Italians or wha'?
— Yeow, Sharon!

— Sharon; here! We're first, righ'.

— Give us a C!!

Bimbo was covered in batter. Sharon was trying to get the spilt fat off her shoes.

— Give us a H!!

It was madness out there; pande-fuckin'-monium.

— Give us an I!!

There was a young one being crushed against the van. Her neck was digging into the counter.

Bimbo joined Jimmy Sr at the hatch.

— Back now! he roared. — Push back there! There's people bein' crushed up here!

— Fuck them!

Jimmy Sr pointed at the young fella who'd said that.

— You're barred!

They cheered, but they quietened after that.

— Give us a P!

The young one was rubbing her neck but she was alright. Jimmy Sr served her first.

— Wha' d'yeh want?

— Give us an S!

Jimmy Sr looked out over the crowd.

— Will somebody shut tha' fuckin' eejit up! he roared.

— Yeow!!

They cheered and clapped, and Jimmy Sr started to enjoy himself. He lifted his arms and acknowledged the applause — Thank you, thank you — and then got back to business.

— Wha' was tha'? he asked the young one.

— Curry chips, she said, raising her eyes to heaven.

— No curry chips, Jimmy Sr told her.

— Why not?

— Cos we're not fuckin' Chinese, said Jimmy Sr. — This is an Irish Chipper.

— That's stupih, said the young one.

— Next!

— Hang on, hang on! A large single an' — an' —

— Hurry —

— A spice-burger.

— A large an' a spice, Sharon, please!! Jimmy Sr roared over his shoulder. — Next. — You with the haircut there; wha' d'yeh want?

— World peace.

— You're barred. Next!

Sharon had a complaint.

— I can't do it all on me fuckin' own!

— Hold the fort there, Bimbo, said Jimmy Sr, and he went to back to give Sharon a hand.

It was like that for over an hour after that. They got into a flow; Bimbo would shout back the order and Jimmy Sr and Sharon would pack it, and Bimbo would repeat the order out loud and Sharon would tell him how much it cost, and that way they started flying. The heat though; they were sorry now they'd got Victor, Bimbo's brother, to block up the window. They had to go the door now and again, Jimmy Sr and Sharon — Bimbo was alright; he had the hatch — and get some proper air. That was how Jimmy Sr caught a kid trying to disconnect the gas. Such a kick he sent at him, he was blessed that it had missed because he'd have killed the poor little fucker.

When the going got rough up at the hatch one of them would go up and help Bimbo, and when it got rough back at HQ one of them would come back from the hatch: they took turns. The only thing was the heat: Jimmy Sr's throat was dry and he didn't have time for a can of 7-Up. Anyway, there wasn't enough room to drink it comfortably; he'd have got an elbow in the neck. Jimmy Sr took off his apron, then his T-shirt, and put the apron back on.

— You should do this, Sharon, look.

— Ha ha.

He checked to make sure that his knickers were well into his trousers and then he was back to work, throwing the burgers onto the hotplate like there was no tomorrow. It didn't work though, taking the T-shirt off, not really; it just gave the flying fat more places to hit.

They'd serve two people and get them out of the way and three more would come out of the pub. It was a killer. Still though, this was what they'd wanted. There was money being made.

— Here! a young fella outside shouted. — These chips are raw!

— Yeh never said yeh wanted them cooked! said Jimmy Sr, and he dashed back to turn the burgers.

He was enjoying himself; the three of them were.

The older lads came out later, Bertie and Paddy and them, and it was more relaxed, a good laugh. It was nearly one o'clock. Jimmy Sr had lost weight, he could tell. He put his hand down the back of his trousers and there was much more room than usual, even with no shirt or vest in there. It was like working in a sauna. He liked the idea of losing a few pounds. He'd say nothing yet to Veronica about it, not for a few days. He'd do a twirl in front of her and see if she noticed.

The place was a mess, and getting dangerous. Sharon had fallen and Bimbo had scorched two of his fingers. It served him right for trying to pick up the burger with his hand cos Jimmy Sr was using the fish slice.

— Night nigh', compadres.

— Good luck, Bertie.

There was no one left. Jimmy Sr closed the hatch. He could see another gang coming up the road and he didn't want to have to start all over again. Anyway, they'd hardly anything left. There were a few chips in the bottom of the bin but they were a bit brown looking. Most of the water was on the floor. It could stay there. They were too shagged to do any cleaning. They made room for themselves on the ledges and shelves and sat up or leaned against them.

— Fuck me, said Jimmy Sr.

— Look at me shoes, said Sharon.

— Buy a new pair.

— Wha' with?

— This, said Bimbo.

He held up a handful of notes, then put them back in the box. He showed them the rest of the cash in the box. He had to squash it down to keep it from falling out; not just green notes either, brown ones as well, and even a couple of blueys.

— Fair enough, wha'.

Someone hit the hatch a wallop.

They ignored it, and stayed quiet.

It felt good, being finished, knackered. They were too tired to grin. Jimmy Sr's ears were buzzing with the tiredness. He got a can from under the hotplate and it slipped out of his hands because of the grease; the flask cup had flowed over.

— Ah Jaysis —

He held the can with his apron, opened it and took a slug: it was horrible and warm.

— Ah — shi'e —

Bimbo got a can and held it up to make a toast.

— Today's chips today, he said.

Jimmy Sr nudged a chip on the floor with his shoe.

— Absolutely, he said.

It had been some day.

At the end of the week — next Friday — he was going to put money on the table in front of Veronica, and say nothing.

They went home.

— Look it.

Sharon showed Jimmy Sr, Veronica and Darren the spots on her left cheek all the way up to her eye, clusters of them in little patches. She'd just found them, up in the bathroom. Her left side was much redder than the right, horrible and raw looking; she couldn't understand it. She wanted to cry; she could feel them getting itchy.

— My God, said Veronica, and went to get a closer look.

Darren was a bit embarrassed.

Jimmy Sr leaned out from his chair to see.

— Gis a look, he said.

— It's some sort of a rash, said Veronica, — or — I don't know.

— That's gas, said Jimmy Sr. — I've them as well; look.

He showed them the right side of his face.

— I shaved over them, he said. — But yeh should be able to still see them.

He rubbed his cheek.

— They're still there alrigh'.

Veronica was confused but Sharon was beginning to understand.

— D'yeh know wha' it is? said Jimmy Sr. — It's the hotplate; the fat splashin' up from the hot plate.

He mimed turning a burger.

— I was on the righ' an' you were on the left, he told Sharon.

He grinned.

— Poor Bimbo must be in tatters, he said. — Cos he was in the middle.

Darren laughed.

By the time Ireland played Egypt, the Sunday after, they'd added sausages to the menu and Jimmy Sr was putting less lard on the hotplate.

Business was hopping.

On Friday they pitched their tent outside the Hikers earlier, at five o'clock, and stuck up posters — Jessica's work — all over the van: £1 Specials — Chips + Anything — 5 to 7.30pm. It worked; the Pound

Specials went down a bomb. Women coming out of Crazy Prices with the night's dinner read the posters and stopped and said to themselves Fuck the dinner; you could see it in their faces. They either bought the chips and anything immediately or went home and sent one of the kids out to get them.

It was Maggie's idea.

— Twelve Poun' Specials, Mister, said one little young one, and that was the record.

By seven, when they were having a rest, Jimmy Sr and Bimbo were talking seriously about getting an engine; then there'd be no stopping them. They'd have to get some sort of a flue put in as well. Even with the hatch and the door open, the fumes were gathering up in the back of the van. You noticed it when you went down there to get more chips from the bin; you came back crying. And the smell off your clothes; no amount of washing could get rid of it.

— It's an occupational hazard, Jimmy Sr told Veronica.

Spots, singed hair and smelly threads; Veronica said that he looked like something out of Holocaust.

— Ha fuckin' ha, said Jimmy Sr.

— A large an' a dunphy.

— Wha'? said Jimmy Sr.

He looked down at the customer, a young fella about young Jimmy's age, with his pals.

— Large an' a dunphy, he said again.

He was grinning.

— What's a dunphy? Jimmy Sr wanted to know.

— A sausage, said the young fella.

— Sausage, large, Jimmy Sr called over his shoulder to Bimbo.

He looked back at the young fella.

— Are yeh goin' to explain this to me? he asked.

— Sausages look like pricks, righ'?

— Okay; fair enough.

— An' Eamon Dunphy's a prick as well, said the young fella.

By Thursday of the second week, the night of the Holland game, the word Sausage had disappeared out of Barrytown. People were asking for a dunphy an' chips, please, or an eamon, a spice burger an' a small single. Some of them didn't even bother eating them; they just bought them for a laugh. Young fellas stood in front of the big screen in the Hikers and waved Jimmy and Bimbo's sausages in batter instead of big inflated bananas.

— This is where the real World Cup starts, said Paddy, when they'd settled down again after the final whistle.

— He's righ', said Jimmy Sr. — For once.

Ireland were through to the knock-out stages.

Jimmy Sr took another deep breath.

— Fuckin' great, isn't it?

They all agreed.

— After all these years, wha', he said.

— COME ON WITHOU'

COME ON WITHIN

YOU'VE NOT SEEN NOTHIn' LIKE THE MIGHTY QUINN —

Bertie summed up the campaign so far.

—We beat England one-all, we lost to Egypt nil-all, an' we drew with the Dutch. That's not bad, is it?

— OOH AH —

PAUL MCGRATH —

SAY OOH AH PAUL MCGRATH —

Jimmy Sr stood up.

—Yeh righ', Bimbo?

The van was outside waiting for them.

It was hard leaving the pub after all that, the match and the excitement: but they did, Bimbo and Jimmy Sr. You had to admire them for it, Jimmy Sr thought anyway.

The day after the Holland game Maggie brought home T-shirts she'd got made for them in town. They had Niall Quinn's head on the front with His Mammy Fed Him On Bimbo's Burgers under it. They were smashing but after two washes Niall Quinn's head had disappeared and the T-shirts didn't make sense any more.

It was great having the few bob in the pocket again. They didn't just count the night's takings and divide it in two. They were more organised than that; it was a business. There was stock to be bought, the engine to save for. Maggie kept the books. They paid themselves a wage and if business was really good they got a bonus as well, an incentive, the same way footballers got paid extra if they won. Jimmy Sr took home a hundred and sixty quid the first week. He had his dole as well. He bought himself a new shirt — Veronica'd been giving him grief about the smell off his clothes — a nice one with grey stripes running down it. He'd read in one of Sharon's magazines that stripes like that made you look thinner but that wasn't why he bought it; he just liked it. He handed most of the money over to Veronica.

—You're not to waste it all on food now, d'yeh hear, he said. — You're to buy somethin' for yourself.

—Yes, master, said Veronica.

The country had gone soccer mad. Oul' ones were explaining offside to each other; the young one at the check-out in the cash-and-carry told Jimmy Sr that Romania hadn't a hope cos Lacatus was suspended because he was on two yellow cards. It was great. There were flags hanging out of nearly every window in Barrytown. It was great for business as well. There were no proper dinners being made at all. Half the mammies in Barrytown were watching the afternoon matches, and after the extra-time and the penalty shoot-outs there was no time left to make the dinner before the next match. The whole place was living on chips.

— Fuck me, said Jimmy Sr. — If Kelly an' Roche do well in the Tour de France we'll be able to retire by the end o' July.

He'd brought home two hundred and forty quid the second week.

They were going to get a video.

— Back to normal then, said Jimmy Sr. — Wha'.

—Yep, said Veronica.

She was going to say something else, something nice, but Germany got a penalty against Czechoslovakia and she wanted to see Lothar Matthaeus taking it; he was her favourite, him and Berti, the Italian. Jimmy Sr liked Schillaci; he reminded him of Leslie, the same eyes.

— Ah, good Jesus, said Jimmy Sr.

He got up off the floor. His trousers were wringing, his back was killing him. He'd been going at the floor with sudsy water and a nailbrush for the last half hour and the floor still looked the wrong colour.

— We're fightin' a losin' battle here, I think, he said to Bimbo.

Bimbo was attacking the gobs of grease on the wall around the hotplate and the fryer. He was making progress but it was like the grease spots were riding each other and breeding, they were all over the wall. Bimbo took a breather. The thing about it was, even if you cleaned all day — and that was what they did for the first week or so — it would be back to dirty normal by the end of the night.

— Look it, said Jimmy Sr. — Tha' grease there —

He pointed at the grease above the fryer.

— It's fresh cos it only got there last nigh', cos it was clean there when we started last nigh'. D'yeh follow?

— Yeah, said Bimbo.

— So, said Jimmy Sr. — It's doing' no harm. It's fresh. It's grand for another couple o' days. Then it'll be gettin' bad an' we'd want to get rid of it cos it'd be a health hazard then, but it's fuckin' harmless now.

Bimbo didn't disagree with him.

— All we have to worry abou' every day before we start is the floor, said Jimmy Sr. — Cos we'll go slidin' an' split ourselves if it's not clean, but that's all.

Bimbo just wanted to check on one thing first. He opened the hatch and then got out of the van and went round to the hatch and looked in, to see if he could see the dirt from out there. He couldn't.

— Okay, he said. — I'm with yeh.

Bimbo couldn't watch, but Jimmy Sr could, no problem; he loved it. Nil-all after extra time, a penalty shoot-out.

— Pennos, said Paddy when they saw the ref blowing the final whistle.

— Fuckin' hell.

— Packie'll save at least one, wait'll yeh see.

— He let in nine against Aberdeen a couple o' weeks ago, remember.

— This is different.

— How is it?

— Fuck off.

It got very quiet. Jimmy Sr's heart was hopping, but he never took his eyes off the screen, except when the young one behind him screamed. She did it after the Romanians got the first penalty. Women had been screaming all through the match but this one stood out because when the ball just got past Packie's fingers there were a couple of hundred groans and only the one scream.

Bertie turned round to the young one.

— Are yeh like tha' in the scratcher? he said.

The whole pub erupted, just when Kevin Sheedy was placing the ball on the spot, like he'd scored it already. There was no way he'd miss it after that.

He buried it.

— YEOWWW!!

— One-all, one-all; fuckin' hell.

Houghton, Townsend, Tony Cascarino.

Four-all.

— Someone's after faintin' over there.

— Fuck'm.

They watched Packie setting himself up in his goal for the fifth time.

— Go on, Packie!

— ONE PACKIE BONNER —

— Shut up; wait.

— He has rosary beads in his bag, yeh know, said some wanker.

— They'll be round his fuckin' neck if he misses this one, said Jimmy Sr.

No one laughed. No one did anything.

Packie dived to the left; he dived and he saved the fuckin' thing.

The screen disappeared as the whole pub jumped. All Jimmy Sr could see was backs and flags and dunphies. He looked for Bimbo, and got his arms around him. They watched the penno again in slow motion. The best part was the way Packie got up and jumped in the air. He seemed to stay in mid-air for ages. They cheered all over again.

— Shhh! Shhh!

— Shhh!

— Shhh!

Someone had to take the last penalty for Ireland.

— Who's tha'?

— O'Leary.

— O'Leary?

Jimmy Sr hadn't even known that O'Leary was playing. He must have come on when Jimmy Sr was in the jacks.

— He'll be grand, said someone. — He takes all of Arsenal's pennos.

— He does in his hole, said an Arsenal supporter. — He never took a penno in his life.

— He'll crack, said Paddy. — Wait'll yeh see.

Jimmy Sr nearly couldn't watch, but he stuck it.

— YEH —

David O'Leary put it away like he was playing with his kids at the beach.

— YESSS!

Jimmy Sr looked carefully to make sure that he'd seen it right. The net was shaking, and O'Leary was covered in Irishmen. He wanted to see it again though. Maybe they were all beating the shite out of O'Leary for missing. No, though; he'd scored. Ireland were through to the quarter-finals and Jimmy Sr started crying.

He wasn't the only one. Bertie was as well. They hugged. Bertie was putting on a few pounds. Jimmy Sr felt even better.

— What a team, wha'. What a fuckin' —

He couldn't finish; a sob had caught up on him.

— Si, said Bertie.

212

They showed the penno again, in slow motion.

— To the righ'; perfect.

— Excellent conversion, said some gobshite.

Where was Bimbo?

There he was, bawling his eyes out. A big stupid lovely grin had split his face in half.

— OLÉ — OLÉ OLÉ OLÉ —

OLÉ —

OLÉ —

Jimmy Sr took a run and a jump at Bimbo and Bimbo caught him.

— ONE DAVE O'LEARY —

— OLÉ — OLÉ OLÉ OLÉ

— THERE'S ONLY ONE DAVE O'LEARY —

They stood there arm in arm and watched O'Leary's penalty again, and again.

— I'll tell yeh one thing, said Larry O'Rourke. — David O'Leary came of age today.

Jimmy Sr loved everyone but that was the stupidest fuckin' thing he'd ever heard in his life.

— He's thirty fuckin' two! he said. — Came of age, me bollix.

— ONE DAVE O'LEEEEARY —

He hugged Bimbo again, and Bertie and Paddy, and he went over and hugged Sharon. She was crying as well and they both laughed. He hugged some of her friends. They all had their green gear on, ribbons and the works. He wanted to hug Sharon's best friend, Jackie, but he couldn't catch her. She was charging around the place, yelling Olé Olé Olé Olé, not singing any more because her throat was gone.

There was Mickah Wallace, Jimmy Jr's pal, standing by himself with his tricolour over his head, like an Irish Blessed Virgin. He let Jimmy Sr hug him.

— I've waited twenty years for this, Mister Rabbitte, he told Jimmy Sr.

He was crying as well.

— Twenty fuckin' years.

He gulped back some snot.

— The first record I ever got was Back Home, the English World Cup record, he said. — In 1970. D'yeh remember it?

— I do, yeah.

— I was only five. I didn't buy it, mind, said Mickah. — I robbed it. — Tweh-twenty fuckin' years.

Jimmy Sr knew he was being told something important but he wasn't sure what.

— D'yeh still have it?

— Wha'?

— Back Home.

— Not at all, said Mickah. — Jaysis. I sold it. I made a young fella buy it off o' me.

Jimmy Jr rescued Jimmy Sr.

— Da.

— Jimmy!

— I didn't see yeh.

Jimmy Jr was in his Celtic away jersey, with a big spill down the front. He nodded at the jacks door.

— It's fuckin' mad in there.

They stood there.

— CEAUSESCU WAS A WANKER

CEAUSESCU WAS A WANKER

LA LA LA LA

LA LA LA — LA

— Fuckin' deadly, isn't it?

— Brilliant. — Brilliant.

They started laughing, and grabbed each other and hugged till their arms hurt. They wiped their eyes and laughed and hugged again.

— I love yeh, son, said Jimmy Sr when they were letting go.

He could say it and no one could hear him, except young Jimmy, because of the singing and roaring and breaking glasses.

— I think you're fuckin' great, said Jimmy Sr.

— Ah fuck off, will yeh, said Jimmy Jr. — Packie saved the fuckin' penalty, not me.

But he liked what he'd heard, Jimmy Sr could tell that. He gave Jimmy Sr a dig in the stomach.

— You're not a bad oul' cunt yourself, he said.

Larry O'Rourke had got up onto a table.

— WHEN BOYHOOD'S FIRE WAS IH-IN MY BLOOD —

I DREAMT OF ANCIE-HENT FREEMEN —

— Ah, somebody shoot tha' fucker!

Jimmy Sr nodded at Mickah. Jimmy Jr looked at him.

— He'll be alrigh' in a bit, he said. — It's a big moment for him, yeh know.

Bimbo tapped Jimmy Sr's shoulder.

— We'd better go, he said.

It was a pity.

— Okay, said Jimmy Sr. — Duty calls, he said to Jimmy Jr.

— How's business?

— Brilliant. Fuckin' great.

— That's great.

— Yeah; great, it is. McDonalds me arse. Seeyeh. — Good luck, Mickah.

But Mickah didn't answer. He stood to attention, the only man with plenty of room in the pub.

— Seeyeh.

— Good luck.

— A NAAY-SHUN ONCE AGAIN —

A NAAAY-SHUN ONCE AGAIN —

Bimbo gave Jimmy Sr a piggy-back to the van. There were kids and mothers out on the streets, waving their flags and throwing their teddy bears up in the air. A car went by with three young lads up on the bonnet. They could hear car horns from miles away.

It was the best day of Jimmy Sr's life. The people he served that night got far more chips than they were entitled to. And they still made a small fortune, sold everything. They hadn't even a Mars Bar left to sell. They closed up at ten, lovely and early, and had a few quiet pints; the singing had stopped. And then he went home and Veronica was in the kitchen and she did a fry for him, and he cried again when he was telling her about the pub and the match and meeting Jimmy Jr. And she called him an eejit. It was the best day of his life.

And then they got beaten by the Italians and that was the end of that.

★   ★   ★

They got in. Bimbo put in the key.

The van had a new engine.

— Here we go.

It went first time.

— Yeow!

They went to Howth.

— Maybe we should get music for it, said Jimmy Sr when they were going through Sutton. They'd stalled at the lights, but they were grand now, picking up a head of steam.

— Like a Mister Whippy van.

— Would tha' not confuse people?

— How d'yeh mean?

— Well, said Bimbo. — They might run out of their houses lookin' for ice-creams an' all we'll be able to give them is chips.

Jimmy Sr thought about this.

— Is there no chip music? he said. — Mind that oul' bitch there. She's goin' to open the door there, look it.

— What d'yeh mean? said Bimbo.

He stopped Jimmy Sr from getting to the horn.

— Yeh should've just taken the door off its fuckin' hinges an' kept goin', said Jimmy Sr.

— The music, said Bimbo.

— Yeah, said Jimmy Sr. — The Teddy Bears' Picnic is the ice-cream song, righ'. Is there no chipper song?

— No, said Bimbo. — I — No, I don't think —

— Your man, look it; don't let him get past yeh! — Ah Jaysis. — I'm drivin' back, righ'.

They went through Howth village and up towards the Summit to see how the van would handle the hill.

They turned back before they got to the top: they had to.

— We won't be goin' up tha' far ever, said Jimmy Sr. She was going a blinder downhill.

— Not at all, Bimbo agreed with him.

— No one eats chips up there, said Jimmy Sr.

— That's righ', said Bimbo.

They went over a dog outside the Abbey Tavern but they didn't stop.

— Don't bother your arse, said Jimmy Sr when he saw Bimbo going for the brake. — We'll send them a wreath. No one saw us.

Bimbo said nothing till they got onto the Harbour Road. He looked behind — there was no rear view mirror, of course — but there was nothing to see except the back of the van.

Then he spoke.

— Wha' kind of a dog was it?

— Jack Russell.

— Ah, God love it.

And Jimmy Sr started laughing and he didn't really stop till they got to the Green Dolphin in Raheny and they went in for a pint cos Bimbo was still shaking a bit.

— Served it righ' for havin' a slash in the middle of the road, said Jimmy Sr.

He paid for the pints.

— Can I drive her the rest of the way? he asked.

— Certainly yeh can, said Bimbo.

— Thanks, said Jimmy Sr, although he didn't really know why; the engine was his as much as Bimbo's. — Good man.

218

Maggie had bought them a space in Dollymount, near the beach, for the summer; she'd found out that you rented the patches from the Corporation and she'd gone in and done it. It was a brilliant idea, and a great patch; right up near the beach at the top of the causeway road, where the buses ended and started. It couldn't have been better. There was a gap in the dunes there where on a good day thousands of people came through at the end of the day, sunburnt and gasping for chips and Cokes. Except there hadn't been a good day yet.

— The greenhouse effect, me bollix, said Jimmy Sr.

There hadn't even been a half decent day.

They climbed up to the top of one of the dunes to have a decco and there wasn't a sinner on the whole fuckin' island, except for themselves and a couple of rich fat oul' ones playing golf down the way, and a few learner drivers on the hard sand, and a couple of young fellas on their horses. It was fuckin' useless. They got back into the van to make themselves something to eat and they were the only customers they had all day. It was money down the drain. Even in the van it was cold.

— It's early days yet, said Bimbo. — The weather'll get better, wait'll yeh see.

He was only saying that cos Maggie'd organised the whole thing; Jimmy Sr could tell.

— It's the worst summer in livin' memory, he said.

—Who says it is? said Bimbo.

— I do, said Jimmy Sr. — I'm fuckin' freezin'.

— It's only July still, said Bimbo. — There's still August an' September left.

One of the horse young fellas was at the hatch, on his piebald.

— Anny rots, Mister? he said.

— Wha'? said Jimmy Sr.

— Anny rots.

Jimmy Sr spoke to Bimbo.

— What's he fuckin' on abou'?

The young fella explained.

— Rotten chips, he said. — For me horse.

— Fuck off, said Jimmy Sr. — There's nothin' rotten in this establishment, Tonto.

— I was only askin', said the young fella.

Jimmy Sr and Bimbo looked at his horse. It wasn't a horse really, more a pony; a big dog.

— How much was he? said Jimmy Sr.

— A hundred, said the young fella.

— Is that all?

— You can have him for a hundred an' fifty, the young fella told them.

They laughed.

The young fella patted the horse's head.

— You'd get your money back no problem, he said. — I'll kill him for yis as well, if yis want.

They laughed again.

— Does he like Twixes? Jimmy Sr asked the young fella.

— He does, yeah, said the young fella. — So do I.

— There yeh go.

He handed out two Twixes and the young fella got the horse in closer to the hatch so he could collect them.

— He likes cans o' Coke as well, he told them.

— He can fuck off down to the shops then, said Jimmy Sr.

The young fella's mate went galloping past on his mule and the young fella got ready to go after him. He stuffed the Twixes into his pocket and geed up the horse the way they did in the pictures, even though he'd no spurs on him, no saddle either.

— Does your bollix not be in bits ridin' around like tha'? Jimmy Sr asked him.

— Not really, said the young fella. — Yeh get used to it.

— You might, said Jimmy Sr. — I wouldn't.

— Yheupp! went the young fella, and he was gone, down the causeway road; they watched him from the door of the van, his feet nearly scraping off the road.

That was the high point of the day.

— He was a nice enough young fella, said Bimbo.

— Yeah, said Jimmy Sr.

That was easily their biggest problem though: young fellas. Jimmy Sr like kids, always had; Bimbo loved them as well but, Jaysis Christ, they were changing their minds, quickly. Everyone loved bold kids. They were cute. There was nothing funnier than hearing a three-year-old say Fuck. This shower weren't cute though. They were cunts, right little cunts; dangerous as well.

There was a gang of them that hung around the Hikers carpark, young fellas, from fourteen to maybe nineteen. Even in the rain, they stayed there. They just put their hoodies up. Some of them always had their hoodies up. They were all small and skinny looking but there was something frightening about them. The way they behaved, you could tell that they didn't give a fuck about anything. When someone parked his car and went into the pub they went over to the car and started messing with it even before the chap had gone inside; they didn't care if he saw them. Jimmy Sr once saw one of them pissing against the window of the off-licence, in broad daylight, not a bother on him. Sometimes they'd have a flagon or a can of lager out and they'd pass it around, drinking in front of people coming in and out of Crazy Prices, people that lived beside their parents. It was sad. When they walked around, like a herd migrating or something, they all tried to walk the same way, the hard men, like their kaks were too tight on them. But that was only natural, he supposed. The worst thing though was, they didn't laugh. All kids went through a phase where they messed, they did things they weren't supposed to; they smoked, they drank, they showed their arses to oul' ones from the back window on the bus. But they did it for a laugh. That was the point of it. It was part of growing up, Jimmy Sr understood that; always had. He'd seen his own kids going through that. If you were lucky you never really grew out of it; a little bit of kid stayed inside you. These kids were different though; they didn't do anything for a laugh. Not that Jimmy Sr could see anyway. They were like fuckin' zombies. When Jimmy Sr saw them, especially when it was raining, he always thought the same thing: they'd be dead before they were twenty.

Thank God, thank God, thank God none of his own kids was like that. Jimmy Jr, Sharon, Darren — he couldn't have had better kids. Leslie — Leslie had been a bit like that, but — no.

The Living Dead, Bertie called them.

Himself and Vera had had problems for a while with their young lad, Trevor, but Bertie had sorted him out.

— How?

— Easy. I promised I'd get him a motorbike if he passed his Inter.

— Is that all?

— Si, said Bertie. — Gas, isn't it? We were worried sick about him; Vera especially. He was — ah, he was gettin' taller an' he never washed himself, his hair, yeh know. He looked like a junkie, yeh know.

Jimmy Sr nodded.

— All he did all fuckin' day was listen to tha' heavy metal shite. Megadeath was one, an' Anthrax. I speet on them. I told her not to be worryin', an' I tried to talk to him, yeh know —

He raised his eyes.

— Man to man. Me hole. I wasn't tha' worried meself, but he was too young to be like tha'; tha' was all I thought.

— So yeh promised him the motorbike.

— Si. An' now he wants to stay in school an' do the Leavin'. First in the family. He's like his da, said Bertie.

— A mercenary bollix.

They laughed.

— He'll go far, said Bimbo.

— Fuckin' sure he will, said Bertie. — No flies on our Trevor.

— Leslie passed his Inter as well, said Jimmy Sr.

— That's righ'.

— Two honours, said Jimmy Sr. — Not red ones either; real ones.

Anyway, the Living Dead gave Jimmy Sr and Bimbo terrible trouble. It was like that film, Assault on Precinct 13, and the van was Precinct 13. It wasn't as bad as that, but it was the same thing. Jimmy Sr and Bimbo could never really relax. The Living Dead would rock the van, three or four of them on each side. The oil poured out of the fryer, all the stuff was knocked to the floor, the cup for the grease under the hot plate went over and the grease got into the Mars Bars. It was hard to get out of the van when it was rocking like that, and it was fuckin' terrifying as well. There wasn't much weight in it at all; they could have toppled it easily enough. The second time they did it Jimmy Sr managed to catch one of them and he gave him a right hiding, up against the side of the van; clobbered every bit of him he could reach. He thought he was teaching him a lesson but when he stopped and let go of him the kid just spat at him. He just spat at him. And walked away, back to the rest of them. They didn't care if they were caught. They didn't say anything to him or shout back at him; they just stared out at him from under their hoodies. He wasn't angry when he climbed back into the van. He was frightened; not that they'd do it again, not that — but that there was nothing he could do to stop them. And, Jesus, they were only kids. Why didn't they laugh or call him a fat fucker or something?

They lit fires under the van; they robbed the bars that held up the hatch; they cut through the gas tubes; they took the bricks from under the wheels.

Jimmy Sr was looking out the hatch, watching the houses go by, when he remembered that the houses shouldn't have been going anywhere. The fuckin' van was moving! It was before they got the engine. Himself and Bimbo baled out the back door but Sharon wouldn't jump. The van didn't crash into anything, and it wasn't much of a hill. It just stopped. The Living Dead had taken the bricks from behind the wheels, that was what had happened. It was funny now but it was far from fuckin' funny at the time.

Jimmy Sr knew them, that was the worst thing about it. The last time he'd walked across O'Connell Bridge he'd seen this knacker kid, a tiny little young fella, crouched in against the granite all by himself, with a plastic bag up to his face. He was sniffing glue. It was terrible — how could his parents let him do that? — but at least he didn't know him. It was like when he heard that Veronica's brother's wife's sister's baby had been found dead in the cot when they got up one morning; it was terrible sad, but he didn't know the people so it was like any baby dying, just sad. But he knew the names of all these kids, most of them. Larry O'Rourke's young lad, for instance; Laurence, he was one of them. It depressed him, so it did. Thank God Leslie was out of it, working away somewhere.

The ordinary kids around, the more normal ones, they were always messing around the van as well. But at least you could get a good laugh out of them, even if they got on your wick. One of them — Jimmy Sr didn't know him, but he liked him — told Bimbo to give him a fiver or he'd pretend to get sick at the hatch every time someone came near the van. And he did it. There was a woman coming towards them, looking like she was making her mind up, and your man bent over and made the noises, and he had something in his mouth and he let it drop onto the road, scrunched-up crisps or something. And that made the woman's mind up for her. Jimmy Sr went after him with one of the bars from the hatch but he wasn't interested in catching him. The ordinary bowsies robbed the bars from the hatch, and messed with the gas and rocked the van as well, but it was different. When they legged it they could hardly run cos they were laughing so much. Jimmy Sr and Bimbo nearly liked it. These kids fancied Sharon as well so they came to look in at her. It would have been good for business, only they never had any fuckin' money. Sometimes, Fridays especially, they were drunk. He didn't like that. They were falling around the place, pushing each other onto the road. They were too young. They got the cider and cans from an off-licence two stops away on the DART; Darren told him that. Jimmy Sr was going to phone the guards, to report the off-licence, but he never got round to it.

One night the kids went too far. They started throwing stones at the van; throwing them hard. Bimbo, Jimmy Sr and Sharon got an almighty fright when they heard the first bash, until they guessed what was happening. They were flinging the stones at the hot plate side. When he saw the dints the stones were making, fuckin' big lumps like boils, Jimmy Sr nearly went through the roof. That was real damage they were doing. He grabbed one of the hatch bars and let an almighty yell out of him when he jumped out the back door. They weren't going to throw any stones at him, he knew that; it was only the noise they were enjoying. So he knew he wasn't exactly jumping to his death, but he still felt good when he landed, turned at them and saw the fear hop into their faces. Then he went for them. They legged it, and he kept after them. A kick up the hole would teach these guys a lesson. They weren't like the Living Dead. There were five of them and when they turned and went up the verge onto the Green there were more of them, a mixed gang, young fellas and young ones, little lads sticking to their big brothers. Jimmy Sr wasn't angry any more. He'd keep going to the middle of the Green, maybe catch one of the little lads or a girlfriend and take them hostage. He was closing in on one tiny kid who was trying to keep his tracksuit bottoms up. Jimmy Sr could hear the panic in the little lad's breath. He'd just enough breath left himself to catch him, and then he'd call it a day.

Then he saw them.

He stopped and nearly fell over.

The twins. He barely saw Linda but it was definitely Tracy, nearly diving into the lane behind the clinic. Grabbing a young fella's jumper to stay up. Then she was gone, but he'd seen enough.

The treacherous little bitches. Wait till he told Sharon.

He turned back to the van. He found the bar where he'd dropped it.

His own daughters, sending young fellas to throw stones at their da. With their new haircuts that he'd fuckin' paid for last Saturday.

He'd scalp the little wagons.

—You've no proof, said Linda.

— I seen yeh, said Jimmy Sr, again.

—You've no witnesses.

— I fuckin' seen yeh.

—Well, it wasn't me annyway, said Tracy.

— Or me, said Linda.

— It was youse, said Jimmy Sr. — An' if I hear anny more lies an' guff ou' o' yis I'll take those fuckin' haircuts back off yis. And another thing. If yis go away before yis have this place cleaned properly — properly now, righ' — I'll ground yis.

He climbed out of the van.

—The floors an' the walls, righ'. An' if yis do a good job I might let yis off from doin' the ceilin'.

He looked in at them.

— An' that'll fuckin' teach yis for hangin' around with gangsters.

Linda crossed her arms and stared back at him.

— I didn't spend a fortune on your hair, said Jimmy Sr, — so yis could get picked up by snot-nosed little corner boys.

228

He loved watching the twins when they were annoyed; they were gas.

— Next time yis are lookin' for young fellas go down to the snobby houses an' get off with some nice respectable lads, righ'.

— Will yeh listen to him, he heard Linda saying to Tracy.

— He hasn't a clue, said Tracy.

— Righ', said Jimmy Sr. — Off yis go. The sooner yeh start the sooner yis'll be finished. Mind yeh don't get your flares dirty now.

— They're not flares, righ'! They're baggies.

He closed the door on them.

They'd do a lousy job, he knew that. It served them right though; it would give them something to think about, that and the hiding Sharon had given them last night. Veronica had had to go into the room to break up the fight.

He listened at the door. He held the handle. He couldn't hear anything. He opened it quickly.

Linda was wiping the walls, kind of. Tracy was pushing a cloth over the floor with her foot.

— Do it properly!

— I am!

— PROPERLY!

— Jesus; there's no need to shout, yeh know.

— I'll fuckin' —

— Can we get the radio? said Linda.

— No!

— Ah, Jesus —

Jimmy Sr shut the door.

★ ★ ★

The weather stayed poxy well into July. But it was alright; the Dollymount patch was a long-term investment, Maggie explained. They took it easier; they only brought the van out at night, except on Fridays at teatime for the £1 Specials. They had time for the odd round of pitch 'n' putt, and their game hadn't suffered too much because of the lack of practice. Jimmy Sr always won.

They stuck close to Barrytown but they kept an eye on the newspapers to see if there was anything worth going further for. Maggie scoured the Independent in the mornings and the Herald later to see if there were any big concerts coming up, or football matches. They were going to get the van as close as they could to Croke Park for the Leinster Final between Dublin and Meath. They'd have to be there before the start because all the Meath lads coming up from the country wouldn't have had their dinners. So they had that Sunday afternoon pencilled in; Maggie'd done out a chart. The Horse Show was coming up as well but they weren't going to bother with that; the horsey crowd didn't eat chips.

— They eat fuckin' caviar an' tha' sort o' shite, said Jimmy Sr.

— An' grouse an' pheasant, said Bimbo.

— Exactly, said Jimmy Sr. — Yeh'd be all fuckin' day tryin' to get the batter to stay on a pheasant.

There were some big concerts coming up as well.

— Darren tells me they're called gigs, Jimmy Sr told Bimbo and Maggie.

Maggie held her biro over the chart.

— What abou' this one on Saturday? she said.

— Who is it again? said Bimbo.

— The The, said Maggie.

— Is tha' their name? said Bimbo. The The, only?

— That's wha' it says here, said Maggie.

She had the Herald open on the kitchen table.

— Well?

— Darren says they're very good, said Jimmy Sr. — He says they're important.

— Will there be many there?

— He doesn't know. He thinks so, but he's not sure.

— Well —

— I think we should give it a bash, said Jimmy Sr.

— Yeah, but —

Maggie took over from Bimbo.

— You'll be lettin' down your regulars.

— There is tha' to consider, said Bimbo. — Yeah.

— Wha' d'yeh mean? said Jimmy Sr.

— It's on on Saturday nigh', said Maggie. — We always do very well outside the Hikers on Saturday nights.

What did she mean, We? She'd never been as much as inside the van in her —

— I see wha' yeh mean, said Jimmy Sr. — There could be thousands at this gig though.

— It's a bit risky but, said Bimbo. — Isn't it?

— Well, said Maggie. — It's up to yourselves —

Jimmy Sr didn't want a row; and, anyway, they were probably right. They decided just to do midweek gigs and to concentrate on the closing-time market at the weekends.

— There's a festival in Thurles, said Maggie.

— It can stay there, said Jimmy Sr.

He'd fight this one; there was no way he was going all the way down to Tipperary just to sell a few chips. But it was alright; Bimbo nearly fell over when Maggie mentioned Thurles.

— Ah, no, said Bimbo.

— Just a thought, said Maggie.

—We'll stick to Dublin, said Bimbo. —Will we, Jimmy?

— Def'ny.

Jimmy Sr felt good after that. He'd been starting to think that Bimbo and Maggie rehearsed these meetings.

Sharon had started going with a chap called Barry, a nice enough fella — some kind of an insurance man; she'd already broken it off twice and him once, but they were back together and madly in love, judging by the size of the love bites Jimmy Sr'd seen on Barry's neck the last time he'd called around. So Sharon wasn't keen on working nights any more. They tried a few nights without her, just the two of them, but it was a killer. So Jimmy Sr said he'd recruit Darren — before Maggie came up with some bright idea. Darren already had his job in the Hikers but he was only getting two nights a week out of that, so Jimmy Sr reckoned he'd jump at the chance of making a few extra shillings. But —

— I'm a vegetarian, Darren told him.

—Wha'!?

Darren shrugged.

—You as well? said Jimmy Sr. — Jaysis. — Hang on but —

He'd been watching Darren eating his dinners and his teas since he was a baby.

— Since when?

— Oh — Tuesday.

— Ah, now here —

— I'd been thinkin' about it for a long time and I just made up me, eh —

— Okay, said Jimmy Sr. — Okay.

He raised his hands.

— Good luck to yeh. — Do vegetarians eat fish?

— Yeah; some do.

— Do you?

— Yeah.

— That's grand so, said Jimmy Sr. — You can just do the fish an' meself an' Bimbo'll handle the rest. How's tha'?

Darren was a broke vegetarian.

— Okay, he said. — Eh — okay.

— Sound, said Jimmy Sr.

They shook on it. That was great. It would be terrific having Darren working beside him, fuckin' marvellous.

— Wha' abou' burgers? said Jimmy Sr.

Darren didn't look happy.

— There's fuck all meat in them, Jimmy Sr assured him.

— No.

— Fair enough, said Jimmy Sr.

He liked the way Darren had said no.

— I was just chancin' me arm, he said. — How's Miranda?

— Okay, said Darren.

— Good, said Jimmy Sr. — She's a lovely-lookin' girl.

Darren wanted to escape but what his da had said there needed some sort of an answer.

— Thanks, he said. — Yeah; she's fine. Someone ran over her dog a few weeks ago, and she was a bit — , but she's alrigh' now.

— Where was tha'? said Jimmy Sr.

— Howth.

— A Jack Russell?

— Eh, yeah. How did yeh know?

— I didn't, Jimmy Sr told him. — It's just, nearly all the dogs yeh see dead on the road seem to be Jack Russells. Did yeh ever notice tha' yourself?

— No.

— Keep an eye ou' for them an' yeh'll see what I mean.

The weather picked up. There were a few good, sunny days on the trot and suddenly everyone was going around looking scalded.

— Thunderbirds are go, said Jimmy Sr.

They got to Dollymount at half-three. Sharon was with them. There was a Mister Whippy on their spot. Bimbo had a photocopy of the Corporation permit in his back pocket. Jimmy Sr took it and went up to have it out with Mister Whippy. He got in the queue, with Sharon. Bimbo stayed with the van. The kid in front of Jimmy Sr ran off with his two 99s to get back to the beach before they melted, and Jimmy Sr was next.

— Yeah? said Mister Whippy. Jimmy Sr looked up at him.

234

— What d'yeh want? said Mister Whippy.

— Justice, said Jimmy Sr.

He held out the permit and waved it.

— Have a decco at tha', he said.

Mister Whippy, a spotty young lad, looked scared.

— What is it? said the young fella.

— Can yeh not read? said Jimmy Sr.

— It's a permit, said Sharon.

— That's righ', said Jimmy Sr. — My glamorous assistant, Sharon, is quite correct there.

Young Mister Whippy was still lost but he was braver as well.

— So wha'? he said.

— So fuck off, said Jimmy Sr.

He took back the permit.

— It's ours, he said. — We paid for this patch here, where you are. We did, you didn't. You've no righ' to be here, so hop it; go on.

Mister Whippy couldn't decide what to do.

— Go on, said Jimmy Sr. — Yeh can go over to the other side o' the roundabout.

— No one'll see me there.

— We'll tell them you're there, said Jimmy Sr. — Won't we?

— Yeah, said Sharon.

— An' anyway, said Jimmy Sr. — Yeh can play your music an' they'll hear yeh.

Mister Whippy still didn't look too sure.

— Listen, said Jimmy Sr. — Shift now or we'll fuckin' ram yeh.

He stepped back from the van and shouted.

— Rev her up there, Bimbo!

Bimbo turned the key and then Mister Whippy got behind the wheel and did the same thing, and moved away around to the far side of the roundabout, away from the dunes.

— Seeyeh, said Sharon and she waved.

Bimbo brought the van up to them.

Mister Whippy turned on The Teddy Bears' Picnic.

— They're playin' our song, Jimmy Sr told Bimbo.

For about a week the weather stayed that way, grand and hot, no sign of a cloud. They came down to Dollier at half-three or so and stayed till half-six and went home with a clatter of new pound coins jingling away in their money box. It was easy enough going; didn't get hectic till after five. Sharon went over to the beach and got some sun and Jimmy Sr and Bimbo hung around the van and watched the world go by. Then coming up to teatime they'd climb into the van and stoke up the furnace. Then the crowds came up over the dunes and the smell hit them, and no one can resist the smell of chips.

The only bad thing was having to stare down at all those peeling faces staring up at you outside the van. Noses, arms, foreheads; it was fuckin' revolting. Red raw young ones with shivery legs would take their bags of stuff and give you their money, turn around to get away from the van and they'd be white on the other side. Sharon wasn't like that; she'd more sense. She did herself front and back and the sides as well, even.

— Like a well-cooked burger, Jimmy Sr told her.

— Jesus!

236

— It's a compliment, it's a compliment.

— Thanks!

The only other bad thing about the beach business was the sand. It got into everything. Even with no wind to blow it they'd find a layer of it on the hatch counter, on the shelves, grains of it floating on top of the cooking oil before they lit the burner; everywhere. Jimmy Sr did a burger for himself and when he bit into it, before his teeth met, he could feel the sand in the bundie. He chewed very carefully. When they got the van back to Bimbo's they had to get damp cloths and go over everything with them, to pick up the sand, but they never got all of it. Jimmy Sr always had a shower before he went out again to do the closing-time business and there was enough sand up his hole and in his ears to build a block of flats. He couldn't understand it because he never went down to the beach, except once or twice to see if there was anything worth looking at; and there never was, hardly ever. He'd keep his eyes on the ground till he got to the beach and then he'd look around him, hoping, and all he ever saw was scorched gobshites getting more scorched. And white lines where bra straps got in the way of the sun. Dollier definitely wasn't like the resort in some island in Greece or somewhere he'd seen in a blue video Bertie'd lent him a few years ago; my Jaysis, the women in that place!; walking around with fuck all on, not a bother on them. Climbing out of the pool so that their tits were squeezed together; bending over so he could see the water dripping off their gee hairs. There were no women like that in Dollymount. It was mostly mammies with their kids. Still though, they were good for business. There was nothing like a screaming kid to get a ma to open her purse. He couldn't see the brassers in that video going mad for chips; and, anyway, they'd probably have wanted them for nothing.

It was busy, getting dark; the Living Dead were out there somewhere. Bimbo had had to dash home for a shite, so Jimmy Sr was by himself at the hatch, taking the orders. And he'd three burgers doing on the hotplate and he asked Darren to turn them for him, and he wouldn't do it.

— I'm not askin' yeh to eat them, said Jimmy Sr, trying not to sound too snotty in front of the customers.

— I only want yeh to turn them fuckin' over.

Darren said nothing, and he didn't do anything either.

— Darren? said Jimmy Sr.

But Darren just started filling the bags with chips.

— Fuck yeh, said Jimmy Sr and he got back to the hotplate and picked the fish slice up off the floor.

The burgers were welded to the plate; they were part of the plate.

— Look wha' you're after doin', said Jimmy Sr.

Darren said nothing.

One of the punters outside spoke up.

— If that's my burger you're messin' with there I'm not takin' it, he told Jimmy Sr.

Jimmy Sr had had enough.

— Righ', he said. — Fuck off then. An' get your burger somewhere else. — Annyone else want to complain?

238

But Bimbo came back and took over at the hatch. And with Bimbo blocking the view Jimmy Sr was able to get the burgers off the hot plate and into their bundies without doing too much damage to them. He dipped them into the deep fat fryer to make them juicy and then trapped them in the bundies before they dripped or fell apart.

— There, he said. — No help to you.

Darren said nothing.

Dunphies were out of the question as well as far as Darren was concerned and they had to go into the deep fat fryer with the fish, so Darren would stand back and get out of Jimmy Sr or Bimbo's way while they fished out the dunphies. It was stupid. Still but, they had to respect Darren's beliefs. Jimmy Sr told that to Maggie after Bimbo had told her about Darren and his vegetarianism.

— At least he has the courage of his convictions, he said.

He wasn't really sure what that meant but it shut Maggie up. Not that she'd been giving out or anything; she'd just thought it was funny that someone called Rabbitte was a vegetarian. Jimmy Sr couldn't see anything particularly funny about that.

Where Darren was way out of line, way out — just the once — was when he objected to the dunphies going into the same cooking oil as the fish.

— Wha'!?

— Part of the meat is left in the oil.

— So?

— It gets into the fish.

— It does in its hole. Nothin' would get through tha' batter. Bimbo made it.

Darren laughed but he kept going on all night about contaminating the oil and he put a face on him every time Jimmy Sr leaned over and dropped a dunphy into the fryer; he got on Jimmy Sr's wick.

No one had ordered a dunphy; he just did it to annoy Darren; he deserved it.

— 'Xcuse me, Darren, till I drop this into the holy of holies.

He blessed the dunphy as it sank down and bobbed up again between two pieces of cod.

— Make sure they don't touch there, said Jimmy Sr. — We don't want any bits o' cod gettin' into the dunphy an' poisonin' someone.

Darren had one last bash at explaining osmosis to Jimmy Sr. He was halfway through it when Jimmy Sr turned on him.

— Spare me the fuckin' lecture, righ', an' just do your fuckin' job.

He flicked a dunphy into the fryer so that it would send some oil flying in Darren's direction. Darren got some of it on his arms. He said nothing but he went outside.

Jimmy Sr's ears hummed while he waited for Darren to come back. He prayed for him to come back but he wouldn't go to the door to look out; he wouldn't even look at it.

He felt Darren going past him, on his way back to the fryer.

— Sorry, he said.

He looked at Darren: he looked fine.

— Okay? said Jimmy Sr.

— Yeah.

— Grand; — sorry.

They were all set to move out. It was the hottest day yet, Jimmy Sr reckoned. All they were waiting for now was Sharon.

— What's she at? said Jimmy Sr. — Jesus tonigh'.

She had Gina with her, in the buggy.

— Mammy can't mind her, she said before Jimmy Sr could ask her. — An' the twins won't.

—Yeh can't bring the baby —

— Give us a hand, said Sharon.

She went round and opened the back door. She climbed in.

— Jesus!

The heat hit her.

Jimmy Sr picked up the buggy with Gina still in it and passed it in to Sharon.

— It's fuckin' dangerous — , he said.

—We'll be grand, said Sharon. —Won't we, Gina?

Gina was looking around. She liked what she saw. She tried to free herself. Sharon sat up on the hatch counter and held the buggy close to her, between her legs.

— I don't know — , said Jimmy Sr.

He shut the door.

Bimbo went very carefully. An oul' one on crutches could have gone faster.

— It'll be fuckin' dark by the time we get there, said Jimmy Sr.

— I don't want to be responsible for an injury, Bimbo told him. — 'Specially to a baby.

But they got there. Jimmy Sr got Gina to sit on a shelf and gave her a Twix to keep her quiet for a bit and Sharon folded the buggy and put it in on top of the driver's seat. It wasn't too bad that way. Bimbo showed Gina how to make batter and he got her down off the shelf and let her dip a slab of cod into it. That was a mistake because now she had to dip everything into it, including herself. But it was nice having her in the van there; it was kind of exciting, as if they were performing for her. Bimbo put her back up on the shelf out of harm's way, and Jimmy Sr gave her the other half of the Twix.

But she nearly fell into the deep fat fryer. She'd crawled nearer to it and she was leaning over to look at the bubbles and the smoke when Jimmy Sr saw her, roared and caught her. He didn't really catch her, cos she wasn't falling, but he told Sharon he did. The poor little thing was wringing with the sweat, so Jimmy Sr put her on the hatch counter to dry. She knocked the salt and pepper and a load of bags out onto the path. A load of young ones saw her and came over to look at her and say hello and wave at her but they didn't buy anything, of course.

— Get us the salt an' pepper there, will yeh, love, Jimmy Sr asked a young one.

— Get it yourself, she said.

They all walked off, laughing.

— Hope yeh got skin cancer! Jimmy Sr roared after them.

— Jesus, Daddy!

— Bitches.

— Bitis! said Gina after them.

— Good girl yourself, said Jimmy Sr.

They couldn't keep her on the counter because she'd get in the way and she was bound to fall out so what Jimmy Sr did was, he went into the dunes and found a plank. He brought it back to the van and gave it a good wipe and used up most of a milk bottle of water to clean it. It was long enough to go over the top of the chip bin and that made a seat for Gina, in the corner, away from danger. She complained a bit; the plank was wet. Bimbo put a cloth under her.

Serving was easier here than at closing time cos there wasn't a mad rush of people. It was good, a gradual, steady flow of customers. Jimmy Sr liked it. It was a good way to start the working day.

— Have yeh anny spicey burgers, Mister?

— They're on the menu, said Jimmy Sr, but not in a snotty way.

— Oh yeah, said the young fella. — How much are they?

Jimmy Sr pointed at the price on the board.

— There; look it.

— Oh yeah.

The kid was a bit simple, he could tell; the way his mouth hung open.

— D'yeh want chips as well? he asked him.

—Yeah.

— Have yeh the money on yeh?

— Me ma's comin', said the kid.

— Fair enough, said Jimmy Sr. — Will she want annythin' herself, would yeh say?

—Wha'?

—Will she be long?

— She's comin'.

— Okay, said Jimmy Sr.

Poor little sap; he'd give him the order even if his ma didn't come. He turned to get a spice-burger.

—Wha' the fuck —

—What'?

—Yeh can't fuckin' do tha' in here!

Sharon was changing Gina's nappy.

Jesus; if a health inspector or a guard was passing and looked in and saw the baby's little arse pointing out at him they'd be rightly fucked. Or Mister Whippy over the other side of the roundabout; if he saw what Sharon was doing he'd race down to Raheny station and report them, and he'd play the Teddy Bears' Picnic all the fuckin' way.

Jimmy Sr slammed down the hatch.

— Back in a minute, he told the kid waiting outside.

— Quick! he said. — Hurry up. An' mind nothin' drops into the chips.

Sharon giggled. Bimbo was battering away. It wasn't dark exactly; you could see everything. It was quite nice really.

— Are yeh finished? said Jimmy Sr.

— Nearly.

Sharon put the old nappy into a plastic bag and put that bag into her proper bag.

244

— Pity the poor fucker tha' robs your handbag, said Jimmy Sr.

They laughed, and Jimmy Sr opened the hatch. The kid was still there.

— Still here, said Jimmy Sr.

— Me ma's comin', said the kid.

— She's a lucky woman, said Jimmy Sr.

— Daddy!

Jimmy Sr slid the spice-burger into the cooking oil.

— Now.

He put a few chips into a bag, nice big ones, and handed them out to the kid.

— Have them while you're waitin', he said.

— A one an' one there, please.

Jimmy Sr looked to see who'd said that. It was a man about his own age, wearing a Hawaii 5-0 shirt and a Bobby Charlton haircut. Bimbo sank the cod into the fryer.

— Grand day again, said Jimmy Sr to the man.

— We're spoilt, said the man.

— What's the water like today? said Jimmy Sr.

— Shockin', said the man. — Filthy dirty, it is. Yeh wouldn't make your worst enemy swim in it.

— Yes, I would, Jimmy Sr told him. — Won't be a minute here.

— No hurry.

Sharon handed out the spice-burger and chips to the young fella. He didn't take them.

— Me ma's comin', he said.

— You're alrigh', said Jimmy Sr. — Go on. She can pay us when she comes; go on.

Gina started singing.

— OLÉ — OLÉ OLÉ OLÉ —

They all joined in.

Jimmy Sr got the cod out the fryer, shook the drops off it and put it in its bag and put that into the brown bag; a grand big piece of fish it was too. Sharon gave him the bag of chips and he slid that in alongside the cod.

— OLÉ — OLÉ OLÉ OLÉ — The works? he asked the man.

He held the salt over the bag.

— Fire away, said the man.

— Righto, said Jimmy Sr. — Say when.

The man took the bag. He handed two of the new pound coins to Jimmy Sr but stopped just short of Jimmy's reach.

— Me ma's comin', he said.

They laughed and he gave the money to Jimmy Sr. Jimmy Sr gave him his change and that was that.

— Good luck now, said Jimmy Sr. — Enjoy your meal.

— Cheerio, said the man.

Jimmy Sr watched him trying to wheel his bike and eat his chips at the same time. There was a woman outside now, trying to get her shower of kids to make up their minds what they wanted.

— Milkshake! said one of them.

They were all over her; it was hard to be sure how many kids she had with her; about six, and another on the way, now that Jimmy Sr looked at her properly.

— It isn't McDonald's, she told the milkshake kid.

— wha' is it? said the kid.

— It's a lurry! said his sister, and she gave him a smack in the mouth, and legged it.

— Look at this, Jimmy Sr said to Sharon.

— Six singles, said the woman when she made it to the counter. — No; seven. Me as well.

— I don't want chips, said one of the boys.

— Well, you're gettin' them! said the woman. — And anyway, you, you're not even one o' mine so yeh should be grateful.

The woman looked at Sharon.

— I only own three o' them, she said.

That was all.

She looked as if she could lie down under the van and go fast asleep, and maybe not wake up again.

— Never again, she said.

— They're lovely, said Sharon.

— They're bastards, said the woman. — Every fuckin' one o' them.

She looked as if she felt better after getting that off her chest, and she straightened up. She patted her stomach.

— This'll be the last, she said. — He can stick it in a milk bottle after tha', so he can.

Sharon was shocked. She'd never seen the woman before.

There was a scream; the littlest lad was having a bucket of crabs and stones and water poured down his togs. The woman patted her stomach again.

— With a bit o' luck this one'll be deaf an' dumb.

She didn't smile: she meant it.

— Righ'! Jimmy Sr yelled. — Line up for your chipses!

— Me!!

— Your mammy first! said Jimmy Sr. — Get back.

— She's always first!

— Get back!

— Not fair —

— Into line, said Jimmy Sr. — Or I'll dump your chips into the sand.

He held a bag of chips up, ready to throw it.

— A straight line. — Salt an' vinegar, love?

— Loads.

That was when Bobby Charlton came back. He threw his bike against the wall of the van.

— Come here — !!

Jimmy Sr dropped the salt.

— Mother o' fuck!

The woman yelped.

— Come here! the man said again.

But the bike slid onto the ground and he tried to pick it up but his leg got on the wrong side of the crossbar, and he'd only one hand to work with because the other one was still holding the chips. He gave up trying to lift the bike and stepped over it, and nearly tripped. He leaned against the van.

He'd given Jimmy Sr time to get his act together.

— What's your problem? said Jimmy Sr.

— I'll tell yeh —

— I'm dealin' with a customer here, Jimmy Sr told him. — You'll have to wait your turn.

The man was right up at the hatch now, like he was going to climb in.

— I'll tell yeh wha' my problem is — , the man started again.

— There's a queue, said the woman.

— There won't be when I'm finished here, said the man.

Jimmy Sr, Sharon and Bimbo were at the hatch. Jimmy Sr handed the singles down to the woman and she handed them on to the kids.

— Excuse me! said the man.

— Calm down, said Bimbo. — Calm down.

— Sap, said Sharon, but not loud.

— Three eighty-five, Sharon told the woman when she looked up.

— Be careful eatin' them, the man told the woman. That sounded bad.

— Oh Christ, said Bimbo.

He looked back at the fryer.

— Righ', said Jimmy Sr, when Sharon had given the woman her change. — What's your problem?

He'd been thinking about it; he hadn't a clue what was going to happen. He stared down at the man.

— It's your problem, said the man.

— Wha' is?

— This.

He held up the bag in his hand, far enough away not to be grabbed.

Jimmy Sr leaned out to see.

— The chips?

— No!

— The fish?

The man looked very upset.

— Fish! he said.

— It's fresh, Bimbo assured him. — It was grand an' hard comin' out o' the —

— Fresh! the man screamed.

Jimmy Sr had to say it again.

— What's your problem?

— Will yeh look it.

But he still wouldn't bring his hand in any closer to the hatch.

— I can't fuckin' see it, said Jimmy Sr. — Wha'ever — Maybe it was maggots.

— I bit into it — , said the man.

— That's wha' you were supposed to do, said Jimmy Sr.

This chap was some tulip.

— Wha' did yeh think yeh were supposed to do with it; ride it?

Now the man did come closer; he banged into the van.

— Oh Jesus, said Sharon.

She got back and went beside Gina.

The man's mouth was open crooked. He really looked like a looper now. They could see into the bag.

— It's not fish — , said Bimbo.

— Oh fuck — . What is it?

Hang on though —

— It's white, said Jimmy Sr.

— It's a nappy! the man told him.

— Wha'! — Fuck off, would yeh.

— He's righ', Jimmy, said Bimbo. — It's a Pamper; folded up. My God, that's shockin'.

— Shut up! Jimmy Sr hissed at him.

— I must have put it in the batter —

— Shut up!

— What is it? said Sharon.

The man wasn't angry-looking now; he looked like he needed comfort.

— Is it a used one? Jimmy Sr asked him, and he crossed his fingers.

— No!

— Ah well, said Jimmy Sr. — That's alrigh' then.

— That's how, said Bimbo. — It'd look like a piece o' cod, folded up like. Ah, that's gas.

— Sorry abou' tha', said Jimmy Sr to the man. — We'll give yeh your money back, an' a can o' Coke; how's tha' sound? Were the chips alrigh'?

The man wasn't won over. He folded the bag into a neater package and put it under his arm.

— I'm goin' to the guards with this, he said.

— Ah, there's no need —

— This is the evidence, the man interrupted Bimbo. He checked to see that the bag was still under his arm.

— You'll be hearin' more about this, he told them. — Don't you worry. I'll never recover from a shock like this.

— A tenner, said Jimmy Sr. — Will tha' do yeh?

— What's your name? he asked Jimmy Sr.

— I don't have to tell you tha', said Jimmy Sr.

— I don't care, said the man. — I've the evidence here.

— Twenty, said Jimmy Sr. — Final offer; go on.

— I've the evidence.

— Shove the fuckin' evidence. We know nothin' about it.

— You're not goin' to bribe me, said the man.

— It's the suppliers yeh should be reportin', said Jimmy Sr, — not us. We know nothin' abou' nappies.

Gina started singing again. Sharon put her hand over Gina's mouth, but the man wasn't listening. He was looking at the sign on the side of the van.

— Which one of yis is Bimbo? he said.

— Ask me arse, said Jimmy Sr.

He pulled Bimbo over to him.

— Get ou' an' start the van.

— But —

— Fuckin' do it!

Bimbo went to the back door.

— Go round the other way, Jimmy Sr told him.

He remembered something.

— The gas!

Bimbo lifted the gas canister and pushed it into the van. He closed his eyes when it scraped on the floor. Jimmy Sr distracted the man.

— It must be terrible bein' baldy with the sun like this, he said. — Is it?

Bimbo got to the driver's door, around the other side of the van, without the man seeing him. He got the buggy off the seat.

— I'm rememberin' all this, the man told Jimmy Sr.

— Good man, said Jimmy Sr.

He took away the hatch bars when he heard the engine starting.

— See yeh now, Baldy Conscience, he said. — Keep in touch.

And he dropped the hatch door. The salt and the vinegar fell onto the path. He shut the back door.

252

— Go on, go on!

The van lurched; Jimmy Sr fell forward, and grabbed a shelf. It skipped again, and then they got going.

Jimmy Sr steadied himself. He leaned against the hatch counter.

— My Jaysis —

— He'll get the registration, said Sharon.

— No, he won't, said Jimmy Sr.

— Why not?

— We don't have one. It's in the shed in Bimbo's. We never stuck it back on. Just as well, wha'.

— He might be followin' us, said Sharon.

She had a point.

Jimmy Sr opened the back door. They were still on the causeway road, and there was your man coming after them, pedalling like fuck.

— I'll get this bollix, said Jimmy Sr.

He looked back, around the van. He stepped over to the hotplate and got a can of Coke from under it. They went over a pothole or something when he was bending over. The hotplate and the fryer were still turned on.

— Jesus; I nearly fuckin' fried myself.

He got to the canister and switched it off.

He weighed the Coke in his hand, then wiped the grease off it on his shirt.

— You'll kill him, said Sharon.

She was probably right. They were heavy things when they were full. He grabbed a few pieces of cod. They were still hard enough.

Bimbo turned left instead of right at the top of the causeway road.

— What's he fuckin' doin'?

— It's so your man can't follow us home, said Sharon.

— Fair enough.

He opened the back door again and the man was still after them, but further back; his legs didn't have it. Jimmy threw a piece of cod anyway, skimmed it, to see how far he could get it. He watched it bounce off the road, well short of the man.

— There's more evidence for yeh!

He shut the door.

Bimbo brought them to Clontarf, then up the Lawrence's Road, onto the Howth Road. He went up Collins' Avenue at Killester, and to the Malahide Road.

Jimmy Sr looked out again, and saw Cadbury's in Coolock.

— We'll end up in fuckin' Galway, he said.

He threw Gina up and caught her, and again, but not too high because he'd already hit her head off the roof, and he was only doing it now to make her forget about it.

They got home. Jimmy Sr and Sharon were melting when they got out the back. Jimmy Sr had to stand in front of the open fridge door.

— We'll steer clear o' Dollier for a while, he said.

— Yeah, said Bimbo.

Bimbo was angry.

— It would never've happened if she'd —

— Shut up, said Jimmy Sr.

Maggie had a great head for ideas; Jimmy Sr had to say that for her. She got flyers printed and sent Wayne and

Glenn and Jessica all around putting them into houses. Linda and Tracy did them as well, until Darren caught them sticking hundreds of the flyers into the letter-box outside the Gem.

BIMBO'S BURGERS
TODAY'S CHIPS TODAY
Wedding Anniversary? Birthday? Or Just Lazy?
Treat Yourself
And
Let Us Cook Your Dinner For You
Ring 374693 and Ask for Maggie

That was what they said, on nice blue paper.

— Four-course meals? said Jimmy Sr when she was telling them about it. — How'll we fuckin' manage tha'?

— Easy, said Maggie.

She'd stick the melon into the fridge in the afternoon so it would be still nice and cold when Bimbo and Jimmy Sr delivered it. They'd use a flask if it was soup; just pour it into the bowls and get it into the houses and onto the tables while there was still steam coming up off it. The main course was no bother because that was what they made all the time anyway.

— What abou' the sweet but? said Jimmy Sr. — The ice-cream'll be water by the time they've got through their main stuff.

He wasn't against the idea; he just saw problems with it.

— Well, said Maggie. — You could keep chunks of ice-cream in a flask as well —

— Wha'; with the soup?

— There's bound to be a mix-up, said Bimbo. — Somewhere along the line.

What they decided on was, one of them would do a legger back to Bimbo's while the customers were laying into the main course and get the ice-cream out of the fridge and hoof it back. That was Darren's job. He didn't mind; he got an almighty slagging from the lads when they saw him running across the Green with a bowl of jelly and ice-cream in each hand but it was better than having to go into the house and serving the customers, like a bleedin' waiter. That was Bimbo's job.

Jimmy Sr shook the flask over the bowl and the last bits of potato slid out and dropped into the soup.

— There now —

There was nothing like a few big chunks of vegetable to make packet soup look like the real thing.

— That's great lookin' soup, said Jimmy Sr. — Wha'.

— Lovely, said Bimbo.

— It's wasted on those fuckers.

— Ah now, said Bimbo.

They were feeding the O'Rourkes tonight, Larry and Mona; their twenty-third wedding anniversary.

— We should make them cough up before we hand over the grub, said Jimmy Sr. — Fuckin' Larry wouldn't give yeh the steam off his piss if you were dyin' o' dehydration.

He took two small pieces of parsley from the bag Maggie'd given him, aimed and dropped one onto the soup in each bowl.

— Nice touch, tha', he said.

Bimbo got into his jacket.

— How's the back, Darren? he asked.

Darren rubbed down Bimbo's back, getting rid of the creases.

Bimbo put the tea-towel over his arm.

The jacket Maggie'd got Bimbo was the stupidest thing Jimmy Sr'd ever seen. He felt humiliated just looking at Bimbo in it. It was white, with goldy buttons, and the sleeves were too long. But it didn't bother Bimbo; he thought he was Lord fuckin' Muck in it — the man in charge.

— Away we go so, said Bimbo.

He checked his watch again.

— Yeah, he said. — They were told to have the table set for half-seven.

He picked up the bowls, using the cuffs to mind his fingers.

— Ring the bell for me, Darren.

— Okay.

— Good lad. Bring the candles as well, will yeh.

— Ah fuck —

— Go on, Darren, said Jimmy Sr. — You're alrigh'; they're vegetarian candles.

— Humour, said Darren.

Bimbo climbed carefully out of the van.

— Get back quick with the main order, Jimmy Sr said after them.

— Will do.

The chips were a definite so Jimmy Sr lowered the basket into the fryer. Larry and Mona wouldn't be long getting rid of the soup. Mind you, they mightn't know what it was. They put water on their cornflakes in that house; so everyone said, anyway.

Bimbo and Darren were back.

— How'd it go?

— It was embarrassin', said Darren.

— How was it? Jimmy Sr asked him.

— He started singin'.

— He's always singin'.

Bimbo took over.

— The minute he saw the candles he started singing to Mona. Tha' one, I can't Help Fallin In Love With You.

— Wha? — WISE MEN SAY —

ONLY FOO-ILS RUSH IN — tha' one?

— Yeah.

— Jaysis. He's gettin' worse. Did they like the soup?

— Stop it, said Bimbo. — Their spoons were clackin' off the bowls. He was singin' an' drinkin' at the same time.

— They didn't think much o' the parsley though, Darren told his da.

— Now there's a surprise, said Jimmy Sr.

— He said if he'd wanted weeds in his dinner he'd've gone ou' the back an' got some of his own.

— Tha' sort o' thing is wasted on shite-bags like them, said Jimmy Sr.

Back to business.

— What's the main course?

— Smoked cod for Larry an' the same for Mona, said Bimbo. — An' they both want a few pineapple fritters as well.

— And onion rings, Darren reminded him.

— Oh, that's righ'. Mona said she'd go a couple of onion rings as well.

— Jaysis, said Jimmy Sr. — They'll keep her up all night if Larry doesn't.

He dropped the orders into the fryer, except the pineapples; they only took a few seconds or they'd turn to mush.

— Do they want wine? said Jimmy Sr when he'd everything else in order.

— Yeah, said Darren.

— Black or blue?

— Blue.

Jimmy Sr ducked in under the hot plate and got out a bottle of Blue Nun.

— Do the business with tha', he said to Darren, and he held the bottle out to him.

— I'd better get back for their sweets, said Darren.

Jimmy Sr turned to Bimbo.

— There, he said. — Suck the cork ou' o' tha'.

Bimbo got working on the bottle with the corkscrew and Jimmy Sr put the two plates on the hatch counter and made a hill of chips on each of them.

— There'll be no complaints abou' the quantity annyway, wha', said Jimmy Sr. — Give someone more than they think they're entitled to and yeh have a friend for life.

— Cos they know we give value for money, said Bimbo.

— Cos they think we're fuckin' saps, said Jimmy Sr.

— The cork's after breakin' on me, said Bimbo.

— Shove it into the bottle.

The plates were full now, too full. Jimmy Sr took some of the chips off and pushed the fish further in, under the chips.

— There, he said. — Can yeh manage?

— No problem, said Bimbo. — I'll have to come back for the wine.

— I'll bring it as far as the door for yeh, said Jimmy Sr.

— Good man; thanks.

Jimmy Sr knew that Bimbo thought he meant O'Rourke's front door but he was only going to go to the van door, for the laugh.

Bimbo wasn't impressed when he got back.

— Very funny, he said.

— Ah, cop on, said Jimmy Sr.

They said nothing for a bit. Then —

— They're havin' a row inside, Bimbo told Jimmy Sr.

— Fuckin' great, said Jimmy Sr. — What abou'?

— Couldn't tell yeh, said Bimbo. — I just gave them their dinners an' got ou'.

— Ah, you're fuckin' useless.

He handed the Blue Nun to Bimbo.

— Go back an' find ou' wha' they're rowin' abou'.

— Who d'yeh think you're orderin' around —?

Darren was back with the jelly and ice-cream.

— Hey, Darren; go in an' see what Larry an' Mona are rowin' abou'.

— Go in yourself.

— Jesus, said Jimmy Sr. — What a staff; such a pair o' fuckin' wasters I'm lumbered with.

He turned to Bimbo and he was glaring at Jimmy Sr; he didn't have time to change his face. It surprised Jimmy Sr.

Eh — are they in the front room or the kitchen or wha'?

— The kitchen, said Bimbo, back to normal.

— Fuck. We could've crept up under the window —

Larry O'Rourke came charging out of the house, trying to get into his jacket. He didn't slam the door.

— How was the cod, Larry? Jimmy Sr asked him.

— Fuck the fuckin' cod, said Larry.

He headed down the road, in a Hikers direction.

— Your jelly an' ice-cream, Larry!

— Fuck the jelly an' the fuckin' ice-cream, they heard.

He turned back to them.

— She can fuckin' eat them! Her mouth's fuckin' big enough!

— Will yeh look who's talkin'! Bimbo said to Jimmy Sr and Darren. — Who's goin' to pay for the dinners?

— Eh — I suppose —

Bimbo looked down the road, then at the house.

— It was Mona phoned Maggie.

— Righ', said Jimmy Sr.

He went up the path, and into the house, with the wine.

Bimbo and Darren waited for him.

Jimmy Sr came back out.

— She wants her jelly.

Darren handed him a bowl.

— Better give her the both o' them, said Jimmy Sr. — She's payin' for them.

— Is she? said Bimbo.

— Fuckin' sure she is.

He went back into the house. Darren and Bimbo got the gas canister back into the van and wiped the shelves. Bimbo mixed some more batter for later that night and Darren fished some loose bits of batter out of the oil in the fryer.

— Maybe she's seducin' him, said Darren.

— Ah no.

They were shutting the back door when Jimmy Sr came out.

—Wha' kept yeh?

— I was havin' a glass o' wine with Mona.

— Is she alrigh'?

— She's grand; not a bother on her.

He waved two tenners at them.

— How's tha', he said. — An' this as well.

He held out a pound coin for Bimbo.

— Your tip, he said. — She says thanks very much. Go on; take it. — D'yis know wha' the row was abou'? said Jimmy Sr when they were all in the van, heading home.

—Wha'?

— His pigeons shitein' on her washin', said Jimmy Sr.

— Ah, is that all?

— She's not a bad-lookin' bird, Mona, said Jimmy Sr. — If she tidied herself up a bit. Sure she's not?

262

Bimbo and Darren didn't say anything. Jimmy Sr wished he'd kept his stupid mouth shut. Darren was blushing beside him; he could nearly feel the heat off him, and he was blushing now himself was well. Bimbo had his mouth in a whistle but there was no noise coming out.

Although they never ran out of ways of flogging their chips and stuff, closing time outside the Hikers was still their bread and butter. Dollymount was grand on a good, sunny day but on a rainy day or even just a cloudy one there wasn't a sinner down there to sell a chip to. And there were never going to be too many good, sunny days in an Irish summer; there was always rain coming at you from somewhere. But people coming out of the pub after a few jars didn't give a shite what the weather was like, they just wanted their chips and maybe a bit of cod with a nice crispy batter on it. Anyway, rain was never that wet when you were half scuttered.

The dinners-for-two with candles and wine hardly paid for themselves. They did them for the crack more than anything else. Bimbo did them to please Maggie, because the idea had been her brainwave, and Jimmy Sr went along with Bimbo.

Only she was always having brainwaves. Sometimes Jimmy Sr felt like telling her to give her fuckin' head a rest.

They came back from Dollier on a Monday late in July covered in sand and with damn all in the money box because there'd been showers on and off all afternoon, and she was there waiting for them, swinging off the front door, with her latest: breakfasts on the Malahide Road.

— You're jokin', said Jimmy Sr, once he knew what she was on about.

She wanted them to park the van at the crossroads in Coolock every morning and make rasher sandwiches for people driving to work.

— Wha' time?

— Half-seven.

— Jaysis —!

— Eight then; it doesn't matter. Durin' the rush hour.

— Look it, said Jimmy Sr. — Maggie. If they're in such a rush they're not goin' to be stoppin' for a rasher sandwich. Or even a rasher an' dunphy sandwich.

— There's plenty of people would love a rasher sandwich on their way to work, said Maggie.

— I know tha', said Jimmy Sr. — But they'll be goin' by us on the bus or they'll be at home in bed cos they're on the dole.

Bimbo was staying a bit quiet, Jimmy Sr thought; very fuckin' quiet.

— The only people who'd drive past that way, said Jimmy Sr, — is the yuppies. An' they can make their own fuckin' breakfasts as far as I'm concerned.

— You just don't want to get up early, said Maggie.

Jimmy Sr ignored this; he wasn't finished.

— Sure, Jaysis, he said. — No yuppie'd be caught dead eatin' a rasher sandwich on his way to work. Think about it.

— You could give it a try, Maggie said to both of them, but especially Bimbo.

— Hang on, said Jimmy Sr.

He wasn't dead yet; and he wasn't getting up at half-six in the morning.

— How far is it from Malahide to town? he asked them. — Abou'?

— Five miles, said Bimbo.

— Abou'?

— Yeah.

Jimmy Sr looked to Maggie to give her a chance; she agreed with Bimbo.

— Five miles so, said Jimmy Sr. — A bit more maybe. It's not very far, is it now? You're not goin' to get hungry travellin' five miles only. Unless you're goin' on your hands an' knees.

— The airport road then, said Maggie. — That'd be better. They'd be comin' from much further on tha' one. Drogheda, and Dundalk — and —

— Belfast, said Bimbo.

— That's righ', said Maggie. — Well —?

— I'm on, said Bimbo. — Jim?

He'd no choice.

— Okay. — Just promise us one thing, he said. — If it works, don't make us go ou' later an' make their fuckin' tea for them as well.

It didn't work. Jimmy Sr made sure it didn't.

— Come here, he said to Bimbo.

They were on the new airport road. It was seven o'clock.

— D'you want to do this every mornin'?

— Wha'? said Bimbo.

— Don't start, said Jimmy Sr. — Do yeh?

— Wha'?

— Want to get up before the fuckin' seagulls every mornin'. Do yeh?

— No.

— Righ'; park over there then.

— Where?

— There.

— Under the bridge?

— Yeah.

They stayed there on the motorway, under the flyover, for an hour and a half. They opened the hatch and all; they didn't cheat. They made three rasher sandwiches, and Jimmy Sr ate two of them and Bimbo ate the other one, and a Twix each as well. They shouldn't have been there but the guards never came near them. They leaned out over the hatch and watched the cars and the trucks blemming past. Then they shut the hatch and went home.

— Not a word, Jimmy Sr warned Bimbo.

— No, said Bimbo. — No.

Jimmy Sr enjoyed getting back to the fort that morning. He let Bimbo do the talking.

— Where did yis park it? she asked him.

— Just there, in Whitehall, said Bimbo. — At the church; where yeh said.

— And no one stopped at all?

— That's righ', said Bimbo.

— No one even slowed down, said Jimmy Sr.

— Ah well — , said Maggie.

That was all; it was grand. Maggie wasn't pushy or a Hitler or anything; she was just a bit too fuckin' enthusiastic.

Bimbo and his kids ate nothing except rashers for two weeks after that, and Maggie brought Wayne and Glenn and Jessica and the other two kids into Stephen's Green in town and they fed seventeen large sliced pans to the ducks.

Bimbo and Maggie were the ones in charge; Jimmy Sr couldn't help thinking that sometimes. Not just Maggie; the both of them.

It wasn't that they ordered him about or anything like that — they'd want to have fuckin' tried. It was just, he was sure they talked about business in bed every night, and he wasn't in bed with them. There was nothing wrong with that; it was only natural, he supposed. He'd have been the same if it'd been Veronica. But sometimes he felt that they'd their minds made up, they'd the day's tactics all worked out, before he rang their bell.

He felt a bit left out; he couldn't help it.

When Maggie'd announced the dinners for two with wine and candles Bimbo didn't say anything but Jimmy Sr could tell that he knew about it already. He didn't stand beside Maggie and nod like he'd heard it all before, but he didn't ask her any questions either: he didn't have to. He might even have come up with the candles bit himself. It was the type of romantic shite that Bimbo always fell for.

267

But, again, there was nothing wrong with it; it was a good idea. It wasn't any less of an idea just cos he hadn't thought of it himself, or because he hadn't been around when Maggie'd thought of it. And anyway, even if he didn't like it, there was nothing he could do about it. He could stay downstairs and watch the telly in Bimbo's till they were finished riding each other or whatever the two of them did when they went to bed and then go up and get in between them and have a chat for a couple of hours, but he couldn't see them agreeing to that.

There was another day; Jimmy Sr was going to play pitch and putt, against Sinbad McCabe. It was the Hon Sec's Prize he was playing him in, and Sinbad McCabe was the Hon Sec himself, and Jimmy Sr hated the cunt. So he really wanted to win it, to beat the bollix in his own cup. He was getting a few sandwiches into him — not rasher ones, mind you — and a bowl of soup, and psyching himself up at the same time. There were two things Jimmy Sr hated about Sinbad McCabe, two main things: the way he always waited till the Hikers was full before he filled in the results on the fixtures board, like it was the Eurovision fuckin' Song Contest he was in charge of, and the way you could see the mark of his underpants through his trousers. There were other things as well but they were the big two. Jimmy Sr was going to look at Sinbad's underpants lines before he took a shot; it would help him concentrate. He wouldn't talk to him either, not a word, and he'd stand right up behind him when Sinbad was putting, as close behind as he could get without actually climbing into his trousers. He was telling Veronica and Sharon this when Bimbo came in.

— What's keepin' yeh? said Bimbo.

— Are yeh comin' to watch me? said Jimmy Sr.

He wasn't sure he wanted Bimbo along with him for this one. Bimbo was too nice to everyone. He'd be chatting away to McCabe and all Jimmy Sr's work would be wasted.

— Wha'? said Bimbo.

He'd come down to hurry Jimmy Sr up; they were bringing the van to Dollier. Maggie and himself had looked out the window, seen all the blue in the sky, and stocked up the van. Only Jimmy Sr hadn't been with them, so he didn't know anything about it. They just expected him to hop. It wasn't fair. It wasn't right.

It upset him. He still beat Sinbad McCabe though.

Another thing he'd thought about a few times, and he couldn't make up his mind about it, if it was important or not: Bimbo had bought the van. Jimmy Sr'd been there beside him when he did it, but Bimbo'd paid for it. He hadn't paid much for it; he didn't think it mattered — he wasn't sure. He didn't feel guilty about it. Maybe he should have given Bimbo his half of the cost of the van. He had the money now. He was welcome to it. What would happen if he did that though? Probably nothing; he didn't know. He'd think about it, maybe talk to Veronica about it. He didn't want to do anything that would mess everything up. At the same time, he was no one's skivvy. Partners was the word Bimbo'd used at the very start, in the Hikers the day they'd pushed the van to Bimbo's. Maybe it was time to remind him of that. He didn't want to hurt Bimbo's feelings though, or even Maggie's. He didn't know.

He'd think about it.

It was great knowing there'd be money there when he put his hand in his pocket; not that he'd much time to spend it. He could go up to the Hikers whenever he wanted, if he wanted to. He sometimes got the paper in the mornings and brought it into the pub and had a quiet pint by himself but it always smelt of last night and polish and the smell that old hoovers left behind them. Except on Saturdays and Sundays; they were better.

He bought himself a suit, a grey one. Veronica liked it. She even came down to the Hikers with him the first Sunday he wore it. It wasn't flashy, and he didn't wear a tie although he'd bought one of them as well.

— Nice suit, compadre, Bertie said.

— Must have cost yeh a few bob, was what Paddy said, but you wouldn't have minded him.

Bimbo didn't say anything but he was wearing a new suit himself the next Sunday, so he must have been impressed, or Maggie'd been.

They were thinking of getting a car; they'd always had one before, or a van, but they'd always had something. Veronica was putting money away.

— We'll have a decent Christmas this year annyway, wha', he said when himself and Veronica were out having a walk alongside the seafront.

— Jimmy.

— Wha'?

— It's August.

— Yeh know what I mean, he said, but they laughed.

They all went to the zoo. Darren and the twins wouldn't come, but the rest of them did; Jimmy Sr and Veronica, Sharon and Gina, and Jimmy Jr and his mot, Aoife. They'd a great day. Gina didn't give a fuck about the animals; she just wanted to go on the slide all day. Jimmy Sr and Jimmy Jr laughed their way around the place. Aoife laughed at nearly everything they said, but especially when Jimmy Sr said that the hippo smelt like Veronica's mother used to, and Veronica agreed with him. She was a lovely girl, Aoife; lovely. They'd a picnic with them. Jimmy Jr slagged Jimmy Sr because he wouldn't sit on the grass cos he'd his new suit on him.

They had a few drinks in the Park Lodge Hotel after the zoo. It was nice in there, after Jimmy Jr got them to turn the telly down. When they were thinking of going home Jimmy Sr ordered a taxi for them, and they went home that way, in style.

— Honk the horn, said Jimmy Sr when your man, the taxi driver, was stopping at their gate.

— Do not, said Veronica.

They all got out while Jimmy Sr settled up with the taxi fella; eight fuckin' quid, but he said nothing, just handed it over to him. It was only money. He made sure he got the right change back off him though. Then he gave him fifty pence.

— There yeh go, said Jimmy Sr. — Buy yourself a hat.

Jimmy Jr wanted to give him half the taxi fare.

— Fuck off ou' o' tha', said Jimmy Sr. — Put it back in your pocket.

— Are yeh sure?

— 'Course I'm sure.

He spoke quieter now.

— I remember when I was skint an' you helped me ou'; I remember tha'.

— Can I have it back? said Jimmy Jr.

They laughed up the hall, into the kitchen, and they wouldn't tell the women what they were laughing about.

It was past midnight, and hectic — mad. They were sliding all over the place but they'd no time to wipe the floor. They were used to it by now, like sailors. Sharon was with them tonight and even she was sweating through her clothes.

— My Jaysis, said Jimmy Sr.

He was getting ready to say what he wanted to say. Himself and Bimbo were at the fryer and the hotplate trying to keep up with Sharon as she called the orders back to them. Bimbo was chasing an onion ring that kept ducking away from the tongs.

Jimmy Sr wiped his brow with his arm.

— D'yeh know wha'? he said.

Here went.

He chuckled first so it would sound right, half a joke.

— This place should be called Bimbo and Jimmy's Burgers, he said.

— No, said Bimbo, very — too fuckin' quickly.

Jimmy Sr's heart was pounding.

— It wouldn't sound righ', said Bimbo.

— Yeah, Jimmy Sr agreed with him. — You're righ'.

— Too long, said Bimbo.

— Exactly, said Jimmy Sr. — I wasn't serious —

— I know tha', — still —

— No, you're righ'.

—You've been great pals for years, said Veronica.

Jimmy Sr nodded.

That was true. Still was.

He nodded again.

—You should try to make sure that it stays that way, said Veronica. — The two of you.

Jimmy Sr kind of laughed.

— Don't worry, love, he said. — Anyway, it's not Bimbo really — I don't know. It's her.

Veronica said nothing.

Darren got out of the way just in time. Jimmy Sr was carrying a brown bag that was already soggy; the arse was going to fall out of it. He'd got his timing wrong; he'd stuck the cod and the spice-burger into the bag but when he went to get the chips there were none left, so while he was putting a new batch into the fryer and waiting for them the cod had got out of the batter and was soaking the bottom of the bag. But he hadn't time to change it. It was getting mad outside again, and it wasn't even dark yet; small gangs of kids had a way of making it seem like they were big gangs of kids. There were only about six waiting to be served but they were all shouting at the same time, and pushing and changing their positions. It was another hot airless bastard of a night, worse than last night.

— Two cods, a spice, three large, Jimmy Sr checked with the young ones who'd ordered them.

— Yeah, she said, like she'd been waiting all day for them.

He slammed in the salt and vinegar and closed the bag.

— A single an' a —

— Wait your turn! said Jimmy Sr.

He turned to Darren and Bimbo.

— One o' yis get over here.

He turned back to the young one.

— There, he said, and he handed her the bag.

— I'm not takin' tha', she said.

— What's your problem? said Jimmy Sr.

— The bag, said the young one. — It'll burst before I get it home to me house.

Jimmy Sr couldn't argue with her; she was right.

— Jesus wept!

He turned to get another bag and bumped into Bimbo. There was no damage done.

— Will yeh watch where you're fuckin' goin'!

— You watch where you're goin' yourself, said Bimbo.

— Where's Darren gone?

— Over to Flemings for water.

— He's no use to us over there, said Jimmy Sr.

Bimbo took over at the hatch.

— Yourself, he said, pointing at a kid.

— Single.

— Annythin' else?

— No.

— One single, Bimbo shouted over his shoulder, into Jimmy Sr's face. — Sorry.

Jimmy Sr handed out the new bag to the young one.

— There now, he said. — Let's see your money.

The young one looked under the bag before she handed over the pound coins, five of them. The coins were warm.

— Your hands are sweaty, Jimmy Sr told her.

— So's your bollix, said the young one, and she just stood there waiting for her change, not a bother on her. She was only about twelve. She stared up at him.

They were all laughing outside.

He took twenty-five pence out of the box. He thought that that was what he owed her, he wasn't sure.

— There, he said.

— 'Bou' time, she said, and she shoved back, to get through the crowd.

She was replaced by a young fella with a pony tail.

— Righ', Geronimo, said Jimmy Sr.

— Me name's not —

— Okay, said Jimmy Sr. — Wha' d'yeh want?

— Curry chips.

— We don't do them.

— Why don't yis?

— Our chips are too good, son, Jimmy Sr told him.

— Wha'?

— We wouldn't insult our chips by ruinin' them with tha' muck, said Jimmy Sr. — They only use curry sauce cos their potatoes are bad, to hide the real taste. Now there's some inside information for yeah.

He was beginning to feel better. Bimbo went back to the hotplate and the fryer. It was about time he did a bit of real work, instead of just hiding in the corner with the fish.

— So, said Jimmy Sr. — Will ordin'y chips do yeh, or wha'?

— Okay, said the young fella. — They'd better be good though.

Jimmy leaned back and took a chip from the rack.

— How's tha' look? he said, and he held up the chip.

They all cheered. There were more of them outside now, about twenty, all of them kids.

— Yeow! Yeh man, yeh!

— They're not chips! a high-pitched young fella in the crowd shouted. — They're potato mickies!

— Gis a bag o' them! said the young fella with the pony tail.

— One single! Jimmy roared back at Bimbo.

Darren was back, with three full milk bottles.

— Wha' kept yeh? said Bimbo.

— I had to negotiate, Darren told him.

Jimmy Sr chose his next customer.

— You with the head, he said.

— A large an' a dunphy.

— Large an' a dunphy! Jimmy Sr roared.

— She was watchin' Jake and the Fat Cunt when I rang the bell, Darren told Bimbo.

— Oh oh, said Bimbo.

276

Missis Fleming had cut off their water supply before, when Jimmy Sr rang the bell during Coronation Street and then knocked on the front-room window when she hadn't answered fast enough for him. They'd had to buy her a box of Terry's Moonlight chocolates, and get Maggie to deliver them, before she'd given them the right of way again.

— A large, a smoked an' a spice! Jimmy Sr roared. — An' hurry up with the large an' the dunphy!

Darren filled a bag with chips and fished a spice-burger out of the fryer.

— He said a dunphy, Bimbo told him.

— It's not for him, said Darren. — It's for Missis Fleming.

He jumped out the back.

— Where's he gone now? said Jimmy Sr. — For fuck sake. We can't let that oul' bitch hold us to ransom. Two large, a bun an' a dunphy — Stop pushin' there; you'll turn us over.

He turned back to Bimbo.

— Why can't she just get a key cut for us, like I said to her? — Two 7-Ups with tha' last one, righ'.

Bimbo was struggling; he could tell.

Good.

Jimmy Sr lobbed in the salt and vinegar, closed the brown bag and handed it out to a young fella.

— One, eh, eighty.

— An' a Twix, said the young fella.

Jimmy Sr got the Twix and went back to the hatch and the young fella'd fucked off without paying. They were all laughing outside. Jimmy Sr had to laugh as well.

— Did yeh see tha'? he asked Bimbo.

— Wha'?

— Mister Rabbitte; here —!

— No skippin' the queue just cos yeh know me name.

— Fuck yeh.

— You're barred.

— He's after barrin' Anto, said another young fella.

— He'll get his da after yeh, Mister Rabbitte.

— He can get his ma after me if he likes, said Jimmy Sr.

They cheered.

— Mind you, said Jimmy Sr. — His da's better lookin'.

— Haaaa!

They were having a great time.

— He'll definitely get his da now.

— Let him, said Jimmy Sr. — I'll let the air ou' of his wheelchair.

He turned to see what was keeping Bimbo. Bimbo was holding a spice-burger over two bags; he didn't know which was which.

— D'yeh want to swap? said Jimmy Sr.

— No! said Bimbo. — No. — Yeah.

Jimmy Sr spoke to his customers.

— I'll have to leave yis now, I'm afraid, he told them. — We're a bit understaffed in the kitchen.

— Bye bye, Mister Rabbitte.

— Good luck now, said Jimmy Sr.

278

He made room for Bimbo.

— There yeh go, he said. — Make sure yeh get their money off them before yeh hand over the goods.

He'd enjoyed that, and the bit of fresh air coming through the hatch had done him the power of good. He slapped on a burger, for himself; he deserved it.

— Batter burger, large, Coke! Bimbo roared.

— I hear yeh, said Jimmy Sr.

He didn't know how anyone could eat those batter burgers; they were disgusting. You could leave one of them swimming around in the fryer for hours and the meat would still be that pink colour and you'd want a chisel to get through the batter. You were dicing with death eating one of those things. Still, they were big though, very good value. He lowered it very carefully into the fat. It was like launching a ship.

Darren was back again.

— Is she happy now? Jimmy Sr asked him.

— Yeah, said Darren. — Sort of.

— Piss on her chips the next time, said Jimmy Sr.

He passed a brown bag back to Bimbo.

— Batter burger, large.

— A Coke as well, Bimbo reminded him.

— That's righ', said Jimmy Sr.

He bent down and got a can from under the hotplate, making sure that his head didn't go too close to it. He wiped the grease off the can with Darren's T-shirt and handed it to Bimbo.

— From the back o' the fridge, he said.

— Two five, Darren told Bimbo.

— Two pound an' fivepence, Bimbo told the young fella at the hatch.

— I've on'y two pounds, said the young fella.

Jimmy Sr took the bag from Bimbo when he heard that. He opened it, got the batter burger out and took a huge bite out of it, and let the rest of it drop back into the bag. He shut the bag, and shoved the chunk of batter burger over to the side of his mouth.

— Two pound, he managed to say, and held the bag out for the young fella.

— Jaysis!! Did yeh see wha' he done!

Bimbo grabbed the bag from him.

— It's all yours, said Jimmy Sr.

They went mad outside.

Jimmy Sr chewed the burger into manageable bits. It wasn't that bad. He went back to his post and turned his burger. Darren was dipping the bits of cod into the fryer, to set the batter. He was laughing as well.

— That's revoltin', he told his da.

— They don't taste tha' bad, said Jimmy Sr, — if yeh don't look at them first. Oh, I forgot but, you're a vegetarian; that's righ'. I suppose yeh think I'm a cannibal, Darren, do yeh?

— No, said Darren. — I just think you're a fuckin' eejit.

They laughed. Jimmy Sr spat the rest of the meat out the back door. His real burger was ready. He didn't bother with sauce.

God, he felt good now.

— Large, smoked! said Bimbo.

— That's your department, Darren, said Jimmy Sr.

The meat was a good safe brown colour.

— Tha' looks better now, doesn't it? he said before he put the top half of the bun on it.

— Small! Bimbo shouted.

— D'yeh not like the smell? he asked him.

— No! said Darren. — Jaysis.

— Yeh must, said Jimmy Sr.

— I don't.

— I don't know — , said Jimmy Sr.

He'd leave Darren alone. He passed a bag back to Bimbo.

— Large, smoked.

— One eighty-five, said Darren.

It was getting dark now. Darren turned on the lamps. Jimmy Sr handed another bag back to Bimbo.

— Small.

— Fifty-five, said Darren.

— I know tha'! said Bimbo.

Jimmy Sr nudged Darren.

— I'm not tha' thick, said Bimbo.

— Yeh fuckin' are! said someone outside.

Darren knew the voice.

— Nappies Harrison, he told Jimmy Sr.

Jimmy Sr went to the hatch.

— Nappies Harrison! he shouted. — You're barred.

They cheered.

— Yeow, Nappies!

— Which one o' yis is Nappies? said Jimmy Sr when they'd settled down a bit.

— Here he is, Mister Rabbitte.

They picked him up, his pals, the lads that played with Darren for Barrytown United.

— Fuck off messin'! Nappies shouted.

They hoisted him up over their heads and shoved him through the hatch. He held onto the sides like Sylvester the Cat but one of the lads took his shoe off and hit Nappies' knuckles with it.

— Aaah!! Fuck yeh! — That's me guitar hand!

— It's your wankin' hand!

Bimbo saved the salt and vinegar and got out of the way. He wasn't impressed.

— For God's sake!

Nappies tumbled over the counter, over the spilt salt and the grease. His foot sent the menu board flying. He'd have landed inside on his head if Jimmy Sr hadn't caught him under his shoulders and held him up till he got his feet off the counter.

Nappies shoved his shirt back into his trousers.

— Look at Nappies' sunburn!

— Give him a job, Mister Rabbitte.

Nappies turned to face the lads outside. He took the red sauce bottle from Bimbo.

— Yaah! Yis cunts, yis!

He squeezed the bottle with both hands before Bimbo could get it back off him; gobs of ketchup rained down on the lads. The van shook. A half-empty can came in through the hatch. It hit no one but it made an almighty bang when it hit the wall and scared the shite out of Bimbo. It dropped onto a shelf and into the fryer and sent a wave of oil onto the floor.

— Oh good Jaysis —!

282

— Here! Jimmy Sr roared, keeping his head well down in case of more cans. — None o' tha'!

— Come on, Bimbo said to Nappies. — Out. It's gone too far. Ou'; come on.

Nappies didn't need to be pushed.

— I didn't ask to come in here, he said. — I was thrun in.

He slid on the oil.

— Jaysis!

He grabbed at the hotplate to hold himself up, but Darren knocked his hand away and he went on his arse, right into the oil.

— Get up, said Bimbo.

Nappies ignored him. He thought he was being cooked. He spoke to Darren.

—What'll I do?

Darren held his hands out for Nappies. He kept his feet out of the oil. Nappies' hands slid out of Darren's. Nappies looked terrified when that happened. He tried to sit up. Darren grabbed his sleeves and dragged him off the oil, to the door.

— Thanks, Darrah.

Nappies was now standing up and looking healthier, ready to start giving out about the state of his clothes. Bimbo was trying to fish the Coke can out of the fryer.

— Everythin's ruined, he said.

He could feel the oil under his runners. He gave up on the can and looked at the floor.

— Bloody bowsies, he said, and he threw a J-cloth onto the floor. —Yeh shouldn't encourage them.

— We want Nappies! We want Nappies!

The lads outside had gathered again.

Jimmy Sr stood at the hatch again.

— What's he worth to yis? he asked.

— Twopence!

Nappies didn't go out the way he'd come in. He was going to, but Jimmy Sr sent him back to the door.

— Oh yeah —

— Mind the oil there, said Bimbo. — Look it.

Nappies climbed down the steps backwards and slowly, because the oil had made his trousers soggy and it was horrible and warm.

— Seeyeh, Darren, he said.

— Good luck, Nappies, said Darren.

He was down on his hunkers squeezing the J-cloth over the chip bin.

There was no one left outside. Jimmy Sr let down the hatch door till they fixed up the mess.

They'd only the one J-cloth, and it was lifting very little of the oil.

— This is crazy, said Darren.

— It's disgraceful, said Bimbo.

— D'yeh think so — ? said Jimmy Sr —

The next thing either of them said could have started a fight, so they said nothing.

It was terrible; the only noise was the shoes on the oil, and the breathing. Then Jimmy Sr remembered something.

— Did yeh ever see Cocktail, Darren? he asked.

— Are yeh jokin' me? said Darren.

— I watched it with Linda an' Tracy there earlier, said Jimmy Sr. — They've seen it thirteen times.

284

— That's just because Tom Cruise flashes his arse in it, Darren told him.

— Does he? I don't think he does, does he? I must've gone to the jacks — . I thought it was quite good, meself.

He saw Darren's face.

— It was shite, he explained. — But good shite, yeh know.

— The routines. Behind the bar. Between Tom Cruise an' your man from Thornbirds. They were fuckin' gas. — Did yeh see any o' them, Bimbo?

The first stone hit the van before Bimbo could answer. It smacked the side over the hotplate, full on. The next one skimmed off the roof.

— Jesus — !!

Jimmy got the door shut.

The next one shook the hatch door.

The Living Dead were outside. They hadn't done this for a good while, more than three weeks. Jimmy Sr had forgotten that they did it.

— The cunts.

Darren knew them. Lar O'Rourke had been in his class in primary school. They knew he was in the van.

The next one hit the side again. Flakes of paint fell on top of the oil.

There was nothing they could do. They'd just have to wait till they stopped. They never did much real damage; they'd never broken the windscreen or the side windows.

The next one was lobbed onto the roof. It made the loudest bang, and the rock stayed on the roof.

Sometimes it wasn't rocks they threw; it was used-up batteries from their ghettoblaster. All they ever played was UB40; nothing else, ever.

Jimmy Sr sang.

— NEARER MY GOD TO THEE —

He didn't lose his temper any more; there was no point.

Another one rolled across the roof.

They'd just have to sit it out. Only they couldn't sit on the floor because of the mess. They had to stand, away from the walls.

— Some nigh', wha', Jimmy Sr said to Bimbo.

—Yeah, said Bimbo. — I hope —

The stone nearly came through the wall.

— Good fuck! said Jimmy Sr.

He touched the dent beside the hatch.

— Someone ou' there's eatin' his greens, wha'.

That was the last one, but it was hard to tell.

They were in the front room.

— FOR GOODNESS SAKE —

I GOT THE HIPPY HIPPY SHAKE —

— Fuck; sorry, Darren.

He'd dropped the Kandee Sauce bottle again.

Darren pushed the Pause button.

Jimmy Sr couldn't get the hang of the sauce bottle. The vinegar was grand; his hand fitted around it properly. It was easy enough to catch. The sauce, though, was a fucker.

Jimmy Sr got the dollop of sauce up off the carpet, most of it. He licked his finger.

— Ready? said Darren.

— Hang on, said Jimmy Sr.

He rubbed the carpet and the stain faded and went. It was grand.

— Righ', said Jimmy Sr.

He'd the vinegar in his left hand and the sauce bottle in his right. He stood beside Darren, a few feet away, to be on the safe side.

— Fire away, Darren.

Darren lifted the Pause button.

— YEAH —

I GOT THE SHAKE —

I GOT THE HIPPY HIPPY SHAKE —

— Vinegar!

They threw up their vinegar bottles.

— I GOT THE HIPPY —

And caught them, together.

— Yeow!

They laughed.

— WUUU —

I CAN'T SIT STILL —

— Sauce!

They did it; the bottles landed back down flat in their right hands.

— YEAH —

I GET MY FILL —

— The both of them!

— NOW WITH THE HIPPY HIPPY SHAKE —

And Veronica came in and caught them.

Darren managed to catch his two bottles but Jimmy Sr lost his concentration completely; he seized up and the bottles went down past his hands and onto the floor. The vinegar stayed there but the sauce bounced and rolled over and some of the goo on the nozzle came off on the carpet. Darren smacked the Pause button.

It took Veronica a while to say anything. She was more surprised than they were. The two of them were in shorts and T-shirts, holding vinegar and ketchup bottles. Maybe they'd been juggling.

That would have explained the ketchup she now saw on the ceiling.

— Ah no, look —!

— Wha'? — Where? — Jaysis, how did tha' get up there?

— I don't know what you two messers are up to —

— We're not messin', Veronica, Jimmy Sr assured her. — It's business.

— Well, you can do it somewhere else, said Veronica. She saw the carpet now.

— I don't believe it —

And now the smell of the vinegar hit her as well.

— It's a routine for the van, Jimmy Sr explained. — We were workin' on it.

He followed Veronica's eyes.

— Don't worry abou' them, he told her. — They'll wash ou'.

Veronica was looking at the marks on the curtains.

— Get out, said Veronica. — Get out; go on. You bloody big eejit, yeh, she said to Jimmy Sr.

She just looked at Darren.

— Come on, Darren, said Jimmy Sr. — We'll go ou' the back, an' leave Veronica alone.

Darren wanted to say something to his mother; not Sorry — he didn't know what.

— Bring the yoke, Darren, said Jimmy Sr. — We'll be ou' the back, Veronica, if anyone calls. — Will I open the windows for yeh there? It might get rid o' the smell —

— No, said Veronica. — Go on.

Darren unplugged the twins' ghettoblaster. He turned it on quickly to check if the batteries were working.

— SHAKE IT TO THE —

Yeah; they were grand.

There was only his mother in the room now, but he still couldn't say anything. He got out the door and followed his da through the kitchen.

He'd left the cassette cover behind him, on the couch. Veronica picked it up.

Cocktail, she read. Original Motion Picture Soundtrack. There was a picture of a nice-looking lad on the front. His mouth was shut but she was sure he had lovely teeth. She read inside to see who he was. Tom Cruise. So that was what he looked like; the twins were always going on about him.

She studied the damage again. It wasn't too bad. The curtains needed a wash anyway. A damp cloth would get rid of the ketchup on the ceiling. Darren could do that.

She went back to the kitchen; she wanted to see what they were at.

— FOR GOODNESS SAKE —

I GOT THE HIPPY HIPPY SHAKE —

YEAH — I GOT THE SHAKE —

She turned on the cold tap and filled the sink although she wasn't going to do anything with the water. She just wanted an excuse to be at the kitchen window.

— WUUU —

I CAN'T SIT STILL —

— Vinegar!

She looked.

They were standing out there, side by side, legs apart.

— WITH THE HIPPY HIPPY SHAKE —

They caught the bottles.

— Yahaa! said Jimmy Sr.

Darren looked around to see if anyone was looking over the hedge at them, and behind him into the field. There wasn't anyone, as far as Veronica could see. There was bound to be someone looking out a window though; there always was. Poor Darren.

— WELL I CAN SHAKE IT TO THE LEFT —

— Concentrate now, Darren.

— I CAN SHAKE IT TO THE RIGHT —

— Sauce!

— I CAN DO THE HIPPY SHAKE-SHAKE —

The sauce bottle hopped off Jimmy Sr's palm but he managed to catch it before it hit the ground, then got back into place.

— WITH ALL OF MY MIGHT —

OOOOOHH —

Darren was quite good at it, streets ahead of the other fool. They threw up both bottles and Darren did

290

a complete spin, in time to catch them. His shorts fitted him as well. Jimmy Sr's were up at the back and down at the front, holding his belly up like a sling.

She turned off the tap.

— FOR GOODNESS SAKE —

She lowered her arms into the water — it was nice — and looked out. She wished Sharon was here, or even the twins; they'd have loved it. Darren flipped the vinegar over his shoulder, and caught it.

— Stop showin' off.

He saw her looking at him; Jimmy Sr did. She looked into the water. She lifted a hand and dropped it, as if she was doing something at the sink.

— YEAH — I GOT THE SHAKE —

I GOT THE HIPPY HIPPY SHAKE —

It got darker. She looked up. She jumped back: Jimmy Sr had his face squashed up to the window. Cold water got through her blouse. She screamed, and laughed. His nose was crooked and white against the glass. He was miming to the Georgia Satellites.

— OOOH I CAN'T SIT STILL —

He kissed the glass. She saw Darren behind him, looking around to see if anyone was looking. Veronica rapped the glass.

— Go away. You're smudging the glass.

— Ah, fuck it, said Jimmy Sr.

But he lowered himself from the ledge and backed into the garden still miming, with his hand clutching his crotch.

SHAKE IT TO THE LEFT —

SHAKE IT TO THE RIGHT —

DO THE HIPPY HIPPY SHAKE —

He turned, and dropped his shorts and wriggled. God, he was terrible. Poor Darren was bright red.

— WITH ALL OF YOUR MIGHT —

— Pull up your trousers! Veronica shouted.

Darren pointed something out to her. She leaned over the sink and saw Mary Caprani, two gardens down, hanging off her clothes-line and gawking in at Jimmy Sr's war dance. Veronica thought she'd fall, the laughing took all her strength. She was bent completely over the sink, her face was against the tap, but she couldn't get up. The face on Mary Caprani; she'd been waiting years to see scandal like this.

Darren tapped Jimmy Sr's shoulder and showed him Mrs Caprani.

Jimmy Sr ran for the back door and tried to rescue his shorts at the same time. He fell into the kitchen.

— Jaysis, Veronica! Did yeh see Radar Caprani lookin' at me?

— Never mind her, said Veronica. — She's probably just jealous.

— Jaysis, said Jimmy Sr.

He was sitting on the floor. He lifted his T-shirt, pulled in his stomach and looked down at his marriage tackle.

— Maybe you're right, he said.

Veronica's blouse was drenched. She'd have to get out of it.

The Satellites were still blemming away outside.

Jimmy Sr grabbed the hem of her skirt when she was getting past him. He joined in with the band.

292

— I CAN'T SIT STILL —

WITH THE HIPPY HIPPY SHAKE —

He put his head in under her skirt.

— Mammy, Darren's playin' our ghetto —

Linda ran into the kitchen.

— Jesus!

Jimmy Sr came out from under the skirt.

— Get ou'!

Linda ran, and so did Veronica.

—They didn't understand, Jimmy Sr told Veronica.

They were in bed. The light was out. Jimmy Sr had been telling Veronica about the Cocktail routine.

— They thought we were messin', doin' it for a laugh.

Veronica sighed. She'd thought that as well. She had to say something.

— I'm sure they didn't, she said.

—They did, said Jimmy Sr. — Maggie did annyway. She wouldn't've just gone back into the house if she hadn't of.

—Well, explain it to her.

— I will not. Why should I?

Veronica sighed again, harder this time; a different sort of sigh.

— It's not my fault if she doesn't recognise a good fuckin' marketin' strategy when she sees it, said Jimmy Sr.

— You're working yourself up again, Veronica told him. — You won't be able to sleep again.

293

— Ah lay off, will yeh. — You're as bad as she is. — Veronica — . — Don't start pretendin' you're asleep; come on — Veronica? —

— Get out o' me fuckin' light, will yeh, said Jimmy Sr.

Then he sort of saw himself, a narky little bollix, the type of little bollix he'd always hated. But at nearly the same time he felt better, and clearer: he'd had an idea.

— D'yeh know wha' we need, Bimbo? he said.

It was half-ten about, outside the Hikers.

He waited for Bimbo to stop what he was doing, opening bags and setting them up in little rows on the counter.

— Wha'? said Bimbo.

— A night on the batter, said Jimmy Sr.

Bimbo looked over at the pile of fish.

— Not tha' sort o' fuckin' batter, said Jimmy Sr. — Tha' just shows yeh we've been workin' too hard if yeh can't remember wha' a night on the batter is.

Bimbo didn't laugh.

— Are yeh on? said Jimmy Sr. — It'll do us good. Wha' d'yeh say?

— Righ', Jim. Okay.

— Good man, said Jimmy Sr.

He clapped his hands.

— We'll have a fuckin' ball.

— That's righ', said Bimbo.

They both laughed now.

Jimmy Sr wanted to check that Bimbo had picked him up right.

294

— Just the two of us, wha'.

— That's righ'.

— Into town, said Jimmy Sr. — Will we go into town?

— Jaysis —

— We may as well, wha'.

— Okay. — Where in town?

— Everyfuckin'where.

They laughed again.

They wore their suits in; Jimmy Sr insisted. They were in the Barrytown DART station now. It was a horrible damp grey shell of a place with plastic wobbly glass in the doors, and a smell. He got the tickets and his change from the young fella behind the glass, a big thick-looking gobshite, and when he turned back he saw Bimbo trying to figure out the timetable on the wall.

— There's one in a minute, Jimmy Sr told him.

— No, said Bimbo. — It's the last one I'm lookin' for, to see wha' time it is.

— Never mind the last one, said Jimmy Sr.

He got Bimbo and shoved him through the door out onto the platform.

There was a fair gang on the southbound platform; a bunch of young fellas near the end probably dodging their fare, a few couples, a family that looked like they were going to visit someone in hospital.

— There's a fine thing over there, said Jimmy Sr. — Look it.

There was a young one by herself on the northbound with a red mini-skirt and a tan and hair that made her head look three times bigger than it should have been.

— Oh yeah, said Bimbo.

— She must be goin' ou' to Howth, said Jimmy Sr.

— Wha' for? said Bimbo.

— The fish, said Jimmy Sr.

There were some things that Bimbo hadn't a clue about. Jimmy Sr could see him deciding if she was really going out to Howth to buy fish.

— I'd say she's meetin' her boyfriend or somethin', said Bimbo.

— Maybe he's a fisherman, said Jimmy Sr.

The DART was coming.

— Here we go, said Jimmy Sr. — Is there a duty-free shop in the last carriage?

Bimbo laughed.

Thank fuck, Jimmy Sr said to himself. He'd been starting to think that Bimbo had lost his sense of humour from leaning over the deep fat fryer for too long.

The trip into town was grand. A scuttered knacker and a couple having a row kept them entertained as far as Connolly. Their carriage was full of dolled-up young ones. And Bimbo began to get more relaxed looking. Things were looking up.

— What's keepin' the cunt? said Jimmy Sr when the train stopped for a minute at the depot behind Fairview Park. — Me mouth's beginnin' to water.

— So's mine, said Bimbo. — There's a few people are goin' to have to go without their chips tonigh', wha'.

— No harm, said Jimmy Sr.

The train staggered, and got going again.

— We're off again, said Jimmy Sr. — 'Bout fuckin' time.

It was going to be a great night; he could feel it now. He was liking Bimbo again, and Bimbo liked him. He was leaning in closer to him, shoulder to shoulder, the two of them together. Away from the van, and Maggie, and the pressure and the rows and all the rest of the shite, they'd have their couple of pints and a good laugh, get locked, and they'd be back to normal, the way they used to be; the way they'd stay.

Bimbo started to get up when the train crept into Connolly.

— Sit down there, said Jimmy Sr.

— Wha'?

— We're gettin' off at Tara.

— Oh.

— We'll have a few in Mulligans first, Jimmy Sr told him.

— Oh, very good.

— The best pint in Dublin.

— So I've heard.

Jimmy Sr knew where he was bringing them; he had a kind of a plan.

By the time they got past the ticket collector they were really excited and they ran around the corner to Mulligans, pushing each other for the mess, and they nearly got knocked down by a fire engine when they were legging it across Tara Street.

— Ring your fuckin' bell! Jimmy Sr yelled after it, and he ran after Bimbo, into Mulligans.

There were two women climbing off their stools when Jimmy Sr found Bimbo at the bar.

— Were yeh keepin' them warm for us, girls? said Jimmy Sr.

One of them stared at him.

— We're not girls, she said.

— That's true, said Jimmy Sr when she'd gone past him.

They got up on the stools. Jimmy Sr rubbed his hands.

— Hah hah!

— Here we are, said Bimbo.

— That's righ', said Jimmy Sr. — An' here's the barman. Two pints, please.

It was a bit awkward sitting in the suits. You had to sit up straight; the jackets made you. And you couldn't just park your elbows and your arms on the counter when you were wearing your good suits; they made you kind of nervous. Still though, they'd need them for later.

— Wha' did you think of your women? said Jimmy Sr.

— Eh —

— Lesbians, I'd say.

— Ah, no.

— I'd say so. Did yeh hear her? We're not girls.

— Tha' doesn't mean —

— Not just tha'. Drinkin' in here, by themselves yeh know. Like men. Here's the pints, look it.

The pints arrived, and Jimmy Sr had an idea. He stood up and got his jacket off and folded it, put it on the stool and carefully sat on it.

— That's better. — My God, that's a great fuckin' pint. — Isn't it?

Most of Bimbo's was gone.

— Lovely.

— A great fuckin' pint.

— Lovely.

They had two more great fuckin' pints, then Jimmy Sr got them up and out before they got too comfortable in there. They put their jackets back on, went for a slash (— The first one's always the best) and headed off for somewhere new.

— Where? said Bimbo.

Doyle's, Bowe's, the Palace; two pints in each of them. They were new places to Bimbo, and to Jimmy Sr although he'd walked past them and had a look in. He'd promised himself that if he ever had any money again he'd inspect them properly. And here he was.

— Good consistent pints, he said. — So far anyway.

— Very good, yeah.

They were in the Palace, standing up against the wall, near the door cos there was no room further in. The women were a disappointment, not what he'd imagined. They were hippyish, scrawny women. He'd expected a bit of glitter; not in Mulligans — they'd gone in there strictly for the pints — but in the other ones. That was why they were in the Palace now, in town, in their suits. Jimmy Sr wanted something to happen. Maybe they should have gone to Howth. Still though, it was good to be just out, with Bimbo, away from everything.

— Yeh finished? he said to Bimbo.

— Are we goin' already?

— This place isn't up to much. Yeh righ'?

— Okay, said Bimbo. — You're the boss.

That's right, Jimmy Sr thought while he waited for Bimbo to get the last of his pint into his mouth; I am the boss.

It had always been that way.

They went outside and it was nice and cool.

— This way, said Jimmy Sr.

Jimmy Sr had always been the one who'd made the decisions, who'd mapped out their weekends for them. Jimmy Sr would say, See yeh in the Hikers after half-twelve mass, and Bimbo would be there. Jimmy Sr would put down Bimbo's name to play pitch and putt and Bimbo would go off and play. Jimmy Sr had rented the pair of caravans in Courtown a couple of years back and the two families had gone down in a convoy and stayed there for the fortnight.

— Where're we goin' now? said Bimbo.

— Somewhere different, said Jimmy Sr. — Wait an' see.

— I'm dyin' for a piddle.

— Fuck off complainin'.

There were huge crowds out, lots of kids — they were on Grafton Street now — big gangs of girls outside McDonalds. Not like the young ones in Barrytown; these young ones were used to money. They were confident, more grown up; they shouted and they didn't mind being heard — they wanted to be heard. They had accents like newsreaders. They'd legs up to their shoulders. Jimmy Sr did a rough count; there were only about three of them that weren't absolutely gorgeous.

This was more like it.

— There aren't any pubs up here, are there?

— Shut up.

Bimbo wanted to get out; Jimmy Sr could tell. He was murdering the Budweiser, guzzling and belching at the same time to get rid of it so they could go. Jimmy Sr wasn't going anywhere yet though. He hated this place, and liked it. It was crazy; himself and Bimbo were the only two men in here who needed braces to hold up their trousers and they were the only two not wearing them. They were also the only two that weren't complete and utter fuckin' eejits, as far as he could see. There was lots of loud laughing, at fuck all. The women though — not all of them that young either.

The crowd kind of shuffled and there was a pair of women beside Bimbo and Jimmy Sr, by themselves. Jimmy Sr nudged Bimbo.

— I don't like your one, he told Bimbo, although he did like her.

— Wha'? said Bimbo.

— Your women there, said Jimmy Sr.

— What abou' them?

— Back me up, said Jimmy Sr. — Howyeh, he said to the one nearest him.

— Oh, she said. — Hi, and they climbed back into the crowd, the two of them, the wagons.

— Stuck-up brassers, said Jimmy Sr. — One o' them was as bandy as fuck, did yeh notice?

But it was a start; he felt great.

He grinned at Bimbo.

— Wha' did yeh think of your women? he said.

— Wha' d'yeh mean?

— Don't start. Did yeh like them?

Bimbo was squirming.

— Did yeh?

— Eh — they were nice enough —

— Nice enough? If — if Sophia Loren came up to yeh an' stuck her diddies in your face would you say tha' she was nice enough?

But he was happy enough.

A woman about his own age bumped into him.

— Mind yourself, love, he said.

— Sorry.

— No problem.

And she was gone but no matter. All he needed was a bit of practice. If she came back in an hour or so he'd get off with her no problem. Not that he'd want to get off with her. Or anyone really. He was just messing; seeing if he could click with a woman if he wanted to. He looked around.

— Over here, he said to Bimbo.

— Why? said Bimbo, but he followed Jimmy Sr. He didn't want to be left alone.

If all Jimmy Sr'd wanted to do was get a woman behind a wall and feel her up or even ride her he wouldn't have come all the way into town; there were plenty of women in Barrytown who'd have come behind the clinic with him; all he'd have to have done was buy them a few bottles of Stag and listen to their problems for a while and tell them that they were still good-looking women when they started crying. He knew them all, and some of them were still good-looking women. But he'd never even been tempted, and not because he'd have been afraid of being caught.

They were in the middle of the crowd now, not at the edge.

What he wanted was to see if he could manage a young one or one of these glamorous, rich-looking, not-so-young ones. He'd back off once he knew it was on the cards; actually getting his hole wasn't what he was after at all — he just wanted to know if he could get his hole.

— D'yeh want another drink, here, Jimmy? Bimbo asked him.

Maybe just the once he'd like to get the leg over one of these kind of women, only the once, in a hotel room or in her apartment, and then he'd be satisfied. Jimmy Sr had never been in a hotel room.

— 'Course I do, Jimmy Sr said to Bimbo.

— Here though?

— Yeah, here. — Only one more, righ'?

Bimbo nodded and slipped through to the bar.

Jimmy Sr smiled at a woman, over a little fella's shoulder. She smiled back quickly, just in case she knew him. Jimmy Sr waited for her to look over his way again, but she didn't. She was about forty but she was wearing a mini-skirt. The little fella must have been worth a fortune.

Bimbo was back.

— It's robbery in here, he said.

— You pay for the style, Jimmy Sr told him.

— Not after I've finished this I don't.

— Okay, okay. — Watch it; brassers at six o' clock!

303

— Wha'?

— Howyeh, girls. D'yis need a drink?

They walked straight past him. They mustn't have known he was talking to them. They must have though; he spoke straight at them.

— Fuckin' bitches, he said. — Look at her. Her; your woman. With your man over there.

— Oh yeah.

— She's fuckin' gorgeous, isn't she?

— Yeah.

— She's got real bedroom eyes, said Jimmy Sr.

She was lovely looking alright.

— Yeah, said Bimbo.

— Bedroom eyes, said Jimmy Sr again. — An' a jacks mouth.

They laughed.

Bimbo's Budweiser was nearly gone.

— Are we goin'? he said.

— Yeah, said Jimmy Sr. — Okay.

Bimbo looked at his watch. It was after eleven.

— I could do with a proper pint, he said.

— Good thinkin' Batman, said Jimmy Sr. — Come on.

— D'yeh know how yeh click with women like tha'? said Jimmy Sr.

— How?

— Money.

— Ah yeah.

It was good to be back in a real pub.

304

Bimbo got two very healthy-looking pints and Jimmy Sr got two more immediately because it was coming up to closing time and Jimmy Jr had warned him that the city centre pubs were fuckers for shutting down on the dot of half-eleven.

They took over two low stools at a table.

— Yeah, said Jimmy Sr. — Nine ou' o' ten women, if they had the choice between money an' looks, they'd go for the money.

— What abou' Maggie an' Veronica?

— Not women like Maggie an' Veronica, said Jimmy Sr. — I'm not talkin' abou' women like tha'. Ordinary women, if yeh know what I mean.

He waited for Bimbo to nod.

— I mean the kind o' women we saw in tha' place back there. Stylish an' glamorous —

— I think Maggie an' —

Jimmy Sr stopped him.

— I know wha' you're going to say, Bimbo. And I agree with yeh. They are as good lookin'. But they're not like those brassers back there, sure they're not?

— No, said Bimbo. — Not really.

— Thank God, wha', said Jimmy Sr. — Can yeh imagine lettin' any o' them floozies rear your kids?

— God, said Bimbo.

Jimmy Sr sat up straight.

— But, let's face it, Bimbo, said Jimmy Sr. — They're rides, aren't they?

— Ah, I don't —

— Go on, yeh cunt. Admit it.

They laughed. That was good, Jimmy Sr thought. They weren't on their way home yet.

— That's the thing though, said Jimmy Sr, back serious. — Veronica an' Maggie. We're lucky fuckin' men. But — they're wives. Am I makin' sense?

— Yeah.

— Those ones back there aren't. They might be married an' tha' but — they're more women than wives, eh — Fuck it, that's the only way I can say it.

— I know wha' yeh mean, said Bimbo.

Jimmy Sr felt so good, like he'd got something huge off his chest.

— Will I see if they'll give us another? he said.

— What abou' —?

— We'll get a taxi. Will I have a bash?

— Okay, said Bimbo. — Yeh'd better make it a short though, Jim. I'm full o' drink.

Jimmy Sr picked on the younger barman and managed to get two Jamesons out of him, and that made him feel even better.

— How's tha'?

— Fair play to yeh, said Bimbo. — Good man.

It was hard getting back down onto the stool, there were so many people around them, but Jimmy Sr did it without pushing anyone too hard. He was dying to get going again with Bimbo.

— Women like tha' —

He waited to see if Bimbo was following him.

— Women like your women go for money, Jimmy Sr told Bimbo. — They'll wet themselves abou' any ugly fucker or spastic just as long as they're rich.

— I don't know, said Bimbo.

— It's true, said Jimmy Sr. — Look at your woman, Jackie Onassis. You're not goin' to tell me tha' she loved your man, Aristotle, are yeh?

— She might've.

— Me arse. Sure, she had a contract an' all drawn up before they got married, guaranteeing her millions o' dollars; millions.

— Tha' doesn't mean tha' —

— An' Grace Kelly.

— Princess Grace?

— She only married Prince what's his fuckin' name cos he was a prince. An' Princess Diana as well.

— Wha' —

— She only married fuckin' Big Ears for the same reason.

— I always thought there was somethin' a bit odd about that' match alrigh'.

— I'm tellin' yeh, Bimbo, said Jimmy Sr. — There are some women would do annythin' for money. The women back there in tha' place would annyway.

— You could never respect a woman like tha', said Bimbo.

— No, Jimmy Sr agreed. — But yeh could ride the arse off her.

They roared.

— It's grand, said Jimmy Sr before they'd really finished laughing. — When yeh think abou' it. If you've money, that is.

— Yeah, said Bimbo. — I suppose. If you're interested in tha' sort o' thing.

— Who wouldn't be? said Jimmy Sr.

Bimbo didn't say anything, and that was good enough for Jimmy Sr. He had Bimbo thinking with his bollix.

The pub was beginning to empty. Jimmy Sr looked at his watch; it wasn't near midnight yet. It was good in a way, because now he could ask Bimbo the question.

— What'll we do now?

Bimbo looked around, like he was waking up.

— Wha' d'yeh mean?

— Where'll we go? said Jimmy Sr.

Bimbo looked at his watch.

— I suppose we'd better head —

— We can't go fuckin' home, said Jimmy Sr. — Not yet. Jaysis; it's our fuckin' big night ou'.

Bimbo was game, Jimmy Sr could tell, but lost. He let him speak first.

— Where can we go? said Bimbo.

— Somewhere where we can get a drink, said Jimmy Sr.

— Ah yeah, said Bimbo. — 'Course.

Jimmy Sr spoke through a yawn.

— We — we could try Leeson Street, I suppose; I don't know. — Wha' d'yeh think? It might be a laugh, wha'.

Jimmy Sr's heart was loafing his breast plate.

So was Bimbo's.

— Would yeh get a pint there? he said.

— Yeh would, yeah, said Jimmy Sr. — No problem.

★ ★ ★

They were on their way.

— Hang on though, said Jimmy Sr out of nowhere. — Wha' colour socks are yeh wearin'?

They stopped. Bimbo looked down. He hoisted up a trouser leg.

— Eh — blue, it looks like —

— Thank God for tha', said Jimmy Sr.

— Why?

— They don't let yeh in if you're wearin' white socks, he told Bimbo. — The bouncers don't. They've been told not to.

— Why's tha'?

— Don't know. Young Jimmy warned me about it. Wankers an' trouble-makers wear white socks.

— Wouldn't yeh think they'd cop on an' wear another colour? said Bimbo.

— Who?

— The wankers.

— True, said Jimmy Sr. — Still, that's wha' makes them wankers, I suppose.

— Yeah. Wha' colour are yeh wearin' yourself?

Jimmy didn't have to look.

— Not white anyway, he said.

They dashed to get into the gang of men going down the basement stairs. They were all pissed and loud, a few drinks away from being sick; business men, they looked like, about the same age as Jimmy Sr and Bimbo. The door opened; the ones in front said something to the bouncer; they all laughed, including

309

Jimmy Sr, and they sailed in, no problem. It cost nothing, just like young Jimmy'd said.

— Thanks very much, Bimbo said when he was going past the bouncer.

— Shut up, for fuck sake! Jimmy Sr whispered. — Good bouncers can smell fear, he told Bimbo. — They're like dogs.

— I only said Thanks to him, said Bimbo.

— Ah, forget it, said Jimmy Sr. — Forget it. They were in now anyway.

— Will we hand in our jackets? said Bimbo.

— No, said Jimmy Sr.

A suit without a jacket was just a pair of trousers; his jacket was staying on.

The wallpaper was that hairy, velvety stuff. This was a good sign, Jimmy Sr decided. There was something about it, something a bit dirty. He could feel the music in the floorboards even before he turned into the dance and bar place. This was the business. He looked to see if Bimbo thought that as well, and caught him gawking into the women's jacks. Two women were standing at the door, one of them holding it open.

— Jesus Christ, Bimbo, d'yeh want to get us fucked ou' before we're even in?

— Wha'?

— Come on.

They were a right pair of bints, your women at the jacks door. Women like that didn't need to piss; they just went in to do their make-up.

The bar was three-sided; the barmen were done up in red waistcoats and dickie-bows, the poor fuckin'

310

saps. It was hot. The dance-floor was over beyond the bar, not nearly as big as Jimmy Sr had imagined. The stools at the bar were all taken. Jimmy Sr led the way around the other side, nearer the dance-floor. There were tables further in, past the dance-floor; the mirrors made it hard to say how far the room went back. The only one dancing was a little daisy jumping around like her fanny was itchy. Every couple of seconds, when you thought you were going to get a goo at her knickers, she pulled down her skirt at the sides. She was very young.

— Are yeh havin' a pint or wha'? Jimmy Sr asked Bimbo.

Bimbo was looking at the young one dancing.

— Is there somethin' wrong with her? said Bimbo.

Good Jesus, there was the poor young one trying to make every man watching her come in their kaks and Bimbo wanted to know if there was something wrong with her!

— A pint? said Jimmy Sr.

— Not here, said Bimbo.

Jimmy Sr agreed with him; a pint of stout in this place would leave them pebble-dashing the jacks for the rest of the weekend.

— Budweiser, said Jimmy Sr.

— Grand.

He had to shout over the music.

There were two women at the bar, not too young and just good looking enough. Jimmy Sr got in between their stools.

— Sorry, girls.

He lassoed a barman on his way past.

— Two pints o' Budweiser, when you're ready!

— Wine bar only.

The barman looked like he'd said this before.

— Wha'?

— No beer or spirits. We've a wine licence only.

— Are yeh serious?

The barman didn't say anything; he just nodded, and went further down the bar.

— Good shite, said Jimmy Sr.

For a second he was lost. Bimbo was at his shoulder.

— Will he not serve yeh? he asked.

— He'll serve me alrigh', said Jimmy Sr. — Only he's fuck all that I want.

One of the women laughed. Jimmy Sr turned to her and grinned; it was that kind of laugh.

He was away here.

— Try the wine, said the woman.

Jimmy Sr stepped back a bit to let Bimbo stand beside him.

— Wha' would yeh recommend? he asked her.

— What's wrong? Bimbo asked him, right into his ear.

— Nothin', said Jimmy Sr.

He tried to use his eyes to point out the women to him but it wasn't easy.

— The house red's very nice, the woman told Jimmy Sr.

— Is tha' righ'? said Jimmy Sr. — Are yis drinkin' it yourselves?

— We are, yes, she said. — Aren't we, Anne Marie?

— Yeah, said her friend.

312

— That's grand so, said Jimmy Sr. — We'll have a drop o' tha'.

Jimmy Sr stepped back a bit more to include the friend, the one called Anne Marie, and he had a quick look at Bimbo to see if he'd copped on, and he had. He was gawking at Anne Marie.

— I'm Jimmy, by the way, he told the girls. — An' this is Bim —

He couldn't remember Bimbo's real name.

— Brendan, said Bimbo.

That was it.

— Brendan, said Jimmy Sr.

— Hello, Brendan, said the woman. — Well, my name's Dawn. And this is Anne Marie.

— Howyis, said Jimmy Sr.

He spoke to Anne Marie.

— Two names, wha'. Is one not good enough for yeh?

She didn't get it. He smiled to let her know he was only messing and turned back to Dawn.

— Better order the oul' vino, he said. — The house somethin', didn't yeh say?

He got in closer to Dawn — great fuckin' name, that — and gave Bimbo loads of room to manoeuvre for himself.

— The house red, said Dawn.

— Grand, said Jimmy Sr. — An' it's the business, is it?

— It's quite nice, said Dawn. — I think myself anyway. And it's quite reasonably priced.

— Never mind the price, said Jimmy Sr. — Let me an' Bim — Brendan worry abou' the price. Here!

He'd captured a barman.

— A bottle o' house red wine, like a good man.

This was great. There weren't bad-looking birds at all. Nicely done up; just the right side of brassy. Somewhere in their thirties. Dawn had the fine set of lungs on her, and her arse fitted nicely on the stool; there was nothing flowing over the sides. Her eyelashes were huge, but they looked real enough. He could see the dark roots in her hair; another couple of months and she'd look like a skunk. But she'd get her hair done again long before that happened. She took care of herself. She'd do grand.

There was something about Anne Marie as well though.

Bimbo edged in closer, but he wouldn't look at her for too long. He leaned on the bar.

The barman had come back with the wine.

— Just park it there, son, Jimmy Sr told the barman.

Anne Marie was fatter than Dawn; not fat though, no way. If he'd been standing right at the bar he'd have been able to see right up to her arse the way her legs were crossed. She was smoking one of those thin cigars. Her expression; it was like she didn't give a shite about anything. He was sure she went like a fuckin' sewing machine, certain of it.

— He wants to know do you want to taste it first, Dawn told Jimmy Sr.

— Fuckin' sure I do, said Jimmy Sr. — Pardon the French, Dawn.

314

He leaned past her, brushed against her — she didn't move back — and picked up the glass. There was only half a mouthful in it. He put his nose to the glass, and sniffed.

— Ah, yes, he said.

Dawn laughed.

— Very ginnick, said Jimmy Sr.

He took a sip, leaned back and gargled. Even Anne Marie laughed. He swallowed.

— A-one, he said.

He gave the barman the thumbs up.

— Pour away, compadre, he said. — How much is tha'?

— Twenty-three pounds, sir.

— Wha'?

He hadn't heard him.

— Twenty-three pounds.

— Grand —

My fuckin' Jesus —!

He handed over a twenty and a fiver. Thank Christ, his hand wasn't shaking.

— There yeh go, he said. — Keep the change.

— Thank you very much, sir.

— No problem.

If he didn't get his hole after forking out twenty-five snots for a poxy bottle of wine he'd — He looked at Bimbo; he looked like he'd got a wallop off a stun-gun. Jimmy Sr grinned and smiled at him, and winked. Bimbo smiled back. Dawn was pouring the drink. Jimmy Sr would have to go to the jacks in a bit to see how much money he'd left. It was a long walk home to Barrytown.

— Cheers, Jimmy.

Dawn was holding her glass up, waiting for the others to join in.

—Yes, indeed, said Jimmy Sr.

He picked up his glass. He had to shout over the music.

— Cheers, eh — Dawn.

He laughed, and so did she.

They all clinked their glasses.

— Cheers, Brendan, said Jimmy Sr.

Bimbo looked to see who he was talking to, then remembered.

— Oh, thanks very much.

Twenty-five fuckin' quid. He could probably have got a wank in a massage parlour for that, and the fuckin' bottle was nearly empty already. He'd have to buy another one in a minute. He put his hand against the bar, across Dawn's back, just barely touching it. She stayed put. Anne Marie helped herself to another glass. She had the look of a dipso about her alright; another year and she'd be in rag order. The music was shite.

— Great sounds, said Dawn.

—Yeah, said Jimmy Sr. — Brilliant.

He nodded his head as he spoke cos it was very loud; the thump-thump-thump crap that young Jimmy used to play when he lived at home. She had to put her mouth up near his ear.

— Wha'? he said.

It was fuckin' ridiculous.

— Are the two of you out on the town for the night? she asked.

She was asking him were they married, Jimmy Sr reckoned.

— Ah no, he said. — No. — Not really. This is nothin' special.

She nodded.

Maybe she didn't care. He put his hand in his pocket to adjust his gooter — the way she kept putting her mouth up to his ear — . Bimbo was chatting away to Anne Marie. Fair play to him. He'd thought that Bimbo might be a liability. But no, they were nodding and yapping away; he was doing his bit. Anne Marie had her glass leaning on her bottom lip. When Dawn turned to get her glass off the bar Jimmy Sr got his hand in under his gooter and yanked it into an upright position — and Anne Marie was looking at him. He pretended he'd spilt some wine on his trousers and he was inspecting them to see if there was a stain.

— What's wrong?

Dawn was looking at him now.

— Ah, nothin'.

He looked: Anne Marie was back looking at Bimbo, and the bulge was going. No harm. — He hoped it wasn't the drink. He was feeling a bit pissed now alright; that wine on top of all the pints.

Dawn got to his ear.

— What do you do, Jimmy?

— When I'm not here, d'yeh mean?

She laughed, and leaned back against his arm and stayed there.

— Self-employed, he told her. — Me an' Bren.

— Ver-y good.

— Caterin'.

— Good.

He could feel the heat coming off Dawn, he was right up against her. And there wasn't a bit of sweat on her. He wondered how she did it.

— It's great bein' your own boss, said Jimmy Sr.

— I'd say you're a tough boss to work for, Jimmy.

— No, said Jimmy Sr. — Not really now. I'm reasonable enough.

Dawn nodded.

— I don't take shite from annyone, Jimmy Sr told her — But once that's established — yeh know.

The DJ was taking a breather, thank fuck. He'd put on a tape, but the noise wasn't half as bad. They could have a chat altogether now, and Jimmy Sr could keep an eye on Bimbo.

— Here!

—Yes, sir? said the barman.

— Another bottle o' house red wine, said Jimmy Sr. — How's it goin'? he asked Bimbo and Anne Marie.

—There y'are, said Bimbo.

Anne Marie was staring at Jimmy Sr, right into his face. He pretended she wasn't. Bimbo was grinning, like he always did when he'd more than ten pints inside in him, and swaying a bit, but not dangerously. The suit made him look less pissed than he was.

Jimmy Sr looked again. Your woman, Anne Marie, was still looking at him.

Then she spoke.

— Your complexions are very good, she said. — Considering.

— Considering what, Anne Marie? said Dawn.

— Where they work.

Bimbo! The fuckin' eejit!

— Where do they work? said Dawn.

— In a van, said Anne Marie.

He'd fuckin' kill him. Grinning away there!

He stayed close up to Dawn — just to remember how it felt.

— Here's the wine, said Bimbo. — My twist. Twenty-three quid, isn't that it?

— They have a chipper van, said Anne Marie.

— That's righ', said Bimbo.

— Brendan's Burgers, said Anne Marie.

Bimbo and Anne Marie were holding hands.

— We're buildin' up a fleet o' them, Jimmy Sr told Dawn. — Wha' d'yeh do yourself, Dawn?

— Do you bring it to football matches and that sort of thing?

She sat up, but she didn't seem to be trying to get away from him. Maybe it would be alright. He was still going to kill Bimbo though, the stupid cunt.

— Sometimes, said Jimmy Sr. — We stay local most o' the time. Our market research has shown tha' reliability is important.

He pushed Dawn's back with his arm, trying to get her to settle into him.

— The punters like to know tha' if they want a single o' chips all they have to do is go out their doors an' we'll be there outside to give them their chips.

— And do you actually make the chips and the burgers yourself?

— Sometimes, said Jimmy Sr, — yeah.

If he pushed against her back any more he'd shove her off the stool.

— Strange thing to do for a living really, isn't it?

— Not really, said Jimmy Sr. — I suppose it might — eh —

This was fuckin' desperate; he was getting nowhere. He'd lose the rag in a minute.

Oh good shite! Bimbo was kissing Anne Marie! It wasn't fuckin' fair. Right up against her, her arms around him, moving up and down his back, then her hands into his hair.

He put his mouth up to Dawn's. She drew back.

— Now now, she said.

Like she had to cope with this all the time.

— Sorry —

Fuck it, he was a fool.

Bimbo and Anne Marie were chewing the faces off each other.

He wanted to cry, and go home. He pointed to Bimbo.

— His nickname's Bimbo, he told Dawn.

He felt really rat-arsed now. He nearly fell over. The arm behind Dawn was killing him but if he took it away that was it, over. He couldn't think of anything to say. He couldn't think. Something funny, anything. The taste of the Guinness was coming up his throat. Anne Marie bit Bimbo's ear.

Jimmy Sr went in on Dawn's mouth again.

— Stop that!

— Come on, said Jimmy Sr.

320

She pushed him away, well able for him; he was fuckin' hopeless.

Bimbo was going to the jacks. Anne Marie held him back and straightened his tie. Then he was gone, past Jimmy Sr.

Dawn didn't look angry or indignant, or anything. Like nothing had happened. She even smiled at him, the bitch.

He moved in again, and she pushed him away again. She pushed him back and picked up her glass at the same time.

— Fuck yeh! said Jimmy Sr, and he went after Bimbo.

The jacks was out the way they'd come in. Jimmy Sr shoved someone out of his way at the door and went in. He fell against the wall inside the door. There was another door. He got that open and there were four sinks and a big mirror in front of him. There was no one at the urinal. Bimbo must have been in one of the cubicles, getting sick with any luck. There were three of them, two of them shut. He got over there and walloped both doors.

— Come ou', yeh cunt yeh!

One of them opened a bit when he thumped it. It wasn't shut at all; there was no one in there. Bimbo was in the middle one so.

— Come on; I know you're in there —

He gave the door a kick. Wood cracked.

— What's wrong with yeh? Bimbo said.

Jimmy Sr heard a zip going up and then the flush. He pushed against the door before Bimbo had it properly open. Bimbo didn't fall back, like Jimmy Sr'd wanted;

321

he could do nothing right tonight. He kicked the door again.

— Get ou'!

— I'm tryin' to —

He saw half of Bimbo's face behind the door. He threw everything against it and it smacked Bimbo's face, and all of the violence went out of him.

He'd hurt Bimbo.

He wanted to lie down on the floor.

Bimbo came out and went over to the mirror. He had his hands over his forehead. Jimmy Sr followed him.

— Are yeh alrigh'?

Bimbo didn't answer.

He studied his forehead. There was a graze, and there'd be a lump. But there was no real damage.

— Sorry, Bimbo — righ'?

Bimbo still didn't say anything.

— Are yeh alrigh'? — Are yeh?

— It's no thanks to you if I am.

— Ah look it; sorry, righ'. — I just lost the head —

Just now, that second, he couldn't even remember why. Then it came back.

—Wha' did yeh go an' tell them abou' the van for?

— Why shouldn't I have? She asked me what I did for a livin', so I told her.

—Well, yeh messed it up for me with your woman —

— How did I? said Bimbo. —You messed it up your-self. It's not my fault if — if she didn't like yeh, is it?

— I was away on a hack until you opened your fuckin' mouth —

— How did I?

322

— You told her abou' the fuckin' van, that's how.

— What's wrong with tha'?

— Ah —

Jimmy Sr didn't know how to answer.

Bimbo was looking at his forehead again.

— Is it not good enough for you now? Bimbo asked him.

— It's not tha' —

— It pays your wages, Bimbo told him.

Jimmy Sr was lost.

— If you don't want to work in it, said Bimbo, — you can leave any time yeh want to. — An' good riddance.

— Ah look it — for fuck sake —

— I'm sick o' you an' your bullyin' — , sick of it —

They were sober and drunk, sober and drunk.

— You got off with your woman an' — Sorry.

Bimbo slumped, like he'd nothing left to hold him up. Jimmy Sr went over and put his hand on his back.

— That's the stupidest row we've ever had, said Bimbo.

— Thick, said Jimmy Sr. — Fuckin' ridiculous.

— We'll go home, will we?

— Wha' abou' Anne Marie? said Jimmy Sr.

— I don't want — Let's go home.

— Okay.

That was the best.

— Fair play to yeh though, said Jimmy Sr. — Anne Marie an' tha'.

Bimbo said nothing. Lucky they'd their jackets on them; they didn't have to go back.

The air was nice, nice and cold. It was heavy going getting up the steps. There was a chap passed out against the railings.

— Will yeh look at him, said Jimmy Sr.

Bimbo said nothing.

They walked down towards Stephen's Green.

— It was a terrible kip, said Jimmy Sr. — Wasn't it?

— They were teachers, said Bimbo. — The two o' them.

— Who? Dawn an' your woman —?

— Yeah. Teachers. — Primary.

— That's desperate —

— They were married as well.

— No.

— Yeah.

Jimmy Sr slipped off the path, and got back on again.

— The filthy bitches, wha'.

They walked on. Jimmy Sr started to sing, to save the night.

— OHHH —

THERE'S HAIRS ON THIS —

An' THERE'S HAIRS ON THA' —

Bimbo stopped to let Jimmy Sr come up beside him.

— An' THERE'S HAIRS ON MY DOG TINE-EEE —

Bimbo joined in.

— AH — BUT I KNOW WHERE —

THE HAIRS GROW BEST —

Jimmy Sr put his arm over Bimbo's shoulders.

— ON THE GIRL I LEFT BEHIND ME.

They were at the corner. There was a taxi coming round with its light on. They stood, leaning into each other, till it came up to them.

It hadn't been a good night at all. It had been a fuckin' disaster. Jimmy Sr's head was starting to ache on and off.

324

They got into the back of the taxi.

— Barrytown, Jimmy Sr told the driver. — Soon home, he said to Bimbo.

— Yeah — , said Bimbo.

He slouched down into the corner and looked out the window. Jimmy Sr did the same thing, on his side.

There was some sort of a riot going on downstairs. He was awake now. His head was killing him. His guts were groaning; he'd be farting all day. The light behind the curtains wasn't too strong. That was good; they probably wouldn't be going to Dollymount in the afternoon. He needed a rest. He didn't want to see Bimbo. He shifted over to a cool bit of the bed. That was nice.

The racket downstairs though; they were all shouting and the dog was yipping away out of him. It didn't sound like a fight though. Maybe there'd been an accident. No; there was laughing as well.

He'd go down and investigate. He needed food inside him anyway if he was going to get back to sleep.

— Oh my fuck —

He'd never make it down to the kitchen. He sat on the edge of the bed. — Last fuckin' night — ; God, he was a fuckin' clown. He slipped down till his head was back on the pillow and lay like that. For ages. And that was how Veronica found him.

— Look at you, she said.

She didn't sound annoyed, the way she usually did when she walked into the mix of drink and farts.

— Darren got his results, she told him.

— What's tha'?

— His Leaving results, said Veronica. — He got them.
Jimmy Sr tried to sit up.

— Well? he said.

— Seven honours, said Veronica. — Isn't that marvellous?

— Seven!?

— Yes!

— How many subjects was he doin', again?

— Guess, said Veronica.

— Seven, said Jimmy Sr. — Jesus, that's brilliant. —
Seven. He must've been the best in the school, was he?

He wished he felt better. Darren deserved better; the
first Rabbitte to do his Leaving and his father couldn't
even get up out of bed properly.

— Is he downstairs, is he?

— Yes. He's down there making coffee like nothing
had happened, special.

— That's Darren. Cool as a —

He couldn't think —

— I'd better go down an' congratulate him —

He stood up and held onto the dressing table.

— I got mine as well, Veronica told him.

That took a while to get through.

— Your results, said Jimmy Sr. — You did the Leavin'
as well.

— I know, said Veronica.

— Yeh passed?

— Of course, said Veronica. — C in Maths and a B
in English. Honours English, that is.

— Ah Veronica, he said. — That's brilliant.

— I'm thrilled.

— So am I, said Jimmy Sr. — I'm very fuckin' hungover as well.

— You should be ashamed of yourself, said Veronica, but she didn't mean it — and that made it worse.

— We'll have to go ou' tonigh', said Jimmy Sr.

— Will you live that long? said Veronica; then — That'd be nice. What about your work?

— Fuck my work. I couldn't look at a chip. Sharon can fill in for me.

He got back to the bed.

— I'll have to congratulate Darren later, he said. — Sorry.

Veronica even made sure that the door didn't slam when she was leaving. He wouldn't sleep. There was too much — Darren would be going to university now. He'd applied for Trinity, Jimmy Sr thought it was, to do something or other. University. For fuck sake. And Veronica — And he couldn't even get up to congratulate them. And last night — He was a useless cunt. He groaned — A complete and utter cunt —

He'd bring Veronica out for a nice meal somewhere, the works; a bottle of house red wine and all.

He was still a cunt.

— It's for the best, Bimbo explained. — It's too messy the other way, so — em; okay?

— Okay, said Jimmy Sr.

He shrugged. He was afraid to say anything else. He didn't think he'd get through it.

— Okay.

Bimbo had just told him that from now on he'd be paying Jimmy Sr a wage. On Thursdays. Instead of the old way, the fifty-fifty arrangement.

— Will yeh have another pint? said Bimbo.

— No. — No, thanks.

— Come on, yeh will. We're in no hurry. We've time for one more.

— Okay.

— Good man.

He should have told him to stick his wages up his hole, that was what he should have done.

Veronica was fast asleep beside him, the selfish bitch.

No, that wasn't fair. She'd listened to him. She'd even told him to give up the van if he wanted to, she wouldn't mind.

He wouldn't do that though. He couldn't go back to what it had been like before they'd bought the van — before Bimbo had bought the fuckin' van. He couldn't do that; get rid of the video again, stop giving the twins proper pocket money and a few quid to Sharon, and everything else as well — food, clothes, good jacks paper, the few pints, even the dog's fuckin' dinner; everything. There was Darren as well now. How many kids went to university with fathers on the labour? No, he'd stick at it.

That was probably what Bimbo wanted him to do; give up. He probably had a cousin of Maggie's or somebody lined up to take over from him. Well, he'd be fuckin' waiting. He'd have to sack him first.

He wasn't going to call him Bimbo any more. Veronica was right; it sounded too cosy.

328

It was his own fault in a way; some of it. He should have bought the half of the van when he'd thought about it. Months ago. He'd thought he was cute, deciding not to bother; there was no need. He'd just been greedy. And now he was working in someone else's chipper van, like working in McDonalds or Burger King. Maggie was probably up at her sewing machine making one of those poxy uniforms for him.

He tried to laugh, quietly.

—Yes, sir, said Jimmy Sr.

— Ah stop tha', said Bimbo, — will yeh.

— Stop wha', sir? said Jimmy Sr.

Bimbo didn't answer. He lifted the chip basket out of the fat, shook it and dropped it back in.

Thursdays, he got paid. Like everyone else.

The second Thursday his pay was in one of the little brown envelopes wages always came in. He looked at it. His name was written on it.

— Where did yeh get the envelope? he asked.

— Easons, said Bimbo.

— Good man, said Jimmy Sr.

But Bimbo was busy in his corner mixing the batter. Jimmy Sr stuck the envelope into his back pocket.

Bimbo was manning the hatch, and sweating.

— Two cod, two large! he shouted again.

He turned and saw Jimmy Sr, leaning against the shelf, pouring himself a cup of tea from his new flask. He was holding a sandwich between his teeth.

— Jimmy! said Bimbo. — For God sake —

Jimmy Sr put down the flask and screwed the top back on it. Then he took the sandwich out of his mouth.

— I'm on me break, he told Bimbo.

Bimbo looked the way he did when he didn't know what was going on.

— I'm entitled to ten minutes' rest for every two hours that I work, said Jimmy Sr.

Bimbo still looked lost.

— I looked it up, said Jimmy Sr.

He saw that Bimbo's face was catching up with his brain.

Bimbo stood back from the hatch. Jimmy Sr took a slug of the tea.

— I needed tha', he said.

— Stop messin', will yeh, said Bimbo.

— I'm not messin', said Jimmy Sr. — I'm entitled to me break.

— Sure Jaysis, said Bimbo, — we did nothin' all nigh' except for a few minutes ago.

— Not the point, said Jimmy Sr. — Not the point at all. I was here. I was available to work.

— Hurry up, will yis!

That came from outside.

— I've five minutes left, Jimmy Sr told Bimbo. — Then I'll sweat for yeh.

— Just get us me fuckin' cod an' chips, will yeh!

Bimbo glared at Jimmy Sr.

Jimmy Sr looked back at him, through the steam coming up off his tea.

330

Bimbo went over and filled two bags with chips and got two cod out of the fryer. Jimmy Sr raised his arm to the small crowd outside and clenched his fist. But no one cheered or clapped or said anything. It was too cold and wet.

Jimmy Sr and Veronica had the front room to themselves. Jimmy Sr'd just been watching the News. Saddam Hussein was still acting the prick over in Iraq. Veronica had her coat on. She'd just come in; she'd been up at the school registering for more night classes — Leaving Cert History and Geography this time.

— Geography? Jimmy Sr'd said when she'd come in. — That's great. You'll be able to find the kettle when you go into the kitchen.

— Humour, said Veronica, imitating Darren.

— Fair play to yeh though, he'd said. — I should do somethin' as well.

They were talking about something different now though. Jimmy Sr was going out to work in a few minutes.

— It's not too bad now, Jimmy Sr told Veronica.

— Good, said Veronica.

— I'm callin' him Bimbo again, said Jimmy Sr.

Veronica smiled.

— I still take me breaks though, said Jimmy Sr. — If I'm goin' to be just a wage earner —

— You'll never be Just anything, Jimmy, don't worry.

— Ah Veronica, said Jimmy Sr. — You say lovely things sometimes.

— Ah —

— Twice a year, abou'.

Veronica slapped him. Jimmy Sr leaned over and kissed her cheek. It was still cold, from outside.

— I'm glad it's better, said Veronica. — It'd be a shame.

Jimmy Sr nodded and sighed.

— I can't get over it though, he said. — I wouldn't mind —

He'd been telling her this for weeks now. She didn't mind though; he was entitled to feel sorry for himself.

— but it was his idea in the first fuckin' place. To be his partner — But there's no point in — It's done, wha'.

Veronica could still get upset thinking about him roaming around the house, stooped and miserable, with nothing to do; trying to smile at her; sitting on the front step watching the girls go by and not even bothering to straighten up for them. Only a few months ago. Waiting for him to creep over to her side of the bed.

— I'll go, said Jimmy Sr.

— Right, said Veronica. — Come into the kitchen and I'll do your flask for you.

— Grand. Will I run up an' put the blanket on for yeh?

— Yes. Thanks.

They sat on the couch together for a little bit longer.

He dreaded climbing into the van. The worst part though was stocking it up, having to go through Bimbo's house, out to the back to the shed; that was fuckin' terrible. She was always there.

— How's Jimmy?

— Grand, Maggie. An' yourself?

The cunt, he hated her. It was easier than hating Bimbo. She was the one.

He paid for everything he took.

— I'm puttin' the twenty-seven pence in, okay?

He held the money over the box.

— Wha'? said Bimbo.

— I took a Twix, said Jimmy Sr.

He showed it to Bimbo.

— There's the money for it, okay?

He dropped it in.

— Ah, there's no need —

— No, said Jimmy Sr. — It's yours.

Bimbo fished the twenty-seven out and handed it back to Jimmy Sr.

— There's no need, he said.

— No, said Jimmy Sr. — It's yours.

And he left Bimbo standing there with his hand stretched out, and wiped the hatch counter. He heard Bimbo throwing the coins into the box.

He did the same thing with Maggie. He was going through the kitchen with a tray of cod. She was at the table cutting pastry into roundy shapes.

— There y'are, Maggie, he said, and he put the twenty-seven pence down on the table in front of her.

She looked up.

— I took a Twix, he told her, and he was out before she'd time to figure it out.

He hadn't taken a Twix at all.

It was enjoyable enough in a sad sort of way, acting the prick.

— Will I turn on the gas?

— Wha' d'yeh mean? said Bimbo.

— Will I turn on the gas? said Jimmy Sr.

They'd just parked outside the Hikers and climbed into the back. It was a very stupid question.

— I don't get yeh, said Bimbo, although Jimmy Sr saw that he was starting to smell a bit of a rat.

— D'yeh want me to turn on the gas? Jimmy Sr asked him.

— Wha' d'yeh need to ask me for? said Bimbo.

— Well, — you're the boss —

— I'll turn it on meself!

He went too far sometimes, like asking Bimbo would he take the chips out of the fryer, would he put the chips into the fryer; he just fell into the habit of asking Bimbo's permission to do everything.

— You'll ask me can yeh wipe your arse next, said Bimbo once.

— No, I won't, said Jimmy Sr. — Me arse is me own.

It was at that moment — the way Bimbo had said it; the pretend annoyance in his voice — that Jimmy Sr realised that Bimbo was enjoying it, being the boss; like he was giving out to a thick lad, a thick kid he liked: he wasn't embarrassed any more.

He'd seen a photograph in the Herald of a field, like a football pitch with an embankment around it, with a sign at the side — Danger No Swimming. It wasn't a field. It was the Vartry reservoir, dried out. And the chap from the Corporation, the spokesman — the fella that used to be a runner for Ireland but never won anything — he said that there was a crisis because it was the mildest September on record. But Jimmy Sr was fuckin' freezing, and so was everyone else. He complained about it but he didn't mind it at all. The Dollymount business was over, so he'd most of the day to himself. He took Gina for walks. They brought the dog with them. He was still trying to teach Larrygogan to fetch a ball, after three years, but Larrygogan was either too thick or too intelligent to do it. Gina fetched the ball instead and Larrygogan went with her.

He'd the best of both worlds now; his days to himself and a job to go to later. He got a good wage on Thursdays, and he'd none of the responsibilities. The hours weren't bad, just a bit unsocial. He was a lucky fuckin' man; he had no problem believing that. He believed it.

So he really couldn't understand why he felt so bad, why at least a couple of times a day, especially when he was hungry or tired, he was close to crying.

He was lonely. That was it.

He was wide awake, lying on the bed, hands behind his head. He'd brought the little electric air heater up to the room with him — to read, he'd said — so he was grand and warm. It was about four o'clock, getting gloomy. He'd stretched back and opened the book but he'd drifted, awake but away from the book. The print was too small; it took too long to read a page. But he didn't blame the book. Maybe it was too warm. He lay back, not thinking, let himself wander. He didn't think about women, Dawn or — . It was like his head got heavier and duller and then it burst out —

Lonely.

It was like he'd learnt something, worked it out for himself. He even smiled.

His eyes filled, the room and the things in it divided and swam, but he kept his hands behind his head. He had to blink. Then he could feel a tear climb out of his right eye and creep along the side of his nose. He lifted his head to see if it went quicker and blinked to feed it more water, and it went off his cheek down the side onto the pillow. Now he wiped his face; it was getting too wet. He didn't stop crying though.

He was safe enough up here.

There was a ball inside him, a ball of hard air, like a fart but too high up to get at. It nearly hurt sometimes. It made him restless, all the time. He squirmed. He sat on the jacks and nothing happened. Pressing made it worse. Hardened it more. He knew he was wasting his time but he went to the jacks anyway. And he knew there was nothing physically wrong with him, even though he could feel it. And he knew as well that he'd felt this way before; it was kind of familiar, definitely familiar. He couldn't remember exactly — . But when he'd noticed himself feeling this way, tight and small and exhausted, he'd recognised it immediately.

He chatted away to Bimbo on the way out to Ballsbridge. Shamrock Rovers were playing in their new ground, the RDS, against St Pats. It had pissed rain the night before — the first decent rain in Dublin for weeks — and again that morning, but it was clearing up nicely for the afternoon. The game was bound to be a cracker and there'd be a huge crowd there. They got a good space to park, up on the path on the river side of the Anglesea Road, and got into the back to get everything ready.

Jimmy Sr took out the letter and left it on the shelf when Bimbo wasn't looking. He took it back again — Bimbo still had his back turned — and opened it up a small bit so that Bimbo would be able to read the top part of the letter and see the letterhead. Then Jimmy Sr got down to work. If Bimbo picked it up or even just saw the top, grand; if he didn't Jimmy Sr'd stick it back in his pocket and keep it for another time.

But Bimbo saw it alright.

Jimmy Sr's face glowed, and not from the heat coming up off the fryer. He saw Bimbo twist his head a bit so he could read the letter without moving it.

He said nothing.

Jimmy Sr left the letter there. He looked at it later himself the way Bimbo had, when Bimbo was busy at the hatch — trying to add up the price of two large cod and a spice-burger, the fuckin' eejit. He couldn't see much of it, only the letterhead and the Dear Mr Rabbitte and half the line under that. It was enough though.

They were waiting now for when the crowd came out after the game.

— Pissed off an' hungry, said Jimmy Sr.

— D'yeh want to go into the match? Bimbo asked Jimmy Sr.

— No; fuck tha'.

— It'll be a cracker, I'd say.

— How will it? said Jimmy Sr. — They're only fuckers that aren't good enough to play in England.

— Ah now —

—You'd see better in St Annes, said Jimmy Sr.

Jimmy Sr had the Sunday World with him and he gave half of it to Bimbo; the inside half, the kids' and the women's pages and the pop stuff and the scandal from Hollywood, the stuff he never bothered reading himself.

They didn't talk.

Jimmy Sr opened his window a bit. It was only a bit after four, more than an hour before the crowd would be coming out. He sighed.

— D'yeh mind waitin'? Bimbo asked him.

— I don't care, said Jimmy Sr. — It makes no difference to me. Just as long as I'm paid, I'll sit here for the rest of the season. It's your money.

—You'll be paid, don't worry, said Bimbo.

— I'd fuckin' better be, said Jimmy Sr, but not too aggressively; messing.

Bimbo kind of laughed.

Then Jimmy Sr thought of something.

— Double time.

—Wha'?

— Double time for Sundays, said Jimmy Sr.

— Now, hang on here —

— Sundays an' bank holidays. Time an' a half for all other overtime.

Bimbo's voice was very loud.

—Who says this is overtime? he said.

—There's no need to shout, said Jimmy Sr. — I can hear yeh.

— How d'yeh mean Overtime?

—That's better.

338

— Well?

— Well wha'?

— Abou' this overtime.

— What abou' it?

— Well —

Bimbo started again.

— Are yeh doin' this out o' spite; is that it?

— No!

— Well, it sounds like tha' to me.

— I'm just lookin' after me welfare, said Jimmy Sr.
— That's all I'm doin'.

— Welfare!? said Bimbo. — Yeh get paid, don't yeh?
Well paid.

— I earn it, said Jimmy Sr.

— Yeah, said Bimbo. — But why d'yeh suddenly
think you're entitled to —

— That's it, said Jimmy Sr. — I AM entitled to it. I
am entitled to it, he said again before Bimbo got the
chance to say anything back. — I work seven days a
week as it is.

— Not days —

— Nights then. That's worse.

Jimmy Sr kept his eyes on the paper and pretended
that he was still reading.

— Seven nights, he said. — How many does tha'
leave me? Eh, wait now till I think, eh — None.

He snapped the paper and stared down at A Little
Bit Of Religion.

— An' now I'm havin' to give up me Sunday
afternoons as well, he said.

— You'll get paid —

— You're the boss, said Jimmy Sr. — I'll go where I'm told but I'm not goin' to be exploited, d'yeh hear me? I want me overtime.

— Who's exploitin' yeh —?

— You are. If yeh don't pay me properly.

— I do pay yeh —

— There's laws, yeh know. We're not in the Dark Ages annymore. — I should be at home with Veronica. An' the kids.

Bimbo waited a bit.

— Is tha' wha' tha' letter's abou'? he then asked.

— Wha' letter?

— The letter inside, on the shelf.

Jimmy Sr bent forward and felt his back pocket, looking for something.

— The letter from the Allied something — the union, said Bimbo.

— Have you been readin' my letters? said Jimmy Sr.

— No! I just saw it there.

The letter had been Bertie's idea. He'd got the name and address for Jimmy Sr from Leo the barman and Jimmy Sr'd written off to them, the Irish National Union of Vintners, Grocers and Allied Trade Assistants, asking how he'd go about joining up. He'd got a letter back from them, inviting him in for a chat. He kept it in his back pocket. He wasn't thinking of joining. He had no time for unions. He'd been in one for years and they'd never done a fuckin' thing for him. They were useless.

— It'll be ammo for yeh, compadre, Bertie'd said.

340

It was a smashing idea. They'd burst their shites laughing. And he was right, Bertie; the letter had been ammunition, like a gun nearly, in his back pocket.

— You've no righ' to be readin' my letters.

— It was just lyin' there.

— Where?

— Inside on the shelf.

Jimmy Sr felt his back pocket again, and looked at Bimbo like he'd done something.

— Is tha' what it's abou'? said Bimbo.

— It's none o' your business what it's abou'. It's private.

— You don't need to be in a union, said Bimbo.

— I'll be the best judge o' tha', said Jimmy Sr; then quieter, — Readin' my fuckin' letters —!

— I didn't read it.

— Why didn't yeh tell me when yeh found it?

— I didn't know you'd lost it.

Jimmy Sr leaned forward, to see out if there was more rain coming.

— Are yeh really joinin' a union? said Bimbo, sounding a bit hurt and tired now.

Jimmy Sr said nothing.

— Are yeh?

Jimmy Sr sat back.

— I'm just lookin' after meself, he said. — An' me family.

Bimbo coughed, and when he spoke there was a shake in his voice.

— I'll tell yeh, he said. — If you join any union there'll be no job here for yeh.

— We'll see abou' tha', said Jimmy Sr.

— I'm tellin' yeh; that'll be it.

— We'll see abou' tha'.

— If it comes to tha' —

— We'll see.

Bimbo got out and went for a stroll up and down the road. Jimmy Sr turned the page and stared at it.

He'd gone down to the shops himself instead of sending the twins down — they wouldn't go for him any more, the bitches — and got them sweets and ice-creams, even a small bar of Dairymilk for the dog. It had been great, marvellous, that night and watching the dog getting sick at the kitchen door had made it greater. Even Veronica had laughed at the poor fuckin' eejit whining to get out and vomiting up his chocolate.

— Just as well it wasn't a big bar you bought him, Darren said.

It had been a lovely moment. Then Gina waddled over to rescue the chocolate and she had her hand in it before Sharon got to her. Jimmy Sr wished he'd a camera. He'd get one.

They'd had a ride that night, him and Veronica; not just a ride either — they'd made love.

— You seem a lot better, Veronica said, before it.

— I am, he'd said.

— Good, she'd said.

— I feel fine now, he'd said. — I'm grand.

— Good, she'd said, and then she'd rolled in up to him.

But it hadn't lasted. Even the next day his head was dark again; he couldn't shake it off. When Darren came

342

into the front room to have a look at Zig and Zag on the telly, Jimmy Sr's jaw hurt. He'd been grinding his teeth. He snapped out of it, but it was like grabbing air before you sink back down into the water again.

He kept snapping out of it, again and again, for the next two days. He'd take deep breaths, force himself to grin, pull in his stomach, think of the ride with Veronica, think of Dawn. But once he stopped being determined he'd slump again. His neck was sore. He felt absolutely shagged. All the time. But he tried; he really did.

He was really nice to Bimbo, extra friendly to him.

— How's it goin', and he patted his back.

He whistled and sang as he worked.

— DUM DEE DEE DUM DEE DEE — DUM — DEE —

But, Christ, when he stopped trying he nearly collapsed into the fryer. You're grand, he told himself. You're grand, you're alright. You're grand. You're a lucky fuckin' man.

But it only happened a couple of times, the two of them feeling good working together. And it wasn't even that good then because they were nervous and cagey, waiting for it to go wrong again.

It was like a film about a marriage breaking up.

— The cod's slow enough tonight —

Bimbo saw Jimmy Sr's face before he'd finished what he'd been going to say, and he stopped. Jimmy Sr tried to save the mood. He straightened up and answered him.

— Yeah, — eh —

But Bimbo was edgy now, expecting a snotty remark, and that stopped Jimmy Sr. They were both afraid to speak. So they didn't. Jimmy Sr felt sad at first, then annoyed, and the fury built up and his neck stiffened and he wanted to let a huge long roar out of him. He wanted to get Bimbo's head and dunk it into the bubbling fat and hold it there. And he supposed Bimbo felt the same. And that made it worse, because it was Bimbo's fault in the first place.

Darren wouldn't work for them any more.

— It's terrible, he explained to Jimmy Sr. — You can't move. Or even open your mouth. — It's pitiful.

—Yeah, Jimmy Sr almost agreed. — Don't tell your mother, though. Just tell her the Hikers pays better or somethin'.

—Why d'you keep doin' it, Da?

— Ah —

And that was as much as he could tell Darren.

— But mind yeh don't tell your mother, okay.

— Don't worry, said Darren.

— It'd only upset her, said Jimmy Sr. — An' there's no need.

There was just the two of them in the van now, except maybe once a week when Sharon was broke or doing nothing better. She wasn't as shy as Darren.

—Wha' are youse two bitchin' abou'? she asked them one night after Jimmy Sr had grabbed the fish-slice off Bimbo and Bimbo'd muttered something about manners. (It had been building up all night, since Bimbo'd looked at his watch when he answered the door to Jimmy Sr, just because Jimmy Sr was maybe ten minutes late at most.

— Take it ou' of me wages, he'd said.

— I didn't say annythin', said Bimbo.

— Me bollix, said Jimmy Sr, just over his breath.

And so on.)

Neither of them answered Sharon.

— Well? she said.

— Ask him, said Bimbo.

— Ask me yourself, pal, said Jimmy Sr.

— Jesus, said Sharon. — It's like babysittin' in here, so it is. For two little brats.

And she slapped both their arses.

— Lay off —!

But she slapped Jimmy Sr again, messing. He had to laugh. So did Bimbo.

— How was it tonight? Veronica asked him when he got into the scratcher and his cold feet woke her up.

— Grand, he said.

Jimmy Sr looked at Bimbo sometimes, and he was still the same man; you could see it in his face. When he was busy, that was when he looked like his old self. Not when he was hassled; when he was dipping the cod into the batter, knowing that time was running out before the crowds came out of the Hikers. In the dark, with only the two lamps lighting up the van. A little bit of his tongue would stick out from between his lips and he'd make a noise that would have been a whistle if his tongue had been in the right place. He was happy, the old Bimbo.

That wagon of a wife of his had ruined him. She'd taken her time doing it, but she'd done it. That was Jimmy Sr's theory anyway. There was no other way of explaining it.

— Look it, he told Bertie. — She was perfectly happy all these years while he was bringin' home a wage.

— Si — , said Bertie in a way that told Jimmy Sr to keep talking.

— She was happy with tha' cos she thought tha' that was as much as she was gettin'. Does tha' make sense, Bertie?

— It does, si. She knew no better.

— Exactly. — Now, but, now. Fuck me, she knows better now. There isn't enough cod in the fuckin' sea for her now. Or chips in the fuckin' ground; Jaysis.

— That's greed for yeh, compadre.

— Who're yeh tellin'.

It was good talking to Bertie. It was great.

— It's her, said Jimmy Sr. — It's not really Bimbo at all.

— D'yeh think so? said Bertie.

— Ah yeah, said Jimmy Sr. — Def'ny.

— I don't know, said Bertie. — Yeh might be righ'. — Would you let your mot rule yeh like tha'?

— No way.

— Why d'yeh think he does then?

— She's different, said Jimmy Sr after a bit. — She's pushier. She's — It wouldn't happen with Veronica, or Vera. He's soft, there's that as well —

That was what he believed; that night. You couldn't be one of the nicest, soundest people ever born and

346

suddenly become a mean, conniving, tight-arsed little cunt; not overnight the way Bimbo had; not unless you were being pushed. He knew what she'd said to Bimbo; he could hear her saying it, — It's either me or him; something like that. The van or Jimmy Sr.

Bimbo was opening up chips bags, getting his fingers in, spreading them inside and flicking the opened bag off them onto the shelf above the fryer. It was tragic.

Other times, he just hated him.

He missed him.

Bertie was great company but Bertie was Bertie. Bertie didn't need anybody. He was as hard as fuckin' rock. Bertie could entertain you all night and listen to your troubles all night but Bertie could never have been your best friend. Bertie didn't need a best friend.

Jimmy Sr wasn't like that though. He wished he was, but he wasn't. When Bertie wasn't around — and he wasn't around a lot — Jimmy Sr never missed him; he didn't feel a hollow. But he missed Bimbo and the fucker was standing beside him shaking the chips.

—Yeah? said Jimmy Sr.

He put the salt and sauce to the side, out of his way.

— Eastern Health Board, said the man outside.

Jimmy Sr was bending to point him to the clinic, beyond the shopping centre, when he noticed the piece of plastic the man was holding up. It was a white identification card. Jimmy Sr didn't take it. He stood back.

He didn't look like an inspector. He looked ordinary.

Then Jimmy Sr remembered; he wasn't the boss.

— There's someone here wants yeh, he told Bimbo.

It wasn't his problem. His heart got faster, then slowed. But his throat was very tight, like something big was coming up. It ached. His face tingled; he felt a bit guilty. That wasn't on though; it wasn't his problem.

Bimbo rubbed his hands on his trousers to get the flour off them as he came over to the hatch. He looked at Jimmy Sr and out at the man, then looked worried.

It was Friday evening, coming up to the Happy Hour; getting dark.

Bimbo rubbed his hands and made himself smile.

— Yes, sir? he said. — Wha' can I do for you?

The man held up the card till Bimbo took it.

— Des O'Callaghan, he said. — I'm an environmental health officer with the Eastern Health Board.

How did you get a job like that? Jimmy Sr wondered. Again it struck him how normal Des O'Callaghan looked. Quite a young man too, for an inspector.

Bimbo's fingers smudged the card so he rubbed it on his shirt, looked to see if it was clean and gave it back to Des O'Callaghan.

— Is somethin' wrong? Bimbo asked him.

Bimbo looked like he needed company so Jimmy Sr moved over closer to him, but he wasn't going to say anything. Bimbo would have to sort out this one out for himself.

— I'm going to have to inspect your premises, said Des O'Callaghan.

— D'yeh have a warrant? said Jimmy Sr.

348

Bimbo looked like he was going to fall, like he wanted to agree with Jimmy Sr but was afraid to.

— I don't need one, Des O'Callaghan told Jimmy Sr, without even a trace of snottiness or sarcasm. He was good. Jimmy Sr was impressed, and scared. — I'm entitled to inspect these premises under the Food Hygiene Act.

Des disappeared and came in the back door.

— Wipe your feet, said Jimmy Sr. — Only coddin' yeh.

Des got down on his hunkers and looked around. Jimmy Sr nudged Bimbo. He waited for Des to run a finger along the floor and then look at it, but he didn't do that. Bimbo thought about getting down beside Des. He bent his knees a bit, then decided not to.

Des was looking under the hotplate now.

— The licence's at home, said Bimbo. — D'you want me —?

It wasn't easy talking to the back of the man's head. Bimbo gave up.

Des stood up. He wasn't taking notes or anything, or ticking things off. He looked into the chip bin. No harm there, thought Jimmy Sr; the chips were only in it a few minutes. Des looked at the milk bottles full of water. Then he touched something for the first time since getting in. He turned one of the taps at the sink and noticed that it was loose and not connected to anything.

— I'm gettin' it fixed, said Bimbo.

Des said nothing.

What was he looking at now? Jimmy Sr wondered. He shifted a bit to see. The walls; he was staring at the walls.

— Is everythin' alrigh'? said Bimbo.

Des still said nothing. Jimmy Sr decided to wipe the hatch counter, to give him something to do. His cloth was bone dry. He nearly had it in the chip bin to rinse it when he saw Des looking at him. He changed his direction just before his hand went into the bin and started wiping the outside of the bin. God, he was a fuckin' eejit; he hadn't thought — He whistled. He turned the bin a bit to see if he'd missed any of it, then stood up and went back to the hatch.

He almost didn't recognise Bimbo, the way he was looking at him. He'd never seen Bimbo look that way before, cold and intelligent. He reddened; he didn't know why. Then his mind caught up with him —

He thinks I ratted on him. He thinks I ratted on him!

He couldn't say anything.

Then Des spoke.

— Can I see your hands, please? he said.

— Wha'?

— Your hands, said Des. — Can I see them, please?

— Why? said Jimmy Sr.

Bimbo already had his hands held out, ready to be handcuffed. Then he turned them and opened his palms. Now Jimmy Sr understood. He did the same. He tried to get Bimbo to see him, without making it obvious to the inspector. He hadn't ratted on him. He had to let him know.

Des looked down at their palms.

— The nails, please.

They flipped their hands over. Bimbo let out a sigh. It sounded cheeky.

— Do we pass? Jimmy Sr asked Des.

If he got snotty with him Bimbo would know that he hadn't done the dirty on him.

— I'm afraid not, said Des.

He looked around again.

Jimmy Sr had to lean back against the counter. Oh fuck — He thought he was going to shite, a cramp ran through him: Bimbo thought it was his fault.

— 'Fraid not, said Des, just short of cheerfully.

Bimbo still had his hands held out. Des nodded at them.

— I'm finished, he told Bimbo.

Bimbo put his hands into his pockets. Jimmy Sr went to put his hand on Bimbo's shoulder, then didn't.

— I'm going to have to close you down, lads, said Des. — I have the power.

Jimmy Sr was surprised he could talk.

— Now, hang on —

— Let me finish, said Des. — Please. — Thanks. Which one of you is the proprietor?

Jimmy Sr pointed.

— He —

— I am, said Bimbo.

Bimbo half-turned, to let Jimmy Sr know that he was to stay out of it.

— I am, Bimbo said again.

— Okay. Mister —?

— Reeves.

— Right, Mister Reeves. — I have to tell you that your van poses a grave and serious danger to public health.

Bimbo looked at the floor. Jimmy Sr did too.

— I'm closing you down now, said Des.

— What abou' our fuckin' jobs? said Jimmy Sr.

— I haven't finished speaking yet, said Des.

Bimbo spoke to Jimmy Sr for the first time since this had started.

— Shut up, will yeh.

He didn't bother looking at him when he said it.

— You close down now, said Des to Bimbo. — The walls are filthy, the floor is filthy, there's no water supply —

— We're gettin' tha' fixed, he told yeh —

— the foodstuffs aren't properly covered and stored, the hotplate is dangerous, the oil in the fryer is — I don't have to tell you. You are personally unclean, especially your colleague behind you. I'm sorry but I'm empowered to make these observations. I've no wish to hurt your feelings.

Jimmy Sr shrugged.

— Your clothes are unsafe and your fingernails are what my mother would call a disgrace.

No one laughed.

— Your hair, both of you, is a threat to public health. I could go on all night. — There are enough breaches of the food hygiene regulations in here to land you a hefty fine and even a custodial sentence.

My fuck —

Des let that sink in.

— Jail, d'yeh mean? said Jimmy Sr.

This was crazy.

— I'm afraid so, yes.

— You're jestin'! Pull the other one, will yeh.

— Shut up, you, said Bimbo. — You've done enough already.

— You're the one goin' to jail, Jimmy Sr told him.

— Just shut up —!

Bimbo looked around the van.

— It's not tha' bad, he said.

— Yes, it is, said Des. — It's worse.

Fair play to yeh, Jimmy Sr thought. Jimmy Sr liked Des.

— We clean it, Bimbo told him.

Des scratched his ear.

— Will I have to go to court? said Bimbo.

— A week, Mister Reeves, said Des. — What I'm going to do is —

He waited a bit.

— I'm going to give you a week to bring your premises into line with Health Board requirements. I'll provide you with a list of what you'll have to do. I'll come back in a week and if I see that you've done your homework we'll forget that I was here this week.

He smiled, then snapped it back.

— It's going to be a busy week, Mister Reeves.

Des was great.

Before Bimbo could thank him he started again.

— However, Mister Reeves, I have to warn you — If you fail to carry out even one of the demands on the list I'll have to close you down. On behalf of the Minister for Health.

Now Bimbo could talk.

— Thanks very much.

Des took a pen and some papers out of his jacket pocket. He clicked the pen and went over to the counter. Jimmy Sr got out of his way. Bimbo followed him. It was some sort of a list; Jimmy Sr couldn't see it properly. Des put a tick beside nearly everything on it.

Would they have to shave their heads? Jimmy Sr wondered. He was feeling good now; he needed deep breaths.

— I'll have to get you to sign this for me, Des told Bimbo. — Just there. — That's right; thank you. — And this one —

He gave Bimbo one of the sheets of paper.

— That's for you, Mister Reeves, he said.

He clicked his pen again and put it back into his pocket with the other papers.

— Well — , he said. — Next week so —

— Yeah, said Bimbo. — I'll get goin' on tha'. All the things — Thanks very much.

— Goodbye, said Des.

— Cheerio, said Jimmy Sr.

— Goodbye, he said to Bimbo.

— Bye bye now, said Bimbo.

Des hopped down the steps, not a bother on him.

— Nice fella, said Jimmy Sr.

— Well — , said Bimbo — I hope you're happy now, that's all I can say.

Jimmy Sr had forgotten.

354

— Wha'? he said.

It was too early to deny anything.

— You know, said Bimbo.

Bimbo wouldn't look at him.

— No, said Jimmy Sr. — Sorry; I don't know.

Bimbo scoffed. He moved for the first time since Des had gone, and turned off the fryer and the hotplate. He hesitated a bit before he turned the dial under the plate, then he did it. He took the baskets out of the fryer.

— Large an' a cod, please.

There was a young one at the hatch.

— We're closed, said Bimbo.

— We may as well get rid o' wha' we have, said Jimmy Sr.

— We're closed, said Bimbo.

— We're shut, love, Jimmy Sr told the young one. — Come back next week, he said loud enough for Bimbo to hear.

Bimbo scoffed again, and this time Jimmy Sr wanted to give him a boot up the hole; he was arguing like a woman. He let the hatch door down and it was dark except for the light coming through the back door.

— I had nothin' to do with this, said Jimmy Sr.

Bimbo said nothing.

— I didn't, Bimbo; I swear.

— Yeah — , said Bimbo.

He went out and lifted the gas canister up into the van.

— I didn't, Jimmy Sr told him. — Des just —

— Des — , said Bimbo.

— I never saw or heard of him before today, said Jimmy Sr.

Bimbo said nothing. He made noises like a strangled laugh, but Jimmy Sr couldn't see his face properly.

— Ah, this is fuckin' crazy, said Jimmy Sr. — Look it, for fuck sake, it had nothin' to do with me —

— So yeh said, said Bimbo.

Jimmy Sr could see enough of him to grab him. He pushed him back; Bimbo fell against the chip bin and the shelf behind him stopped him from going back further. The bin went over and there was water everywhere. His legs were soaked but Jimmy Sr ignored it. He had Bimbo by the shirt, and he was up over him because Bimbo's legs had slipped. He shook him.

— Are yeh listenin' to me!?

He shook him again. One of the buttons went.

— Are yeh!?

Bimbo slid back more. He was kneeling in the water. Jimmy Sr could have kneed his thick face for him. He took one hand off the shirt and grabbed hair.

— Let me up —!

— I will. I will. Just listen! —

Jimmy Sr had to calm himself. He was all set to pulverise Bimbo. If Bimbo said one thing wrong he'd destroy him. Bimbo stayed still.

— Now — Your man comin' here — it had nothin' to do with me, righ'. I didn't rat on yeh —

He didn't want to kill him now. He stepped back to give Bimbo room. He held out his hand to help Bimbo up. Bimbo pushed it away.

— I can manage meself.

356

He could hear Bimbo grabbing air, like he'd been running. There was a growl in his breathing as well. Jimmy Sr was the same.

— D'yeh believe me? he said.

Bimbo began to lift the bin, then let it go.

— Yeah, he said. — Yeah. I believe yeh.

— Sorry — for —

— Forget it, forget it. — Forget it.

Jimmy Sr was exhausted.

— We'll fix it up, don't wo —

Jimmy Sr was knocked back before he realised he'd been hit. It wasn't hard enough to throw him back against the counter but he slid before he steadied himself. Bimbo had thumped him, hard on the chest; but it made more noise than pain. His knuckles would be killing him.

This was terrible. They were coming up to the end. Jimmy Sr gasped a few times and massaged his chest. He was close to crying. And wrecking the place.

— If — , Bimbo started.

He was the same as Jimmy Sr, nearly crying.

— If it hadn't been your man, he said, — it would've been somethin' else.

— What's tha' supposed to mean?

Bimbo didn't say anything for a while; ages. Jimmy Sr could hear him breathing, and himself; and his heart.

A stone hit the outside of the van. They both jumped.

— Fuck —

Jimmy Sr tried to laugh but only a croak came out. Another stone walloped the wall behind Bimbo.

—Yeh were goin' to get me anyway, said Bimbo then.
— Weren't yeh?
— Wha' d'yeh mean —?
— One way or another.
Another stone. It rolled over the roof.
—You were goin' to get me —
— Fuck off, will yeh.
— The union —
— Fuck off; Jaysis.
— Anythin' to get at me —
— Shut up.
— Even spreadin' rumours abou' me an' tha' woman —
— Shut fuckin' up!
— Make me.
He heard Bimbo move closer to him.
— I said nothin' about yeh.
—Yeh did.
— I didn't.
—You were the only one tha' seen me!
—Well, it wasn't me, righ'!
Bimbo'd stopped.
Just as well for himself.
He heard Bimbo giggle, forcing himself.
— Am I tha' bad? he said.
The air seemed wet.
—Yeah, said Jimmy Sr.
He wiped his nose.
— I pay yeh well, don't I? — Don't I, Jimmy?
—Yeh do, — yeah.
—Well then?
He was pleading with him. But it was too late.

358

— When we started ou' — , said Jimmy Sr. — When we —

He tried to dry his face.

— When we got the van —

— When I bought the van, d'yeh mean? said Bimbo. — When I bought the van; is tha' what yeh mean?

He was gloating, the cunt. Trying to explain was a waste of time.

The stones had stopped.

— Forget it, said Jimmy Sr.

Gina came into the van. Sharon had lifted her in.

— Out, said Bimbo.

Sharon was in.

— Get her out, said Bimbo.

— Don't talk —

— Out!!

Gina started bawling.

Jimmy Sr was on top of Bimbo. He had him in a headlock. He tried to get at his face, to get a clean thump in. Bimbo was thumping his sides, his arse; he got Jimmy Sr in the bollix, but not hard enough. Sharon and Gina were gone. Jimmy Sr gave up on the fist and opened his hand; he got his thumb to Bimbo's face somewhere and pressed. Bimbo whined. He found a wad of Jimmy Sr's fat over his trousers and he squeezed, dug his nails into it. Jesus, it was agony — Jimmy Sr let go of him and got back. He tried to kick him but he couldn't reach. He slipped. He grazed his arm on the counter trying to stay up.

That was it; there was no mending anything now.

— I'm goin', he said.

He climbed out of the van. It was dark now. It could have been any time of night. He wiped his face. He'd go home. No, he'd walk a bit first. His eyes would be red. He'd get his breath back to normal first.

He was glad.

He turned around and headed for the coast road. He had to go past the van. He didn't look at it.

Bimbo caught up with him.

— Come on back.

— Fuck off.

— Come on —

— Fuck off.

— Jimmy —

— Fuck off.

Bimbo stayed with him.

He only wanted Jimmy Sr back so that he wouldn't feel guilty; he needed him to go back to work for him. He could ask Jimmy Sr's arse if he thought —

Bimbo grabbed at Jimmy Sr's arm, trying to stop him. Jimmy Sr turned on him, and they were fighting again, in a clinch, gasping before they'd started. Bimbo's head hit Jimmy Sr's mouth.

— Sorry —

They held onto each other, heaving. There were people coming up from the bus-stop

Bimbo spoke.

— Let's go for a pint.

— Okay.

They drank and stared at each other. Afraid to speak. They looked away. Into their pints. Everywhere. When

Jimmy Sr saw Bimbo looking at him he looked back until Bimbo gave up.

A lounge boy went by.

— Two pints, said Jimmy Sr.

His voice sounded grand now. He was dry again. He leaned over to get his hand into his pocket when he saw the young fella putting the pints on his tray and coming over to them. Bimbo tried to beat him to it.

— I'll —

— No way, said Jimmy Sr.

He took the pints from the young fella and passed one over to Bimbo.

— There.

He hoped no one came in, Bertie or Paddy. Bimbo had finished his first pint. He held up the one Jimmy Sr'd just bought.

— Cheers.

Jimmy Sr waited. He felt good now. He was almost happy, in a very unhappy kind of way. He'd made his decision, done what he should have done weeks ago. He lifted his pint.

— Cheers.

The young fella was going by again.

— Two pints, like a good man, said Bimbo. — We may as well, he said to Jimmy Sr.

Jimmy Sr shrugged.

— Fair enough.

— For old time's sake.

— Fuck off.

— Ah, Jimmy —

— Ah Jimmy nothin'. — I won't be goin' back, yeh
know.
— Yeah.
— It's the only way.
— But — No, you're righ'.
The young fella unloaded the tray.
— I'll pay yeh your redundancy money though,
Bimbo told Jimmy Sr. — Alrigh'?
— Thanks very fuckin' much, said Jimmy Sr.
He thought of something else.
— I'll buy a fuckin' chipper van with it.
They tried not to look as if they were staring each
other out of it. Jimmy Sr coughed, cleared his throat,
thought about going into the jacks to spit. He examined
the head of his pint.
— Wha' happened, Jimmy? Bimbo asked.
It took Jimmy Sr a while to understand.
— Fuck off, would yeh, he said.
He didn't care what had happened any more. It was
over and done with. He'd no time any more for that
What Happened shite.
— Two pints, he shouted.

Five or six pints later — Jimmy Sr'd lost count —
Bimbo was looking demolished. Jimmy Sr was holding
his own, he thought; knackered, yeah, but not rat-arsed.
He nearly missed the door when he'd gone to the jacks
the last time but he was grand. There was still no sign
of Bertie or Paddy.
Bimbo was pathetic, sinking down further into his
chair, like someone had let his air out. He was licking

362

up to Jimmy Sr now because the No Hard Feelings wankology had failed.

— Come on, Jim, — come on.

Jimmy Sr let Bimbo keep his hand stretched out over the table, waiting for Jimmy Sr to shake it. Bimbo took his hand down. Jimmy Sr didn't have any feelings at all now but he wasn't particularly interested in making Bimbo feel any better. The cunt deserved to suffer. He should just have got up and gone home and left Bimbo on his own. But he couldn't.

Bimbo'd told him that he didn't know what he'd do now without him, told him that it wouldn't be the same without him, told him that the sun, moon and fuckin' stars shone out of his fuckin' hole; desperate for Jimmy Sr to give him a sign that he still liked him.

Bimbo put his hand out again, then forgot what he was doing. The man was demolished.

He saw Jimmy Sr.

— The best — fuckin' — worker in the wor — the fuckin' world, he said.

Jimmy Sr looked around.

— Fifty-fifty, said Bimbo.

He sat up.

— Wha' d'yeh say-y? — Fif'y-fifty.

— What're yeh fuckin' sayin', man?

— Fif'y-fif'y, said Bimbo. — Half for me an' — half for — The way it was —

— No.

Maybe though —

— No way.

— Go on. Par'ners —

— Forget it — Fuck tha'; no way.

This pint had got very warm. It wasn't nice at all.

Bimbo slipped back down. He walloped the table with his knees when he was trying to get up again. The glasses wobbled.

— Mind!

— S-sorry 'bou' —

He tried to put his hand on Jimmy Sr's leg. He couldn't reach.

— Jimmy — you're my bes' frien' —

— No, I amn't, said Jimmy Sr. — Fuck tha'.

—Yeh are —

— Forget it, pal — I've learnt me lesson; fuck tha'.

He knocked back the pint before he remembered that it was horrible. Bimbo was muttering. Jimmy Sr kept the glass at his mouth in case he couldn't keep it down. He badly needed a cold one; then he'd be alright.

— I'll kill it, said Bimbo.

— Wha'? said Jimmy Sr.

— Tha' poxy van, said Bimbo.

He staggered up. He staggered, but he stayed up.

— Come on, Jim, he said. — C'me on.

Bimbo drove. He went up on the roundabout near the coast road and he fell asleep twice but he got the van to Dollymount, in between the dunes and out onto the sand; through the soft stuff (—We're stuck. No — Go on, go on; we're movin') and out to the hard sand.

They got out. The wind was lovely. The tide was out, way out.

— Come on, Jim, said Bimbo, and he went to get back in.

— Hang on here, said Jimmy Sr.

He held Bimbo's shoulder.

— What're yeh doin'?

He knew what Bimbo was doing.

— You'll regret it, he said.

— No, I won't, said Bimbo. — Not me.

Jimmy Sr got in with him.

He headed for the water. It was hard to see where it started. There were no waves, no white ones. Jimmy Sr heard it. They were in it now. He saw it now, lit up in front of him and out the side window; only a few inches. Bimbo kept going. Jimmy Sr wasn't scared. They stopped. The van coughed and died. Bimbo turned the key. Jimmy Sr looked down. There was water at his feet. Bimbo had to push to get his door open.

— Mission acc-accomplished, he said. — Come on, Jim.

He bailed out. Jimmy Sr heard the splash. Jimmy Sr did the same. He lowered himself down (— Jeeesus!!) into two feet of water, freezing fuckin' water; it lapped up to near his bollix.

— Aaaahh! Jesus; shi'e!

He'd never felt soberer.

— Where are yeh, yeh fuckin' eejit?

He found Bimbo behind the van, pushing it, trying to get it further into the water, getting nowhere.

— Give us a hand!

Jimmy Sr waded over and put his arms around Bimbo's waist and lifted him away from the van.

— Come on, he said.

Bimbo didn't fight.

Jimmy Sr let him down.

— Come on.

They waded, then walked, back to the shore. Jimmy Sr looked back. They'd only come about thirty yards. He could see the top of the van's wheels; the water only reached the bottom of the burger sign. When the tide came in though, it would disappear then.

He took his shoes off.

— I did it, said Bimbo.

He sat down. In a half inch of water.

— I did it, Jim.

— Good man, said Jimmy Sr. — Come on before we die.

Bimbo stood up. He caught up with Jimmy Sr. He put his arm around Jimmy Sr's shoulders. Jimmy Sr shrugged it off. He tried again. Jimmy Sr shrugged his arm away again.

When they got to the dry sand Jimmy Sr turned to look. Bimbo was ten yards behind him; he'd turned sooner. The van seemed to be deeper in the water.

— You'll be able to get it when the tide goes out again, Jimmy Sr told him.

Bimbo said nothing.

Jimmy Sr turned back and headed up to the dunes.

Veronica woke up while he was getting his clothes off. She smelt the sea in the room. It was getting bright outside. He sat on the bed beside her.

— Give us a hug, Veronica, will yeh. — I need a hug.

Also available in ISIS Large Print:

The Commitments

Roddy Doyle

The first book in the Barrytown Trilogy — now a hit musical in London's West End!

A pungent, steaming crock full of inimitably Irish imagination   **New York Times**

Barrytown, Dublin, has something to sing about. The Commitments are spreading the gospel of Soul. Ably managed by Jimmy Rabitte, brilliantly coached by Joel "The Lips" Fagan, their twin assault on Motown and Barrytown takes them by leaps and bounds from the parish hall to immortality on vinyl. But can The Commitments live up to their name?

This funky, rude, unpretentious first novel traces the short, funny, and furious career of a group of working-class Irish kids who form a band, The Commitments. Their mission: to bring soul to Dublin.

ISBN 978-0-7531-9258-0 (hb)
ISBN 978-0-7531-9259-7 (pb)

The Snapper

Roddy Doyle

The second book in the Barrytown Trilogy

Meet the Rabbitte family — a motley bunch of loveable ne'er-do-wells whose everyday purgatory is rich with hangovers, dogshit and dirty dishes. When the older sister announces her pregnancy, the family are forced to rally together and discover the strangeness of intimacy. But the question remains: which friend of the family is the father of Sharon's child?

ISBN 978-0-7531-9260-3 (hb)
ISBN 978-0-7531-9261-0 (pb)